Wycked Crush

Wycked Obsession – Book 1

Wynne Roman

WYCKED CRUSH
Wycked Obsession Series — Book 1
Copyright ©2017 by Wendy Ferguson
All Rights Reserved
Edited by Loredana Elsberry Schwartz
Proofreading by Kathy Hafer
Cover Design by Tatiana Vila, Vila Design
Formatting by Carlos Garzona, Vila Design

TABLE OF CONTENTS

PROLOGUE

BREE

I've waited so long.

Now, finally, Ajia is touching me. His eyes are soft and…is it love I see in their unique caramel color? I've crushed on him for so long—five whole years—and he's finally seeing me as a woman. Not just a kid who's trailed along behind her big brother and his band.

Me and Ajia. Just like I've always known it should be.

His fingers cup my breast and he squeezes. Hard. But—wait a minute. What? Something's wrong. He's crushing me. Pinching me. It's not…right. Ajia's touch wouldn't be like this.

"I knew you'd feel this way."

The low, guttural voice rips me out of my dream—oh, God, it's only a dream—and I wake up on high alert. I open my eyes to *him* in my room, standing over me.

Not Ajia, the man I want like no other, but Gabe. My stepfather.

I shriek and shove my hands against his chest. He stumbles back, leaving my breasts exposed because he pushed my T-shirt up. Thank God, I'm wearing a sports bra.

I jerk my shirt down to cover my chest. It's an old Pearl Jam T-shirt that belongs to my brother Knox. It's way too big for me—

exactly the way I want it. Disgusting as it might sound, I've started wearing baggy clothes so my *stepfather* won't notice me.

It doesn't seem to be working.

He blinks and then his lips curve into a small smile. "I didn't mean to scare you, sweetie." He takes a step toward me. "I just—"

"I don't give a damn what you were *just* thinking." I push up on my knees, and if looks could kill, he should be a pile of ashes by now. "Stay away from me, Gabe. Don't ever touch me again."

"Aw, Bree." He gives me a look I've seen him give my mother a hundred times. Maybe he thinks it's seductive. It makes me sick. "Don't talk like that."

"What the fuck is wrong with you?" I demand. "You're my *stepfather,* for Christ's sake. My mother loves you!"

"And I love her." He gives me that same awful smile. "But you...you're like she must have been as a teenager. Imagine. Fucking both versions of the same woman. And within hours of each other."

For a minute, I think I'll throw up. Gabe's been coming on to me for months now, ever since he and my mom got married. It's been a soft press up until now. Things he always claimed were accidental, or I'd misunderstood his intentions.

He's younger than Mom by about five years, good enough looking, I suppose—or at least I thought so when she first started to date him. Dark hair always perfectly styled, dark eyes, clean shaven. He dressed in suits and cotton pants with button-down shirts. Conservative and professional, I thought.

I was so fucking wrong.

At first I thought it was just a new husband figuring out how to fit in with a ready-made family. A forty-something, never-before-married stepfather learning to live with a nineteen-year-old stepdaughter in the same house. Touching my shoulder, my hip, watching me in that pervy way I now hate. I tried to blow it off. Walk away. Eventually I learned to make sure I was never alone with him.

Most especially, I never meant for anybody to find out. I'd thought I could handle it. Handle him. It was Knox who caught Gabe once, rubbing his hand up and down my spine, grabbing my ass before I could step away. The memory pierces me again.

"What the fuck?" Knox had asked the instant I'd gotten him away from Gabe.

I hadn't been able to meet his eyes. "It's…nothing."

"It didn't look like nothing."

I'd lifted one shoulder. "Yeah, he's been a little too…friendly."

"That fucker coming on to you?"

I'd shaken my head. "No. Not really. Just…well, like what you saw. It makes me uncomfortable, but I'm not sure he realizes what he's doing."

"Fuck that," Knox had snapped. "He knows."

"Knox." I'd grabbed his arm so he'd know I was serious. "I can handle it. It's nothing. I'll be fine."

"C'mon, Bree. You know better." He'd frowned in that overprotective way of his. "He—"

"He's Mom's husband and she loves him. She waited a long time to get married again after Dad took off. I'm not getting in the way of that."

"You aren't doing shit. It's him and his wandering dick."

"Well, his dick isn't going to wander in my direction. I promise."

I'd meant it then, and I mean it now. Every single day. Even if he's getting braver. The idea of even being in the same room with Gabe Richmond is enough to make me want to puke.

After I convinced Knox to let it go then, I've kept as much of it from my brother as I can. Was that a mistake?

"Get out of here, Gabe." A rage is growing in me, and I put every bit of fury into my voice. "I'm not sleeping with you. I'm not doing *anything* with you."

"Oh, Bree, honey." He shakes his head. "You don't know how good we'll be. We—"

"Gabe? Honey, I'm home! Bree?"

My mother's voice rings from another part of the house, and relief floods through me. A tension I hadn't even been aware of eases. It's always like that. I just react however I need to in order to get away.

But I'm safe now. Mom's home, and he won't try anything else. Not today.

Still kneeling on the bed, I sit back on my heels. Gabe shoots me a dark look. "You won't say a word if you know what's good for you."

What does he think he can do that's worse than what he's already tried? But he's right. I *won't* say anything—and not for his sake.

He's still standing in the doorway when Mom walks up. Everybody always says we're mirror images of each other. Her hair's shorter than mine, shoulder length but the same coffee color, and I inherited her brilliant green eyes. She's dressed in what she calls business casual, a plain gray shift dress and teal-colored blazer.

She looks between us. "What's going on?"

"I just came to check on Bree. She was being awfully quiet in here." He gestures to my bedroom.

I point to my phone, headphones still attached. "I was listening to the new album. I guess—" I swallow "—I fell asleep."

Mom smiles easily. "How many times have you listened to Knox's new album already?"

You can do this. I can look my mom in the face and carry on a decent conversation. "It's not just Knox's album, Mom. It's all the guys in Wycked Obsession."

"Yes, yes, I know. And I'm proud of them all. But Knox is the only one who's actually my son."

She turns to Gabe, her smile softening to one of love. The kind of smile I'll give Ajia someday, if I ever get the chance.

The kind of smile that asshole Gabe doesn't deserve.

"Now, aren't you taking me out for Mexican tonight?" she asks him in a throaty voice and slides her arm through his.

He smiles back, and the whole scene just makes me sick. Sicker than when he touched me—and I didn't think that was possible.

"Sure, honey," he says and then looks at me. "You want to come along, Bree?"

"Uh, no." It comes out too flat, and so I add, "I'm going to see Knox."

Something flickers in Gabe's eyes, and it makes me smile. Does he think I'm going to tell my brother? I don't say anything else.

"Sure." Mom nods. "You want to spend time with your brother before the boys leave on tour, don't you?"

"Yeah. That's it."

4

Knox and his band have a rental house where they've stayed the last six months. I didn't have any plans to go there tonight; we planned to hook up tomorrow. That's changing right now.

Wycked Obsession's become the biggest band to come out of Austin in years, and I've tried not to be too much of a pest since they got back from their first tour. Things are different now—*the guys* are different. They've had new experiences. Fame. Adoration. Fans and groupies and shit we all used to joke about. It's all real for them now.

But, I need them tonight. Whatever part of their life they can share. I need the guys who are as much brothers to me as Knox. And I need Ajia, however I can get him. Even if he doesn't know how I feel. Will probably never know.

Tonight, of all nights, I want to think about loving Ajia and how I'm going to spend the summer avoiding my stepfather's advances.

CHAPTER 1

BREE

I stand in the driveway of my brother's house and frown.

Shit. Shit, shit, shit.

He's having a party. Well, *they're* having a party.

Why didn't I expect it? A pre-tour party and a chance to celebrate the release of their second album, *Wicked Is As Wycked Does.* This is for their friends and their hometown fans. Different, I guess, from tour parties. Especially *this* tour, when they'll be opening for Edge of Return, just about the biggest rock band in the world right now.

They didn't invite me.

It hurts. I get it—sort of—but that doesn't make me feel any better. Knox doesn't want me hanging out with their musician friends. Groupies and sluts, he calls them, but maybe that's just for my benefit. To get his way and keep me from getting to know people he things might be a bad influence.

Hysterical laughter bubbles up in my chest. I'm living with Gabe fucking Richmond, for Christ's sake! So maybe it's more complicated than that, but I don't give a shit right now. I hate my life—and I *really* hate witnessing the one-night stand hook-up thing that's part of the whole rock star lifestyle.

It's become part of the Wycked Obsession lifestyle, and Ajia's living it every goddamn day.

Well, fuck that. Fuck rock stars and my stepfather and my piece of shit life. I'm crashing.

I stalk up the driveway and through the front door before I can even think about it. Noise overpowers me at once. Voices and the pounding rhythm of music. Not Wycked Obsession's music but...*Highway to Hell* by AC/DC.

Great. They're into 80s metal tonight.

The crowd moves like it's alive, and I slip into the kitchen to stash my purse in one of the cupboards. Why not? They never keep any food there, anyway.

It's hotter than hell in the house, and I notice the open sliding glass door. May in Austin—of course it's freaking hot! Did they remember to turn off the AC with the door open?

I'm stalling, and I know it. Maybe I was brave a few minutes ago, but it's all starting to fade, now that I'm faced with the reality of finding Knox. I'm pretty sure he won't make me leave. And if he tries? Well, I don't want to pull the Gabe card in front of everybody, but I'll do it if I have to.

"Hey, you need a beer?" Some guy shoves a Shiner Bock in my hand, and I smile a thanks. Deliberately, I wander away before he can say anything else.

A corner of the living room's a safe place to watch the action while I search for Knox. He's a couple of inches over six feet tall, so I should be able to find him easily enough. As always, a passing jealous thought reminds me that he has the height. Knox takes after Dad and I, as Gabe so disgustingly reminded me, look just like Mom. All 5'4" of me.

My brother is nowhere to be seen, but I'm not looking as hard as I should. Not for him, anyway. Ajia's the one I really want to find.

Ajia Stone. Lead singer of Wycked Obsession. The hotter-than-hell guy with the throaty, husky voice that generates love, lust, and orgasms, according to fan gossip. He's one of my brother's best friends. One of *my* friends.

And the man I can't seem to get over.

I was 14 when I first met Ajia. He and Knox were putting Wycked Obsession together, and I was the tag-along. Ajia was 19, out of my reach purely because of our age difference, but I crushed on him, anyway.

Well, I'm 19 now, almost 20, he's 24—and just as much out of my reach. He's a rising rock star with access to any girl he wants. Worse, my little schoolgirl crush has become so much more. I never wanted any other guy, and so I'm a 19-year-old virgin who's Ajia's *friend.* Like the band mascot.

7

Worse, he calls me *kitten,* like I'm some kind of pet.

There's a reason for it, not that I like remembering it. I was babysitting a friend's kitten the day I met him. An unexpected birthday present for my friend Heather, I'd drawn kitten-sitting duty when her family had gone on a planned vacation to Disney World. Knox and I had never had a pet, and I was a little obsessive about making sure that Whiskers went home as healthy and happy as when she came to me. Somehow, that earned me the nickname *kitten,* and I've been stuck with it ever since.

Ajia might be missing, but I spot Noah, the band's drummer. He's huge, like 6'4" or 6'5", with an upper body honed by years of playing the drums. Except for his darker hair, he could give Chris Hemsworth's Thor a run for his money. He even has the long hair and firm jaw that hints at superhero status. I teased him about it so much, he eventually had Thor's hammer tattooed on his bicep. He's kind of become known for it, and now he takes off his shirt about halfway through every show and throws it to the crowd.

I grin in spite of my party-crashing status. I love Noah like a brother, but I'm a realist, as well. He's also kind of a wild man, and right now he has a girl under each arm. Nope. Not talking to him at the moment.

Zayne and Rye aren't too far away, I notice as I sip my beer. They're standing pretty close together, talking to a group of girls. They're a really stunning combination—tatted up, long-haired music gods. Rye plays keyboards, and his pitch-black hair and matching eyes attract more attention than he ever seems comfortable with. Zayne's the bassist, with chocolatey brown hair and striking hazel eyes. He seems to like being noticed just fine.

They're like a couple more brothers to me, but no way am I approaching them with a whole *group* of fans around them. Knox's sister or not, girls don't like me being around their idols. It's jealousy, pure and simple, and it's also so goddamn stupid! I'm the band mascot, after all.

"What the fuck are you doing here?"

The voice comes from the right, close to my ear, and I squeak as I turn.

"Knox. You scared me, you fucker." I have to give as good as I get with these guys.

"Who told you about the party?"

"Nobody."

"Was it Rye?" He narrows his eyes, so dark suddenly they're more gray than blue.

"No! I kind of ended up here by mistake."

"Mistake?" Knox shoves a wave of dark hair away from his face and gives me that piercing look that sees way too much.

"Not really mistake," I correct as I drink my beer. Damn, but I always get nervous when my brother starts his protective thing. It's so freaking unnecessary. Most of the time.

"I...meant to come here," I add, "but I didn't know about the party."

"So you decided to stay."

"Yes."

The song changes to Guns N' Roses, *Welcome to the Jungle,* one of Knox's favorites. Maybe it'll put him in a better mood. He lets out a sigh to go along with the frown.

Is he weakening?

"You know I don't like you around this kind of shit." He jerks his head toward the rest of the room.

"What, watching you and the guys hook up with as many girls as you can convince to sleep with you?"

His gaze sharpens. "Can't say there's much sleeping that goes on."

"Okay." I pissed him off. Fine. He's pissing me off, too. "Then watching y'all hook up with as many girls as you can fuck."

He sucks in a tight hiss. "Goddamn it, Bree!"

I stare at him with what's supposed to be wide-eyed innocence. "You think I don't know how this works? I'm not a kid anymore."

"So?"

"Wycked Obsession is hotter than a Texas summer," I snap, like I'm not proud as hell of the guys. *Wicked Is As Wycked Does* is climbing the charts, they play *Tonight* on the radio every freaking hour, and you're leaving for three months to tour with Edge of Return. You're honest-to-God rock stars now, and you're taking advantage of the—perks."

"The perks." Finally, Knox grins. "Wonder what the fans would say if they heard you say that."

I shrug. "They wouldn't care. All they want is to fuck one of you."

9

His grin dies a sudden, ugly death. "Stop saying shit like that."

"You shouldn't have taught me the words, then."

"Hey, baby." A hand with long, pointy fingernails painted red slides around my brother's chest. The rest of the girl follows, her skirt so short it barely covers her ass and top so low it hardly hides her nipples. "You said you were coming right back."

"I need a couple of minutes." Knox doesn't even look at her.

"Who's this?" she demands, her eyes narrow and angry. Her voice is sharp enough to cut steel.

"My sister." Knox drops his gaze to hers. I can't see his expression, but I know what it means when he says, "Maybe I'll catch up with you later."

So does she. "Knox…baby."

"Later."

She glares at me and slinks away. Later means never when my brother says it like that. She fucked up, and she knows it.

"Sorry." I don't sound it.

"You gonna tell me why you're here?"

I sigh. Knox has a one-track mind about some things, and I learned long ago that I'm one of them.

"Later. I'll tell you later when all this—" I wave one hand "—isn't going on."

"So you're just going to hang out here?"

I take a drink of my beer—a long one this time—and give him a look that says, *Listen to me! For once in your life, just* listen. "Look, Knox. You can kick me out. I'll sit outside on the curb. Sleep in the bushes. Whatever. You're stuck with me tonight, and we'll talk about it tomorrow."

"Bree—"

"Baby girl!"

That's my other nickname. All the guys call me that, even though I'm not that much younger than they are. Ajia's the oldest in years, but they all have worlds of experience over me, so I guess the name fits. It doesn't matter. I've never been able to convince them to stop using it.

"Noah."

I grin at the drummer. His girls trail behind him, looking less pissed than Knox's groupie. Maybe they don't care so much since they're already looking like a threesome.

"I wondered if you'd show up." He grins back.

"She wasn't invited," Knox puts in.

"Asshole," I say just as Noah offers his own opinion.

"Don't be a fucker, man. You know Bree-baby is always welcome."

"Thanks, Noah." I give him a big hug and slide a shitty smile in my brother's direction.

"Uh, the…other guys know you're here?" asks Noah.

I shake my head. "No. Don't think so. I saw Zayne and Rye. Where's Ajia?" I ask as casually as I can.

Noah shrugs, but he doesn't make eye contact with me. I tell myself it isn't because he suspects how I feel about Ajia, but a part of me is afraid he guessed. I've been wondering that for a while now.

"Haven't seen him lately," he finally says.

Knox stares at me, and I know what he's thinking. The same thing I'm thinking. If Ajia isn't around, then he's off somewhere with…someone. Some chick. A slut, I insist to myself, whether it's true or even fair. All I can think of is him kissing another girl, touching her, fucking her.

My breath catches and the bottom drops out of my stomach.

"Look, you guys go do…whatever." I force the words out, but they come easier as I speak. "It's your party. Just ignore me. I'll mingle, and if I get bored, I'll go to the music room. You won't even know I'm here."

The music room is actually the garage, but the guys put some soundproofing in there, keep most of their instruments there, added some furniture and a window AC unit. It's gotta be cooler in there, and I won't have to worry about turning around to find Ajia sucking face with some slut.

"You sure about that, baby girl?"

I smile at Noah for trying to makeup for Knox's shitty attitude. He's protective, too, but in a different way. If nobody gets hurt, if it's legal—or close enough—and everybody involved is an adult, Noah's all for it. My being here pretty much fits all his criteria.

"Go on." I step from in between the guys. "I'm going to get another beer. Don't let me cramp your style." And then I just walk away.

For the next couple of hours, I work my way through the crowd. I talk to a few of the guys' friends, some I know from school and others from the club circuit back when Wycked Obsession played every damn gig they could get. Most of the girls ignore me, but I know a few of them. I even get a chance to talk to Zayne and Rye…and then finally I see Ajia.

He stands across the room from me—with someone. An octopus, I think with a look that should disintegrate her on the spot. She has her hands all over him. I'm sure as hell not going up to him now, but I'm torn. I don't want him to see me like this, all brokenhearted and aching for him, but another part of me wants him to notice me. He doesn't.

He's totally preoccupied with *her.*

Asshole. I'm pissed off and sick, even knowing I have no right to be. *Don't forget what you've always known,* I remind myself. Ajia's flat-ass fucking hot, almost pretty in a handsome sort of way. His features are fine and perfect. His hair is wavy, like Knox's, and they both wear it long, past their shoulders. Ajia's is a golden blond color, his eyes a caramel brown. The combination is unexpected and alluring.

He's tall, maybe 6'2", and muscular. He doesn't have Noah's upper body, but Ajia works out and looks pretty damned impressive. He's also tattooed, sleeves on his arms, part of his chest, and some stuff on his back. Knox told me they'd all added the new album title somewhere on their bodies, but I haven't seen any of the finished work yet.

I have to force myself to look away. No way can I talk to him now. Not with Ursula hanging off him. A smile makes me feel only slightly better, but I like comparing the fangirl to the villain from *The Little Mermaid.* Maybe it's childish, but I don't care.

It's a distraction, but I force myself to listen to Mötley Crüe's *Kickstart My Heart,* Poison's *Every Rose Has Its Thorn,* Whitesnake's *Here I Go Again,* and Warrant's *Heaven.* I've heard them all—dozens of times over the years—along with Classic Rock, Blues, 90s Grunge, Alt. Rock, and Indie Rock. In fact, I can't hear any goddamn song at all without associating the music with Knox, Ajia, and Wycked Obsession.

Hell, I've spent the last two years at the Butler School of Music, going for a degree in Composition because of the band. How fucked up is that?

By the time one o'clock rolls around, I'm done. My emotions are raw, and I never wanted to be a part of the whole party scene in the first place. It only got worse after seeing Ajia like that. Knox made me feel like shit, too, and no matter how hard I try to forget, the thing with Gabe still preys on my mind. I need to get away, sack out in the music room and just get some sleep so I can talk to Knox tomorrow.

The music room *is* cooler and quieter. I turn off the lights and stretch out on the ratty old couch the guys dumped there. I wish I'd brought a toothbrush or looked for an extra one here, but no way am I fighting that crowd again. I'll have to make do until morning.

I don't expect to fall asleep easily, but I must have. One minute there's silence, and then suddenly there are noises. Realizing I'm awake, I lie quietly, listening and hoping it isn't a rat or something. Doesn't matter that I grew up in Texas; I hate that kind of thing!

No, it isn't a rat, I decide. Not the four-legged kind, anyway. The noises aren't right for that. It's people, and they're—

"What the ever-loving fuck?"

The words are out before I can stop them. *Holy hell!* The last thing I want is to be an audience for some couple getting it on.

The overhead light snaps on, and I get my first glimpse of the spectacle. A girl's on her knees with some guy's dick in her mouth. She's sucking, moving her head back and forth and making soft, greedy noises low in her throat. She pulls back, blinking and giving me an unobstructed view of a long, thick, hard cock that looks way more impressive than anything I've ever imagined.

"Ajia?" she snaps, stroking the length of his cock once, twice, but it's too late. My gaze jerks upward and I stare into his face. His caramel eyes look odd, sharp and piercing, as always, and yet heavy with desire. His gaze catches mine and he blinks.

I'm up off the couch in an instant, suddenly on fire and not in a good way. *"Oh, Jesus."*

They stand between me and the door, but I can't stay there. I try to keep from looking down again, but I can't help it. Ajia's dick is still hard, and long, well-manicured fingers still stroke him.

"Jesus." I say it again, and somehow I can finally move.

"Bree," he says in a hoarse voice as I brush past him on my way to the door. I cut it too close, and my shoulder rubs against his.

"Jesus." I'm begging by this time, and then finally—somehow—I'm on the other side of the door.

Ajia and…that girl. She was sucking him off. Stroking him off. I want to close my eyes, but I'm afraid to. Afraid that's all I'll be able to see. Where else can I look? It's all there, and it won't go away.

"What the ever-loving fuck?" I whisper to myself again.

"Baby girl?" Noah suddenly stands in front of me.

"Hey." I want to smile, but I can't.

"What's wrong?"

I shake my head. *I just interrupted Ajia getting sucked off by some chick and it's breaking my freaking heart.* I can't say it.

"I just need a couple of minutes." I clear my throat. "It hasn't been the greatest night." *That* is an understatement—but why did my voice have to sound so goddamn *weak?*

"You—"

Noah breaks off when the door behind me opens. *Shit.* I should have kept moving. Why didn't I? I really don't want to do this now.

"Bree?" Ajia's voice is soft.

I don't look back; I don't have to. It's all on Noah's face. The recognition. The understanding. The…sorrow? Yeah. He knows how I feel. How I *really* feel about Ajia.

Noah hauls me against his chest and gives me a hug. It's comforting, and I hug him back.

"Go to my room," he says against my hair. "Sleep in my bed tonight. I'll take the couch."

I want to laugh, but it won't come. Instead, I pull back from him. "That's sweet, but you know you don't fit on the couch."

His eyes crinkle with a smile, and he winks at me. "You inviting me to spend the night with you, baby girl?"

"You wish." Somehow, I manage a smile.

He nods. "Okay. Go on, then." He gives me a little push, like I'm a kid or something.

Oh, that's right. The band mascot. Like their pet. Their baby girl.

14

A sad place twists inside me, but it isn't Noah's fault. It's nobody's fault but my own, longing for shit that can never be mine. Like some sort of freaking masochist.

I reach out for a quick squeeze of his hand. "Thanks, Noah."

"Don't mention it."

I walk off without ever looking at Ajia, and then I hear a grunt from behind me. "What the fuck, Ajia?" Noah's voice sounds sharp, like a whip. "Just once, couldn't you learn to keep your dick in your pants?"

CHAPTER 2

AJIA

"Shut the fuck up, Noah." I bite the words off, my jaw clenched, and turn to the girl next to me. Hailey? Harley? "I'm gonna have to take a raincheck, honey. Something came up."

"Yeah. I know just what that is." She rubs her hand over my crotch and smiles. It's probably supposed to be sexy. It isn't.

"No." I push her away. "Something else. Band shit."

"Was it that little bitch who interrupted?"

"Bree's not a bitch," I snap. Defending her comes automatically. It's that way for all of us. Bree is...special. Always has been.

"Okay. Well, I'm not really into threesomes, you know. You got the whole package here, baby." What's Her Name throws her arms wide and shoves her chest out like she's trying to remind me of her fake tits. "If you want her, too, I guess I can put up with a lot to fuck Ajia Stone."

God, she even says my name wrong. It's pronounced *Asia,* like the continent. The spelling of my name has pretty much pissed me off for most of my life. *I* didn't choose it. Can't *somebody* get it fucking right?

The rest of it...I don't even go there. Chicks always want to fuck the rock star. Doesn't matter which one. Front men and guitarists like Knox and me are always targets, but everybody in the band gets more than our share of pussy. It's like a goddamn game or something, and I'm so fucking sick of it.

So why do I keep playing?

16

But I know why. It's because I'm such a piece of shit. I don't deserve anything better. And now Bree saw this chick sucking my cock. Jesus-fucking-Christ.

"Look, sorry." I don't even try to be nice. She called Bree a bitch. "It's not gonna happen tonight. I got shit to take care of." I stalk off without a look back.

"Where you going?" Noah calls after me.

"I told you! To take care of shit."

He ought to fucking know. We rented a four-bedroom place in Austin after the last tour. A place to share, to practice, write music, and figure out what the fuck we're doing. Our first album took off kind of unexpectedly, and then we started touring to promote it. We didn't have a lot of time to think or even *breathe* on tour, and we finally got the last six months to put together the album that became *Wicked Is As Wycked Does.*

We'd written most of the songs. This was time to polish and record. Time to plan. Time to get to know our manager and the people at our record label. We did all that and more, and day after tomorrow, we're leaving on tour again. Or is it tomorrow already? Whenever, we've got three months across the South, West, and Midwest.

Three months before we'll be anywhere near Austin again. I can't leave Bree with her last image of me being sucked off by some random chick.

Noah's words come back to me. *Just once, couldn't you learn to keep your dick in your pants?*

It beats the alternative. If whipping my cock out for every girl who's interested keeps me from thinking about—well…old crap that can't be changed, then I'm all for it. Besides, it's the perfect description of my life.

Ajia Stone, fucker.

I stop in front of Noah's door and give it a quick tap. I don't wait to be invited in.

The room is dim, the only light coming from a lamp on the bedside table. It creates a lot of shadows. Maybe that's good. I won't have to look Bree in the eye.

She's sitting on the end of the bed, staring at the floor. Sad. Lost maybe. Did I do that to her? I've always known she had a little crush on me, but that can't be enough to make her look like that. Can it?

"Bree."

"Uhm." It takes a minute before she looks at me. In my general direction, anyway. "Hey."

"You okay?"

Her gaze slides away. "Embarrassed, but I'll live."

I sit next to her, almost close enough for our hips to touch. Too much, maybe, but I want—*need*—her to be comfortable around me again. "I'm sorry you saw that."

She nods but doesn't look at me.

"I didn't know you were there." Lame fucking excuse.

Her laugh is cut off, a kind of choked sound. "Yeah, I know. You were…busy. It's funny." She doesn't sound amused. "I thought the garage'd be safer than the bedrooms."

"Bree…" Fuck. How can I tell her I don't bring random hook-ups back to the place I *sleep?* "Kitten—"

"Don't worry. I know I wasn't supposed to be here. Knox already bitched me out." She sounds hurt. "I didn't mean to crash, but—"

"Ajia, you fucker!" Knox barges through the door. So Noah tattled.

"Shut up, Knox. I'm talking to Bree right now. I'll deal with you later."

"You'll deal with me right fucking now. Leave my sister out of this. She's—"

"Right here, Knox. I can speak for myself."

I swallow a smile. One thing about Bree, she can hold her own against her brother.

"Look, Bree—"

"No, you look," she interrupts and throws her head back to glare at Knox. I've seen Bree in lots of different moods. This is her pissed off one. The one she brings out when her brother gets on her last nerve.

"Just stop this *protective shit.*" Even Knox can't miss how furious she is—can he? "I'm sick of it. I don't need it. Not where the band is concerned. So I woke up to see Ajia getting a blowjob. At some point, I could have caught you doing the same thing, or Zayne eating some girl out, or Noah in a threesome. So the fuck what."

I choke off a strangled sound. Damn. I've always admired Bree's honesty, but…Jesus! Where the fuck did this shit come from?

18

She stares at Knox, but he only shakes his head, his eyes bugged wide. "Goddammit, Bree, you're not supposed to know about that shit."

Exactly.

Her shoulders slump. "Knox, you dumbass. I'm nineteen now. *Nineteen!* Twenty this summer. You know I'm at least as old as most of the girls you guys fuck around with. Older than some."

He blinks, his mouth open but nothing comes out. I can't help laughing. "She's got you there, dude."

Me, too, actually. She's at least as old as Blowjob Girl. I mean, I know I'm an asshole, but have we really been pretending that Bree isn't grown up, same as us?

I slant a glance in her direction. She's dressed in some baggy white shorts, but—damn! She's got legs. Tanned and sleek, they go all the way to heaven.

Holy shit. I am *not* thinking that way!

At least she's wearing an old Pearl Jam T-shirt of Knox's. It's way too big for her, and I can't tell anything about her shape underneath it. Good thing.

He starts to laugh all of a sudden, a weird, stupid sound. I look at him, equal parts relief and confusion, but he's staring at Bree. "Jesus, you're right," he says, shaking his head. "It's fucking insane! I keep thinking you're still the kid you were when we started this thing."

"I'm not. You grew up, and so did I." She points to her chest.

"Yeah, okay." Knox lets out a long breath. "I get it. Fuck." He shakes his head. "Look, I'm not going to change overnight, but I'll try to do better. Okay?"

"Yeah." She smiles, the first I've seen since I flipped on the light in the garage. Maybe she doesn't need to be protected from real-life shit, but—

Wait. What did she say? *Just stop this protective shit. I'm sick of it. I don't need it. Not where the band is concerned.*

"Hey, just a minute."

"What?" Knox and Bree look at me. I stare at her.

"You said you don't need protecting where the band is concerned. So what *do* you need protecting from?"

Maybe she didn't mean the band in general. Did she mean...*me?*

19

Her eyes pop wide, and I notice them for the first time. Kind of a dark green, or maybe sort of brownish? The shadows make it hard to know for sure. Why didn't I ever pay attention before? And why am I looking now?

"Bree?" Knox asks.

The wheels are turning in her brain; I can almost see it. Something's going on, something she doesn't want to say. Shit.

"Well..." She has kind of a swagger in her voice, a sure sign she's nervous. "I was wondering. I thought maybe I could, you know, housesit for y'all this summer. Stay here in the house and just, like, watch over things."

"You wanna stay here?" Knox repeats.

"Yeah. It'd be...great."

"You want to party or something?" So maybe it isn't about me, but it pisses me off to think about her partying without the rest of us there to look out for her.

"No, it's not like that." She shakes her head. "I just—"

"Doesn't matter," Knox interrupts. "We can't say yes even if we wanted to. The lease is up. We let it go for this tour."

"You're moving out?"

"Movers are coming tomorrow afternoon—well, *this* afternoon. Everything we don't take with us is going in storage."

Bree sort of sinks into herself, almost like she's folding up, trying to find some strength or something. She's *never* acted like that before.

"What's wrong, kitten?" I can't catch her gaze.

"I was just...well, I hoped—" She shakes her head.

"Bree?" Knox sounds concerned, but at least he isn't pushing too hard. It's like a goddamn miracle or something. Maybe he really *is* listening to her for a change.

She doesn't answer, just stares at her lap and her twitching fingers.

"Baby girl?" I try again.

She looks at me then, her eyes damp and almost stricken. When she drops her lashes, the tears spilled down her cheeks.

"Aw, don't cry, kitten." I haul her into my arms and shoot a fierce glance at Knox. *What the fuck?* He shakes his head like he hasn't a fucking clue.

"Bree?" He kneels down in front of her. "What's wrong? What happened?"

She sniffs but doesn't move. Her arms are around my waist, her breasts soft against my chest. She has a little more upstairs than I realized.

Nope. Should *not* have noticed that. I should push her away and get the hell out of there. I don't, of course. No way can I.

"It's...Gabe," she says finally.

Gabe? As in Gabe Richmond? Knox's and her stepfather?

"That motherfucker." Knox shoots to his feet as he swears. "That son of a bitch tried to touch you again, didn't he?"

"What the hell?" I look between siblings. "Are you telling me that Gabe—" I can't even fucking say it.

"He came into my room this time," she whispers against my chest. I think she'd push herself inside me if she could. "I was sleeping. I—" she swallows "—woke up and he was touching me."

"I'll kill him." Knox whirls toward the door.

"I'll help." I try to peel Bree away from me.

"No! Stop! You can't!" It's almost a scream.

Knox glares at her. "Why the fuck not?"

"You...know why." She sits up and pulls away from me. Some part of me doesn't want to let her go. "We've talked about this, Knox."

"You've talked—" I look between them. "This isn't new?"

She shakes her head, and her long brown hair dances around her shoulders. I've never noticed *that* before, either.

"No." She doesn't look at me. "It's been happening for...a while."

"Since he moved into the house," adds Knox grimly.

"I've been trying to avoid him." Fuck. She sounds so desperate about it. "Never be alone with him. You know."

"And it's not working," Knox puts in flatly.

"Wait a minute." I aim for clarity. "He's a grown-ass man and you—" I look at Bree "—grown up or not, you're still technically a teenager. What the fuck's he think he's doing?"

She shudders. "Today was the worst. He told me...he wants Mom *and* me. The younger version."

"That's fucking sick."

"You haven't told your mom?"

She shakes her head and sends a pleading look at Knox. "We *can't* tell her. We've talked about that."

"Tell me, then." I grab her hand. For her or me? I only know this whole thing has my gut churning.

Bree dips her head. "Dad broke Mom's heart when he took off, A." A spark of relief soothes me if she can call me by the nickname only she uses.

"It took her a long time to get over it," she adds after a second. "She worked like hell as a single mom to support us. When she found Gabe…it was like she came back to life. I'm not taking that from her."

"Sis—"

"No!" Bree straightens her spine but doesn't pull her hand from mine. "I told you. There are two outcomes if I say anything. One is that she doesn't believe me and it ruins our relationship. Two is that she believes me and it ruins her marriage. Either way, she loses, and I won't be a part of it."

"You really want your mom to be with a guy like that? If he tries shit with his own…stepdaughter—" goddamn, it's hard to *think,* let alone *say* "—you think he won't try with somebody else?"

Bree swallows hard. "I don't know, but I can't be the one to break her heart. *I can't.*"

Fuck. I get it. That doesn't mean I like it, but I let it go—for now.

"Okay…so…" I can't think of anything else to say.

"I don't know." Bree sighs. "I got rid of him today, but he's pushing. Getting braver. I don't want to spend the summer around him. You know, with you guys gone."

Knox slumps against the door and shoves his hands into his hair. "Son of a bitch. You're right. Okay." He stiffens, straightens. "Then we do the only thing we can."

"What's that?" She sounds so goddamn tired.

"You're going on tour with us."

CHAPTER 3

BREE

On tour with Wycked Obsession. Living on the same tour bus as the band. Seeing Ajia every day.

Every. Single. Day.

Seeing the groupies mob him. Seeing them touch him. Kiss him. Maybe another girl and another blowjob?

Nope. I can't go there. Can't do it.

But…this is my chance to get away from Gabe without having to explain one damn thing to Mom. She knows how I feel about Knox and Wycked Obsession's success. How proud I am, and how I've been a fixture with the band from the beginning. It's summer vacation; she probably won't even ask many questions. Probably would love a chance to be alone with Gabe.

Gag.

Ajia's question comes back to me. *You haven't told your mom?* How can I be the one to destroy her trust? Either in me or in Gabe, whichever way it goes?

But how can I keep my mouth shut and let her stay married to an asshole like that?

I have no answers. Not for those questions. Instead, I think about how I'm trading my claim of hating Knox's protective bullshit for taking on the whole Wycked Obsession entourage as my protectors. But then, away from Gabe, what do I really need protecting from?

Not Ajia. That's for sure.

"What about the band? You think the rest of the guys—"

"You know we all love you, baby girl." Ajia's still holding my hand, I realize suddenly, and he squeezes.

The excitement that wants to bubble up inside of me fizzles away. Yeah, they love me. Baby girl. Kitten. Band mascot.

"Thanks." I try to smile and pull my hand free. "But you've had me tagging along for—"

"No way are you staying in Austin with that fucker."

I look at Ajia. He sounds as fierce as Knox, and he's frowning in a way I haven't seen before.

"Okay…" I look between my two favorite guys. "But how's this going to work? You got a little bed in the corner for me?"

I don't know where that came from. Maybe I'm a little more sensitive than I realized. Sometimes, it's just all too much.

"Don't be a bitch, Bree," snaps Knox.

"Sorry."

"We'll work it out. I'll smooth it all over with Mom."

I don't doubt that. He's always had her wrapped around his little finger. Knox wants it, Knox gets it. And in this case, maybe it'll work to my advantage, too.

I know just how serious he is when I try to sneak out of the house the next morning. No clean clothes, no toothbrush. I *have* to get home and clean up.

"Morning, baby girl." Noah's scrunched up on the couch.

"Hey, Noah." I wave. "What time did things wind up this morning?"

He shrugs.

"Thanks for the bed."

"Anything for you, Bree. You know that."

"Yeah, well…" I flush.

"Hear you're coming on tour with us."

"Knox told you?"

"Yep."

Noah stretches and sits up. He isn't wearing a shirt, and I can see for myself just how impressive his chest, pecs, and biceps really are. Thor's hammer stands out prominently. No wonder girls want him, even two at a time.

"You okay with that?" I ask.

"You're not staying here with that fucker!"

"Jesus. Knox told you *that,* too?"

24

Noah looks offended. "Course! We all talked about it last night."

"This morning," I correct him. "Shit. So everybody knows."

"Just the band."

That's enough. I drop my gaze.

"What's wrong, baby girl?" Noah pads across the room and throws an arm around my shoulders. "You okay? You're not still upset about Ajia are you?"

"No!" My cheeks burn but I shake my head. Maybe I am, but I'm not admitting that to *anybody*. "I just feel...kinda dirty over this Gabe thing, you know? Disgusted. He's married to my mom!"

"This is on him, not you." Knox said the same thing.

"Yeah." I sigh. "Maybe I'll feel a little better when I know I'm away from him."

"Good girl."

"Okay, I'm off." I slip out of Noah's grip. "I'm going to the house to clean up and get packed."

"Want some company?"

"What? No. You've got stuff to do."

"You sure you want to go there alone?"

"I...oh. Because of Gabe?" I shake my head. "No, it's okay. He won't be there. He's at work."

"You sure?"

"I'm sure." I smile and hug Noah. "I'll see y'all later. Have Knox text me with the details."

I'm home, in and out of the shower, and packing my suitcase within the hour. From that point, it takes longer. I have to really *think* about what I'm taking. The guys have all complained about the lack of space on a tour bus, and I know I'm not allowed much. Everything I take must have a purpose.

One thing is sure. I'm *done* with all that baggy crap I wore to keep Gabe from noticing me. I'm not going all slutty or anything, but I want to dress in cute clothes that make me feel like a girl. Happy. Attractive.

Even if Ajia doesn't notice.

I pick out a favorite skirt—striped patterns of blue, yellow, and black—and a white blouse with short sleeves and V-neck. The skirt is short and hugs my hips, and I love how it makes me feel feminine, while the blouse shows the little bit of cleavage I have.

I know I'll spend most of the tour in yoga pants, jeans, and shorts, but I want to at least start out feeling good about myself.

Like Bree Gallagher, woman, not baby girl Bree, Wycked Obsession's band mascot.

A little eye shadow, mascara, lip gloss, and I'm ready. I've never been much for a lot of makeup, but I do what I can. The guys wear eyeliner on stage. Maybe I should get some tips from them.

I step back into my room, grinning, but it dies a quick, sudden death. Somebody's there.

Knox asks, "You ready?" and I scream.

He shakes his head. "Goddammit, Bree, what's wrong with you?"

"You scared me, you dick!"

"Thought I'd help with your suitcase."

"Yeah." I take a deep breath to slow my heartbeat. "Thanks. Sorry. I'm just a little…nervous."

"Okay, I—"

A clatter in the hallway interrupts.

"What the fuck?" Noah arrives first.

"Bree! Kitten, you okay?" Ajia is a close second.

"Goddammit, Bree, what happened?" Zayne brings up the rear, looking a little worse for the wear after last night's party.

Oh, wait. Rye's there, too. He just doesn't say anything.

"Guys, it's fine." I shake my head.

"I scared her." Knox grabs my suitcase.

"Jesus, you gave us all a fucking heart attack." Zayne frowns.

"Sorry." I pick up my backpack and purse. Ajia takes the bag from me. "Maybe I'm a little jumpy."

"No worries." Noah slings one arm around my shoulders. "Let's get out of this hell hole."

"Hell hole?" I laugh.

"Hey, we got a limo outside, a brand-new tour bus, and three months of open road ahead of us," he brags.

"You guys got a new tour bus?" I'm impressed.

"New to us," explains Rye. He's the quiet, calm member of the band. "Edge of Return's on our label. They got a new bus for the tour, so we got their old one. Refurbished."

"Rumor has it, there's an extra-large bathroom." Zayne wiggles his eyebrows. "And bigger bunks."

"I'll believe it when I see it." I laugh, remembering their old bus. Nothing wrong with it, but it was certainly nothing fancy.

We pile into the limo—provided by the label because it's delivering us straight to where the tour bus is parked—and the guys chat about the tour, meeting up with the guys from Edge of Return, and album stuff. I sit next to Rye and don't pay much attention.

"You really okay, Bree?" Rye takes my hand.

I smiled at him. He's the sweetest, kindest man I've ever met, but he always has a look of sadness, maybe even regret, that tries to hide deep in his eyes. I've never been able to completely cheer him out of it.

"I'm good, sweetie." I lay my head on his shoulder. "Now that I'm with y'all. And leaving Austin."

"Glad you're coming with us." He sounds like he means it.

He lets go of my hand and puts his arm around me. I ride the rest of the way tucked against him. We're kind of a handsy group, I guess, but there's never been anything weird about it. Nothing sexual. We're just...close.

Not like with Gabe. The guys and I have seen each other through too much for that.

Except for me with Ajia. It's never been uncomfortable, but now that I saw some chick with her mouth on his dick, it's all different. How do I fix something like that?

We pull up to the recording studio before I can answer. The label works with this studio, and I guess that's where the tour bus is parked. All the activity is around back.

"What the fuck?" Noah says suddenly, using the phrase he relies on more than anything else. "You puttin' the moves on our baby girl?" He glares at Rye, but I recognize the teasing in his eyes.

"Don't be a dickhead." Rye hugs me closer. "Just making her comfortable."

"That's right," Knox agrees as the limo door opens. "He's not doing a damn thing, because Bree's off limits."

Zayne's the first one out. We all follow, and I'm the last one out. Ajia is there to help me.

"You okay, kitten?"

I blow out a heavy breath. Under other circumstances, I might like all the attention, but not after Ajia's little performance last night. And not after everybody knows what Gabe did. Or tried to do.

27

"Fine." I smile without looking at him. "Thanks."

Standing in the parking lot, I get my first good look at the new tour bus. Wycked Obsession's logo and *Wicked Is As Wycked Does* are painted on both sides of the bus. It's bigger than the other tour bus, newer, but I see the old tour bus parked just behind it. It has a new paint job, as well.

"Is that the old bus?"

Rye answers. "Yeah. It's for Baz and the crew."

Baz is their manager. His real name is Basil, I think—some old family name or something, Knox said—but I've been warned to *never* call him anything but Baz. I'm sure not going to piss him off *now*. I haven't seen him in a while and wonder if he knows I'm tagging along…and if he does, how he feels about it.

"There's another truck—" Rye pulls me aside and points farther down, "—for our instruments, equipment, that sort of thing."

It has the same Wycked Obsession paint job. I can't help but laugh. "Damn. Y'all are big time now."

He laughs with me. "Remember that old piece of shit van Zayne had? The thing barely got us to our gigs."

"How could I forget? Worst shocks ever. And not enough seats. I had to sit on the floor every flipping time."

"Hey, y'all! Inside!"

Knox is standing on the first step into the bus. He beckons, but I notice the limo driver delivering my suitcase and backpack to where others are loading the storage compartments under the bus. I snatch up my backpack—it'll get me through the first couple of days—and follow Rye into the bus.

"Holy shit!"

Cream-colored leather couches line each side of the bus, with a flat screen TV mounted on the wall. Farther back is a U-shaped booth, and behind that a kitchenette.

I follow the others and spot the bathroom—it *is* bigger, with a tub even—and then the bunks. Six on one side, three on the other. *That's* where they got room for the larger bath. Custom made for Edge of Return?

The guys are huddled around the bunks, picking their own personal space for the next three months. I take a quick look myself. I think these bunks *are* bigger than the other tour bus. Maybe that's another reason why there aren't as many.

I turn to ask, but the guys are all crowded around the back of the bus.

"We've got a surprise for you, kitten." Ajia reaches for my hand, and I let him take it. I've been avoiding him as much as possible since they picked me up at the house, but I knew it couldn't last.

"Wow." I look around. "An actual bedroom."

"It's all yours."

I pull my hand from Ajia's and backed away. "No."

"Don't you like it, baby girl?" Noah asks from behind me.

"Doesn't matter. I'm not taking the bedroom."

"But you're the only girl."

"Thanks for noticing, Zayne, but I'm still not taking the bedroom. I'm not even an official member of the band. I should probably be riding on the other bus with the crew."

"No fucking way." Knox's voice is flat.

"Yeah, yeah. But the answer's still no."

"Bree…" Ajia gives me a serious look. I hold my body still but shake my head and look back.

"What if we compromise?" he asks. "Sort of…rotate."

"Well…okay." I nod once. "We rotate."

They try to get me to go first, but I know better. If they get me in there, they won't want to change. Rock, paper, scissors works out the schedule—each of us for a week—and I'm number four. Noah gets it first.

He flops on the bed. "Excellent! Starting the tour in style."

"One request." I glare at him from the doorway.

"What?"

"Keep it down when you bring your girls back here. And no naked chicks running around the bus."

"Aw, baby girl."

"I'm serious." I try not to grin. "My bunk is right there." I point to one on the other side of the bedroom wall. "I don't want to listen to the sound of you fucking all night long."

"Goddammit, Bree!"

"Shut up, Knox."

I don't look at my brother—or anyone else. Somehow Noah's the only one I trust in this. The only one who knows how I feel.

"I promise," Noah says, but I see the devil dancing in his eyes.

"I mean it." I turn to look at the others, lounging on the couches behind me. "Y'all might be rock stars, but we're not living like this is a frat house on wheels."

Noah laughs from behind me and pushes me out toward the others. "See? I knew this was gonna work out having you along, baby girl. You'll take care of us."

"Yeah. Like a babysitter," I grump.

"Sister," says Knox.

"Friend," suggests Rye.

"Mom?" asks Zayne with a shit-eating grin.

"Wife," says Ajia, and then he shakes his head like he wishes he hadn't said anything.

"That's it!" Noah spins me around like we were dancing. "Bree-baby, you can be our wife!"

"She's my sister, you dumb fuck."

"Okay." Noah nods. "You're Knox's sister and wife to the rest of us."

I look at Ajia. I can't help it. His hair's pulled back today, and it makes his caramel eyes bright. Noticeable. He looks back, like he's aware of every single molecule around us, and yet like he isn't even there.

I get it. I feel a little like that myself.

I turn to the rest of them and force a grin. "You got champagne or something? We gotta toast! We're on fucking tour!"

CHAPTER 4

AJIA

The tour starts in Houston.

It's only a few hours' drive from Austin, and we're there by mid-morning. I have a vague recollection of heading out, maybe around five or six a.m. The band spent the night on the bus since we already moved out of the house, and we're all still in bed when we pull out.

I don't have any trouble going right back to sleep. Good thing, because I had a hard enough time falling asleep the night before. Bree's in the bunk right below me.

Who decided that?

Don't think she realized it when she picked it. Her wide eyes gave her away when I crawled in above her. Guess she couldn't figure out how to change things up after that.

She's still embarrassed about the scene in the garage; I can tell by the way her eyes skitter away from mine. I'm not, although I wish *she* hadn't been the one to see it. You can't live on a tour bus with four other guys and be uncomfortable about your sex life. We've all heard the others in foreplay, mid-fuck, and afterwards. Seen and done some shit, too. Together and separately. I just never counted on Bree being a part of it…or her knowing anything about what we did.

She's different from other girls. She's our baby girl. But now that she's seen my cock…well, *it* wants her to see it again.

And more.

My body and my mind have gone to war over her, and that's just fucking unacceptable.

31

Breeanne Gallagher is *off limits*. Always has been. She's Knox's little sister. She was a kid when we met, babysitting some schizophrenic little kitten that made her crazy, and I've made sure she stayed safely that way in my mind. Then she saw my dick. She started talking about blowjobs, girls being eaten out, and threesomes. She snuggled up against me, her bare legs tanned and slim and gorgeous, and she pressed her soft, plush tits against me. *Jesus Christ!*

Even worse is the fact that her fucking stepfather *hit on her.*

Talk about fucking unacceptable.

Shit.

She isn't a little girl anymore, and my fucking prick knows it.

I had a hard-on when I fell asleep last night, and it's still there when we leave Austin. Both are because she's so close. Is it my imagination, or can I smell the sweet scent of strawberry that I always associate with her?

Fuck. As relieved as I am that we got her out of Austin and away from that prick of a stepfather, I know it's going to be a long fucking tour if she's sleeping beneath me every night.

And *not* the kind of *beneath me* that my dick suddenly wants.

I try to settle down. Close my eyes. Count to ten. Go over the lyrics for *Tonight,* our new single. Run down my choices for the set list we'll use in concert.

Relax and breathe…

"Ajia."

She slips into my bunk.

"Bree…"

I can't believe she's here.

She presses her body against mine. "I couldn't wait. I couldn't sleep, knowing you were right here."

"What do you want, Bree?" I force myself to ask the question.

"You. What did you think?"

"But Bree…baby…"

"But what?" She presses her lips to the base of my throat, drags them up to my jaw, stops at the corner of my mouth. "I want you, you want me. What more is there to say?"

"Jesus."

She kisses me, and at the same time I feel her hand slide down my stomach, my hips, and then she has me. Her fingers wrap around my dick and caress, up and down. I've never been so hard.

"Bree." I breathe her name against her lips, and then our mouths find each other. I catch her tongue with mine, find the hot recesses of her mouth, test the ridges of her teeth. Her breath catches, and I stroke my tongue through the whole of her mouth.

God, she tastes good.

She pulls away. Her mouth, open and kissing, slips over my chest, my abs, down farther, and then she pushes my boxers away. Her hands and mouth find my cock, and she presses a tender kiss against the head.

"I've wanted to do this for so long, A," she says. "When I saw you letting that other girl go down on you, I knew I had to take her place."

"Bree—"

My voice breaks off when she takes me in her mouth. She's hot and moist, and her tongue swirls around the head. She finds that special spot just below the head and teases it with her tongue, then pulls me farther in, until her mouth is halfway down my shaft. I know I'm probably too big for her to take all of me, but goddamn...this feels so fucking good!

"That's it, baby." I flex my hips, and she groans softly. She likes it.

She sucks harder and cups my balls. She caresses me, and then her mouth is there, before she licks all the way back to the tip. She takes me between her lips again, and this time I go deep enough to feel the back of her throat. My baby girl doesn't even gag.

Goddamn but she knows what she's doing! She licks and sucks, and I'm damn near lost. I know I ought to reach for her, caress her, give her the same kind of pleasure she's giving me, but I can't seem to move. All I can do is give myself over to her and let her bring me to the point where I have to come or lose my fucking mind.

"Ajia." She groans my name.

"Ajia!"

I groan.

"You gonna stay in bed all fucking day? Bree's cooking us breakfast!"

Fuuuuuck!

Her hot mouth and soft hands are gone. It was only a dream.

A fucking dream, and I'm in my bunk—alone—with Noah shouting at me.

I groan again.

"You got a girl in there?"

"No, asshole. I was asleep."

"Well, get up. Bree's cooking bacon and eggs, and we gotta meet Edge of Return in less than an hour."

I look down at myself. My cock is hard as a fucking rock, and I can see a small damp spot at the front of my boxers. Precum. I didn't actually come, but my body sure as hell wants to.

Nothing I can do about it now.

I climb out of the bunk and pull on a pair of jeans, zipped—not easy since I'm still hard—but unbuttoned. "Got time for a shower?" I ask, still turned away from the others.

"If you hurry." Bree answers without looking at me. "Just scrambling the eggs now."

"Right."

I grab clean clothes, hold them in front of me to disguise my hard-on, and slip into the bathroom. All the bunks lift for storage underneath, and today I'm glad for the convenience. I don't much care if the others wanted to call me on my morning wood, but I don't need Bree seeing or hearing about my boner.

I shed yesterday's clothes and step into the shower. I should make it icy cold, but first things first. I need to take care of the reasons for a shower, because my hard-on isn't going away. I swallow another groan.

I close my eyes, fist the base, and slide my hand up my cock. *Jesus.* I try to go back to images from the dream, but it's different now. Bree's in the shower with me. On her knees in front of me, finishing what we started earlier. Her mouth is over me, taking me in, her tongue swirling around the head, and then she's sucking me deep. My hand follows her rhythm, and my hips flex.

She pulls away, licks the length of my shaft and whispers, "Come for me, baby."

She takes me again, all the way. My fist tightens, and I stroke myself hard. She moans, and I see her hand slip between her thighs. She's touching herself, and that's all I need.

My balls draw up and I feel the familiar tingle at the base of my spine. I drop my head forward and finally come. Hard. I growl long and deep in my throat.

Christ! It's the first day of the tour, and I'm already jerking off in the shower.

I clean myself up, dry off, and dress with sudden speed. I *have* to figure out how to keep my mind occupied if I don't want to fight a constant hard-on for the next three months.

"Just in time," Bree says as I step out of the steamy bathroom. She hands me a plate of bacon and eggs scrambled with onion, red peppers, jalapenos, and cheese. It's a favorite she's been making for us for years.

I sit in the booth and she hands me a cup of coffee. The others are acting like starving animals, already eating without saying a word.

"You eat?" I turn to her.

It's the first time I've really looked at her this morning. Images from my dream, my shower, shoulder for position in my head, but I force them out. Bree deserves better than that.

She's dressed in a pair of ragged cut-offs and a racer-back tank top that says *Keep Austin Weird.* Bare feet, and I notice her toenails are painted bright red. Kind of like the color of Wycked Obsessions' logo. Her dark hair is pulled back into a ponytail that swings as she moves.

She looks fan-fucking-tastic, and my dick approves.

She stares back at me. "I've got mine here." She lifts a plate, smaller than what she gave the rest of us.

"That enough?"

"Plenty." She almost smiles.

"Sit down." I gesture to the table. "You're not waiting on us."

She drags a slow gaze around the table and finally nods.

"Slide over." I shove at Knox next to me, and everybody moves a little to the right. She has no choice but to sit next to me.

I take a bite and savor the crunchy pepper and spice of jalapeno mixed with the eggs. Bacon is perfect, crispy but not overdone.

"You haven't lost your touch, kitten."

"Thanks, Bree." Rye smiles from across the table. "Best breakfast I've had in a long time."

"You're welcome, sweetie." She smiles, but I can feel a tension radiating from her. No matter how close we've all been, going on tour with the five us can't be easy.

"What're you doing today?" asks Knox from my right. He must be talking to Bree; Wycked Obsession already has our day scheduled.

"Figure out how shit works around here," she says. "Unpack some of my stuff. Talk to Baz. I already know what y'all like to eat, so I'll put together some menus. You know."

"Wife stuff," puts in Noah.

We all look at him. "What?" he demands, and then Bree laughs. It releases some of her unease.

"Yeah. Wife stuff."

He nods. "We'll be around."

"We're meeting Edge of Return," I tell her. "Interview with a local TV station. Finalize our set list. Rehearse."

I don't know why I'm telling her all this.

"No radio station?" she asks, and I smile. She knows her shit.

"Edge of Return did a morning show today," Zayne tells her. "We do it tomorrow."

"We're here two nights?"

"Two shows in Houston," I tell her. "Talent usually gets a hotel if we spend more than a night, but I guess not at the beginning."

"Talent?" She looks around at all of us. "That's y'all. I'm just the…wife." She grins, but it looks a little awkward. "Think I'll stay on the bus."

"You can take turns sleeping with us," Noah says. He sits back with a casual smile. "You know, like that *Sister Wives* show, except the opposite."

That just pisses me off. It started as a joke, but it's getting fucking old now. Noah's a shit-stirrer and I know it, but suddenly I want to punch him in the face.

"She gets her own room—" Knox frowns his way around the table "—and you fuckers are out of luck. I worked it out with Baz."

"Knox." Bree leans forward to catch her brother's eye. "You don't have to do that. I'll be fine here. I—"

"Forget it. We're at a hotel, you're at a hotel. No discussion."

"Fine."

36

She flops back against the booth, shoulders stiff, and her breasts are just suddenly *there*. Not like they hadn't been or even that I haven't known on some level that she's grown into a woman's body. But—damn. She has actual tits and cleavage and I know they'll fit perfectly in my big hands.

And I *don't* need to tell myself how wrong that is.

"Let's go." Zayne pushes out of the booth and the others start to move. "We've got about ten minutes."

"Uh, don't forget..." Bree says calmly as she continues to eat.

"Forget what?" Zayne stops.

"I might be your collective wife, but I'm not your maid. Plates in the sink, gentlemen. I'll take care of the rest."

Rye blinks with a smile and is the first to comply. The rest follow suit, all sliding out on the opposite side because Bree and I take up the other end.

"Thanks, Bree!" He waves on his way out.

Zayne is right behind him. "Yeah. Thanks."

"Thanks, baby girl." Noah kisses the top of her head.

"Thanks," Knox mutters and then looks at me. "You coming?"

"In a minute." I point to my plate. I have a couple of bites left.

He nods, and then it's just Bree and me. I don't move away from her.

"You got them to cooperate." I clean my plate.

"It's early. Think it'll last two weeks?"

"Maybe." I laugh.

"Can I tell you a secret?"

I lean aside to look straight at her. "Sure."

She points over her shoulder with one thumb. "There's a dishwasher."

I laugh and can't help thinking how different she is from every other chick I've ever known. Ordinary. Focused on something besides my fame or my dick.

"You're shitting me," I say with a grin.

"Nope." She shakes her head. "I found it this morning. It's small, at least half the size of a regular dishwasher, but it's there."

"Edge of Return must live damn well. Wonder what their new tour bus is like."

She laughs and gets to her feet. "I can't even imagine. Maybe that'll be y'all after this tour."

I shrug. "Got plenty of money right now. This fame shit…it's harder to deal with." *That's* the understatement of the year.

She is in the kitchenette, scraping dirty plates into the garbage, but looks up at me through the fringe of her eyelashes. "You okay, Ajia?"

She wants to know what was wrong with me? There's so much I could say. And not just about the other night in the garage. Old shit. Ugly shit. Shit that would turn her stomach. Some of it I don't understand, even now, but I swallow it all.

"Sure. It's been six months of ordinary-guy mode. Just getting back into my rock star personality."

"Okay." Her smile is crooked. She straightens and takes my plate from me. "You guys are good, you know. Like—*really good.*"

I grin. "You're gonna see for yourself. You're coming to the show tonight, right?"

Her smile broadens. "Wouldn't miss it."

"Come inside if you get bored." I nod toward the arena. "I'll show you around."

Her eyes dart away, come back, and she then gives me another, more careful smile. "Okay. I'll do that."

"See you later, kitten." I head down the aisle toward the front of the bus. "Oh, and Bree?" I stop at the top of the steps and look back.

"Yeah?"

"Thanks for breakfast. I…liked it. A lot."

CHAPTER 5

BREE

It's almost time for Wycked Obsession to take the stage, and it's the first time I've gone backstage all day.

Ajia's offer to show me around left me breathless and excited for most of the day. I couldn't let myself take him up on it, though. Not today. Not so soon after the episode in the music room. Instead, I tried to keep myself too busy to think about it.

Besides, I know he—all the band, really—has too many legit responsibilities right now. A secret, dreamy part of me hopes it can happen later in the tour.

I slip through the darkness and make my way to the side of the backstage area. I have an all-access pass, thanks to Baz. We had a quick chat earlier, and I'm relieved that he's okay with me coming along. Pretty sure Knox told him about Gabe.

God. I shouldn't be embarrassed—it's on Gabe, as everybody keeps reminding me—but it's just so...*eeewwww!* I felt guilty when I talked to my mom this morning. She sounded okay about me going on tour with the band; Knox explained it would be good experience for my degree. Even so, I could tell she was surprised, maybe even hurt, that I hadn't talked to her about it myself. It made me feel bad; I'd all but convinced myself she'd be glad for a chance to be alone with that asshole.

It also reminds me of Ajia's questions. *You really want your mom to be with a guy like that? If he tries shit with his own...stepdaughter—you think he won't try with somebody else?* But my answer remains as true as when I said it. *I can't be the one to break her heart.* I can't.

39

A long, low note captures my attention, and I look out onto the stage. Teasing enticement from Zayne's bass. The low rumble of crowd noise turns into a shriek. Zayne plucks his bass again, and then the thudding demand of Noah's bass drum joins in. The screams get louder. Rye suddenly runs the scales on his keyboard. Spotlights shine on them, one by one, while the rest of the stage remains dark. My heart's pounding because I know what's next.

The opening guitar riff of *Run,* the band's first single, sends the crowd into a growing frenzy, and a fourth spotlight shines on my brother. The other three are positioned equally around the back of the stage, while Knox stands closer to me, at the front. He doesn't look at me, the audience, or anywhere except his guitar. His hair hangs down over his face and his fingers produce musical magic.

And then a voice. *His* voice.

Run, baby, run.
You cannot hide from me.
Are you really sure you want to go?
You know I can set you free.

The words are a sensual demand. Ajia's voice carries a husky echo with a certain ragged breathiness that tells every woman in the audience she'd be a fool to go. He can make them live…love…come. They scream their satisfaction and move closer to the stage.

I can't look away from him.

He stands cupping the microphone to him like a lover. His head drops low, waves of blond hair concealing his face, but I know his eyes are closed. I'd bet money on it. He wears black leather pants that caress him like a second skin and black motorcycle boots. His shirt's a white button down, with the sleeves rolled up to his elbows. It's untucked, unbuttoned, and I get a flash of six-pack abs.

Oh, God.

My nipples are suddenly stiff and aching, and my sex is damp. I swallow a groan of arousal.

Like thousands of other women in the audience.

I close my eyes and try to breathe, but *that* image returns. Ajia in that groupie's mouth. The hard length of his cock. Its stunning girth. He's crooning the words of the song in his low, sexy voice.

Jesus, I could come right there!

My eyes pop open, and I force myself to look at the crowd. At the looks of ecstasy on all those female faces. At the shrieks and screams. I am *so* not alone in this.

Who will be the lucky girl tonight?

He sings the first verse again.

Run, baby, run.

No one wants to go anywhere. We all want *him.*

You cannot hide from me.

A thousand voices shout his name. Somehow, I don't.

Are you really sure you want to go?

Hell, no. I will crawl on my hands and knees to get to him.

You know I can set you free.

His mouth, his lips and tongue, his hands. Holy mother of God, his cock. They can give me a freedom that I can only imagine. But I'm only Knox's sister. Band mascot. *Kitten.*

The crowd is frenzied by the end of the song. Me, too, but I stand my ground and watch Ajia greet the audience.

"Hello, Houston!" he screams with a grin.

They scream back.

"We're Wycked Obsession, and we're here to get your night started right. Are you *ready?*"

Screaming. Shouts I can't understand.

"I said, are you *fucking ready?*"

More screams, and this time I can make out one woman's shriek. "Ajia! I wanna have your baby!"

I send a murderous gaze out into the audience, but he just laughs. "Whoa, there, honey. Don't think we're ready for that yet."

The crowd screams for more, but I'm just pissed. *Honey?* And *we?* He doesn't think *we're* ready for that? Why is he even *associating* himself with her?

Ajia's arm comes up, Noah counts off the beat, and Knox leads them into the opening of *No Doubt,* their first single to make it into the top five. I hear the music, the lyrics, but only distantly. My mind is in shock.

What is *wrong* with me?

This is the first show of the tour, and I'm totally eaten up with jealousy over fans he can't even see? How will I survive the next three months with the band if I'm a basket case already? Knowing that every time he's alone, he might be with another woman. Doing all the things with her that I want him to do to me.

Worse, it's none of my business. I have nothing to say about it, because I'm only Bree.

Baby girl. Kitten. Suddenly I hate those nicknames.

This is getting fucking ridiculous!

So, what are you going to do about it? I don't just ask myself, I demand it. *You gonna play Knox's star-struck little sister, or are you gonna do something about how you feel?*

Do something?

Do something? Like what?

What are all the clichés? Shit or get off the pot. Fish or cut bait. Step up or step off.

What does any of that even mean? Like Nike? *Just do it.*

Do what? Can I really, like, try something? Get him to notice me?

I look down at myself. I gotta admit, I dressed pretty carefully for the concert. I don't know why I try so hard; I'm in *way* over my head when compared to the way all the groupies act and dress.

I'm wearing a brand-new skirt, shorter and tighter than anything else I own. It's white with a pattern of impressionistic flowers in pink, gray and black streaked all over it. I added a blousy pale pink tank top with spaghetti straps. The hem of my top and waistband of my skirt barely touch. I have some pink gladiator sandals at home that would look perfect with it, but I settle for some strappy white flat sandals that I packed because they'll go with anything.

Fuck it. Maybe I *can* do this.

I look at Ajia. He's strutting around the stage like he owns it—and he does. He fucking does. And I know then that I want to own him almost as much as I want him to own me.

A lot of shit is happening backstage after Wycked Obsession's performance. They're coming off, Edge of Return are going on, and I'm in the way. I almost run over a young, pimply-faced guy, and I mumble my apologies. Shit! I need to get the hell out of there, so I escape to the dressing room.

Why the hell don't they just call it the backstage party room? I ask myself, and not for the first time. A lot more of *that* goes on, or at least that's what I saw the couple of times I visited on the last tour. Knox kept me on a short leash then, but I'm *not* having it tonight.

I help myself to a vodka and Sprite from the table laid generously with food and booze. I find a spot on the couch and settle in to wait. Maybe I can come up with an idea of just how the hell I think I can get Ajia to notice me as a woman.

Then—*damn*—I'm not alone long enough to reach any conclusions.

The guys come racing into the room like a litter of lab puppies, laughing and joking and jumping around. Well, some of them. Rye, Noah, and Knox come in. No sign of Zayne or Ajia.

My resolve hardens.

Noah is shirtless. He always wears a Wycked Obsession T-shirt on stage and then throws it into the crowd. His hair is plastered to his head from sweating.

I get up for hugs. "You guys were awesome!"

"We were, weren't we?" laughs Noah. He hugs me again.

"Whew—you smell like sweat!" I laugh with him.

He shrugs. "Hard work out there, baby girl. You saying I need a shower?"

"Well…" I pretend to think about it.

He grabs me, Rye grabs my drink, and then Noah has me pinned on the couch. "Say I smell good and I'll let you up. Like a flower."

"A flower?"

"A tulip.

"Do tulips smell?"

"A rose."

"I don't like the smell of roses."

"Aw, you're gonna get it, baby girl."

He tickles me and my top rides up above my waist. I don't care. I can't stop squirming or screaming or laughing. I have no power against being tickled.

"You got five seconds to get in the shower," Knox yells, "or I'm going first."

That's what gets Noah's attention? He hops up as fast as he tumbled me down. "Gotta go, baby girl." He grins. "I'm always first in the shower."

I grumble to myself, straighten my top, and stand so I can pull my skirt back into place. I look up to see Ajia standing just inside the door. A girl no older than me is clutching his arm.

My stomach clenches and I blink. He stares back with the strangest look. Is he pissed? Jealous? Amused? I can't tell, and then I decide it doesn't matter. My next step is what's important.

I grab my drink from Rye with a smile and saunter over to Ajia.

"You were great, sweetie." I rely on the same endearment I use with the other guys. Why do I use it so rarely with Ajia? I laugh and shake my head. "What am I saying?" I reach for his free arm with my drinkless hand. "You were...amazing."

His eyes darken to a rich, whiskey brown, and that's when I get brave. I press myself against him and wrap my arms around his neck. I have to go up on my tiptoes to do it and watch the angle of my red cup, but I use the distractions to my advantage. I tuck my face against his neck and breathe in that delicious scent of sandalwood, musk, and Ajia, and then his arms are around my waist.

I drop my head back so I can look straight into his face. "Congratulations."

He smiles. "Thanks, kitten."

I'm not crazy about him calling me *kitten* at this particular moment, but I let it go. It's at least personal between us.

"Ajia."

The whiny voice of the girl next to him interrupts. I want to say something nasty, shove her as far away as possible or—well, it doesn't matter. It isn't gonna happen, and so I do the next best thing.

I unwind my arms from his neck and, using my red Solo cup as my excuse, balance myself against him as I sink back to my feet. As in...I drag my breasts down his chest until I'm standing flat footed again. His shirt is still unbuttoned, another reason for my nipples to go hard. They aren't shy about making an appearance through my clothes, and they aren't the only thing that's hard.

I recognize the impressive ridge in Ajia's leather pants for exactly what it is. I don't actually take any credit for his hard-on, but at least being next to me didn't chase it away. I wait against him as long as I dare and then take a single step back. His hands are still at my waist, skin against skin, I realize suddenly. My shirt rode up, but I have no intention of pulling it back into place.

I kind of like it when he does it for me. Mostly, though, I wish he'd pull it up over my head and maybe even get serious about getting me out of the rest of my clothes.

"Ajia." Whiny Voice again.

I step back slowly, give him what I hope is a steamy smile, and stroll back to the refreshment table. The room's starting to fill up, mostly groupies and fangirls, but there are also a few guys I don't recognize. I don't care. Nobody says anything to me, and why would they? They don't know me except as the chick who was just talking to Ajia. I'm nobody to them, and I'm not about to announce myself as Knox's little sister.

How lame is that?

Noah is out of the shower—that was quick—and stands near the booze, pouring himself a drink. I stop next to him, ignoring the giggling girls on his other side.

"Having fun there, baby girl?" He looks at me.

I peek at him through my lashes and pour some vodka into my cup. "Maybe."

"Good thing Knox's in the shower. He missed the ending to that little scene."

"What scene?"

He takes a drink. "You know what you're doing, Bree?"

I fill my glass with Sprite. "No. Not sure that I do."

He laughs. "At least you're honest."

I slug back a big drink. "What should I do? Just watch while he fucks his way through the tour?"

Noah's gaze flicks between Ajia and me. "I dunno. Might be safer."

"Safer for who?"

He shrugs. "Knox isn't gonna like it."

I laugh but it sounds harsh. "Knox doesn't like anything where I'm concerned."

"He's your brother. He loves you."

My smile becomes more genuine. "Yeah, he does. And he's protective as shit. But he's having a hard time letting me grow up, and I'm not waiting."

Noah grins. "Well, this ought to be interesting."

"What?" I ask, pretending I'm innocent.

45

He steps close until we're practically touching, and then he bends down to press his lips close to my ear. "Watching you go after Ajia."

I pull back enough to look him straight on. "You make it sound like a game or something."

"Isn't it?"

"No." I frown. "I've never been more serious."

Our faces are close enough together that I can see a riot of thoughts chasing through Noah's pretty blue eyes. "You might want to be careful."

"Careful of what?"

"Ajia. He's…been through some shit."

I shoot Noah a look. One that says, *are you fucking kidding me?*

"We've all been through some shit, Noah," I remind him. "Maybe you remember the story of the last guy who hit on me? My *stepfather.*"

A second later his grin is back. "Yep. It's gonna be good. Ajia doesn't have a chance in hell."

I can't help it. I grin back and tug him close for a hug. "I hope you're right, sweetie."

"Don't worry, baby girl. You need any help, I'm your wingman."

I give him a knowing smile. "Just for that, I'll do *you* a favor. Go back to your girls." I point to his other side. "They're…anxious."

Noah shouts his laughter. "Is that a nice way of saying they're horny?"

"Yeah. They wanna fuck a rock star."

He lifts his eyebrows. "So do you."

I turn automatically, look to where I last saw Ajia. He isn't there. Neither is the chick who was pawing his arm and whining for his attention. I search the room but don't see them, so I turn back to Noah. He has an arm around one fangirl, while another whispers in his ear.

I take a long, deep drink from my cup.

That's right, Bree, I tell myself. *Partying with rock stars, living the rocker life, and you think you've got a chance in hell with a man like Ajia? Are you thinking with your head, your heart—or your pussy?*

And what does it matter? Brave or weak, I'm either in or out.

46

How much risk can I afford?

"Thirty minutes, guys!"

It's Baz shouting from just inside the doorway. I head for Knox, fresh from his shower.

"What happens in thirty minutes?"

"Limo. We're heading downtown to Edge of Return's afterparty."

"They're still on stage!"

He shrugs. "They'll follow when they're done."

"I—" I'm not sure what to say. Am I invited? Should I ask or just slip out and head for the tour bus? It isn't always easy to know where to fit when you're the band mascot.

"You going with us?" asks Rye from behind me. He's out of the shower, too.

Sheesh, how do they manage to get cleaned up so fast?

"Course she's going with us," snaps Knox. "Bree goes where the band goes."

I guess that answers my question. I'm not quite sure how I feel about it, though. It's great that Knox isn't as uptight about my partying, living on the fringes of rock star life, but it would be kind of nice to be included because they *want* me there. Not just because I'm part of the entourage.

Oh, get freaking over yourself! My conscience has little patience with self-pity. *Go and have a good time!*

If ever I need to find an answer to my question—am I in or out?—this seems like the perfect opportunity.

CHAPTER 6

AJIA

"So, this is how rock stars live."

Bree sits back on a sofa in the VIP section of a club in downtown Houston. All of us are partying with Edge of Return, celebrating the start of the tour. They have an upstairs room with a balcony that looks out over the main bar and dance floor. A DJ plays *Something from Nothing* by the Foo Fighters, and the place rocks.

I don't know the guys in the other band well, but they seem to be a lot like us. They hit it big fast, a couple years ahead of Wycked Obsession, and they're riding the wave. Nothing wrong with that.

I'm on the other end of the sofa, while Knox sits in a plush chair by Bree. The crowd's an eclectic mix. I recognize a couple of movie stars from Texas, other musicians, and a supermodel with a very impressive female entourage. I also spot a couple of well-known sports figures, a few other minor celebrities, and some obvious groupies.

The faces get more impressive with every tour. But—fuck. I'm just an ordinary guy with some pretty good pipes. Mad Spencer, Edge of Return's lead singer, is better. Worse, all this shit keeps me tied into that rock star thing that buried Ajia Stone, the man. Do I even know who he is anymore? Is he worth finding again?

I'm almost glad for the interruption when a huge guy approaches. He holds out a hand. "Hey, I'm Tom. Just wanted to say you guys were great tonight. Congratulations."

"Thanks, man." I stand and we shake hands. "Glad you enjoyed it."

He and Knox exchange a couple of words, and then he's gone.

Bree looks from Knox to me. "Doesn't he play for the Texans?"

"Yeah. Defensive End." I sit back down.

She stares at me. "You know football?"

I laugh. "C'mon, Bree. I grew up in Texas. You know a man in Texas who doesn't know football?"

She grins. "Good point."

She leans toward Knox, and they fall into a discussion of…who knows? I can't really hear them except for an occasional word or two, and I don't try to eavesdrop. Pretty sure they'd have included me if I wanted, but I'm preoccupied.

I can't forget the way Bree slid herself down my body and rubbed her nipples over my chest. My cock perks up at just the memory.

What was she thinking?

And what the fuck was *I* thinking to let her? To dream about her? Or stroke myself off in the shower thinking about her?

I'm not a forever kind of guy. I've known it for a long time, learned it the hard way, and it's not the kind of lesson a man forgets. I don't deserve to even attempt that entirely fictional happily-ever-after crap, and I sure as hell am not tempting fate by trying to pretend otherwise.

Besides, Bree's a kid, for fuck's sake. Knox's little sister. Off limits. She has been for as long as I've known her—and rightly so.

I'm at least as old as most of the girls you guys fuck around with.

Hearing her say those words, and knowing she saw that chick with my dick in her mouth, did something. Changed things around in my head. I'm fighting to push her back into that tidy little box that keeps her safe from assholes like me—and then she has to stroke herself over me like a purring goddamn kitten.

Fuck.

"I'm getting a drink." I push to my feet. "Y'all want anything?"

Knox waves his empty Corona bottle, and I nod. Bree's glass is half-full, and she shakes her head. "I'm good."

The bar's located along the far wall, and I glance around for the bartender. Zayne's making the moves on some woman from the supermodel's group, Rye's deep in conversation with a woman I remember from the TV station, while Noah's entertaining the groupies. Business as usual.

49

I wait until the bartender gets to me. He sends a waitress over to Knox with his beer, while I listen to Coldplay's *Adventure of a Lifetime.*

"Good song." A female voice comes from behind me.

I turn to see the supermodel standing just behind me. "Yeah. Coldplay's always classic."

She steps closer and runs a finger down my arm. "You know...*Tonight* is my favorite song."

"Really?" I don't believe her, but it doesn't matter. That isn't what this is about.

"Did you write it?"

"No. That one's Rye's." I point. "Our keyboardist."

She blinks but then she smiles. It doesn't take a genius to figure out what she's after. Sex radiates from her.

"Nobody could sing it like you," she purrs.

Yeah, purrs. No other way to describe it. Part of me wants to laugh. A supermodel and a rock star. A fucking cliché...and that's my life.

The bartender hands me my beer, and I lead her away from the bar to an empty space closer to Knox. Not really quiet or out of the way, but it doesn't matter. She wants to be seen with me, to fuck me, and that's supposed to be the goal on my part, too.

Better to fuck a random chick, supermodel or not, than think about other shit. Especially Knox's little sister.

"So..." She presses herself against my side and whispers, "Any chance I can get a *private* concert?"

I can almost look her eye to eye. Doesn't happen too often, but she has those long model legs and wears four-inch fuck-me heels. I get a flashing image of her standing in front of me wearing nothing but those shoes.

"A private concert?" I ask with a practiced smile. My cock decides to take notice. "Or something a little more...personal?"

She smiles back. "Singer's choice. In everything."

So she's up for whatever I want? She rubs her hand over my crotch and my dick gets a little more serious.

Yeah, I could fuck her. And tomorrow? Another concert, another woman to fuck, and then go on to the next show. I have three months of that to look forward to.

I smile again, but it's automatic. Nothing of me in it. That's how I can do it, fuck a different girl every night.

"What do you say, baby?" She leans in for a kiss, but I turn my head. I don't kiss on the mouth. Ever.

I glance at her but don't meet her eyes. "We got time. Let's see where this goes."

The words are barely out of my mouth when Knox moves into my line of vision. He's with one of Supermodel's friends.

"Keep an eye on Bree," he mutters as they pass by. "We're going to...dance."

I slide a quick gaze in Bree's direction. She's there on the couch alone, her drink almost gone. She's messing with her phone and doesn't look around.

Goddammit. But I nod.

Fucking Knox. What the hell happened? He was doing his protective big brother shit, but now he's going off with some random woman? Worse, he trusts me to protect his baby sister, and he shouldn't. He really fucking shouldn't. *I* don't trust me that way anymore.

Besides, I have Supermodel rubbing her tits against me again. I take a long pull from my beer as she starts chattering about something. Some photo shoot in Hawaii? I listen with half an ear and search the room for Noah, Zayne, or Rye. They can help with Bree, but Noah and Zayne are missing, and Rye's got his back to me.

Finally I glance back in Bree's direction to see Ayden, the bassist from Edge of Return, next to her. They're laughing and talking and seem kind of friendly.

Shit. He's *way* fucking out of her league. He's even older than me. I take a step in their direction when Supermodel grabs my arm and presses her breasts against my chest. "Don't you think so, baby?"

"Uh—what?"

"We ought to get out of here." She rubs her palm over my semi-erection. "I think you'd like to get to know me a little better." She laughs. "Or maybe a *lot* better."

Coldplay turned into Maroon 5's *Don't Wanna Know,* but now that bleeds seamlessly into Demi Lovato's *Confident.* Bree squeals, a sound I've heard a million times, and she's on her feet. "I love this song!" she cries, and then Ayden leads her downstairs to the dance floor.

I want to be glad. If Knox is on the dance floor, *he* can look out for his sister. *If* he knows she's there. Or if he's even still at the club. He turned over responsibility for his sister the minute he tagged me. It's how we've done it for years. If Knox isn't there, one of the rest of us steps up. No questions.

So why does it irritate the shit out of me tonight? And that's a dumbass question, because I know. And that pisses me off even more.

"You wanna dance?" I ask Supermodel.

"What?" She frowns at me.

"Going to the dance floor."

"But I thought—" The frown becomes more pronounced. Enough that the beautiful face doesn't look quite so attractive anymore. "We're getting out of here, right?"

"Sorry." I shake my head. "Not tonight." I walk away but toss over my shoulder, "Nice to meet you."

A screech follows me, but I'm just not that interested.

I spot Bree while I'm still on the stairs. She isn't especially tall, but Ayden is. She's wearing that little pink top, and it looks almost neon in the flashing lights. They seemed to be having a good time, but—damn! She moves her hips in a way that looks way too sensual, especially in that short, tight skirt. Her arms are up over her head, and I spot a band of flesh between the hem of her shirt and her waistband.

Ayden doesn't seem to notice anything. He's there dancing with her, yeah, but three other chicks have discovered him. Bree doesn't seem to care. She just keeps dancing, moving like I've never seen her before. Like the music is part of her.

I wonder suddenly how much she's had to drink, especially when a strange guy comes up behind her. His hands are on her hips and she looks at him, dances a few steps. He leans forward, she shakes her head and turns away, but then he touches her again.

I shove my way through the crowd. "There you are, baby girl!"

I can't tell if she hears me, but I know the instant she sees me. Her body changes somehow. I can't tell exactly what happens, but it softens or invites me or some damn thing. She smiles and her hips sway *hello*.

She drops her arms from above her head, and I grab her hand, pull her toward me.

"Hey," shouts Anonymous Guy, and he follows with a frown. "We were dancing."

I wrap my arm around Bree's shoulders and shoot a *don't-fuck-with-me* look at the guy. "Saw your hands on my girl."

"Your—" He looks from me to Bree and then back again. "Hey, aren't you Ajia Stone?" He doesn't get my name right, either, but it's kinda close.

"Yeah."

"And this is your girl?"

"Yep."

He holds up his hands. "Sorry, man. I didn't know."

Bree squirms against me, and so I tighten my arm. "No worries. This time." I pull her closer. "C'mon, baby girl, let's dance."

My hands are on her hips, and I keep us moving.

She shifts close enough to shout in my ear. "That was shitty."

"What?"

"You lied to that guy to blow him off."

"So what? Did you wanna dance with him?"

She pulls back. "That's not the point. I'm just trying to have a little fun."

"You can't trust guys like that."

She stares at me. "You mean guys like you?"

Fuck. "Yeah. Guys like me."

We dance for a bit, and then she asks, "What are you doing here? Where's your girlfriend?"

"She's not my girlfriend."

"Okay. Tonight's fuck, then."

I jerked her against me as the song changes. *Closer* by the Chainsmokers. "Don't talk like that."

She tilts her head back. "Why not? It's true."

I press her head against my chest. "Just dance."

It takes only a few seconds before her arms go around my waist, her hands at my back. *They should be around my neck.*

Bad thought. Totally inappropriate. That would put Bree on her tiptoes, her body pressing against mine from shoulder to hip. Her breasts pillowed against my chest, her crotch cradling my cock.

Nope. No way should I be thinking that shit. So why can't I stop?

"Why are you doing this?" I can barely hear her over the music.

"Doing what?"

"Dancing with me."

I don't answer. Not sure what I want to say.

"Ajia?"

"Knox is busy. Ayden got distracted. Don't want you out here alone." I settle on that much of the truth. So why *not* tell her that her brother asked me to keep an eye on her?

Just stop this protective shit. I'm sick of it. I don't need it.

She told us that in Austin. She'll be pissed if she thinks it's still going on.

She drops her head back, but I can't read her expression with the shifting shadows from the flashing lights. "So, you're here babysitting the kid." The edge in her voice is sharp.

"I don't do shit I don't want to do."

"And you want to be here with me," she scoffs.

"Bree—"

"Like this?" It's like she's been reading my mind. Her grip suddenly slips from my waist, she pushes her palms up my abdomen, and then her arms wrap around my neck. She presses her torso against mine, her breasts flat against my chest, and her crotch cups the ridge of my erection.

Oh, fuck. When did I get so hard?

"Or like this?" she whispers against my neck, and then I feel the swipe of her tongue over my jawline.

I swallow. "What—how much have you had to drink?"

She laughs softly and closes her teeth over one corner of my bottom lip. "Not nearly enough." She licks the same spot. "You want to be with me like this?"

Her lips are on mine then, soft and expressive, but there's an honesty about her kiss. An uncertainty that keeps me from kissing her back. She doesn't quite taste me and I don't taste her, and I know in a sudden flash of understanding it's because of her innocence.

She might be the same physical age as the chicks the band parties with, but she's years behind in actual experience.

She presses her mouth against mine, harder, but I hold still. Slowly, she pulls away to sink back on her heels, her body touching mine in ways that should be illegal. "I guess not. Not like that at all."

"Fuck me," I mutter as I tighten my arms around her. "I fucking tried."

My mouth slams against hers. I slide my tongue along the seam of her lips, and the instant they part, I push inside her mouth. Finally, I can taste her, the faint citrus from whatever she's been drinking and something that's uniquely Bree. It's like no one I've ever kissed before.

Kissed?

My brain goes on instant alert, a part of me so very freaking aware that I don't kiss women—*ever!* But here I am with my tongue seeking the hidden depths of Bree's mouth. I feel like Indiana-fucking-Jones looking for the lost ark, and the only way to find it is through her kisses.

I lose the thought as she lets out a soft, sighing moan. Her hands are in my hair, tangling through the length of it and holding my head so she can move her mouth, her lips, her tongue against mine.

She kisses me back like she'll die if she doesn't. Maybe she won't, but I will.

I cup my hands around her ass and haul her close against my hard-on. My hips flex against hers, and I don't doubt what I want. Hell, we can both feel it. I only need a couple of minutes, just long enough to find some privacy, and then I'll be balls deep inside this woman.

I want—

A heavy hand slams down on my shoulder. "You really think this is a good fucking idea?"

I jerk my mouth from Bree's so I can tell this asshole to leave us alone. Then I see Noah standing on the dance floor next to us.

"What…" I demand as Bree moans my name. An instant later she recognizes the interruption.

"Noah?"

He leans forward and drops an arm over each of our shoulders. "Personally," he says in a low voice, "I don't care if you two fuck like rabbits." He looks at me. "I'll fucking kill you if you hurt her, but if you're two healthy adults looking to hook up, I say *go for it.*" He looks between us again. "But do you really want to do it in the middle of a goddamn club full of cell phone cameras and video? You want to see this on TMZ or some internet fan site tomorrow? Where *anybody* can see it?"

Anybody, meaning Knox.

He looks at that shit. He wants to know what people are saying about us. He posts on Twitter and Facebook and Instagram and a bunch of other social media sites, for Christ's sake.

Holy hell.

I drop my arms from around Bree and step back. My hard-on doesn't go away—I still want her like a drowning man wants dry land—but my brain somehow grabs some of the blood flow.

"You're right." I haul in a ragged breath.

"Ajia?"

Bree doesn't seem to recover so well. She looks confused, raw, in pain. Shattered. Not that there's a fucking thing I can do about it.

I spin on my heel. "See that she gets home, Noah." And then I lose myself in the crowd.

Chapter 7

BREE

I avoid Ajia as much as I can for a couple of days. It isn't hard. He's ignoring me, too. I don't go to the second Houston show. When he's on the tour bus, he either watches movies, plays video games with the guys, or disappears into his bunk. I stick to my little area, too. If the guys are there, I read in my bunk, write in my journal, or use the booth in the small dining area. When I'm there alone, I pretty much have the run of the bus. I watch what I want to watch, bake, text with my mom.

It's not ideal, but I need the time. Time to answer the question *honestly* this time.

Am I in or out?

I write a lot about it in my journal. Like pros and cons. Snippets of feelings. Hopes and fears. Lyrics—or poetry, really, as I don't have any steady music to go with anything. It changes, depending on my mood.

I was reckless the other night. I gave literally *no thought* to my actions. Alcohol gave me courage I couldn't back up. I let my heart—and maybe a few other body parts—take chances that were too risky.

Now I'm paying the price.

It hurt when Ajia walked away in the club. A lot. I didn't cry, but I could tell Noah expected me to. He acted so sweet, calling a cab, and getting us out of there. I tried to convince him to stay, to let me go back alone.

"Nothing doing." He insisted with a grin that looked a little forced to me. "I need my beauty sleep! I've got the bedroom this week, remember."

"And here I thought you were going to use it for fu—"

He put a finger over my lips. "Forget about it. We're just two friends who are looking after each other right now. You're the wife, remember? I'm taking care of you."

I try to smile but can't. "I'm sorry I ruined your night."

His grin becomes more genuine. "There'll be other nights, baby girl. Lots of 'em."

Since then, I've had time to think. Once I got over the initial hurt of Ajia turning his back on me like that, I start to remember other things. He rescued me from that anonymous guy, even though I didn't really need saving, and then he danced with me. He kissed me—holy hell, did he kiss me!—and I know damn well he got hard from it.

That has to mean something. Doesn't it?

I give it all a fair amount of thought in the hours when I'm alone, scribbling madly in my journal, and then, eventually, the answer hits. It's solid. Unmistakable. As real as the air in my lungs.

If I don't *really* try, I'll never know.

Yeah, it could all go to shit. I could make a complete ass of myself, but in the end, I'll know I tried. Gave it my best shot and took responsibility for my own happiness.

I've been holding on to *what if* for a long damn time, and all it's done is make me miserable. Nothing will change—certainly not my chance for happiness—if I keep doing the same thing. Or try things half-assed. I need to do it for real.

But I need a little time to figure out my next step.

We're in El Paso for two shows, kind of a shock when I heard we'd be stopping here. I know if Knox had anything to say about it, we'd drive hundreds of miles out of our way to *avoid* El Paso. Rumor has it that the record label or Edge of Return or somebody owes the venue there a favor. A big one, I guess. So here we are, and I'm going shopping.

I can think, maybe plan, while I shop.

Knox sits in the booth, working on his computer. I peek over his shoulder to look out the window. A taxi is making its way toward the tour bus, and so I grab my purse and start down the aisle.

"See you later," I call softly, hoping he's so caught up in whatever he's doing that he won't notice me leave.

"Where you going?"

Damn. So much for that idea. Still, my brother doesn't look up.

"To the grocery store."

"What?" *Now* his head snaps back.

"We need fresh stuff. Baz got just enough to get us through the first few days. I'm going to get the rest of what we need."

Knox frowns. "You're not going out in this shithole town all by yourself."

"Knox…"

"Not negotiable, baby girl."

I sigh. It isn't much of a surprise that my brother calls El Paso a *shithole town.* He doesn't mean it about El Paso exactly; it's just that our father was born here. Every time Dad needed a break—to gamble, drink, hook up with other women—he'd disappear and go back to where he grew up. Then one day, he didn't come home again.

Knox was 12 and I was 8.

"We still need groceries." I try to sound reasonable.

"Ajia, go with her."

I spin around to see him standing next to the kitchenette. I didn't know he was up, but there he is, dressed in his usual dark jeans and T-shirt.

"I can go by myself."

"Told you." Knox sits back in the booth. "Not negotiable. Not in *El Pisshole.*"

"You know this hatred you have for El Paso is unnatural."

"Don't give a shit. Ajia?"

He stands unmoving until finally he blinks and shakes his head. "Why me?"

So he still doesn't want to be around me. It hurts, but I push the feelings away. I don't have room for distractions right now.

"I'm doing this social media shit." Knox slings a hand toward his laptop. "Unless you want to do it?"

Ajia shakes his head.

"Zayne's asleep, Noah and Rye went out for coffee. That leaves you standing in the kitchen with your thumb up your ass. Or the big rock star too good to go shopping?"

59

"Fine." Ajia comes toward me but doesn't look anywhere near my face, my eyes.

"Knox...really." I try again. "I can—"

"What part of *not negotiable* you having trouble with, Bree? Not? Or negotiable?"

I blow out a harsh breath. "Fine." I repeat Ajia's word and take a step toward the door.

"And next time you go anywhere, have Baz call you a car. No more taxis."

"What?" I stop and turn back. "What do you mean, no more taxis?"

Knox shakes his head. "Increased security. Edge of Return had trouble with some stalker or something. Don't know the details. Just know the label says we're getting security."

"Fine," I say again. No point in arguing with my brother about it. He's already non-negotiable about me going to the freaking store alone just because we're in El Paso. If there's a security problem for anybody on the tour for *any* reason, he won't be giving me a free pass.

"No more taxis after this one," I agree, grasping that last moment of independence.

"And Bree?" Knox calls as I turn to the exit.

"What?"

"Get some bananas."

"Ass," I mutter under my breath, and I hear a chuckle from behind me. Ajia. He's going to the store with me.

I'm not sure if I'm happy about it or not.

He surprises me by opening the car door for me, but then I wonder why. There isn't a woman in Texas who's opened a door for herself—ever—if there's a man within a fifty-foot radius. It's like Texas men are born with an extra door-opening gene or something.

I give the cab driver instructions for where I want to go and then, finally, glance at Ajia. He's looking out the window.

"Sorry you got roped into this."

He shrugs but doesn't look at me. "No problem."

I almost let it go. The shy, weak part of me wants to. But another part, the grown-up part that's opening up, coming to life and seeing the possibilities, won't shut up.

"Right," I say. "No problem." I laugh and it sounds unpleasant, even to me. "That's why you won't even look at me."

He turns his head slowly. His blond hair shifts lushly over his shoulders, and I have a sudden, overwhelming urge to touch it. I know better.

"Like this?" he demands, and his eyes are like liquid caramel. Hot and...pissed?

"What? Why should *you* be mad at *me*? *You're* the one who left me standing alone in the middle of the dance floor!"

He blinks. "Noah was there."

"Noah wasn't just kissing me like his life depended on it."

"I don't kiss women like my life depends on it. I don't—" He drops his gaze.

"You don't what?"

He shakes his head.

"Come on, A! You don't *what?*"

I'm furious suddenly. He screwed with me by walking away after a kiss that rocked my fucking world, by completely avoiding me for three days, and now he doesn't want to explain?

No. Fucking. Way.

"What?" I demand again, fiercely this time.

"I don't kiss," he snaps, pinning me with a furious gaze. "I don't kiss on the mouth. Ever."

I sit back against the seat. "But...you kissed me."

"Yeah. I fucking did."

I stare at him, and he stares back. There's a lot of shit going on behind his eyes, but I can't make out any of it. Maybe it's just as well, because I don't know what the hell is going on inside me.

He doesn't kiss on the mouth. Ever. But he kissed me. Like he meant it.

Relief settles my nerves when we pull up to the grocery store. What can I say to Ajia when he doesn't look like he wants to talk to me at all? It's easier to just get out of the taxi. And when Ajia pays the cab driver before I can, I walk away.

I need a moment.

Shopping carts are outside, and I grab one as I head into the store. Produce is first, and I assemble the things I want. I wish Knox were there so I could show him I already had bananas on my list.

61

Next comes dairy, and from there I head up and down the aisles until I get to the other refrigerated items. I find Ajia there with a tube of chocolate chip cookies.

He looks at me, his gaze hooded. Fine. I can't talk to him about this shit right now, anyway. Not at the freaking *grocery store.*

"You used to make cookies for us."

I nod. "I did. You always liked chocolate chip."

He nods back. "My favorite. Without nuts."

I take the tube from him. "Female." I can't help grinning as I put it back.

"What?"

"You like female cookies. Without nuts."

He snorts. "Yeah, I guess I do."

"I'll make you cookies." I start for the baking aisle. "But not from a tube. I'll make them from scratch."

"Kitten!" he calls from behind, but I keep going.

He catches up with me as I toss flour, sugar, brown sugar, and chocolate chips into the cart. I've been up and down most of the aisles by now, and the buggy's getting pretty full.

"Jesus," he grunts when he stops next to me. "You feeding the whole fucking tour?"

I laugh shortly. "The five of you will eat this in three days."

"And where you going to store it all? Pretty sure I didn't notice a pantry in that tiny kitchen."

"You don't notice anything except the food that comes out of that tiny kitchen." I snort. "But if you must know, I had an idea. I'll use the storage under one of the empty bunks for my pantry."

He cocks his head and looks at me with a bright expression that surprises me. "That's brilliant! Hell, I never thought of that."

"That's why *I'm* the wife." I say it with just enough sarcasm to be sure he won't take me seriously.

"Bree...kitten—"

"Oh, my God! Ajia Stone!"

Two girls, maybe fifteen or sixteen, rush up to us. One stops on Ajia's left, the other on the right. They're pretty in a high school sort of way, and I realize suddenly that they're just a little older than I was when I first met Ajia. God, I can *so* understand the attraction.

"Is it really you?" asks the girl on the left. She grips his arm and won't let go.

"Oh, my God! We *love* Wycked Obsession!" squeals the girl on the right. She takes hold of Ajia's other arm.

I notice a tightening around his mouth, a flash in his eyes, and I know why. Of course I know why. Man-slut or not, he hates it when fans touch him without asking. None of the guys really like it, and I don't blame them. Personal space is, well...personal.

Ajia recovers quickly enough and pastes a flirty grin on his face. "Thanks, girls. It's always nice to know the fans are there for us."

"You're in town for the concerts, right?"

He nods. "Two shows."

They squeal and jump up and down. "We have tickets for tomorrow night," says Right.

"Oh, God," says Left. "I can't believe Ajia Stone is shopping in our store!"

"Ajia is *not* shopping," I point out dryly. "*I* am doing the shopping. He's just my...bodyguard."

He shoots me a look that clearly says, *What the fuck?* I just grin back and respond with my own expression. *Thought you'd like that better than* babysitter.

The girls turn to me suddenly, as though I didn't exist before I opened my mouth. Which, for them, is probably true. They both stare, and then Right says, "Who are you?"

Ajia's grin takes on a wicked curve. "This is Bree. She's Knox Gallagher's baby sister!"

"Oohh!" They shriek again, like being related to Knox is some great lifetime achievement. "Where is he? Is he here?"

"No. He's...busy this morning." I'm not about to say anything about what he's doing or where we're staying. Living on the tour bus with this new security issue warns me to keep my mouth shut.

"You're on tour with them?"

"Yep." I send Ajia a look that says, *All summer, baby.*

"You're so lucky."

Ajia extricates himself from the hold they have on him and steps around Right to stand behind me. Not quite sure why he moved, except I guess he had enough of them touching him.

"Bree was our first fan." He rests his hands on my shoulders. "She's like our mascot. A member of the band."

There it is again. Band mascot. The ass.

Worse, the soft, love-struck looks they gave him would be a joke if I didn't understand them so well. And he knows just how to make it happen. Double ass.

I lean into him, enough that his chest presses against my back. I meant to put him in his place, but suddenly *I'm* the one who's breathless.

"We're like…one big…happy…family."

I get the words out, but they sound ridiculously ragged. He's only standing behind me, for God's sake, but he's close enough that the scent of sandalwood and Ajia makes all my girl parts tighten.

And what about his guy parts? If I push my ass backward, will I bump against his erection?

"We better get going, kitten," he says suddenly, his mouth closer to my ear than I realized. "Our ice cream is going to melt."

"Uh. Okay."

God. I sound less intelligent than the fangirls who stare at Ajia with all the adoration their 15-year-old hearts can muster.

"I'll bet you girls would like an autograph, wouldn't you?" I force myself to ask.

"Yes! Please!" They're like an echo of each other. "And a picture!"

"Will you sign my boobs?" asks Left, trying to be cool, but it comes out sounding too breathless and innocent.

Ajia laughs. "Nope." He shakes his head. "Try again in three or four years."

She flushes, but Right smiles widely. "How about the back of our shirts?"

He pulls a Sharpie from his pocket—all the guys have learned to carry them—and grins wickedly. "Okay, honey. Bend over."

They both squeal again, and I wonder suddenly why somebody in the store hasn't come over to investigate these high-pitched screams. It doesn't seem to matter much as Ajia scrawls his name and the date on the back of each shirt. I take a picture with each of their cell phones.

"Have fun at the concert tomorrow night." He smiles with genuine appreciation this time. "I'll look for you in the crowd."

They screech again, but by this time Ajia has his arms on either side of me. He's pushing the cart forward, crowding me between the handlebar and his chest.

"Jesus," he mutters when we reach the end of the aisle. "I think I'm deaf."

I laugh. "Nothing quite like a young girl's high-pitched squeal, is there?"

He lets go of the cart and moves to my side. I notice the sudden loss of heat and closeness, but I know better than to say anything. Not here and not now.

Besides, I don't know what the hell to say. We've been too close these last few minutes, and I'm *way* too distracted.

"Uh, you know we don't have ice cream," I say instead.

Ajia laughs. "Doesn't matter. I needed to get out of there."

"You won't be able to find them in the crowd."

"I won't remember to look."

I push the cart up to a checkout stand. "Why didn't you offer them backstage passes?"

He shoots me a frown. "They're kids. You know what kind of shit goes on backstage."

"Yeah. I do. Since when does that bother you?"

"I don't mess around with girls who are still in high school. None of us do."

"Just girls in college?" I smirk. "Or is *nineteen* too young now?"

He looks at his phone without responding to my question. I know he heard me—I can tell by the way his expression tightened—but he types something, waits, and then types again.

"Car will be here in ten minutes," he says as he shoves his phone into his back pocket.

"You called a car?"

"Knox said no taxis."

"Since when do you listen to what my brother says?"

Ajia drops his lashes enough that I can't read his expression. "Since some mystery security shit is going on and we're alone in an unfamiliar place."

"But it's Edge of Return's problem. We're just—"

"Following the label's rules."

"Is this more protective shit, A? Because if it is—"

"Don't, Bree."

"Don't what?"

He looks at me again, his eyes suddenly churning with a bright golden fire. "Don't talk to me about being an adult. About not

65

needing anybody to look out for you." His voice is tight. "Don't even *try* it."

"But—"

"Listen to me," he snaps as he begins literally throwing things onto the conveyor belt. He stops only long enough to pin me with a sharp, penetrating gaze. "I have two things to say about your *protective shit.* Gabe Richmond and Ajia Stone."

"Ajia—"

"Let. It. Go." He stops moving long enough to stare at me with a withering look. *"That* says everything you need to know about men, life, and this fucking tour."

CHAPTER 8

AJIA

I go back to avoiding Bree as much as I can after our shopping trip. Dumbass that I am, I said too much. Saying shit I want to keep secret is bad enough. But, no. I have to say crap that doesn't make any sense. That only leads to trouble.

It's a relief when we roll into Phoenix. It means, finally, a couple of nights in a hotel. Three nights, Baz said, because of a screwed-up schedule. We have a show, a free night when Edge of Return plays some kind of private gig, and then another show.

The security people join us here, but we don't notice them much. One guy, Kel, is assigned to us, but we can still come and go as we want. Thank God, because it's fucking creepy.

Nobody in Wycked Obsession is complaining about any of it. We get a whole fucking day and night to do nothing. A day and night when we aren't on the road? Hell, yeah.

Three days and nights out of that goddamn bus so I can put some distance between Bree and me.

I hate to be such an asshole. She isn't doing anything wrong; she's just *there*. Smelling like strawberries. Present and so close. She's still sleeping in the bunk below me.

Christ, she makes me think of shit I walked away from a long goddamn time ago. I didn't fuck my way through a never-ending list of nameless, faceless girls who don't give a shit about me because I'm hot and sexy. I'm a commodity. I make sure they come first, and they get to tell their friends they fucked a rock star.

Yeah, I come. I forget shit for a while. It makes me feel alive for a few minutes…and then I remember what a piece of shit I am. What I've done and the lives I ruined.

I'm not laying all that on Bree, no matter how much I want her, because with her, it will *never* be one and done. I want to protect her from all the bad shit…and especially me.

Fuck.

It's our free day, and I'm in my bedroom in the suite I share with Rye. I *hate* admitting it, but the truth is I *want* Bree. Like I've never wanted another woman. And that's, literally, *never.*

A shitty little voice inside me keeps whispering. *You get with Bree, and it'll be like nothing you ever had before. You'll feel things with her. She might even fix you…heal you.*

Fuck that.

I'm not broken. Don't need fixing, and nothing in me can be healed. Yeah, I have a past. Everybody does. And that's exactly where that shit needs to stay: in the past.

But…it colors stuff. Screws with you. And I'm not letting any of my shit touch Bree. She doesn't know about Lara, about Mason and Jill, about the accident. About…any of it. Not many people do. I told the guys in the band, and that's where it ends. Bree will never be tainted by my fuck-ups. She's special, and I've always known that. Now that things have changed between us, even if it's only in my mind, I know something else.

She is way too good for a piece of shit like me.

And *that* isn't just in my mind.

I grunt and dig through my bag, change into shorts and a T-shirt. A place like this will have a gym. I'll bury all this useless shit under some weights and cardio. Couple of hours ought to do it.

I find Rye in the main living area. He's pulling a bottle of water from the refrigerator. "Going to the gym?" he asks as he tosses me the bottle and grabs another for himself.

"Yeah. You?"

He shrugs. "See you there later. Noah and Zayne're out scouting."

I laugh. "Looking for chicks?"

Rye grins and shakes his head. It's an old story with those two. They fuck around way more than I do. Or maybe they're just different from me. More fun. Playful. I'm into one night stands where we don't know each other's names. Noah likes his threesomes, and Zayne doesn't mind an audience. Knox has a bit of a kink that he doesn't talk much about, but I don't get into it. If he wants to tie some chick up and she's into it, who am I to say anything about it?

Rye's different from the rest of us. He's more…selective. Goes for a certain type of woman, but it's still never more than a hookup. Never seems like he's looking, but if he runs across his type, he'll take her on.

Pretty sure Zayne and Noah *look* for Rye's type and hook him up. Like they're some kind of pimps or something. We all know it, and it makes me laugh.

"What?"

I shake my head. "Nothing. See you later."

I bust my ass in the gym for almost an hour before Rye shows up. He does some cardio, some free weights, and finishes up about the same time I do. We shower and head down the street to a nearby Mexican restaurant. Everybody else is MIA.

A couple of beers and a skillet of fajitas later, Rye's phone buzzes. He looks at me. "Hunting party surfaces."

"Where are they?" I take a hit from my Corona.

"Hotel. Party in Noah and Zayne's room."

Like that comes as a surprise. I smile and shake my head.

"Knox's with 'em."

"Where's Bree?" The question comes automatically. She and her brother are sharing a suite. "He didn't fucking take her along to scout *women,* did he?"

Rye texts and replies when his phone pings. "Guess she went shopping this afternoon. She's with them now."

Fuck. I close my eyes. Here we go again. Another party, more drinking, more women, and Bree will be there, watching it all. While my cock gets as hard as granite thinking about *her.*

I wave the waitress over. "Two shots. Patron."

Rye eyes me. "Tequila?"

"Might as well get started now."

We toss back the shots as soon as we get them, and I order another round.

"What are you gonna do?"

I stare at Rye with a deliberately blank expression. "About what?"

He shoots me a look that says, *Don't take me for a dumbass.* "Bree."

"What about her?"

"Did you fuck her?"

"Jesus!" I search for the waitress and our tequila, but nothing is in our vicinity. "Jesus," I say again. "Didn't expect that from you, Rye."

"Did you?"

"No!" I grab my water glass and take a long drink. "Hell, no. When would I have had the chance?"

"You want to."

I flop back against the booth. "Who says?"

"Your face, every time you look at her."

"What the ever-loving fuck?"

The waitress arrives with our drinks. I take them both, shoot one and look at Rye as I toss back the second. I don't waste time with salt or a lime, just order another round.

"You kissed her." He sounds almost casual, but I know better. Hell, yes, I know better.

"You don't know what the fuck you're talking about."

"I saw you. On the dance floor."

I blow out a ragged breath. "I don't kiss women."

"I know." He angles one head in my direction. "But you kissed Bree."

"Fuuuuck."

"She wants you, you know."

I shove a hand into my hair and wish suddenly that I'd pulled it back. It's too much. Clothes are too much. I just want to be blissfully alone, naked and floating where none of this shit matters.

"It's just a little crush." I hate the desperation in my voice.

Rye laughs, and it almost sounds like he's sympathetic. "It was a little crush when she was fifteen, bro. She's almost twenty now, gonna start her third year of college this fall. She caught you getting sucked off by some groupie. You think she doesn't know about shit?"

I stiffen. "Who told you about that?"

He gives me another of those *dumbass* looks.

"Fucking Noah," I mutter.

The next shots arrive, but I just look at mine. After a minute, Rye salts his hand, licks the salt, kicks back the shot, and sucks his slice of lime.

"I wanna say that what you do with Bree is your business," he says finally. "But you know that ain't true. Knox will kill your ass if you sleep with his sister, and the rest of us will break every fucking bone in your body if you hurt her. So, if you're thinking about going any farther with this shit, prepare yourself for the consequences. It ain't gonna be pretty if you make the wrong choice."

♪

I wrestle with Rye's words as we start back toward the hotel. Everything he says is true. Hell, I've been telling myself the same damn things. I just hadn't realized, until I heard the words aloud, how much I hoped to find a loophole. A way out.

A way to have Bree, at least for a little while.

A really dumbass thing to think about, a rusty voice of conscience reminds me. *She'll never be anybody's one and done, and you don't let girls into your life who are anything else.*

Not anymore. I had one—once—and it turned into the worst fucking mistake of my life. Not her fault. Mine. Totally mine, and I'll live with that every day of my worthless life. That's why Bree has to stay safe. Away from me. I've made as much of an exception for her as I can. She might not know it, but that's just as well.

She can only be Bree…our baby girl. *My kitten.*

Five years into Wycked Obsession, and she used to be only that. Now…she's so much more.

Fuck. A dozen other curses roll through my mind.

She deserves a guy who can love her, who's bright and clear and not filled with the pain and shit that follows me around. I hide what I am, what I did. Had years of practice at it. The ugliness is still there, though. Deep down. Killing and maiming people doesn't go away. It eats away at you every fucking day, and so I bury it with meaningless sex, too much booze, and the knowledge that I deserve every fucking thing I get.

Except the success. That threw me when it started. I'm no more comfortable with it now. It shouldn't be mine. The rest of the band deserves it, though, and that's the only way I can accept it.

Well, that, and knowing the only place I feel at home, where I feel alive and at peace with myself, is on stage. Or when the band jams, writes, records.

So why the fuck do I suddenly have these thoughts about—*these feelings for*—Bree? Where did they fucking come from, and how the fuck can I get rid of them?

Rye and I take the elevator at the hotel and go straight to Zayne and Noah's room. Music filters into the hallway. It sounds like stuff we used to cover. *Rockstar* by Nickelback. Fucking hilarious. The door is propped open with the swing bar that locks hotel room doors.

"Hey!" Zayne waves his red plastic cup the instant he sees us. "Where you assholes been?"

I shrug and Rye shakes his head.

"Havin' a party," announces Noah unnecessarily. He has a girl on his lap and one hanging around his neck.

"Come meet the girls!" shouts Knox, who has a chick perched on his knee.

I see a couple other girls—one who looks exactly like Rye's type—and I shoot him a grin. He looks back, his eyes dark, almost sad, but then he grins back and heads across the room.

Everybody looks pretty drunk already, and I'm on the edge of a buzz. The only one who looks remotely sober is Bree. She sits at the table with the rest of them, a red Solo cup in her hands, and gives me a look that I swear says, *What are* you *going to do?*

I'm not sure what she's asking, or maybe I don't want to know. I don't have a fucking answer, and so I blink and look away.

I wander into the kitchen, grab a cup, and mix myself a rocks margarita. It tastes shitty—the tequila and mix are cheap—but I drink it anyway. Maybe I'll get drunk enough tonight to get whiskey dick and not have to worry about wanting to bury myself balls deep in Bree's welcoming body.

Fuck.

I find an empty seat across the table from her. It's a good thing, or so I think at first. She's far enough away that I can't smell her scent or feel the soft heat of her body. I just didn't count on looking at her, seeing the light flush on her cheeks, the invitation of her mouth, the desire...and uncertainty in her sparkling green eyes. She's wearing her Keep Austin Weird T-shirt. Was it always so tight across her tits? I forget about that as I notice her mink-colored hair draped all around her shoulders.

Jesus, now that I see her in this new way—now that I've *tasted* her—I can't think of anything else.

Introductions are made, but I don't give a shit about who the other chicks are. Won't ever see them again, can't remember their faces if I close my eyes. I nod and toss out that shit-eating grin that lets me get my way more often than not.

Everybody's drinking, joking and laughing. We talk about Wycked Obsession stuff that excites the fangirls, joke in that sexy way men and women do, until one of the women says, "Let's play a game!"

I don't know who said it because I'm pretending not to look at Bree. I groan, along with Rye, but Noah laughs.

"What kind of game?"

"How about...Flip, Sip, or Strip?"

It might have been the same chick who suggested a game in the first place—I can't tell—but it doesn't matter. "No!" snaps Knox.

The woman on Zayne's lap pouts—it must have been her—but nobody says a word. The guys know why Knox refused.

Bree.

I shoot a stealthy gaze in her direction and see she's blushing. She knows, too. Or is it the idea of playing a game where we'd all start stripping that has her cheeks so pink?

"How about Truth or Dare?" suggests Noah.

I groan again, but nobody else seemed to care that much. The chick who sits next to me, wearing some kind of skin-tight dress that barely contains her tits or covers her ass, wiggles in excitement. "Ajia!" I tense as she claws at my arm. "I dare you to kiss me."

I stare at her hand clutching my forearm and slowly drag my gaze up to her face. She's probably pretty enough—or would be if she didn't have so much makeup caked on and more eyeliner than I wear on stage—but nothing about her appeals to me.

"That's not how it works, honey," I say as I force a grin.

"It's not?" She fake-pouts, like it's supposed to be sexy. It isn't.

"Besides," puts in Knox. "Ajia never kisses on the mouth."

My gaze zooms to Bree's; I can't help it. She stares back at me, but I can't read a goddamn thing in her eyes.

"What do you mean?" demands Tight Dress.

I shrug. "I don't kiss. Not on the mouth."

"How come?"

I weigh my answer. Most women never notice after I give them their first orgasm, but I've come up with a few bullshit reasons over the years.

"Fuck that. We playing or not?"

It's Rye who interrupts the moment, and I shoot him a look. He's staring at Noah with a frown. I bet he did it for Bree. Our conversation at the restaurant reminds me just how much Rye knows. Doesn't matter. I'm relieved. *Kissing* is still part of an open wound between Bree and me.

"You start, Beater," Rye said. "It was your idea."

"Oohh," squeals the woman hanging around Noah's neck. She sucks on his earlobe. "Beater! Is that your nickname?"

He grins over his shoulder and gives her a quick kiss. "Among others."

"Does everybody have a nickname?" screeches the girl next to me. Why the hell do these girls' voices always get like five octaves higher that way? "What's yours?" she demands as she tightens her claws on my arm.

"Fuck this," snaps Zayne. "Are we playing this goddamn game or not?"

Noah looks at the chick on his lap. "Okay, babe. Truth or dare?"

She makes a squeaky sound, too, but it isn't quite as offensive as Tight Dress next to me.

"Truth!" she shouts, surprising me. I figured sure she'd ask Noah for a dare.

"You ever fuck a rock star?" he asks immediately.

"Noah!" She wiggles on his lap.

"Well?"

"Nooooo," she admits slowly. "But…"

"But?" he asks with a sly wink.

"I'm hoping to change that tonight."

We all laugh, even Knox and Bree. I'm kind of surprised that he's going along with any of this shit. But maybe, as long as Bree isn't stripping as part of the game, he figures he'll keep his word.

I'm not going to change overnight, but I'll try to do better. He made the promise in Austin.

The questions go around, most of the girls opting for truth this early in the game. Everybody's drinking, but maybe we all have to imbibe a little more before we're brave enough for a dare.

I don't pay much attention until it's Bree's turn. Knox looks at her. "Truth or dare?"

She smirks. The women might have been strangers to us, but Bree knows the band. Better than we know ourselves, I think sometimes.

"Dare."

The guys hoot, and Knox nods like he's taking it seriously. "Okay. I dare you to go to your room and stay there the rest of the night."

There's a second of charged silence. I see Bree's face go white, the way she swallows and then closes her eyes. I know what she's hiding. I've seen the pain she conceals. Hell, I've put it there.

"No fucking way," shouts Noah as he glares at Knox. "I call that an invalid fucking dare."

"Jesus, Knox," says Rye.

"When did you get to be such a fucking prick?" demands Zayne.

Knox looks at me, and I shake my head. *Bad fucking idea,* my eyes insist, even though a part of me wishes she'd do it. It would be so much simpler on so many levels.

At least for me. Now who's the prick?

"Hey!" He tries to laugh it off and gives Bree a light punch on the shoulder. "I was just kidding."

"Were you?" She stares him down.

He blinks. "Yeah. Of course." He smiles, but even I can see it's a shitty effort. "You know that, baby girl."

She shakes her head but doesn't say anything.

"So what's your dare?" I ask him before he—or anybody else—can make things worse.

"Uh…" He pauses and then smiles. "Okay, I dare you to let us blindfold you. You have to feel somebody else's face and tell us who it is by touch alone."

Bree's wide eyes reveal her surprise. Hell, *I'm* surprised! What's his game? But when I think about it, I guess he thinks it's safe somehow. She'll be touching only a face, one that belongs to another woman or a man who's like a brother to her.

Except me...and Knox doesn't fucking know that.

I refuse to look at him or any of the other guys.

Bree's brave, though, and she nods. "All right."

"Son of a bitch, Knox." Noah laughs. "Last time we played Truth or Dare, that was *his* dare," he tells Bree.

Shit, I'd forgotten that.

"And he blew it, right?" She laughs, too, but only looks at Knox. It's kind of a rough sound, and I know she hasn't forgiven him for his original dare.

"Bad," says Zayne, and then everybody laughs. Except me.

Fuck. Now that I remember, I remember *all of it.* Knox blew it all right, but he ended up practically fucking that girl right there in front of us. The way it was, she came all over his fingers before she gave him a blow-job.

Dumb fucking asshole.

"Somebody get a blindfold," cries Knox, and one look at Bree tells me she's determined to do it. My dick twitches at the idea as Zayne races for the bedroom and returns waving a pillow case.

Bree's eyes widen, but she takes a breath. I shouldn't notice the way her breasts move, but I do.

"You can fold it over my eyes," she says firmly, "but don't put it over my head. I...don't like that."

"Sure, baby girl." Zayne grins, twists the pillow case around and then ties it around her face. He waves a hand in front of her, really close, but she doesn't flinch.

She can't see anything.

"Okay." Zayne turns to look at the rest of us. "Who's offering up their face?"

CHAPTER 9

BREE

Zayne's pillowcase makes a pretty effective blindfold. I can't see a thing.

What the hell did I agree to? It seemed harmless enough, especially when the guys joke about Knox being such a failure at it. But sitting here, waiting and completely unable to see, I wonder if I'm messing up.

It's not that I don't trust the guys. I do. I just don't want to look like a complete idiot in front of the fangirls. They might be my age, but I can tell they're way more experienced than me. They don't have Knox freaking Gallagher for a brother, who pretty much does whatever he can to wreck most chances I've ever had with a guy.

Or a five-year crush on Ajia freaking Stone that keeps me from really even *looking* at another guy.

God, I'm so screwed.

I hear movement, whispering, giggles, and laughter. The others moved away from the table, and I can't make out much more than a muddle of sound. Male voices rumble, almost like an argument, but I can't hear the actual words over Justin Timberlake's *Sexyback*.

"Okay," says Knox finally, sounding like he's across the room. For some reason, I've been assuming it won't be his face I touch, and this seems to confirm it. "You ready?"

"Yes." I nod. Nerves dance through my stomach.

I hear more movement shuffling around me, and then someone turns my chair away from the table.

"Open your legs," says Noah, sounding like he's nearby. "You know. So your…person can get closer."

"Okay." I do it.

I sense more movement, and then a body stands between my thighs.

I know two things immediately. It's a man. He's too big, has too much presence, for it to be one of the too-skinny fangirls. He smells masculine, like sandalwood and a very certain scent that belongs to only one man.

It's Ajia.

That must have been what the argument was about. Somebody wanted him to do it, and he doesn't want to.

A sad, empty space opens up in my stomach, stirring my nervousness into a frenzy. After all that's happened between Ajia and me, he doesn't like it. Doesn't want it. The idea of risking my heart any more than I already have shrivels. I've known he doesn't really want it—me—but every time I get reminded, it hurts like hell again.

"You gonna start?" Knox demands.

"Uh, yeah." I'm not going to waste this opportunity. It'll probably be the only chance I ever get to touch any part of Ajia the way I want to.

I reach out, not sure where my hands will land. I find his shoulders, broad and solid and muscular. I curl my fingers for a gentle squeeze, but I know I can't get by with much extra-curricular groping.

Everybody's watching.

I pat my way inward, finding the column of his neck, and his hair tangles around my fingers. It's long and soft, but that can be said for any of the guys; they all have long hair.

I trace the curve of his ears, massage a spot just behind his earlobe. His skin is soft and warm. He shifts slightly, and I hear a soft catch in his breathing.

Ears, I tell myself. He likes to be touched there. I'll never have the chance again, but still I commit the secret to memory.

I splay my fingers wider to push his hair back from his face. God, I want to shove my hands forward so I can grip his head and pull him closer, but I know I can't. Instead, I work my way up until they're resting near his hairline. I lift my hands then, just a little. Enough to sweep light, caressing fingertips over his forehead.

It's an easy touch, sensual, sexual even. At least to me, without my eyes. I'm afraid it reveals too much, and so I force myself to work harder. Trace the arch of his eyebrows. Rest the flat tips of my fingers against the skin around his eyes.

Don't tease him like a lover, I tell myself with ragged insistence. *You're supposed to be finding out who's kneeling between your thighs.*

Oh, God.

The song playing in the background changes to Gnarles Barkley's *Crazy,* and I know before the lyrics start it's meant for me. I *am* crazy. I wanted—and got—safely away from Gabe, only to lose myself in the intimacy of life on the road with Ajia.

And now I want more. So much more.

I lighten my touch as I trace all the contours of Ajia's eyes. His eyelids close beneath my fingertips, and I feel the sweep of his eyelashes. I wish I could kiss him there, feel the feathery brush of his lashes against my lips. I even start to lean forward, and then the sound of movement, followed by a giggle—shushed and cut-off— reminds me of where I am.

Ajia is crouched between my legs, yes, but we have an audience. This isn't romantic or even sexual. It's a game. A goddamned drinking game.

So why are my nipples stiff beneath my bra and T-shirt? And why am I wet and aching between my legs? If I could see him, would Ajia have a hard-on?

God, how I wish it could be true!

I flatten my fingers again and stroke down over the slope of his nose, up to the curve of his cheekbones, then lower again to his jawline and the brush of a couple days' worth of beard.

Then, I'm right there. Touching his lips. I press against them softly. Tenderly. Longingly.

He doesn't kiss girls. Not on the mouth.

But he kissed me.

"So who do you think it is?" Knox demands suddenly, laughing.

The sound of my brother's voice brings back all the other noise in the room. It all died away for me, and I didn't realize it until it returns. I didn't hear the rest of *Crazy,* didn't hear movement or chatter or laughter. I only knew the touch of Ajia's skin—his mouth—against my hand.

I rub my fingers over his lips again, back and forth, until they part just a fraction. It's all I need. I push one finger between them, against his teeth, and then my index finger is in his mouth, stroking over the wet heat of his tongue.

"Bree?"

I wait long enough for Ajia to lick around my finger, suck it deep into his mouth, and I lose a soft, ragged breath.

"It's Ajia," I admit softly.

I'm not pretending that I don't know. Not for some stupid drinking game. Not when I want him to understand that I will *always know him*, any time, any place.

Besides, if he didn't know it before, he had to have known I recognized him the second I stuck my finger in his mouth. The way he licked and sucked my finger tells me so.

I pull the blindfold off and stare at him. He hasn't moved. I can't look away from the sight of him, still kneeling between my thighs and my finger still lodged in his mouth. His tongue still circles it round and round.

"How the hell did you get it?" demands Zayne, and I try to blink myself back to awareness. "We thought for sure the last one you'd guess was Pipes."

The scrawny, fake-boobed blonde who's been throwing herself at Ajia all night screeches. "Pipes! So you all *do* have nicknames!"

Ajia jerks my finger from his mouth, pulls back and pushes to his feet. His eyes are fastened on mine, and neither of us can blink. God, how I wish we were alone.

"Bree?" It's Rye's voice that prods me.

I force myself to look at him. "I don't know. I just tried to imagine the features in my mind as I went, and something told me it was Ajia."

It's a shitty explanation, but I can't tell them the truth. Not any of it. That's between Ajia and me.

"So does Ajia have to drink?" demands Knox. His arm is slung around Ciara or Cherry or something like that. The chick who's sitting on his lap. "Since she got it right?"

"No, dumbass," laughs Noah. "*You* have to drink. You made the dare."

"Huh." He shakes his head. "Right." He shoots me a mildly offended look. "Shoulda made you take the first one."

"And I should punch you in the face." I refuse to let him hurt my feelings this time. "It's not like one drink is going to make a difference in your current asinine condition."

He looks at the girl painted against his side and laughs. "Guess you're right, sis."

Everybody else laughs, too. They get up, move around, get drinks and some of them even make out. I figure it must be the end of the game, so I get up for more vodka. It's lousy vodka, but I'm getting used to it. Hell, I *need* it after that intimacy with Ajia. I used to expect rock stars to splurge on good booze, I think as I add Sprite to my drink. But it's got to have been my brother who picked it out. Knox is always a cheapskate.

I turn back to the main room and see Knox cozied up with Ajia. They're talking—not about my little display, I hope—and I see them exchange...what? Not sure, but I get a sick feeling in my stomach.

God, they didn't bet on the dare, did they?

"Okay, everybody," shouts Noah, waving his hand around. "Break's over. We haven't even gone all the way around the table yet."

"We've had our turns." Knox points to the fake-looking chick plastered against his side. "Chanel and I have...something else to do."

Chanel! That's her name.

The fangirls giggle, Zayne and Noah shout obscene suggestions, and I frown at my brother. Jesus, he'd better understand the message my expression is trying to shout.

You're a pig for fucking a groupie you know you won't see again. But if you have *to do it, get the loud shit out of the way before I get back to my room!*

He gives me a drunken smile, waves, and follows Chanel to the door. She's into it as much as he is. And why the fuck doesn't that bother him? Knowing he's as much a notch on her belt as she is on his?

It shouldn't mean a damn thing to me. It's the lifestyle of a rock star. I've known about it for years, especially since the very first sign of Wycked Obsession's success. It's just that it's climbed to such astronomical levels since their first album. Besides, it's one thing to hear about the guys nailing girls when they're on tour and I'm safe at home, but it's a whole different beast to actually witness *my brother* doing it.

Eeewwww!

"Okay, Bree." Noah calls on me as I take my seat. "You're up."

I swallow like half my drink and try to get my mind back in the game. Away from the memory of Ajia's face beneath my fingers. From how it felt to have my finger in his mouth. Away from wondering if Knox and Ajia bet on whether I could identify him, and away from knowing my brother's down the hall in our suite fucking some girl he'll never see again.

I turn to the handsy girl who sits at the end of the table. She's between Ajia and me, and that's enough to make me hate her.

I've had both my question and my dare prepared for most of the game. "Okay," I say. "Truth or dare?"

She squeals and I can't help poking one finger in my ear. Jesus, can she screech any louder?

"I take dare!"

She bounces on her chair, looking from me to Ajia. Like she thinks I'm going to give her something that could possibly involve him?

No way in hell, bitch.

I nod and smile. "Touch your tongue to your nose."

She blinks. *"What?"*

"Touch your tongue to your nose." I stick out my tongue and wiggle it. "I can't do it. I want to see if you can."

She looks from me to Ajia again. He smiles like he's encouraging her, but his eyes are mostly empty.

"Go ahead, honey," he says. "Try it."

It would piss me off that he calls her honey, except I know that's what he and all the guys call women when they can't remember their names. In a twisted way, it kind of satisfies me.

She giggles, which sounds almost as irritating as her screams, and I try to pretend it doesn't bother me. The truth is, everything about her pisses me off, and it isn't even really her fault.

Everybody laughs when she can't do it. Her tongue doesn't come anywhere close to her nose, and so she has to drink. She practically drains her freaking glass and then shoots Ajia a wicked smile.

"Okay, baby." She smirks at him. "Truth or dare."

"Truth," he says easily and leans back.

I shake my head when that seems to surprise her. Jesus! She's like the clichéd fangirl in every possible way. Ajia's shown her like minimal attention, and she thinks he's going to pick a *dare* from her?

She smiles then, slowly, and says, "Why don't you kiss on the mouth?"

I can't read his expression, which is something pretty new between us. Why does it keep happening lately?

"It's against my religion," he says with all seriousness.

What? I grab my red plastic cup and try to hide a laugh behind pretending to take a sip.

His religion? I'm pretty sure he believes in God, but his *religion?*

Far as I know, he doesn't have one.

Fangirl, on the other hand, takes him seriously. "Oohh." She nods. "What religion are you?"

He shakes his head. "One question. And I don't talk about it. It's…personal."

She nods again, and I keep pretending to drink my vodka. I don't dare look at Noah or Zayne. They know exactly how to destroy me with nothing more than a look, and I'll be howling with laughter. So will they.

I wonder why they aren't laughing, anyway, and then it hits me. They probably think they're helping him *get* with that girl. Like they want him to fuck her.

Assholes. I frown. I hate them all right now.

I quit paying attention as the game continues. I'm just pissed. The chicks keep trying to make everything sexual, and the guys just…well, they're fucking with the girls. Leading them on and then backing off. It must be some kind of game they play with groupies. Maybe it makes for better hook-up sex, keeping the girls on edge. They don't know if they're getting laid or not until the very end.

I'm *so* going to have a talk with these assholes.

"Truth or dare." I finally zone back into the game when the chick on Zayne's lap prompts him.

"Dare," he says with a wicked grin.

She looks around the table. "Can I dare somebody else?"

He lifts an eyebrow. "Why?"

"It might be fun." She whispers something in his ear, then leans in for a long, luxurious kiss.

"Sure." Zayne shrugs when his mouth is free again. "Why not? You drink if they refuse the dare. You drink if they fuck it up. Right?"

He looks around the table, and everybody else pretty much agrees. I don't really care. I'm sick of the game, anyway. Not so much the game itself, but the groupies who keep trying to turn it into some kind of sexual marathon or orgy or something.

"Okay," says Zayne's girl. "I dare Liza to make out with Ajia. Five minutes. On the couch."

My heart starts to pound, and I can't breathe. I blink fast until the only thing I can do is close my eyes. I don't need to see in order to hear a new screech from the Squealer.

Her name, apparently, is Liza.

I shouldn't feel so blindsided, but I do. There's been a sexual undertone to the whole night, but—*Jesus!* I never thought it would end up like *this*.

Say no, I think to myself. *Please, Ajia, say no!*

Movement. Chairs scraping across the floor. Laughter. More shrieking.

"I wanna see how good he is if he doesn't kiss."

I hear the comment from Zayne's chick, and I want to char her to absolute fucking ashes. And even though I know I shouldn't, my eyes open.

Liza has Ajia over by the couch. She pushes at his shoulders, and he kind of flops down, his back to me. She's on him in an instant, straddling his lap. I have no trouble picturing the horrifying image of her dress pushed all the way to her waist.

I'm losing my ability to breathe as she pulls his T-shirt over his head and tosses it aside. His hair flutters around his shoulders, and I remember how soft and silky it felt, tangled around my fingers. They twitch with the memory.

I lose the sensation in an instant when she shoves the top of her tube dress down, and her boobs pop out for everybody to see. They're twice the size of mine and way too perky to be real. I hear one of the guys hoot—Zayne, I think—but I can't look away. It's like I'm frozen in place, watching the proverbial train wreck.

She leans forward, kissing Ajia's neck, his chest, and pressing her tits against him. He doesn't move, and so she starts squirming on his lap. She looks at him, her head cocked to one side, and then she parts her lips in a slow, sexy smile. She straightens, pulls his hand to her breast, and presses his palm against her. His fingers squeeze a couple of times, and she moans. Her head falls back, and his thumb strokes once, twice, across her stiff nipple. She groans, and his fingers keep moving.

I'm going to be sick. I do my best to swallow it back while my mind spins like it's caught in a tornado. I still can't move, can't look anywhere else, even though my mind is screaming at him.

God, Ajia! Stop. Just—please. Stop!

Nothing changes until she leans forward again, bringing her other boob to his mouth. "There you go, baby," she murmurs, thrusting her nipple against his lips. "I'm all yours."

I can't see for sure that he's taken her into his mouth, but I can tell his head is moving. It doesn't matter. They're both naked to the waist, he's caressing her breasts and I know how this goes. I saw the evidence that night in the garage.

They won't stop here.

I stand up so suddenly the chair clatters back behind me. I ignore it.

"I have to go." I step back and swallow again. "I'm not feeling well all of a sudden."

"Bree!" It's Rye's voice, but I wave him off and spin for the door.

"She can't hold her liquor, can she?" demands one of the girls.

"Goddamn, you fuckers."

The snarl comes from Noah, but I can't let it stop me. I'm out the door and racing down the hall before anybody can say one more fucking word. It's all a goddamn nightmare, and I just want free of it.

Of them. Of the sight of Ajia playing with another woman's tits and knowing it isn't going to end there.

That he'll never be with me like that. That he'll give himself to almost anyone else, as long as she isn't me.

CHAPTER 10

AJIA

Noah's shout is followed by a slamming door. The noise sends off an explosion in my brain, and I realize in an entirely new way that I'm sprawled on the sofa with some topless chick shoving her tits at me. And I'm letting her.

What the fuck is wrong with me?

I shove the girl off my lap and stand up. I hardly notice when she tumbles to the floor. Where the fuck is my shirt?

I spot it on the floor halfway across the room and stalk over to grab it. I tug it over my head and shove my hair away from my face. Fucking shit.

I hear the woman—Lizzie or Lisa or something—screech behind me. "Ajia! What the fuck?" I ignore her and look around the room. It's like everything is different, but it's exactly the same.

Noah is on his feet, as pissed as I've ever seen him. "Yeah, Ajia. What the ever-loving fuck?"

I scrub one hand over my face. "Don't start with me, Noah," I snap. "You fuckers set this up."

He takes a step toward me. *"I* didn't have a goddamn thing to do with this fucking farce."

I whip a furious gaze to Zayne. "What about you, asshole?"

Zayne looks between Noah and me. He squints like he's totally confused. Drunk or high, more like it. "What the fuck happened?"

The groupies around him look just as fucked up. Christ! How did this all get so goddamn, disgustingly *dysfunctional?*

"Ajia?" The chick I was supposed to be making out with grabs my arm, but I jerk away.

"Don't touch me." I glare at her and put as much distance between us as I can. "And pull your fucking top up, for Christ's sake."

"Don't try to blame anybody else, you asshole." Noah is relentless. "You knew what you were doing. You *always* know what the fuck you're doing. Take some fucking responsibility for yourself for a change."

He's right. He's so fucking right, and there isn't anything I can say. No way to defend myself. I *knew* I was playing a dangerous game when I let Tight Dress lead me over to the couch. I knew it could—and probably would—get out of hand. And I let it happen anyway.

No! You didn't let *it happen. You* did *it. You knew what you were doing and you fucking did it, anyway!* My conscience won't let me off the hook. *All because you got freaked out when Bree touched you like she did. What a sorry piece of shit.*

I didn't want to be the one whose face she touched. I knew that having her hands on me that way—in any way—would turn me into a raging, testosterone-filled monster that I couldn't let loose. Not here and not now, and so I argued against it. It had every potential to turn into a shit storm. Just like it did.

Zayne and Knox were so sure she'd guess anybody but me. How are they so fucking clueless?

"I still don't get what the fuck happened!" Zayne looks around the room like a drunken owl.

Rye shoots him a death-ray look. "Bree didn't like some half-naked chick shoving her tits in Ajia's face."

Zayne blinks a couple of times and then finally nods like he got it. "Oh." He doesn't get shit.

"And she didn't fucking like Ajia touching some half-naked chick." Noah just can't leave well enough alone.

"Oh." Zayne nods again like it made more sense. "Like the chick in the garage."

Goddamn stupid fucker. And me? The rest of us? We're all playing with these girls' lives like they're so freaking expendable.

"But, Ajia," Linda, or whatever her name is, says from behind me. She moves closer. "Don't you want to—"

I turn on her. "No! I don't want to. I don't want anything to fucking do with you. Leave me alone."

I storm away from her and go straight for the door.

"Hey, asshole, where ya goin'?" calls Zayne over the suddenly frantic whispering of the chicks.

I glare at him over my shoulder. "Where the fuck do you think?"

The door slams as I leave. It's the most satisfying thing to happen since Bree stuck her finger in my mouth. I shove the memory away and make it halfway down the hall before I hear my name.

"Ajia. Wait."

It's Rye. "What?"

"What are you going to do?"

"What the fuck do you think?" I snap. "Apologize to her." I hadn't seen the look on her face, but I heard the ragged sound of her voice. It was enough.

Shit's already in an uproar between us, and now pretending that fucking ugly little scene didn't happen isn't going to fix anything.

"What're you going to say?"

I stare at him for a second. "Don't you think that's between me and her?"

He lifts one shoulder. "Maybe. Under other circumstances. Tonight? Not so sure. Maybe tonight you've fucked with her enough."

I drop my head, shove my hands over my face and into my hair. "Jesus, Rye. What the fuck happened tonight? What's wrong with me?"

"You want her."

"Yeah." It takes me a minute to admit it out loud. "I do."

"So why do you keep doing shit to hurt her?"

It feels like I can't stand suddenly, and so I lean back against the wall. I shake my head.

"I don't know, man." Rye is the one person I know I can be honest with. He knows my shit. He's got some shit of his own to deal with.

"I don't mean to," I add after a minute. "But…"

"What?"

I close my eyes and bang my head back against the wall. *Jesus.*

"Ajia?"

I blow out a heavy breath. "I'm fucking scared. Okay?"

"Of what?"

"You know. Of her, man. *Of her.* Of what could happen."

"You're scared of being with Bree?" He sounds surprised.

"Shit, yeah. Of fucking course."

"Ajia. Dude, c'mon. She's—"

"Bree. Baby girl. I know! She's like the sixth member of Wycked Obsession. But…"

"You have feelings for her."

I stare at him. "Of course I have feelings for her. We've all got feelings for her. There's nobody—"

"Yours are different." There's no question in his voice.

"Yeah. I guess. They're starting to be."

"You gonna do anything about it?"

"I don't fucking know." I shake my head. "I shouldn't, you know? I'm all fucked up. Jaded. And she's…Bree. Sweet and fun and funny. She'll kick any one of our asses. But she's, I don't know…innocent, I guess."

Rye gives a soft laugh. "You calling a girl who can cuss better than the rest of us innocent?"

I smile a little. "That's all bullshit, and you know it. She learned how to fit in. A bunch of fucking rowdy rockers who don't have an inch of decency among us."

"That ain't innocence, dude." He steps closer, his voice low. "It's inexperience."

"Same difference," I insist.

"No. It isn't. But you can be damn sure she ain't gonna stay that way for long. If you don't step up—" he shakes his head "—somebody else will."

I straighten away from the wall. "Is that a threat? *You* gonna be the one to step up?"

Rye laughs. "Hell, no. My feelings for Bree haven't changed. But this tour…" He pauses. "There are fucking guys everywhere. Drivers, roadies, merch. Hell, Edge of Reason. And none of 'em are blind."

"Then you think I should…step up."

"Ain't for me to say. I just know that you gotta do one or the other. Take your chance or back off. No in-between."

"Shit." I shove my hands through my hair again and glance down the hall. "I gotta go, man. I gotta…fix this somehow."

"Good luck, man."

Rye turns back toward Zayne and Noah's suite. He doesn't say it, but we both know what he's thinking.

You're gonna need it.

♫

I don't have any trouble getting into Bree's suite. I have Knox's key card.

The place is quiet, the living area dark. I stand inside the doorway long enough that my eyes adjust to the heavy shadows. I try not to think as I wait. *Thinking* isn't going to help, not one goddamn bit.

I swallow a sigh, one of those get-it-fucking-over-with-because-it-isn't-going-to-get-any-easier sighs, and try to pretend that I'm not a little freaked out. It's really, really quiet, except for the hum of the AC unit. What if I'm wrong and Bree *didn't* come back to her room?

I take a careful step toward the bedrooms, and that's when I hear it. The sound is muffled enough I'm not exactly sure what it is. Breath? A sigh? Tears? It's something, and it came from behind the only closed door.

It opens easily, and I can see well enough to spot a pile of clothes on the floor by the bed. Bree is on the bed, her back to me, wearing a tank top and panties, as far as I can guess. *Thank God,* I think, it's too dark for details.

"Bree? Sweetheart?" I say as I lightly touch her shoulder.

She gives a soft yelp and whips around on the bed. She scrambles away from me before I can say another word, so I hold my hands up in front of me, hoping she can see them.

"There you are, baby girl. It's okay. It's just me."

She makes an odd noise, like an angry breath. "How did you get in here?"

"Knox's key." I hold up the card but keep my movements slow. I don't want to shake her up any more than she already is.

"Where's he?"

"We switched rooms tonight. He wanted…well, to be alone with his…girl."

"He didn't want me to hear them fucking, you mean."

"Uh…" Shit. I hate it when she's like this, even if it *is* my fault. "Yeah."

"So what are *you* doing here? You don't care if I hear *you* fucking?"

Goddammit.

"Bree…kitten. It's not like that." I try to maintain my shit, but a part of me wants to punch something. Like a very solid fucking wall.

"What's it like, then?"

"I…I need to talk to you."

She shakes her head and pushes herself up to sit. As far away from me as she can get. "Pretty sure there's nothing to say."

"No. Fuck, no. There's a lot to say."

"Then maybe now isn't the time to say it."

"No," I say again. "It has to be now."

"Think your girlfriend would disagree."

"She's not my girlfriend!" I shove my hand through my hair. "Jesus, Bree, you know that."

"Okay." She doesn't move. "Fuck buddy. Tonight's hook-up. The one who's going to blow you, fuck you, do whatever the rock star wants."

"Goddamn it, Bree!" I can't hold back the words anymore. *"Jesus Christ!"*

She looks at me with what the shadows pretend is innocence. I don't believe it for a second. She's pushing me, hard, and she means to do it.

Worse, she deserves to. I can't argue that she deserves to do a lot worse to me.

"You know me, *sweetie.*" The endearment she uses with the rest of the guys sounds like an insult. "I call 'em like I see 'em. I see through the bullshit. Can't get by with making shit up when you've got a brother like Knox Gallagher."

"I know, sweetheart."

I try to be sweet, because she deserves it, but I'm so fucking pissed. Not at her, but at myself. At the rest of the band. At the women we always attract. At…life. It's so fucking unfair!

I thought I'd come to terms with what my life would be. With taking only what I deserved and leaving the good shit, the sweet shit, for others. The night of that last party in Austin changed everything. And tonight totally destroyed it.

"Look, honey." I try again and kneel carefully on the edge of the bed.

"Don't call me that!"

I stop before I understand the words. "What?"

"Don't call me honey. Ever. You call all the groupies and fangirls *honey* when you don't know or can't remember their names."

"Okay, Bree. Kitten."

I move slowly, pull off my boots and push myself up to lean back against the headboard. I stretch my legs out across the mattress and hold one hand out to her. I shouldn't—Christ knows, I shouldn't—but she's hurting, and I have to do *something*.

"What do you want?" she demands irritably.

"Come here."

"No. Go back to Tits and—"

"I'm not going back and I'll never see her again." *Fuck!* I have to swallow the word. It isn't what Bree needs right now…but what about what *I* need?

Jesus. It hits me again. I have to do *something*.

"I know you didn't actually *come* sitting there on the sofa with her, so—"

"Motherfucker!" I can't hold it back this time. The word explodes, and Bree flinches. I hate that, but at the same time I hope she gets it that she can only push me so far. "We are *not* talking about that."

She doesn't respond, and so I slowly reach for her hand. I link our fingers and tug as gently as I can. "C'mon, baby. C'mere."

"Why?"

"Because we *are* going to talk about some other shit. And I don't want you sitting on the other side of the room."

"I'm not on the other side of the room. I'm on the other side of the bed. *My* bed."

I tighten my fingers around hers. "And we can stay this way. All night if you want to. Not going anywhere until we talk."

"What do you want to talk about?"

"Bree…" I tug lightly on her hand.

She hesitates another second and then finally scoots so she's leaning against the headboard next to me. I don't let go of her hand.

92

"I know I upset you, baby, but it was nothing." I try to make light of it without explaining shit. Not that I expect to get by with much, but I'm weak enough that I have to give it a shot.

"Nothing," she repeats.

"That's right." I don't get too excited about her agreement. I know women well enough to know better. "Just messing around with a fan."

"Messing around." She repeats that, as well. *Shit.* The tone of her voice doesn't sound good. "So feeling some chick up and sucking on her tits is *messing around.*"

Fuck. I blow out a breath. Knew she wasn't going to make it easy for me.

Bree stares straight ahead, her hand lifeless in mine. At least she's still there with me.

"It was the booze. The game. It all kind of got away from me."

"Don't try to bullshit me, A." Finally, she looks at me. "Nothing ever *gets away from you.* You knew exactly what you were doing. The whole fucking time. You..." Her voice cracks. "You knew, and you did it anyway. Even after the other night. Even knowing it would hurt me."

She leans close enough that I can see the shadowy pain in her eyes, the way her eyelashes are damp and spiked together. *"You did it. Anyway."*

"Bree." I pull her against me, her head on my shoulder, and wrap both arms around her. She stiffens but doesn't move away.

"Baby, I am so sorry. I was...fucked up. I shouldn't have done it. Didn't like it when I did it. But—fuck! I don't know how to explain it."

"Well, let me explain something to *you.*" She still doesn't move, doesn't soften. It's almost worse that she just lays resting against me as she talks. "I've had a crush on you since I was fifteen. The first day we met. I was babysitting Whiskers, and you've called me kitten ever since. You know all this shit—everybody knows this shit! Me crushing on you wasn't the secret I thought it was. I'm not as good at hiding my feelings as I thought I was."

I don't know what to say, but it doesn't matter when she continues.

"It was bad enough to hear shit about you. See shit on the internet and those TV gossip programs. I could pretend, though. Tell

93

myself that it was the paparazzi making up shit or putting a spin on things that weren't there. That was probably even true some of the time."

"You know it was, kitten. We've talked about it."

"And then I saw that chick sucking you off. Stroking you off. I saw the look on your face when she was doing it."

My insides clench, and for a minute I can't breathe.

"Then tonight you let that other chick crawl all over you. You put your hands on her, took her in your mouth. And that's when I knew."

"Knew what?" I really don't want to ask.

"It doesn't matter if I've grown up. If I've loved you for five years and I've saved myself for you. I'll never have you. You'll never be mine. You'll never want me like you want those other girls."

My heart feels like it's going to pound out of my chest. I can only answer half of what she says. "Baby, those girls don't mean anything to me."

"Don't lie, A. For God's sake, don't do that. And even if that *were* true and they don't mean shit to you, they mean a fuck of a lot to me. And, honestly, I can't keep pretending that they don't mean more to you than I do."

"Bree! Goddammit! That's not true!"

Somehow, I get my hands on her arms, and I twist her around so she straddles my lap about mid-thigh. I glare at her.

"Ajia?"

"No. Now *you* listen. You mean a fuck of a lot more to me than some faceless groupie whose name I can't even remember. *I kissed you,* for Christ's sake. I don't kiss anybody. Ever. I told you that."

"That is such bullshit." She twists against my hold but I don't let go.

"No," I snap. "It's intimate."

"Intimate, my ass. *Intimate* is when you stick your cock in somebody. *Intimate* is when you put it between some chick's lips or put your mouth on her pussy. *That's* intimate, you asshole!"

"That's just sex," I insist. "It doesn't mean shit."

She shook her head. "Spoken like a true rock star. You invent these excuses so you can have whatever you want. Parties, pleasure, and pussies. But get around *real* feelings—around somebody who wants more than your dick or your money or your fame—and you freak out. Well, fine. Then freak. Fucking. Out."

She tries to crawl off me, but I hold her tight. "I thought I could play your game," she says, sounding suddenly ragged. "I realized that this tour with you was my chance to show you things could be different. *I'm* different. I'm an adult now. A woman who could—" she waves her hand suddenly, a shadow slicing through the darkness "—it doesn't matter. I was fooling myself. I get it now. I have nothing you want, and so I'm gonna protect myself the only way I can."

"What are you talking about?"

"I'm gonna learn how to get over you."

CHAPTER 11

BREE

The words shock me when I actually hear them echo in the room. I hadn't really planned to say anything like that, hadn't gotten that far when Ajia came barging into the room. Mostly, my mind is all jumbled and circling through a minefield of pain, humiliation, and absolute fury. Part of me wants to curl up in a ball and feel *really* sorry for myself. The rest of me wants to punch Ajia in the throat.

Now the room gets quiet in an uncomfortable sort of way when he finally says, "Smartest thing you could do, kitten. We both know it."

The words hurt because I know, even though he *said* I matter to him, *this* is the truth. "Such an easy answer."

His fingers tighten around my arms. "Nothing fucking easy about it, baby. Don't kid yourself."

Is he talking about for him? Or for me? I can't let it matter. Now that the idea has surfaced, I have to stick up for myself.

"I have a favor to ask, then."

He's looking at me. I can feel the weight of his gaze, but the darkness keeps me from being able to judge his expression.

"What?"

"Could you...kind of...keep me in mind? Or at least...you know, when you're with those other girls, could you just do it—" I pause for a trace of strength "—where I can't really see you?"

"Oh, baby." He pulls me against him suddenly, moving faster than I can see in the shadows, and then I'm sprawled across his chest. One hand strokes over the back of my head. "How can you do it?"

"Do what?" I whisper in confusion.

He shakes his head; I can feel it. "I can't mean that much to you. I'm not worth it."

I hesitate, unsure how to proceed. Is this more bullshit to get him off the hook, or is this a deep moment of truth for him?

"I'm not sure which of us should be more offended," I finally answer. "You, because you think so badly of yourself, or me, because you think I'm such a lousy judge of character."

He snorts. "I just know the truth."

"What truth?"

"I've done shit. Made mistakes. You—don't go there."

"Like you're the only one," I snap. I wriggle in Ajia's grip, but he doesn't let go. "Don't try to pull that crap with me."

"What crap?"

"Don't play that game of tortured bad boy. You do it better than almost anybody, except maybe Rye, but I know better."

"No," he says flatly, so different from seconds ago. "You don't."

He's gone stiff, the muscles of his chest and abdomen hard against me, even through the barrier of his thin T-shirt. I squirm uselessly for a softer position that Ajia's body can't provide. Especially not with that *other* hardness. Lower. The thick ridge of his cock presses boldly against my belly.

"So..." Why does my voice have to sound so goddamn breathy? "Explain these great mistakes to me."

He shifts, though I can't tell whether it is to move away or press himself closer against me. "No." His voice registers soft but harsh. "Not tonight."

"Why not?"

"You've—enough shit's gone down tonight. Not going there."

I know that tone of voice. Experience—years as Ajia's *friend*—has taught me the futility of being able to convince him to say more when he doesn't want to. And yet I just lie there, draped all over him like a limp towel. I try to hold myself still and yet can't quite manage it.

"Are you thinking about them? Her?"

"Who?"

"That girl from earlier."

"No!" He turns suddenly, rolling me onto my back. His hips and legs hold me in place, pressing me down into the bed. "Fuck no! Why would you ask that?"

He pushes up on his arms and stares at me. It pushes his lower body closer. I recognize the rough irritation in his voice, but the darkness robs me of the chance to find any clear idea of his expression.

I swallow and raise one leg just enough to rub against his crotch. "Just wondered."

The moment freezes, like all the air was suddenly sucked out of the room, and then it roars back in with a new heaviness. It pushes against me, anchors me tight against Ajia, until the whole damn thing blows up. He shoves away and surges from the bed.

"Fuck." His voice rips through the night. I can see just enough to recognize the movement as he shoves his hands through his hair. *"Jesus Christ."*

"Ajia?" I know what freaked him out. It freaks me out a little, too. But he has to own that, not me.

He steps back. "Go to bed, Bree."

"I am in bed."

"Then go to sleep."

I push up on one elbow. He was hard. Lying in bed with me, he got a hard-on. I can't let myself take it as any great sign of...well, anything. I bet just about any woman would have gotten him that way if they were lying in a bed together. Hell, maybe he started that way.

It's the fact that he got an erection being there with *me* that he hates.

"Sure." I grab at the covers like they're a lifeline, tearing them back so I can slide beneath the protection. "Right."

"I...I'll be in Knox's room. If you need anything."

"I won't." I turn my back to him.

He stands by the bed for a while. I know it, can feel him. Finally—I don't know how long it takes—he says a soft, "Goodnight, kitten," and is gone.

♫

I sprawl on the couch in the garage music room, sitting but taking up more than my share of space. I look around and decide it's okay. Nobody else is here.

I drop my head back, enjoying the moment until I hear…sounds. Not sure what they are, I force my eyelids open and look around. Nothing. Then I hear them again and realize they're coming from behind me.

I turn my head just enough to catch sight of Knox in the corner of my eye. He's got some girl in his arms, and they're pressed together like lovers. I swallow an annoyed laugh. I know my brother and love *is the last thing on his mind.*

It's fucking, pure and simple.

I turn away and realize that the rest of the band is there, too. They wander around the room, messing with their instruments and talking, but I can't hear them. I look back at Knox—for help?—but his shirt is off and the chick is naked!

God, no. *I do* not *want to see that shit. Not when it's my* brother!

I look around—anywhere—and notice that the guys are leaning against the wall, watching as a line of bikini-clad women saunter past. They have kind of a plastic look to them that makes me think Barbie, *like the doll, and I laugh. Ajia frowns at me, puts a finger to his lips and shakes his head. "Sshhhh," he says firmly.*

I nod to show I understand, but the longer I sit there watching the Barbies parade, the madder I get. Fuck the dolls—and fuck the guys. And who's Ajia to shush me?

I push up off the couch to call him out on it, but suddenly I'm in line with them. A brilliant spotlight tracks my progress. The Barbies are all wearing the same pink string bikini, but when I look down, I realize that I'm *naked!*

Naked? What the hell am I doing naked? *In this line? Traipsing up and down in front of Noah, Rye, Zayne…and Ajia!*

Horror scrapes over my nerves, but I can't do anything except keep moving forward as part of the Barbie line. I get to Ajia first— but hadn't he been on the other end?—and he looks at me from head to toe.

"No. No, no, no." He shakes his head sharply, and his golden blond hair swings around his shoulders. Fear keeps me watching that instead of looking at his face.

"What are you doing here, Bree?" he demands sharply. "You don't belong with these girls."

"I know," I mutter, wishing not for the first time that I did. That I deserve a pink bikini and that Ajia said yes *instead of* no *to me.*

"Go sit down."

He gives me a little push toward the couch, and I go. Humiliation washes over me, staining me with a blush of fever, and I keep my head down. I sink down on the couch, still naked, and pull my hair over my shoulders to cover my breasts. Thank God it's long enough!

I can't do much about the rest of me, so I fold my hands and leave them on my lap to cover my vagina. Thinking a more clinical word helps me think of my body less...personally. I don't feel quite so inadequate.

"Don't cover yourself, Bree."

The voice is too close, and I look aside to see my stepfather next to me. He sits sideways, his arm along the back of the sofa and his eyes are riveted on me. On my body.

"Gabe!" I gasp. "Jesus, get away from me!"

I scoot away from him, but I can't seem to put any real space between us. He keeps smiling, his eyes sharp and piercing like he can see beneath my hair, under my clenched hands.

"You know I want you," he says, and then he shifts so he can reach me with one hand. "It doesn't matter if he doesn't." He points an accusing finger at Ajia. "I do."

"I don't care! Don't touch me!"

I scream the words and shoot a frantic gaze all around the room. Knox and his girl are caught up in each other. Zayne and Noah are laughing, twirling girls around like ballerinas on a music box, while Rye sits behind Noah's drum kit, crashing the cymbals every time a new girl steps up.

"Guys!" I shout. "Help me! Please!"

Ajia can't be bothered. He presses his lips against the next-in-line bikini-clad Barbie, taking her mouth in a kiss that should incinerate them both.

"You don't kiss!" I yell, as though I need to remind him. "You told me! You only kissed me!"

He lifts his head. "That was a mistake." And then he kisses the new girl again and again and again.

I want to cry, scream—do something—but the moment escapes unfinished when Gabe's fingers brush the hair away from my breasts. He palms their fullness, pinches my nipples, and squirms around on the couch until I look down. His penis is out of his pants, and he's stroking it up and down.

"God, you sick fucker!" I scream again. "Get away from me. Leave me alone! I don't want you!"

"C'mon, Bree. You're my baby. You can call me daddy. Just think...fucking my baby girl."

"Oh, God!" Nausea threatens to swamp me, and I swallow heavily. Please! *I pray silently.* This can't be happening!

"Let me in." Gabe drops his hand from my breasts and lays his palm over my clenched fist. He wants to touch my vagina!

"No! Jesus, no!"

I try to squirm away again, but I can't seem to put any space between us. I find little relief when Gabe seems to reconsider, because he's still touching me. He's simply moved his hand to the back of my neck and forces me forward.

"C'mon, Bree. You know you want it."

It takes no more than an instant, and then I realize exactly what he wants from me. A blow-job. He wants me to suck him off!

"No!" I squirm against his hold, but he's strong. Way stronger than I expected, and he keeps pushing my head down. His dick gets closer and closer to my mouth, and I keep turning my head. He uses his hand to slap his prick against one cheek, then the other.

"Stop it! No! Please!"

I'm sobbing. I know it, hating the weakness, but all strength deserts me. "Ajia!" I scream, praying—dear God, begging—*he stops kissing that chick and look at me! "Please! Help me!"*

"You're okay, baby." Gabe's dick keeps stroking my cheeks.

"No!"

"It's a dream, sweetheart. Just a bad fucking dream. C'mere. I've got you. I'm here."

Something around me changes. What? How? The music room, the spotlight, the Barbies...everything disappears. It's dark and quiet, and Gabe is nowhere in the heavy shadows.

Or is he? Jesus, is he hiding? Waiting for me to let down my guard?

I move, or try to when I realize arms, warm and comforting, hold me close. Fingers, soft and gentle, caress my cheek, and the scent of sandalwood comforts me.

"Ajia?" I whisper. It can't be anyone else.

"There you go, baby. I've got you. Everything's all right."

I let out a ragged sigh and shudder as I try to stem my tears. He'll keep Gabe from me—won't he? He and Knox pretty much told me that! But then he told me no, that kissing me was a mistake, and he'd kissed that other girl.

A dream, a soft voice reminds me. The Barbies, the mean words, the strange way the bandmates acted...a stupid fucking nightmare.

"God." I snuggle closer to him and rub my cheek against his chest. Some faint warning from far in the back of my mind cautions me away from such recklessness, but the alarm sounds too soft to stop me. I need the reassurance of Ajia's presence, his body, if only for a little while.

"It was just a bad dream, kitten," he repeats. "You're okay. I'm here with you."

A bad dream. A *nightmare.*

Breath heaves from me, and I try to blink away the tears. I can't stop them completely and choke back a sob, fighting the sensation of Gabe grabbing me, touching me, forcing my head down toward his crotch. I'm not good enough, strong enough, and it won't give me any peace.

I need something more. Something to make me forget.

I push myself against Ajia, not really meaning to or thinking or questioning what I'm doing. I just need to feel his closeness. Connect with something—someone—who can bind me to reality. To the world outside my nightmare.

I swallow and rub my cheek against Ajia's chest again. It feels so warm and reassuring...and very naked. That, finally, draws my eyes open.

He's half-sitting, half-kneeling on the bed, his arms tight around me and his skin smooth against my face. He's never had much chest hair as far as I know, but I've never really been close enough to *feel* him. Not like this. His legs, one tucked under mine, are different altogether. They're rough with hair, and in a blinding instant, I realize I've never felt *them,* either.

Is he naked?

"You wanna talk about it?"

Only *that* question can claim enough of my attention to let go of thoughts about his possible nudity.

"Ajia." I sniff and can't stop from snuggling closer again. "Hold me. Please?"

His arms tighten around me, hands smoothing up and down my back. I breathe deeply, greedy for any and every sensation that his touch produces.

"Sure, baby," he says after a moment. "I've got you." Then we're moving. He shifts around until he's sitting with his back against the headboard and me tucked against his side. He adjusts the covers, pulls them over us both, and tightens his arms around me once more. "There," he says softly. "You're safe."

"Safe," I murmur against his chest and sort of nod.

"Safe," he agrees. "You okay, kitten?"

I breathe long and hard again, mostly as an excuse to take in every bit of sandalwood and Ajia's own, personal scent. "I don't know."

"You wanna talk about it?" he tries again.

"No." I shake my head. "Maybe. Yes?"

He strokes one hand over my hair. "It can't be so bad. Tell me, baby. What happened?"

Fresh tears leak from the corners of my eyes. They'd mostly stopped, but now, facing it again, they're back. I hate it. The tears, the feelings, everything it means. It all felt *so real!*

"God," I sigh thickly. "I feel like such an idiot."

"Hey, no reason for that. It's okay. It was a dream. A pretty fucking bad one, seems like, but it can't hurt you."

"He. It was…Gabe." At least that's part of it.

Ajia stiffens until he feels like a living statue. "Your fucking stepfather." It's not a question.

"Yeah. He was the worst part. Acting all…pervy and disgusting."

"He's like a thousand miles away. Forget about him."

I swallow. He's right. "I know. But there was other stuff, really weird, you know? You were there. So was Knox. He was making out with some chick, Rye was playing the drums, and you, Zayne and Noah were judging a bunch of Barbies who were marching in pink bikinis." It seems the safest—if dumbest—way to describe it.

Ajia blows out a soft laugh. "Sounds interesting."

"You'd say that." I sigh, trying to sound teasing, but it comes out more grumpy. Exactly like I feel. "I think you were head judge or something."

He doesn't say anything, and so I finally offer, "We were in the garage music room in Austin. I was on the couch, watching the Barbies parade around." I can't tell him what he said, or how I felt watching him kiss another girl. "Then Gabe was there, and he kept trying to force me to...ugh." I shudder.

"What?" Can he sound any more concerned? Disgusted? "What did he want you to do, baby?"

"Suck him off."

"Jesus." Ajia's arms tighten around me. Does he mean it as reassurance? Comfort? Or does he get the symbolism? Why my brain invented that crap in *that* location?

I don't ask the questions aloud, or even try to answer them for myself. I just open my mouth to say...what? I have no idea. Then the rest of it comes tumbling out. "I kept yelling 'no' and calling for help. I called for you." I don't intend to make it sound like an accusation, but it kind of does. "Nobody came—y'all were just doing your thing with the other chicks—and then he...his dick—"

"Shh, baby. I'm sorry." His embrace gentles into comforting, and I feel the press of his lips against the top of my head. "I'd never let Gabe hurt you like that. I promise you. No matter what."

I swallow. I want to accept his declaration, to believe him, but the memory of betrayal—real and imagined—holds strong, like it's new and real. "But you did. You didn't care. You were busy. You..."

"What?"

"You were kissing another girl. One of the Barbies."

Electricity crackles around us. I created it. I know I did, but I can't quite figure how to make it go away.

"I told you I don't kiss women. Not on the mouth."

He sounds kind of desperate, but I can't let it go. "You were, though. And it was...like you kissed me."

"Bree..."

I tilt my head back far enough to find Ajia's face through the darkness. The shadows still protect his expression, but I don't need to see him to realize his struggle. We've already talked about it, and he's pretty much hated those conversations.

"I don't kiss on the mouth. Ever."

"But...you kissed me."

"Yeah. I fucking did."

And just tonight?

"You mean a fuck of a lot more to me than some faceless groupie whose name I can't even remember. I kissed you, for Christ's sake. I don't kiss anybody. Ever. I told you that."

"You can't deny it," I insist because the words won't stay inside. "You kissed me like you wanted to. Like you *meant it*. And being here with me, earlier tonight..." I hesitate, but only for a heartbeat. "You liked it. I know you did."

I spread my fingers wide and trace them over the muscles of his abdomen and down farther, to the waistband of his boxers. So he isn't naked. Disappointment pierces me. "I know you did," I repeat, "because your body told me."

"Oh, Jesus. Fucking. Christ."

His fingers wrap around my wrist, stopping me from going any farther. I tug, his grip tightens, and my breath catches.

"You're playing with fire, baby."

"No," I sigh. "I *am* fire. And you made me that way."

CHAPTER 12

AJIA

This is not supposed to happen. I do not fucking mean to kiss her. I left her room to avoid it. Forced myself to go into Knox's bedroom, tossing and turning until I could finally fall asleep, and then I heard her cries. *Help! No! My name.* That almost tore me to pieces. No idea what the fuck was happening. I was out of bed and down the hall before I had the thought to even move.

I don't know what I expected, but not Bree thrashing around on the bed, caught in some nightmare. She was scared, heartbroken, desperate; I heard it all in her voice, saw it in the way she moved. And so I did the only thing I could: I took her in my arms.

It's as right as it is wrong, and now I hold her tight against me, her mouth trapped by mine. Her lips are soft, her breath moist, and my tongue plunges forward to taste every bit of her. I angle my head to deepen the kiss, and she offers herself to me without hesitating. Her tongue dances with mine, seeking and seducing and desiring, and a part of me knows I'm lost.

I should be scared to fucking death, but my brain's too scrambled for that right now.

I *do* know that I shouldn't be here with her like this. Been running from it since that night in Austin. It was what—only a couple of weeks ago? How the hell has everything changed since then? Better...and worse. Hearing her admit to her crush for me, even though I've known about it for a while now, changed things. Again. Seeing her as a woman. A living, breathing, very fucking desirable woman. And knowing how I've hurt her by being a douche with other chicks.

106

I can't do it anymore. Can't keep hurting her because I'm a goddamn coward. Can't pretend that I don't want her. Because I do.

Jesus, do I want her.

I kiss her again, take her mouth just like my cock wants to fit in her pussy. I don't deserve her, but it doesn't stop me this time. Been fighting that battle with myself for a while now, and doing a shit job of it. She's the only one whose been a casualty in my half-assed struggle—well, her and any shred of decency I ever had—and I can't keep doing it to her.

To us.

Maybe she deserves a hell of a lot better, but for some fucking reason, she wants me.

I won't fuck her. Not tonight, and maybe not ever. She deserves better than me at my best, no matter what she thinks. But tonight, after I played stupid fucking games with some chick who meant nothing to me, I'm only gonna think about Bree. What she needs, what she deserves...what she wants.

Maybe I'm as fucked up as I think, but right now I don't give a shit about that or the consequences. All the reasons why I'm a lousy choice for her. *Right now,* I want nothing more than to watch her come apart against my hands, my mouth.

I'm not really thinking about what I'm doing, but my hands are moving, my body right behind them. I turn so she's pinned beneath me on the bed. Shoving my fingers through her hair, I push it away from her face and stroke the softness of her cheeks, her jaw, her neck. She moans, giving me the chance to slide my tongue up over the roof of her mouth, around her teeth, along her lips.

Her breasts arch against my chest, and her nipples poke me. I'm suddenly on fire, just like Bree claimed I did to her. I have to touch her, skin-to-skin.

I delay the moment, though. To tease her? Me? I cup her breast through the thin fabric of her tank top. She isn't wearing a bra and fits against my hand like she was made for me. I scrape my palm over her peaked nipple and then move it in light, tight circles, keeping up the rhythm of palming her tits and teasing her nipples. She moans again, louder this time, and thrusts her chest forward.

I turn my hand, drag the backs of my fingers down her side until I reach the hem of her shirt. "I want to see you. Touch you," I mutter against her mouth and trace my thumb over a patch of skin just above her panties.

"Yes." It's more breath than word.

Yeah, it's dark in the room and I won't be able to see much. I don't care. That's not the point.

I move my hand up, fingertips barely stroking her stomach, her waist, the underside of her breasts, and then her lush curves. Her shirt drags up with my wrist. The heavy shadows reveal only shades of gray, but they're enough. "Jesus, baby. You're beautiful. Who knew you were hiding tits like these?"

She pulls my hand to her perfectly formed breasts, pressing my palm against the crest. I love the message she's sending and drag my thumb over her nipple, again and again. I take her mouth in another long, soul-stealing kiss, but it can't last.

I need to taste her.

I drop my head to circle her other nipple with my tongue. Again and again. Bree gasps and arches her back, her tits pushing forward. I suck her into my mouth, teasing one nipple with my tongue and the other with my thumb.

She needs this. *I* need it. And more.

I slide down her body but keep my fingers on her breasts, playing with her nipples. She writhes against my hands, moaning soft encouragement. She's sensitive there. I smile to myself, enjoying her sexy secret.

I kiss her body, mouth open and tongue seeking. I taste her stomach, push her panties down so I can get to her hips, her mound. "What's this?" I lick her there, just above her pussy. "You're bare."

"I…" I hear her struggle for breath. "Waxed. Everything."

"It's sexy, you know that, right?" I drop kisses along the same path my tongue followed.

"I…" That breathiness again, maybe because I still play with her nipples. "Wanted to be…pretty."

"Pretty?" I lick her again. "For me?"

"Yes! *God, yes.*"

Her hips flex, and I know what she wants. Same thing I want.

I slip farther down, neglecting the hard-on that doesn't want to be ignored. Thank God I have my boxers on, because Mr. Johnson isn't coming out to play. Not tonight.

It's easy to think only about Bree when her legs part so willingly. I drag her panties off one leg so I can kneel between her thighs, kiss them, then drag my tongue down to her knees and back up. First one leg and then the other. She sighs and squirms against my mouth.

"You like that, baby?"

"Yes. Oh…yes."

I do it again, stretch out with my legs behind me and shoulders spreading her thighs wide. I drop a light, teasing kiss right above her clit, and then drag my tongue flat from bottom to top. And again.

She keens a sharp cry of need. I recognize it perfectly, and so I keep doing it until even I'm crazy with need. Not for me but for her. I find the bud of her clit with the tip of my tongue, and she all but comes up off the bed.

"Oh, God! *Ajia!*"

I smile against her and do it again. "You like that, don't you, baby?"

"Yes." Her breath cracks on a half-laugh. "Jesus, are you kidding me?"

I do it once more, then take her gently in my mouth and suck, just a little. I'm not usually so careful with women, but this is Bree. I want it to be good for her. Better than any high school or college dudes who're all about their own pleasure.

I suck again, lightly, and swirl my tongue around her clit. She gasps and then her hands shove into my hair. She holds me close against her, and her hips pick up a quick rhythm.

Jesus, she's so sensitive! Never knew a girl to get so turned on so quick. It makes me smile, feel powerful and masculine, and I lick her again.

Her fingers clench in my hair, her hips flex, and I know she won't last long. I shift so I can slide one finger inside her.

Jesus, she's wet. And tight. More than any other girl I've known. Ever.

Bree groans low in her throat as I push my finger in and out. Carefully, I add another, scissoring both as I move them inside her. She holds still for a minute, but I keep soft pressure against her clit with my tongue and soon she moves with the lure of my hand.

"You're so tight, baby." I suck gently on her clit, plunge my fingers in and out. "So perfect."

"Yes. *Please.*" Her hips thrust.

"Please what?" I tease.

"Please! You…know." Her hips arch again.

"You wanna come?" I massage her clit with my tongue.

"Yes. God, yes."

"Tell me." I hold steady, not really sure how I can do it. "Tell me what you want, baby."

"Jesus, Ajia. Make me come! *Please!*"

Her hips move with demand, and I smile against her. I've always loved her honesty, and now I love that she asked for what she wanted. I move my hand faster, more urgently, and curl my fingers forward, seeking her sweet spot. I give up the soft, gentle tug on her clit and use my lips, my tongue, my teeth…my whole mouth to carry her forward.

"Ajia!" She squirms against my face, tightens her hands in my hair, and then she's there. Her hips buck sharply, and I taste her release against my mouth, feel her pussy tighten around my fingers.

Jesus. Having her come against my mouth, around my fingers, sends a shot of need straight to my cock. It's better than I ever expected…and not enough. Nowhere near enough.

Never had a woman respond to me like that. As quick, as hot, come as hard.

Keeping my fingers moving, slower, I lick her through her orgasm. I peer up the length of her body as she shudders against me, her face relaxed with a heavy, satisfied smile. Grinning, I pull my fingers from her, lick each one, slow and careful and greedy. She can see me, and I work it. I want her to know how good she tastes.

I move back up, pull her in my arms and hold her close. She gives a little shudder now and then, a post-orgasmic reaction that satisfies me to the depths of my soul.

"You're an oral sex girl, huh?" I ask with a contented smile.

She nods against my shoulder. "I guess I am," she sighs.

"You ought to know by now, baby. Don't tell me those college boys don't know how to go down on a girl." It bugs the shit out of me suddenly to imagine her with some other dude like that, but I don't have any room to complain and I know it.

I'm a manwhore, after all.

She lifts a shoulder in a cute little shrug. "I don't know. They might be pretty good at it. I just…haven't done that with any of them."

I push up on one elbow, smooth the backs of my fingers over her cheek. "Baby, you've got a beautiful pussy! Amazing responses. Those boys can't tell that?"

"Well, I…"

"What?" I ask when she turns her face against my chest. Not crazy about reminding her of other guys, but I need her to know how beautiful she is. How sensual and desirable. How well she's made for love.

I stroke my hand down her spine. It pulls her shirt down, and I hate to see her very fine tits covered up, but something has her uncomfortable. That's more important.

"I haven't…really—er…"

Her voice dies, and I kiss the top of her head. "Haven't what, baby?"

"I haven't been with any guy. Like that. Or…at all."

"You—" I swallow as the truth of what she's saying hits me. "You're a virgin?"

"Sort of." She keeps her face hidden. "Except for oral sex with you just now. I've kissed other guys, but that's pretty much…it."

Sweet fucking Christ.

A virgin. My Bree is a virgin, and I just went down on her like she was some experienced chick. Like she knew what to expect. Jesus!

"Oh, baby." I smooth a hand over her hair, brush it away from her face, and urge her head back so she can look up at me. I don't know why, since we can see so little, but I do it, anyway.

I kiss her with all the tenderness I can gather. I haven't kissed a woman in *years*, except for Bree, but my desire for her demands that I do it right. Suddenly, I wouldn't want it any other way.

"I'm sorry," I whisper against her mouth.

"For what?" she pulls back. Blinks. Her voice sounds a little careful, almost awkward. "Are you sorry we—"

"No, baby. Not that. I should have taken my time. Been more—"

"Oh, no, A!" She snuggles tighter against me and kisses my neck. "It was *perfect.*"

111

I try to laugh but it's not very good. "You don't have anything to compare it to."

Her tongue is doing crazy things to my neck, behind my ear, and then her teeth close over my earlobe. *Jesus.* My hips flex against her, my cock rock hard, and I shift away.

"I don't need anything else to compare it to," she whispers. "You're a very good teacher."

She bites my earlobe with a bit more pressure, and my body responds again. I try to put more space between my hips and hers, but she's not having it. She strokes her palm over the length of my cock. Does it again. I don't mean to, but still I push against her hand, and her fingers close around me.

Thank God for my boxers. If she touches me skin-to-skin, my good intentions will go up like fucking smoke.

"Not a good idea, baby." I pull her hand free and twine my fingers with hers.

"Why?"

Does she really sound so sad?

"Not about me tonight. I—" How can I say I don't deserve it without bringing up memories of that groupie chick? Or Garage Chick. I don't want to spoil it and so I kiss her instead. "You're the virgin here. You're going to stay that way."

"Don't you want me?"

I laugh, but it's ragged. Harsh. "Oh, I want you, baby. Bad. But we're still not doing it tonight." I'm determined and reach down to help her pull her panties back into place.

"But...sometime?"

I hear the desire in the word. *Sometime?* Do I really think I can fight her after this?

"Yeah. Sometime." I tuck her against me. "Now let me hold you while you go to sleep."

"You won't leave?"

"Nope. I'm here. I'll keep you safe." From everything except me.

"I—okay." She snuggles tight against my side and kisses my chest. "If you're sure."

"I'm sure."

"Okay," she says again. "Night, Ajia."

"Night, baby."

♪

Noise, soft and out of place, brings me to *almost* awake. I lay there, half-listening, while the rest of me identifies the other stuff around me. One breath I'm trying to put it together, and the next I know.

Bree is tucked against me, her head on my shoulder, one arm slung over my chest and her leg draped over my already hard dick. Or maybe it's still hard. Not sure that my hard-on ever really went away after I cockblocked myself last night.

I shift, moving kind of into her and one hand idly stroking over her arm. I'm more aware of what I'm doing after I start, but I'm not really awake enough to think about stopping, or even if I should. Her skin is soft and smooth, and I want to touch more of her.

I blink, turn my head so I can drop a kiss on Bree's forehead.

"Morning, kiddies."

I close my eyes in a slow blink and reverse my turn. I go farther, slant a look toward the door, and then drop my eyelids again. *Fuck.*

Noah leans against the doorframe, which doesn't concern me so much. It's Knox, standing next to the goddamn bed. He glares at me like one pissed off motherfucker.

"What. The. Fuck."

Bree chooses that minute to wake up. She wiggles next to me, stretching with a soft, contented sigh and slowly opens her eyes. I know the instant she spots her brother; she goes all tense and stiff. She'd even pull away, if I let her, but I don't. I tighten my grip around her. I know better than to let either of us act like we're guilty of something.

"Morning." I respond to Noah.

Knox steps closer to the bed. "Again, Ajia. What the fuck?"

"It's not what you think," Bree insists, and I wonder if she just made things worse.

"You two in the same bed?"

Knox sounds pissed off enough that I'm not sure why he hasn't jerked my ass out of bed. Maybe it's because he's hung over.

"Yes." Bree answers primly.

"Then it's exactly what I think."

113

"Knox—" I start but she interrupts.

"Don't start this shit, Knox."

"What shit? I didn't start any goddamn thing. Looks like this fucker did."

Why the hell is Noah standing there grinning?

"Nobody started anything." I try to sound unconcerned.

"Then what the fuck are you doing in bed with my sister?"

"I had a nightmare." Bree sounds a little more defensive than is probably good for the situation, but I can't really blame her. It *is* an awkward fucking position to be in.

"So, what? You rushed in to fuck her awake?"

"Knox!"

Bree might be shocked, but I'm suddenly pissed. Knox can say anything he wants about me, because it's probably all true. But not about his sister, and he damn well knows it.

I smooth a hand over her hair and turn so she's laying on the bed next to me, then I swing my legs over the side of the bed and sit straight. "Apologize to your sister."

"Why?"

"The only one who got fucked last night was you. And probably Noah." I fling one hand in his direction. "Nothing like that happened between Bree and me."

So maybe I'm not exactly telling the truth. Something *did* happen. I kissed her like I hadn't kissed a woman since Lara, and Bree came all over my face, my hand. It's the best fucking memory I have. Ever. Knox's protective bullshit isn't going to ruin it. Not for me, and not for her.

We've got enough shit to work through without her brother interfering.

"Nice boxers," Noah points out. My morning wood is mostly gone, thank God. By now, I figure I look pretty ordinary.

"We're not exactly naked here, Knox," Bree points out as she crawls from behind my back to kneel next to me.

"He's in boxers, you're in panties and a tank. Yeah, that's real fucking reassuring."

"Oh, get over your fucking self," Bree snaps. "I had a nightmare. Ajia woke up when I screamed, and he came running. He didn't take time to think, 'Oh, maybe I should put on a three-piece suit in case Knox comes in and jumps to the wrong conclusion.' He just knew I needed something—somebody—and *you* weren't here to help."

"We traded rooms—"

"Exactly!" She sits back on her heels. "You wanted privacy to fuck your groupie and left Ajia to take care of me. Now you're pissed because he did it?"

Knox frowns between us. "Doesn't explain why you ended up in the same bed."

"Oh, for Christ's sake, Knox." I'm done with all this bullshit. Maybe because I *do* have something to hide. Or because Noah's just standing there, arms over his chest and grinning like a fucking clown.

"What?"

"Bree had a fucking nightmare. It upset her. She was crying, for fuck's sake. I stayed until she fell asleep, and I guess I fell asleep, too."

"You were crying?" Finally, something else catches Knox's attention.

"Can we have this discussion later?" Bree asks as she shifts around, trying to get off the bed, I guess. She kind of tilts in my direction, and I reach out to steady her. Knox grunts, and I hear a stifled chuckle from Noah.

Assholes.

"Why? So you two can cuddle up and get your stories straight?" Knox demands.

"Jesus, when did you get to be such a paranoid fucker?"

He points to the floor. "When I see your boots tossed on top of my sister's clothes."

CHAPTER 13

BREE

I flop back onto the bed and stare at the pile of clothes I threw on the floor last night. Ajia's motorcycle boots lay in what looks like a drunken heap on top of them. I suppose they *could* look a little suspicious, but they shouldn't. Ajia took them off when he first came in to talk to me about Tits. I guess neither of us thought much about them after that.

I know I didn't.

"You notice the rest of his clothes aren't there," I point out with every bit of reason I can find.

"Yeah? I notice he doesn't have them *on,* either."

I sigh. "Knox, there is a perfectly good explanation for everything. If you'll let me take a shower and get a cup of coffee, I'll tell you the whole freaking story."

"Oh, so there is a fucking story." He glares at me. Or is it Ajia?

"No. Except for the bullshit you've invented in your head. But I'll tell you everything that happened." I bump shoulders with Ajia but don't look at him. "We both will."

"Well..."

"C'mon."

I've got about a million other things I'd rather think about—like the memory of how it felt to have Ajia's mouth on me, his fingers inside me, and if there's a chance anything else can happen again. We have to talk, but that isn't going to happen until my brother gets over himself.

"Dude." Noah straightens from his place in the doorway. "Let our baby girl have her shower and coffee. Nobody's going anywhere. If it turns out Ajia fucked up, I'll *help you* beat the shit out of him."

Noah's smiling, but it's shitty enough that I wish he didn't know how things were between Ajia and me. He means it. He *will* beat the shit out of Ajia. Any of the guys will if they think he did something to hurt me.

"Do I look like I need defending?" I ask the question but nobody responds.

"You coming?" Knox demands, glaring at Ajia.

He's torn. I can see it in his face. He knows we need to talk as much as I do, but we can't do it now. Part of me is relieved. What if he tells me last night was a mistake? That he regrets what we did?

The weak, insecure part of me wants to wind up that thinking into imagining something terrible, something that will end badly and break my heart. A faint voice of better judgment insists I slow down.

Don't get ahead of yourself, it reminds me. *If that's how it happens, then you'll know. It's that simple. You decided the* what ifs *were killing you. Either way, you'll have your answer. You've been afraid it would go to shit, and you knew the risk when you took it.*

"You okay, kitten?"

Ajia's concern warms me. "I'm good." I smile softly.

He opens his mouth like he has something else to say, then his gaze flicks around the room. Knox looms there like some giant gargoyle or something. Ajia just nods and disappears from the room.

"Bree—"

"Get out, Knox." I grab my makeup bag and a change of underwear from my open suitcase. "You wanna talk, we'll fucking talk. But not until I've had my shower. And get me a double espresso skinny mocha with whip."

Then I'm outta there, and I don't give a shit if my brother still looks pissed off.

I don't hurry through my shower, hair, or makeup routine. Ajia and I didn't do anything wrong, and I'm not going to let Knox treat it that way. Yeah, so we made it to third base. It was fantastic. Far better than any fantasy I'd ever had about being with Ajia. I wouldn't trade it for anything in the world. But that's between him and me. None of Knox's business.

And if you think he's going to leave it there, you're crazy.

My conscience is right. Knox isn't going to be okay with what happened—so it's a good thing I have no intention of telling him. I wouldn't tell him if I'd gone that far with any other guy. I've never told him about any boys I ever kissed. Just because he knows Ajia— or *because* of it—I'm not giving him any reason to bring out the big-gun protective shit again.

I dress simply in a pair of ripped jeans, a red Wycked Obsession tank top, and my white flipflops. My hair is kind of coffee-colored, and I leave it loose around my shoulders and down my back. The contrast of my dark hair against the red shirt is good. Attractive. We aren't on the tour bus, where it doesn't matter if I look sloppy. We're in Phoenix, and I want to look decent if anybody sees me with the band.

Really? a sly voice demands. *You sure you aren't dressing up for Ajia?*

Maybe. I've learned some hard lessons about lying to myself. So what if I am? Besides, this is hardly *dressing up.* And who's it hurt?

I find the whole band in the living area. Every last freaking one of them. A box of donuts sits on the coffee table next to what I assume is my double espresso skinny mocha with whip.

I snatch up my cup. "So what's going on? We having an intervention?" I try to make it sound kind of funny, but it falls flat.

"Probably should have done it before now." It's Rye who answers.

Shit. I take a long drink of mocha, letting the coffee, chocolate, and whipped cream melt over my tongue. Zayne and Knox are on the sofa that faces me, Noah's in a square-shaped chair, and Rye and Ajia are on opposite ends of the sofa nearest where I stand. They're all dressed a lot like me—ripped jeans and T-shirts—and are looking anywhere but at me.

I choose my seat deliberately and sink down between Rye and Ajia. Neither of them moves.

"Okay," I say. "Y'all are making way too much of this. *Nothing happened.*"

"We were there, baby girl," Noah reminds me with surprising gentleness.

Is this about more than Knox and him finding Ajia and me in bed together? "Maybe so," I agree. "But you're still making more of it than you need to."

"Start at the beginning," Knox snaps. He doesn't like me sitting next to Ajia, I can tell. That pisses me off.

"The beginning? Which beginning? Like the fact that our *stepfather* can't keep his hands off me so I came on tour with y'all? Or your dare that I leave the party and go back to my room?"

He flushes. "Bree…"

"I'm not shitting you about last night, Knox. That hurt my feelings!"

I hadn't really thought about bringing that up, but it's true. And, now that it's out, I realize it's also when I started to get a little edgy last night. Like I didn't belong. Like they all would have been better off—had more fun—if I hadn't been there. My vulnerabilities had cruised to the surface, and the rest had been practically inevitable.

"You trying to make this my fault?" Knox scowls.

"No. You said start at the beginning, so I did. At least for *this* stupidity." I wave my hand around the room. "You really embarrassed me last night—not that I expect you to take responsibility for it. You never have before. And you were too freaking busy looking for a place to fuck your groupie chick so *I wouldn't hear.*" I emphasize the words to remind him that *he's* the one who wanted to change rooms. "You didn't give a shit what happened to me. Then, after you left with her, things got…a little more out of hand."

"What does that mean?"

I'm surprised he doesn't argue with me, that he leaves it at that simple demand. Does he *get it* on any level, or is he still trying to pretend that he's above any responsibility?

I look around at the rest of the guys. They either look away or their expressions are blank. Noah gives a slight shake of his head. So there's another wrinkle. Nobody told Knox about Tits. Cowards. I glare at them all.

"One of the chicks dared her friend to make out with Ajia." I sigh. "I took exception when she took out her tits and started rubbing them all over his face, and I left."

Knox pushes forward on his seat. "Ajia, goddamn it, you fucker. After that night in Austin—"

We are *so* not going there!

"Shut up, Knox." I snap and point at him like my finger has some kind of magical power. "Just listen. You weren't there, so you don't get to say a goddamn thing about what happened."

Nobody else says anything, so I do. "Ajia followed me to apologize and make sure I was all right. I was already in bed, and we talked. I guess that's when he took his boots off." I shrug. "He must have forgotten them when he went to bed."

"I went to bed alone." Finally, Ajia says something. He flicks a quick glance in my direction that I want to mean, *I got this,* but maybe that's my own wishful thinking. I want so bad to mean something to him besides *baby girl, the band mascot.*

"And yet that's not where I found you this morning."

"And *I* told you what happened," Ajia insists before I can say anything. "I woke up in the middle of the night, Bree was screaming, and so I hustled my ass down the hall to see what was wrong. I didn't stop to think I was only in my boxers. It really didn't fucking matter at the moment."

I glare at Knox. "And *he* woke me up from the nightmare. Remember that little fucking detail?"

My brother isn't giving in. He's staring at all of us like he's pissed at everybody. I don't care. He has no right to be upset about any damn thing. He's mostly—or at least *partly*—to blame. And right now, I'm getting more and more pissed at *him.*

Noah leans forward with an uncharacteristically serious look. "What'd you dream about, baby girl?"

"Her fucking stepfather, what d'you think?"

I give Ajia a look that says *enough.* Not sure he sees it though. He's glaring at Knox.

"Fuck." It's like an echo all around me. Even Zayne, who looks like death warmed over, rouses enough to curse.

"Oh, don't worry," I snap, suddenly sick of the whole damn farce. "Y'all were there, too. Knox? You were busy making out with some naked groupie. Noah, you and Zayne and Ajia were judging a bunch of Barbies in pink bikinis. Rye, you were playing the drums, crashing the symbols every time a new Barbie stepped up. And me?" I pin every one of them with a furious gaze. "I was fighting off my goddamn stepfather, who wanted me to give him a blowjob. I yelled and yelled, but you were all too fucking busy with your chicks to pay attention to me."

"Jesus."

I think it's Rye who said it, but I keep talking. "So just fucking excuse me, Knox Gallagher, if I needed somebody to hold me and tell me they'd protect me from that asshole. And forgive me for sleeping and dreaming in the middle of the fucking night when you were too busy with your fuck buddy so that your *friend* had to comfort me. And for God's sake, I'm so fucking sorry that I was tired and emotional and we somehow fell asleep next to each other."

The more I talked, the more shit came out. Stuff I hadn't really thought of—yet, anyway, since I hadn't had a chance to process anything—but the whole asinine situation began to blow itself open as I defended myself against Knox's stupidity.

And when the fuck did my hand end up in Ajia's? Did he do it, or did I?

He leans in, effectively blocking me from seeing Knox. "You okay, baby?" His fingers tighten around mine.

I blink and look at my lap, away from the intensity of his whiskey-colored eyes. I see the conflict there, I understand it, but I see something else, too. Things have changed between us, and he's not pretending. Not now, at least.

What does that mean? I can't answer.

"Bree?"

I let out a breath I didn't realize I was holding and nod to Ajia. He gives my hand a squeeze, then lets go and leans back. I stare at my brother.

"What?" I demand.

"I fucked up, didn't I?"

I nod.

"And you still didn't apologize," Ajia points out in a frosty voice, apparently remembering that Knox had never complied earlier.

I shake my head. "I don't care so much about that." I fix a glare on my brother. "I care that you don't want me to have an ordinary life for a normal nineteen-year-old woman."

He flushes. "I just want you to be safe."

121

I take a breath. "And you think if I *had* slept with Ajia—as in *sleeping with* meaning *sex*—" I can't call it fucking right now "—I wouldn't have been *safe?"*

Knox's eyes bug wide, and I hear a sharp grunt from Ajia. I don't look at him or Noah or Rye, who seems suddenly stiff beside me.

"Bree…" Knox can't seem to say anything else, and he shakes his head.

"Listen, sweetie." I try to soften my approach. "I'm a big girl now. I don't want to be twenty years old and sneaking around with some guy behind my brother's back. Or trying to avoid my pervert stepfather. I'm just an ordinary girl with an extraordinary brother and some really extraordinary friends." I open my hands to indicate the room. "And with all that, I wanna be *normal."*

They all have the deer-in-headlights look, and it's Rye who finally takes my hand. "We all love you."

I squeeze his fingers. "And I love you, too."

"We act like a bunch of adolescent fucking douches." He's probably the only one with the balls to look me in the face when he says it. Maybe even the only one to see that part of it.

"Pretty much." I smile. "And not just about me."

I stand and look at them all. "We better all be good here, because I'm done. Y'all know what happened, you don't have to beat the fuck out of Ajia, and you're on official notice that I'm a normal almost-twenty-year-old woman who intends to have a normal life. Even if that means…" I pause deliberately and then say with a wicked wink, *"Sex!*

"Now, I'm outta here!"

Nobody says a word as I leave. I head straight for my bedroom to…I don't know. I just needed to get away from all that protective male testosterone. Plus, I want to look at Ajia, touch him, talk to him, and none of that is possible right now.

Maybe that's a good thing, I decide as I turn to straighten up my suitcase and see his boots still in a heap next to my bed. I gather them up and put them outside the door in a tidy pair. Maybe I ought to think about what happened—and what I want from here on out.

What's there to think about? a voice inside me screeches. *You want to be with him—and go a lot farther than third base!*

Do I really need to think about it anymore? Haven't I already overthought it to the point of insanity?

I want Ajia. He wants me. At least some part of him wants me. And the rest of him doesn't like it.

That's easy to see. Even understand, I suppose. The hard part is finding out what he's willing to do about it.

I know how far I'm willing to go. I've always known, I suppose, even when I knew I had no chance in hell of ever making him see me as anything except his friend's baby sister. And yet some tiny, ridiculously determined spark of desire must have found a safe place to hide deep within me, because hope never completely died somehow.

Now, here I am. Shit happened. Icky shit. Shit that hurt. But somehow, it's changed things between Ajia and me...and I don't know what the hell we're going to do about it.

CHAPTER 14

AJIA

I don't get a chance to really *talk* to Bree for a day or two. We see each other but we're never alone, and neither of us can say what we need to in front of anybody else. Are the others deliberately sticking around us, or is it just normal on-tour closeness? I can't be sure, so I try to ignore it. Even when Knox watches me with a creepy, thoughtful look on his face.

Asshole.

He doesn't really deserve that. Not in this case. I did have my mouth on his sister's pussy, my fingers inside her. But I haven't forgiven him for saying some of the shit he did—and for not apologizing to Bree.

You rushed in to fuck her awake?

I didn't, but we came close enough.

And what are you going to do about it now? Maybe you ought to be giving some thought to that shit!

Yeah, maybe I should, but I don't. Not really. Not when the band is around every fucking second. Through sound check, being onstage, during the show itself, or on the tour bus. Later, when I'm alone—*really* alone—I probably won't be able to think about anything else. But right now, I have to think about anything *but* her.

It's a little bit of a relief that Bree acts like she feels pretty much the same way.

We're all glad to leave Phoenix behind, and L.A. is a decent alternative. We're doing a few shows in Southern California, as well as meeting with the label and doing some other industry stuff.

Interviews, a photo shoot, and, I've heard, a couple of parties. Not afterparties, but label shit.

Fuck.

The fall-out of our last party is too fresh.

We're in individual hotel rooms this time, but nobody asks why. It's always different in every hotel. As long as we get time out of the bus, we're happy. Especially me. Time to think—and a chance for Bree and me to talk alone.

The photo shoot is first on our schedule, and we take a car to some photographer's loft. Bree stays at the hotel, but I don't know what she's doing while we're gone. Knox tried to make her promise to not leave the hotel. She turned her back on him and walked away.

The photographer shoots the whole band first, and then I'm first up alone. I'm dressed in black leather pants and a white shirt that's kind of like the one I sometimes wear onstage. This one's bigger, blousy they call it, and it streams out behind me from the big fan they turn on. It blows my fricking hair around, too, and I hate that. And I'm barefoot! Christ.

They have me move in all kinds of poses. The only thing that gives me the ability to pretend to be what they're after is that they play Wycked Obsession music. It gets me in touch with the songs, feelings from writing and recording. Guess it works, because they act like I'm some kind of cover model or something.

God, what bullshit.

It's a big loft, and one side is set up with a bed and all kinds of gauzy white shit. That's next. Shirt off, pants unbuttoned, and they want me to stick my hand under the waistband like I'm touching myself. Jesus. Mr. Johnson is *not* getting turned on by this.

I know they do shit like this. I've seen pictures. I've learned to pose. But I don't really like this sexy stuff. It's kind of fucked up in my mind. Yeah, I know women find me attractive for whatever fucking reason and I hook up with 'em, but I don't go *looking* for it. I don't encourage them to come after me, and that's what this feels like.

Look at me, girls. I'm the vocalist. Wanna fuck me? Here I am!

Nope. Not really into it.

Especially when I can't stop thinking about Bree.

We go through more shots, more poses, more fake expressions, and finally I'm done. *Get used to it!* I tell myself, but I hated the whole thing when I posed alone.

Knox is next, and I head over to where Rye sits waiting his turn. I drop into the chair next to him. "Where're the others?"

"Zayne's in wardrobe and Noah's in makeup."

I snort. They change it up for individuals and close-ups. "What a load of shit."

Rye grins. "What? You didn't like playing Mister Hot-and-Sexy-Come-Fuck-Me-Rock-Star?"

I flip him off. "Your turn's coming, asshole."

He laughs. "Nah. I'm the keyboardist. Nobody pays attention to the guys in the back."

"Bullshit." I shake my head. "You're the sad, tortured one. Chicks love that."

He kind of jerks his head to one side and narrows his eyes. "Who said that?"

"Bree."

He keeps staring at me. Finally, he shakes his head and shrugs. "All that shit you two said. That true?"

I stare back. "Yeah."

"You fuck her?"

"You asked that before. Answer's the same."

There must have been something in my voice. Don't know what, but Rye blinks and glances from side to side. "She get you off?"

I stiffen. "No."

"But you made her come."

I hesitate for half a breath, but it's too long. "Not answering that, Rye."

"You don't have to."

Fuck, no, I don't have to, and now he knows goddamn everything. Why didn't I expect this? Have some kind of bullshit answer ready?

"So you're going for it with her?"

I lift one shoulder. "I shouldn't. Know I'm not good enough for her, but—"

"Jesus, Ajia." He blows out a harsh breath. "How long're you gonna punish yourself?"

I glare at him. "You know it's true."

"It ain't true. It's a bunch of bullshit, and you know it. It was an accident!"

"Doesn't matter," I insist, feeling a little sick. "Ends the same way. I'm here, and Lara's—"

"Dead. Yeah, I get it."

Pain scrapes through me. "Yeah. Dead. Mason's fucked up on pills and never gonna walk without a limp, and Jill's like a kid who'll never grow up. Because of me. So don't say—"

"You really think Lara'd want you to punish yourself for the rest of your life? You know Mason doesn't hold a grudge. He made his own choices. And Jill loves you. She lights up every time you visit her."

Fuck. My heart beats hard, like it's gonna pound right outta my chest. Rye knows the most about my past mistakes. He's got his own shit to deal with, and we've talked sometimes. But…goddamn.

"Rye…" I don't really know what to say.

"Look, man, I'm not gonna tell you not to do this. I know Bree's different, and I know you have feelings for her. But give her the real you. Not some guy fucked up by the past, and not some manufactured rock star bullshit. The Ajia Stone nobody else knows."

The Ajia Stone nobody else knows. He's the one who's the piece of shit. Ajia-the-rock-star at least has some musical talent going for him.

I don't have a chance to put any of it into words before Rye gets called into makeup. I watch as they finish up with Knox and then put Zayne, Noah, and Rye through the same paces as me. The photographer seems happy with everything, and we're finally given the go-ahead to get back into our street clothes.

Knox hangs back to do something about marketing and all that social media crap, and the rest of us take a limo back to the hotel. I separate from the others at the elevator. Don't know what they're doing, and I don't care. We've got some time before sound check, and I like the idea of a couple hours by the pool. Maybe a swim and some sun will bake the uncertainty out of my system.

I tie my hair back—no freaking manbun for me—and throw on a pair of board shorts, sunglasses, and an Astros cap. I grab a towel and a bottle of water, and I'm outta there.

The pool is less crowded than I expect. Maybe everybody in the hotel is off doing a gazillion other things that Southern California has to offer. All I care is that it gives me a pretty good choice of seats, and then I see her.

Bree's stretched out on a lounger, her hair pulled back in a ponytail a lot like mine, and her eyes covered by some gaudy-looking sunglasses. She's wearing a tiny yellow bikini decorated with a bunch of colorful flowers. It isn't the most revealing thing I've ever seen. At least her tits are completely covered and the bottom doesn't sit too low over her pussy, but this is Bree, goddammit! I don't want a bunch of strange assholes looking at her!

You hear yourself? You've got no right to say anything about it. You haven't claimed her.

The other side of my brain is a bigger pervert. *Jesus! She rocks that fucking bikini. Look at those tits! Those hips. Remember how she tastes? The little sounds she makes when she comes?*

"Hey there, baby." I drag a lounge chair up next to hers.

Her head pops up. "Ajia!"

She smiles but I can't tell anything else behind those sunglasses. Fair enough. She can't read me behind my aviator glasses, either.

"How was the photo shoot?"

"Ridiculous."

"What happened?"

I shrug and drop down to sit on my chair. "Nothing. Just a bunch of standing around and making faces at the camera. Except—"

"What?"

I give her a half-smile. I can almost laugh about it now. "They had this bed, and I had to lie there and stick my hand down my pants."

She kind of snorts, and it sounds cute. "Okay, so I might like to see that one, but...did they make Knox do it, too?"

I laugh. "I don't know, kitten. I did *not* watch that part."

She laughs, too. "Well, please warn me after you see the proofs. That's one of those things that I can't unsee, and then I'll have to poke my eyes out or something."

So maybe we broke the ice a little. I like the idea, since I don't know what the fuck I'm doing.

"You got barbecue sauce on you?"

She looks down at herself. "Sunscreen?" She nods. "Yeah. You?"

I shake my head. "Forgot."

She leans down to reach into the bag next to her chair. It draws attention to her cleavage, and I love the sight as much as I hate myself for looking. But—damn. This woman has some seriously beautiful tits!

"Here." She hands me a bottle. "Put it on. Everywhere."

"Everywhere?" I don't mean to say it with that flirty lilt in my voice, but the word is out before I can think.

She stares at me. "If you're bringing *him* out in the sun, then, yeah. Everywhere."

I squeeze some sunscreen on my hands and start rubbing it over my arms. "Him?"

"Him." She nods decisively. "You're the boy, so your dangly bits are *him*. And my lady parts are *her,* since I'm the girl."

I'm pretty careful about getting the lotion rubbed in. Last thing I need is to be onstage sunburned. My skin crawls just thinking about it. Besides, it keeps me from looking at her after that little announcement. Finally, though, I can't resist any longer.

"Dangly bits?" I laugh as soon as the words are out.

"Fine." She looks from side to side. "Penis. Dick. Your cock." She tries to follow it up with a shit-eating grin, but I see the blush on her cheeks that wasn't there a minute ago.

"Yeah." I'm rubbing sunscreen on my chest, so I peek over the top of my shades. "So lady parts means your *vagina.*" I pause for effect. "That beautiful virgin pussy of yours."

"Ajia!" Her voice comes out sounding like a scandalized whisper, and that cute blush races down her neck to her chest. "Somebody might hear!"

"Nope." I move on to lather up my legs. "Nobody close enough. They might take a picture, but—" I tap my Astro's cap "—I'm in disguise."

Bree laughs. "That's your disguise? I'd recognize you a mile away in that hat."

"That's cause you know me, baby. Most people...they aren't looking."

"You sure about that?"

"Yep. This is Southern California. Stars around here are a dime a dozen. Nobody gives a shit about some B or C-list rocker." I hand back the sunscreen and try to get the last of it off my fingers by rubbing the back of my neck.

"What about your back?"

"Can't reach," I say carefully. "You offering?"

She stares, and I wish she'd take off those goddamn sunglasses so I could see her eyes. "Maybe."

I open my arms. "Go for it."

She watches me a few seconds longer, then pushes up from her lounger and circles around behind me. I try to tell myself this game isn't dangerous. We're out in public, after all. Doesn't matter. I know better. She wants me—hell, she thinks she loves me, even if it's just a leftover childhood crush—and I sure as hell want her. We're both adults. No reason we can't spend some fan-fucking-tastic time together. Except for Knox, but she's made it damn clear that she isn't going to let her brother get in the way of this.

And me?

My conversation with Rye comes back to me. *Give her the real you. Not some guy fucked up by the past, and not some manufactured rock star bullshit. The Ajia Stone nobody else knows.*

If we do this, she deserves that much. Doesn't she?

Her hands are soft and warm on my back. She shoves my ponytail over my shoulder and rubs lotion over my neck and shoulder blades, down my spine.

"I haven't seen your back up close before." She's rubbing more sunscreen but seems to be tracing the contour of my biggest tattoo. "Who's Cecelia?"

"Patron Saint of Musicians."

Her hands stop for a second. "Are you Catholic?"

"Nope." *The real you. The Ajia Stone nobody else knows.* "I was really...lucky as a kid," I finally admit. "Seems like somebody was looking out for me. Musta wanted me to stick around. Finally decided it must be Saint Cecelia."

She keeps rubbing. I don't know what she's thinking, but I know what she's seeing. A tat of a beautiful dark-haired woman dressed in gold and white, flowers in her hair, and a harp in her hands. I got her after *Run* started to get Wycked Obsession noticed.

Bree's sudden squeal comes as a surprise. "What?"

"Oh, my God!" she snickers. "You got *Wicked Is As Wycked Does* as a tramp stamp?"

I glance over my shoulder. "I don't think it's called a tramp stamp on men."

She rubs lotion down there. "I don't care. It's…"

"What?" I dare her with my tone, my look, even though she can't read my expression behind my aviators. "It's what?"

"Slutty."

I push my sunglasses down my nose far enough for her to see my eyes. The words are out before I can think about them. "That's what I am, aren't I?"

She hesitates, her hands on my lower back, and then she reaches up to reveal her own expression as she settles her sunglasses on top of her head. "You don't have to be."

"I'm a rock star, right? Sing some songs and fuck some girls. It's what I'm good at."

I hate the words. Hate that I said them, and especially hate that I said them to Bree. But she *has* to know what she's getting into with me. Doesn't she? I can't take the chance that she doesn't.

"No." She leans forward and places a soft, gentle kiss on my shoulder. The back of my neck. Her arms circle around me and link together over my middle. "You're anything but that to me. You're the guy who's called me kitten since the day we met because I was so OCD over babysitting that stupid cat. You're the guy who came to my high school concerts and plays with Knox and my mom, because I didn't have any other family to come. You're the guy who threatened to beat up my prom date if he touched me, and you're the guy who whistled and clapped and raised such a ruckus when I graduated from high school that I was actually embarrassed." She kisses my shoulder again. "You're anything but a rock star or a slut to me."

Jesus.

I don't mean to, but I wrap my arm around her neck and pull her down for a kiss. I catch her bottom lip between my teeth and suck it into my mouth, then bring my tongue into play as I stroke the contours of her mouth, her lips, her teeth. My tongue pushes forward, and hers comes up to meet it. Her fingers clutch my biceps, and I've got one hand wrapped around her waist.

The kiss goes on. Changes. Deepens. Retreats and then resumes. Everything I ever wondered if a kiss could be.

For a guy who doesn't kiss—ever—I've sure done a fuck of a lot of it lately.

We kiss until neither of us can breathe, and I finally tear my mouth from hers. She rests her forehead against mine, and our breath is heavy and ragged. I can feel her breasts heave against my back, and my cock has surged to hard, granite life.

"Bree," I pant. "Baby."

"Ajia." Nobody says my name as perfectly as she does.

"Are we really gonna do this?"

She pulls back. "Do you want to?"

I close my eyes and slowly pull my aviators from my face. *"Fuck."* I let out a low breath. "I shouldn't. I should fucking leave you alone and let you find a guy you deserve. But…"

"But?" Her eyes are wide and bright in the sunlight.

I pull her close enough to catch her lips in another, this-time-gentle kiss. "I want you. And not just in bed. I like you, kitten. You're fun and funny. We have a history. And I…wanna know what else there could be."

If I've got anything else in me.

"Ajia." She whispers my name, and this time she kisses me like a soft promise.

"I don't have a good track record, baby. You know that. I don't fucking know what this means."

"Day by day," she murmurs against my mouth. "I don't know, either, so we take it day by day and see where it takes us."

"And your brother?"

She pulls back just a little and shakes her head. "I don't want to tell him yet. I want us to have a chance to figure this thing out without him getting in the way."

It makes sense. I even agree. But…

"If he finds out on his own, he'll take it wrong. You know that." I brush the backs of my fingers down her cheek. "And he's gonna hate it, no matter what."

Her hand comes round and cups my cheek. "This isn't about Knox, A. It's about us. You and me. And I'm not going to let him freaking screw it up. I want it to be just you and me for a little while."

A thought occurs to me. "Like you don't want to tell your mom about Gabe?"

"Fuck." She mutters it softly, but I hear it.

"You can't hide shit from people, baby. Not this kind of shit. Important shit. It comes out the wrong way, and everything's fucked. Unless…"

"Unless what?"

"Maybe you don't want people to know you're hooking up with manwhore Ajia Stone. Maybe—"

"Shut it."

"What?"

"Just shut up. Jesus! I want everybody to know that I want you and you want me! But there isn't really anything to know yet. We haven't even—you know."

"Fucked?"

She scowls. "Is that all it's gonna mean to you? Another girl to fuck?"

I frown back. "You know it isn't."

"So we haven't even *slept together*. And you know what's going to happen when we go public? Besides Knox and all his bullshit, your fans are gonna hate me. They're already jealous of me being Knox's sister. Once I'm anything other than that, I'm dead meat. I want just a little time to get to know this different side of you. Ajia, the man who kisses *me* and nobody else. The man who makes me come and holds me when I'm scared. I don't want that to be up for public consumption."

I get it. I do. And even knowing it has the potential of turning into a shit storm just like the others we've been through in the past couple of weeks, I don't have the heart to turn her down.

"You got it, baby." I give her a quick, promising kiss. "We'll keep each other's secrets for now—but it can't last long. You know that, right?"

"I know." She kisses me back. "I don't really want it to. But there's one other thing you ought to know."

"What?"

"You're mine now. No sharing. So you better find a good way to let your groupies down easy, Pipes, or it ain't gonna be fucking pretty. Knox finding out will be the least of our problems."

"You talking violence, kitten?"

"Yes. No more Tits. Or Garage Girl. You ready for that?"

I don't hesitate. For better or worse, I've made up my mind. "I'm ready, baby. Are you?"

CHAPTER 15

BREE

I dress carefully for the concert. I'm not quite sure what I'm doing, but I know I want to look nice for Ajia. Not slutty, but I want him to know I'm the woman for him. I don't have a lot of choices, though—which I suppose is good. If I change things up too much, Knox might get suspicious.

I did some shopping in Phoenix, and I found a cute pleated skirt in a floral pattern of pink, turquoise, and white. I can pair that with my pink spaghetti tank and white sandals, and I'm good to go.

I take extra time with my hair and makeup. I leave my hair long and loose because guys like long hair—right? It's silly, because Ajia has seen me looking about as bad as a person can look. Still, I know the groupies are going to be there and all over him, just like every other show, and I want him to see me at my best. Remind him of his promise.

No more Tits. Or Garage Girl. You ready for that?

I'm ready, baby. Are you?

I text Baz that I'm ready to go, and he replies that he has a Town Car waiting to take me from the hotel to the venue. It seems silly that I can't just take a cab, but the security restrictions haven't changed. Kel and some other guys are usually around, but nobody will tell us much. All I know for sure is that one of the Edge of Return guys had a stalker, maybe even threats, and Wycked Obsession gets the same security. The team is good—I don't notice them all that much—and they seem to make Knox happy.

The driver drops me off at the venue, and I make my way to the back. I've learned to keep my laminated backstage pass on me all the time, and it gets me wherever I want to go. The roadies, merch guys, and other crew recognize me by now, and I wave at everybody.

"Hi, Bree!" The pimply-faced guy I almost ran over that first night always greets me, and I give him a friendly smile. His name is Steve, he said, and he seems like a nice enough guy. He's no Ajia, but nobody else can compare. Not even the guys from Edge of Return.

"Lookin' good, honey," shouts Ayden as I pass the open door of their dressing room. Maddox, their lead singer, gives me a thumbs up, and I wave back at them.

My guys are in their dressing room, a couple of doors down. Noah's sitting on one end of the sofa, drumming a steady beat with his fingers. Rye's on the other end, head back and eyes closed, flexing his fingers. Knox is standing over a table, pen in hand. I'd bet the price of ticket sales for the night that my control-freak brother is going over the set list one more time. Zayne's sprawled out on the other sofa like he's comatose.

And Ajia? He's in the bathroom, shower on hot and steam filling the room. He spends some time that way before every concert. It's for his vocal cords. He started doing it a couple of years ago after he quit smoking. Because of my nagging, I'm proud to add.

I don't say anything, just let the guys go through their pre-show ritual until Noah notices me. "Hey, baby girl." He smiles.

"Hi."

"New duds?"

I smile. "I bought some stuff in Phoenix. I was getting really tired of the two skirts I brought."

"You look nice," says Rye, and I cross to give him a kiss on his head.

"Thanks, sweetie."

I head over to Knox and hug him around the middle from behind. "I love you, bro."

He turns and wraps his arms around me for a real hug. It isn't something he does a lot—at least not this kind of hug—and I know our bickering has bugged him, too. "You good?" he asks and lets me go.

"Yep." I grin at him. "Ready to rock out with y'all."

"You better get out there, then. We're on in less than ten."

I wish I had an excuse to wait for Ajia to make an appearance, but I know I can't do it. Keep it copacetic, as Knox would say. Things are too…unstable right now.

Ajia and I need time.

I have a certain general area where I like to watch the shows. It gives me the best view of Ajia, but I let Knox think it's so I can see him. I find my spot and settle in to be out of the way *and* comfortable. Others shift around in the backstage darkness, and I can sense the anxious crowd out front.

I stand there for a few minutes when I hear a voice. "You always watch from here."

Glancing aside, I smile. "Hi, Steve." I nod. "Yeah, it's the best seat in the house."

He points to the stool in his hand. "Thought you might want to actually sit for a change."

"Wow!" My smile grows. "Thanks, Steve! That's really sweet of you."

He moves the stool into place for me, and even holds my hand as I hike my butt up. It pushes my skirt up pretty high, and I wish it was too dark for him to notice, but I think he does. His eyes are glued to my legs.

"Well…" Finally, he looks at me and then nods kind of jerky. "Enjoy the show."

"I will. And thanks again, Steve! I really appreciate it!"

I sense movement on the stage at almost the same time and forget all about Steve and his friendly gesture. I focus all my attention on the shadows in front of me until I hear the familiar twang of Zayne's bass. Noah's bass drum follows, Rye's keyboard, and then they open up with *Run*. They like to start with that song, maybe for sentimental reasons. I always like to see Ajia when the spotlight first hits him, like he's making love to the microphone.

He's dressed a little differently tonight, all in black. Instead of an open button-down shirt, he's wearing a black tank. Part of me is disappointed, because I got a really good look at his chest when we were at the pool. Saw his tattoos closer than I ever had. Before, I was always trying not to look, or I forced myself to look away before anybody knew what I was thinking. Now I know that he has Wycked Obsession's logo on his right pec, an odd winged heart on his left, and the names of each of the band's single releases in script down his right side. His sleeve is made up of a microphone, guitar, drums, keyboard, musical notes, and all things musical entwined with each other. I plan to trace every single line on his body with my tongue.

Most of me, though, is super satisfied that no groupie or fangirl is going to get a chance to look at his chest tonight. Touch him skin-to-skin. At least not there. *You're mine now,* I told him. *No sharing.* I mean it.

Ajia goes through his usual courting of the audience after the first number. He doesn't call back but points and waves when women call out how much they love him. He gets Knox to step forward for his share of catcalls.

No Doubt is next, a song I've always loved. Knox wrote the music, Ajia the lyrics, about his fantasy romance with his ninth-grade English teacher. He's never admitted publicly who it's about, and I've always loved knowing that little secret.

No doubt that I want you.
No doubt that I need you.
No doubt that we'd be good.
But I can't have you.
Shouldn't take you.
Should have left you alone
Right where you stood.

Is it my imagination or does he turn to glance in my direction as he sings? I'm in no mood for his second thoughts, and so I do the only thing I can. I show him how the music and his fuck-me voice overtake me. I sway from side to side and imagine Ajia's arms around me, moving with me, his mouth on mine. I keep my eyes open and watch him through every single note. I know he can feel the pull of my gaze, and our eyes catch and hold for the last few seconds of the song.

It's true, he seems to say.

You're mine now, I tell him again. *And I'm yours.*

The crowd erupts with the last notes. They always do. It's a fan favorite with a harder beat and faster tempo. It's not about seduction. It's about the urgent need between lovers who know what they want and can't wait, even if it's a little illicit. In that way, it *is* me tonight. I want—need—Ajia in a way I never did before. I know what his hands feel like on my body, how his mouth tastes, and the warm strength of his body against mine. I'm tired of waiting.

The lights go out, leaving me in blessed darkness. I'm glad suddenly. I take a deep breath and pretend that my nipples aren't stiff and aching, my panties wet, my legs trembling. The anticipation of being with Ajia again is killing me.

I force myself to look anywhere but at him during the next couple of songs. I watch Knox breeze through the tricky guitar solo in *Leaving You Behind,* and follow Zayne's heavy bass line in *Lonely.* Noah's a wild man behind the drums, shirtless now after he sent it flying into the crowd. Rye's understated keyboard melodies always haunt me, and love for these amazing guys fills me to overflowing.

I'm caught up watching them in a way I haven't been in years. Not since they first started playing clubs and gaining a following. Is it because of my changing relationship with Ajia? Or because of our little *intervention* in Phoenix? Whatever explains the way I feel, I love these guys, and I'm captivated by their performance.

They play with perfection, ending with their current hit *Tonight,* before I realize how much time has passed. It's Rye's song, but I swear Ajia looks at me when he sings the opening lines.

I'm yours for tonight,

Baby, it's all right.

God, I hope he means it.

The lights go down, and screams and applause send the band offstage. They don't go through the back but come my way, and I give every one of them a triumphant, loving hug, sweaty or not.

"You guys were fantastic tonight!"

"You had the best seat in the house." Knox indicates my stool.

I grin. "Yeah. Steve brought it out for me."

"Steve?" Ajia asks sounding funny.

"Yeah." I look at him. "A roadie. He's about my age." I lower my voice, in case he's anywhere around. "Acne?"

"Steve," he repeats.

I shrug. "He said he thought I might like to sit for a change."

"Is that so?"

Is Ajia—could he be—*jealous?* Of something as simple as some ordinary, pimply guy offering me a place to sit backstage? No. I'm overreacting. I can't believe anything like that. He's *Ajia Stone,* for God's sake, and I've loved him for five years. He knows that.

"Let's head back to the green room." Noah slings an arm around my shoulders. "I need a shower."

I slip my arm around his waist. "Boy, do you! And you're the first, right?"

"Always, baby girl. Always."

We laugh and work our way down the darkened hallway, avoiding the controlled chaos that is backstage. I notice Steve watching from a distance and wave my thanks again. He doesn't wave back, but I don't pay much attention as we step over cables, around boxes and totes and trunks. Finally, we reach the hallway leading to the dressing rooms.

"Ajia!"

"Knox!"

"Noah!"

Women cry out their names—every one of the band members—and come rushing up to us. I usually miss this part, because I head for the dressing room before the last song is quite over. This time I'm caught in the middle of it—and I hate the way the chicks descend on us like...I don't know, some kind of sci-fi invaders or something. Those aliens in *Independence Day.*

Groupies grab at the guys, try to pull them into embraces and kiss them. We keep moving, and Zayne seems to be the only one into it tonight.

"Hey, sweetheart!" Noah waves at the girls and keeps walking, pulling me along.

"Hey, girls!" Rye grins with a salute. "Hope you liked the show!"

The chicks squeal and Knox turns to walk backward. "Good to see y'all here."

Ajia's back in the rear of our little parade and gets caught up with one particularly persistent fan. I turn the instant I hear the squeal—bad memories of Tits, I guess—and see her grab his arm and press her chest against him. He doesn't hesitate, just pats her on the shoulder with a distant smile I've seen before. It comes out whenever the price of fame gets too high for him.

"Thanks for coming out tonight, honey."

He somehow disentangles himself and follows us into the dressing room. I'm not quite sure how he did it, and I'm not foolish enough to think that the girls aren't following us into what they consider party central, but I feel like grinning. Two days ago, he would have slung his arm around her shoulders and dragged her along.

Today, I staked my claim and he agreed.

The green room is full just like I expected, people milling about, drinking the booze, and eating the food spread out in generous supply. Southern California knows how to treat the talent. The alcohol is expensive and the snacks are more than chips and dip. I'm too nervous to eat, though, so it doesn't really matter.

I'm yours for tonight,
Baby, it's all right.

Ajia sang those words to me—and he didn't fall into that groupie's grip. *Holy shit.*

"Here, baby girl." Noah shoos everybody off one of the couches and plops me down in the middle. "You want vodka and Sprite? They got the good stuff."

I grin. "You know you're corrupting a minor."

Noah laughs. "Hell, baby girl, we corrupted you a long time ago."

I share the laugh and salute him with a nod. "Guess you're right, sweetie. Yeah, vodka and Sprite."

"Here you go, kitten."

Ajia hands me a drink before Noah can even move, and he sinks into the seat next to me. He's got something for himself in his red Solo cup, but I haven't a clue what.

"That how it is now?" Noah asks with raised eyebrows and a shit-eating grin.

Ajia shrugs. "Get in the shower. You stink."

Noah laughs again and heads toward the bathroom. "Watch your back, asshole."

I look curiously at Ajia. "Watch your back?"

He shrugs and takes a drink. "Guess I better not fuck this up." He angles his head carefully in my direction.

I blink and nod, not sure how I feel about all this. Oh, I love the part with Ajia and me together—or almost joined. But Noah's interference? I'm not surprised that he sees what's happening, but I really don't want anyone else getting involved.

"How we doing here?" Rye drops down onto the seat on my other side and looks at us with his own shit-eating grin.

"Good," I say slowly and look between him and Ajia. And then I know. "Fuck."

Rye raises his brows. "What?"

"You know." I look at Ajia again. "He knows."

Ajia shoves his hair back from his face. "He doesn't know shit."

I look between them. "He knows enough."

Rye grabs my hand and tugs me against him. "Don't worry, baby girl. My lips are sealed." He zips his other hand over his mouth like he's fastening it closed.

"But Knox—"

"Ajia ain't told me nothing," says Rye gently, squeezing my hand. "I'm guessing at shit. If Knox'd open his damn eyes, he could guess, too. But he ain't gonna, and you better do something about that before it all goes to shit."

I nod. "A couple of days? Just enough to…you know."

He grins and looks over my head at Ajia. "That what they calling it these days?"

I turn to see Ajia grin back.

"That's not what I mean." I try to sound serious, even firm, but I can't help laughing. I love Rye as much as I love Knox and Noah, and I trust him just as much. "I just want us to have a little…private time."

Rye nods, serious now. "I get it, baby girl. Just be prepared. This is gonna shake things up. You know that, right?"

I nod and feel Ajia lean close. It probably looks like he's paying attention to the conversation between Rye and me—at least that's what I hope it looks like—but I feel a gentle push of his shoulder against my spine. I'm not in this alone.

"Things are already shaken up," I reply. "Thought I pretty much did that in Phoenix."

It's like the words suddenly echo between us. *You're on official notice that I'm a normal almost-twenty-year-old woman who intends to have a normal life. Even if that means…sex!*

Rye blinks and leans back. "Guess you did that after all, Bree."

"What's up, kiddies?" Freshly showered Noah sticks his head between Rye's and mine. "You taking care of the wife?"

Nobody has a chance to answer before there's a ruckus at the door.

"What the fuck?" It's Zayne with a startlingly slutty-looking girl plastered to his side. He looks a little wild, wound-up, and he waves one hand around like a drunken conductor. "We havin' a party or what?"

I slant a glance in Ajia's direction. "He's fucked up."

He nods and looks at the others. "You think he's using again?" he asks under his breath.

"I've been noticing that he disappears," says Noah. "Goddamn asshole."

Rye sighs. "Thought he was still clean. If he's using, it started on tour."

"Fuck," says Noah.

I push to my feet and hand my glass to Ajia.

"Kitten..."

"I have to," I say as I walk away. "You know I do."

And I guess they all do, because nobody tries to stop me.

"Hey, Zayne," I say as I slip up next to him. His pupils are dilated, and I know he's high on something.

"Baby girl!" he shouts and throws his arms around me. "You like the show?"

"Loved it!" I put all the enthusiasm I can into my voice and hold him close. "Y'all are awesome."

"Especially the bass line?"

"Especially the bass *player.*" I give him my best grin.

His arms tighten around me, and he places a big, smacking kiss on the top of my head. "Jesus, I love you, baby girl."

"And I love you, too, Zayne. But I'm kinda worried about you."

"What?" He leans back and stares at me as Slut Girl starts to whine.

"Zayne! I thought you were gonna be with me tonight!"

He waves her away. "I am. Later. Right now I wanna talk to my wife." He laughs like it's the funniest thing he's ever heard.

"Your *wife?*" screeches Slut Girl, and it's like everything in the room stops.

I swallow a long, deep sigh. Fucking rock stars. "It's a joke," I say to her with a fake smile. It's all I have. "I'm Knox's sister, and I'm on tour with the band."

"Your wife?" she shouts again, not seeming to get what I'm saying.

143

"Cool it, babe," slurs Zayne and he plants another loud kiss on me, this one on my forehead.

"Zayne, you fucker—"

"You hogging our wife?" demands Noah from behind me, cutting off Slut Girl before she can get wound up, and pulls me out of Zayne's grasp. He tucks me back against his chest.

"C'mon, man, you gotta share," says Rye, coming up on one side of me.

"You don't like our joke?" asks Ajia, slipping into place on the other side.

Slut Girl blinks and looks between us all. "What?"

"It's a joke," Noah explains. "Bree's Knox's sister. She came on tour with us. Cooks for us and shit, and we started calling her our wife. Just a dumbass joke."

I force myself to smile, but I really want to smack Zayne for starting this stupidity in the first place and Slut Girl for not listening when I said virtually the same thing.

"What's going on?" Knox shows up—almost too late, as always.

"We're havin' a party!" Zayne's smile is expansive. "Bree's bein' a good wife, and I got myself a little action for tonight." He leans toward Slut Girl. "Where you been, Knoxie boy?"

"*Fuck.*" My brother gets it.

"Let's all go back to the hotel," I say suddenly. "We can party in your room, Zayne."

I've seen Zayne out of control one too many times, and that's just from alcohol. He gets angry. Mean. He starts throwing shit. It hasn't happened since the last tour, and I don't want to see it happen on this one. Especially not when we're so close to L.A. and the label. Hell, some rep might even be in the audience!

"Party in my room?" Zayne repeats.

"Yeah." I nod. "You said you wanted to."

"I did?"

I wait for somebody to back my idea up. Ajia is the first one to get it. "Sure, man. Don't you remember? You said you wanted to find a girl—" he points at Slut Girl "—and bring her back for a little party."

"Oh…" He nods like that's the smartest thing he can think of. "Well, hell, yeah. What the fuck are we waiting for?"

"Baz's got the limo out back," says Knox. "Let's go."

"Y'all comin' to the party in my room, too?" Zayne calls over his shoulder as Noah leads him and Slut Girl out of the room.

"Of course!" I sound far too enthusiastic, but I don't want to take a chance that he'll get all pissy about it. I shoot looks that say *you're going* at all the guys. "Lead the way, sweetie. We're right behind you."

"Fuck me," says Ajia behind me with a growl.

It's not exactly the way either of us intended for the night to go. But this is Zayne, he's family, and if he's in trouble... I can't be sure he is; I don't know if any of this actually means anything. But I don't care. I'll make sure we do whatever we have to in order to get Zayne through the night.

I look over my shoulder and catch Ajia's gaze with mine. *This doesn't change things,* I remind him with a look of promise, and he nods.

I know, he seems to say—and I try to make it enough. For now.

CHAPTER 16

AJIA

Fucking Zayne. I'm gonna kick his ass if he's using again. We all did shit on the last tour that got out of control. We got back to Austin kind of fucked up. Couple of days of non-stop sleep, checking into the real world again, and we agreed that kind of shit was gonna burn us out quick and dirty. I've already watched Mason, my buddy from high school, lose himself to painkillers and prescription meds; I don't want to see anybody else go down any part of that road.

We agreed to cut out the drugs. Within reason, we'd kill our brain cells the old-fashioned way, with booze. Maybe a little weed now and then, and we're all sticking to the bargain.

Or I thought we were.

I glance across Zayne's hotel room to where he's lounging on the bed, a bottle of tequila in one hand and that slutty-looking girl draped all over him. Bree sits on the end of the bed, trying her best to keep the conversation moving, easy and lighthearted.

It kind of hits me then that she'd been through this kind of shit before with us. And she knows what Zayne can be like. She's still trying. I hate that. He's got a point where he's an ugly drunk and his highs make him an asshole. If he's mixing shit, who the fuck knows when he'll hit his limit?

Fuck.

This is *so* not what I had planned for tonight. It puts a bad spin on the whole fucking night. I hate that Bree's taken this frontline protective role with Zayne. She feels obligated as the only woman, I guess. Or like he's another brother. I don't know, and I don't care.

I've seen him in action. He could tear her to shreds and never even realize the hurt he caused.

Or care, until it's way too late.

I wanted to slip away unnoticed with Bree, spend some time alone with her. Fucking? Maybe. But she's a virgin, and I'm worried as fuck about being her first. Never been anybody's first except for Lara, and that was a long, *long* time ago. So long I can barely remember it. I was a lot younger and stupider then.

Maybe I just don't want to remember it.

Lara.

Fuck. I don't want to think about her, either. Not tonight. Not her or Mason or Jill or any of it, but I'm not stupid. If things go anywhere with Bree, it's going to come out. Rye knows it all, Knox and Noah know enough. And if Bree's thinking about getting involved with me, she maybe even deserves to know about my past.

But not yet. She wants a chance for it to be just us, without outside interference? Me, too. We'll keep our secret from Knox until the time is right, but before then I'll have to tell her the ugly truth about who Ajia Stone really is.

What a piece of shit loser she thinks she loves.

I make myself look back at Zayne. He's kissing the slutty-looking girl, his hand stuck up under her too-tight skirt, and Bree's trying to look anywhere but at what he's doing.

That's enough.

"C'mon, kitten." I cross the room and reach for her hand. "Think it's about time you got outta here."

"Ajia—"

"What the fuck, dude?" Zayne has a sudden moment of awareness. "You stealin' the wife?"

Jesus. Why's he suddenly stuck on that? Yeah, it's been a joke between us all for weeks, but it doesn't come up this much.

"She doesn't need to see this, man." I point to him and the girl.

"What?" His tone sharpens.

"Remember what happened in Phoenix?" I demand with a fierceness that surprises even me. "And in Austin right before we left?" I have to force that one out, but it's only fair. I *was* responsible for both fuck-ups.

Zayne blinks like he's thinking about what I said. "Oh!" he says finally. "The girl with the tits. And the one who was sucking you off!"

He had to fucking say it out loud. "Yeah, man. That."

He frowns at Bree. "You don't like to watch, baby girl?"

She stiffens, and her fingers tighten around mine. I gotta admire her ability to recover, though, because she laughs like it's nothing. "Not with you, Zayne. You're like my brother."

He nods like that makes some kind of twisted sense, and the slutty girl starts rubbing her hand over his crotch. Holy hell!

I lead Bree away before anything else can happen. I give Knox a look.

"I'm taking Bree to her room. She doesn't need to see that shit." I jerk my head toward Zayne. "You got a problem with it?"

Knox is on the room's other bed, messing around with a girl he brought from the venue. She's not as slutty as Zayne's girl, but she's a one-and-done girl. No question about it. What the fuck is he thinking, doing this again? And in front of Bree? Especially after the shit storm in Phoenix.

He stares at me with a *fuck-you* expression.

I give him back the same look. "You wanna take her?"

"Knox," Bree snaps and tightens her fingers around mine again. I don't think anybody else can tell. "If you don't stop being a fucker about this…"

"What?" he demands. "What're you gonna do?"

"Wouldn't you like to know?" Her scowl is stern. "You think I'm gonna tell you? I'm not! You won't expect it, and then one day—*wham!* Something is gonna blow up in your face, and you'll know it was me."

Noah laughs from his chair across the room. At least he and Rye were smart enough not to come back with women. "You better listen to her, dude. You know better than to fuck with our baby girl."

"Fine." Knox agrees reluctantly, but he's not happy. He glares at me. "I'm calling your room in ten minutes."

"You know the number," I call over my shoulder as I pull Bree toward the door.

"And hers, too!"

"Go for it, man."

Her room's a couple of doors down, with Knox's in between hers and Zayne's. I'm on the opposite side at the other end of the hall. I'm not usually a paranoid motherfucker, but I can't help wondering this time.

Bree opens her door and steps inside, then turns back to face me. "Are you coming in?"

I shake my head. "I want to, baby." I reach for her, cup her cheek in my palm and stroke my fingers over her soft skin. "You know I do. But I can't."

"Knox." She scowls.

"Doubt if he was kidding about calling us. He's gonna check up on you."

Her eyes soften. "Will you kiss me at least?"

I smile and step into her room. The door clicks shut behind me. I catch her mouth with mine and bite at the fullness of her bottom lip. She gives me a soft moan, and her lips part under mine. I slip my tongue forward, and she welcomes me in her mouth.

Her hands rest on my upper chest, clutch my shirt, and I've got hold of her hip. I want to bring her forward, hold her against me so she can feel how hard I am, but I know better. Knox doesn't trust me right now, and he could decide to check up on us at any time.

And if Bree and I are going to sleep together, I'm not going to rush it.

I pull back with a harsh breath. It's all so fucked up.

"Are you going back to the party?"

I shake my head. "It's not a party. It's just the rest of us trying to keep an eye on Zayne. If he's got shit, he won't use in front of us. He's got enough of an audience for anything else."

"You think he'd—do that?"

I nod, hoping she'll let it go at that.

"Has he—" She cuts off the word and pauses for a second. "Have you seen him…?"

I nod again. "He…likes it when people watch."

She leans forward, rests her cheek against my chest. "Ajia." She sighs. "I…" She shakes her head. "I don't even know what to say."

"I know, baby," I answer when she can't finish. I wish I hadn't told her that stuff, but chances are that she'll see worse than Zayne's little performance tonight before this tour is over.

"I'll see you in the morning." I give her another quick, hard kiss, and then I'm outta there, while I still can go.

Something wakes me. A noise? The AC's come on and gone off all night, but it isn't that. I'm awake enough now to recognize the knock when it comes again.

I turn on the bedside lamp, stumble from the bed to the door and look through the peep hole. Bree.

What the fuck?

I open the door. "Bree…baby."

She's wearing what she calls sleep shorts and a tank. I'm in my boxers, and she drags her gaze all over me.

My dick perks up at the attention. "Come in." I pull her into the room before anybody can walk by. As if they would at—I glance over my shoulder—3:12 a.m.

"What are you doing here, baby?" I ask when I get her inside with the door locked behind us.

She shakes her head, and her hair shifts over her shoulders like a chocolate waterfall. Stupid metaphor, but the brain isn't working quite right yet.

"I can't listen to them one more second."

"Listen to who?"

"Knox."

"He been giving you a hard time?"

She shakes her head again and steps around me into the room. "No. It's him and his fuck buddy."

My brain catches up. "They're in the room next to you."

Bree nods. "And she's *loud.*"

I try not to smile.

"Plus, my brother must have some kind of wicked stamina or something." She shudders like the idea of Knox having sex creeps her out.

"Too bad he didn't get whisky dick," I say mildly and follow her into the room.

"Oh, for that small favor." She looks at me, more serious than amused. "If I hear her scream, 'Oh, Knox! C'mon! Spank me, dude,

150

and make me come on your cock again!' I'm going to do my own share of screaming."

My amusement vanishes. Did she know about her brother's kink? My guess is not. I don't think he's deep into it. It's just more fucking around than anything, according to his bragging. It's still not the kind of thing he'd share with his sister.

"C'mere, baby." I pull her into my arms. "Sorry about that. He's been trying to keep that kind of shit away from you. Guess he kind of lost track tonight."

She rubs her cheek over my chest. I like the feel of her soft skin against mine.

"I don't give a damn about him having sex. Really." She pulls back to look up at me. Her eyes are a deep, earnest green. "He's just such a goddamn hypocrite!" She blinks. "And I don't really want to hear him groaning, 'That's it, honey. Take my cock down your throat.'"

Fuck.

Can't really blame her there. If I had a sister, I wouldn't want to hear that shit.

"You know the worst?" she asks and drops her gaze.

"Jesus, there's something worse than that?"

Her smile is crooked, and she doesn't look at me. "It made me want—you know. Something. Sex—with you." She sneaks a peek upward through her lashes. "Maybe I'm not ready to be spanked, but…"

Tension shoots through me. "But what, baby?"

She leans back and finally brings her gaze to mine. "I know the mechanics of sex. I'm not a prude. But I'm not…experienced. Hearing all that tonight makes me sure that I want to do…things with you. I never had any interest with other boys—men—but I—" She cuts off the words.

"What, kitten? Why didn't you want it with other guys?" I know the answer, but I want—*need*—to hear the words.

"You know why, A." She kisses my chest, light and easy. "Because of you. I only wanted you."

Because of me. "You weren't tempted?" I can't help asking.

She shakes her head. "None of them were you."

"And now?"

She kisses my chest again, harder and longer, swirls her tongue in a tight circle and doesn't take her eyes from mine. "You tell me. I want you more than I ever have, and I don't want to wait."

I don't want to wait, either. Rye's advice ghosts through my mind. *I just know that you gotta do one or the other. Take your chance or back off. No in-between.*

"Come here, baby." I take her hand and pull her to stand next to the bed. "I'm past waiting." I don't know what else to say.

"You mean it?" She looks up at me with equal parts desire and uncertainty. Those fucking bedroom eyes kill me.

"We're going to take this slow," I insist.

"After the other night...you don't have to go *too* slow."

I smile with wicked satisfaction. "I know. But this is different."

"Is it?" Her gaze slides away.

"What's wrong?"

"I...what if I—I'm not good at it? Or I don't...please you? There have been so many others. Women who know...how."

I smile to myself, but I don't let it reach my face. No way am I going to let her know how fucking adorable she sounds.

"Don't think about any of that, baby. I'm in charge, yeah? You don't worry about anything."

"Nothing?"

I shake my head. "Do you trust me?"

She nods so earnestly. I smile. "Of course."

"So it's all on me. And I promise you—" I push her hair back from her face "—if you like it, then *I'm* going to love every second of it."

I kiss her then, softer than I want to, softer than I have in the past, but this is different. Tonight is different. She's mine in a way I never expected, and the idea that she's never let another guy do the things she's allowing me is the only thing that gives me the strength to be gentle.

I pull back, bring one hand up to stroke the backs of my fingers down her cheek. "You know you're beautiful, baby. Right?"

She shakes her head, and her hair falls over her shoulders, draping over my wrist. I drag my thumb over her bottom lip before she can say anything. "Let me show you," I say, and I drop my hands to the hem of her tank top.

I hear her breath catch and sense her nervousness, but I don't give her much time to worry it. I've already touched her, tasted her, seen her in the shadows. Now I want to do it all in the light.

I slide the tips of my fingers along her skin, up to her hips, her waist, the bottom curve of her breasts. I tug the shirt up and over her head, toss it aside, and then she stands before me topless.

"Jesus, baby. You really are gorgeous." I *have* to reach for her, slip my fingers over her nipples, so lightly it's barely a touch. It doesn't have to be more. She hisses in a sharp breath and arches toward my hand.

I do it again. Her cheeks flush pink, but she holds herself still this time. I can only stare. My imagination and the taste, the touch, of her gave me an idea of how beautiful she might be. Seeing her tits like this…I'm sunk.

I drop to my knees and drag my hands over her hips as I go. Her sleep shorts come with me, and then she steps carefully out of them. She's naked, and she's mine.

I lean forward and place an open-mouthed kiss just above her pussy. "You are so beautiful, baby. I—you don't know how much I want you." And it's true. My cock is as hard as it's ever been.

"Show me," she whispers and threads her fingers through my hair.

I give her a quick lick and stand. Somehow, I want to be naked for her, too. She must want it, too, because she reaches out to help as I shove my boxers from my hips.

"*Ajia.*"

My name is no more than a breath. She wraps her fingers around me, and my hips move on their own. She peeks up at me through her lashes.

"I've seen pictures," she whispers. "You're nothing like that. You're so much…bigger."

I can't help smiling. What guy doesn't want to hear his girl say he's got a big dick? As much as it makes me sound like the douche I am, she isn't the first to say it. It's the first time I've cared, though.

"Your hand feels so good on me," I say.

She shakes her head just a little and looks down. "But I can barely wrap my fingers around you. Are my hands really that small? Or…"

I place my hand over hers and stroke us both up and down the length. "Doesn't matter, baby. What matters is you're here, and I want you. *Jesus, do I want you.*"

She follows my rhythm easily, tilts forward enough to place a soft kiss in the middle of my chest, and then she peeks up at me. "Are you sure it'll work?"

"What, baby?" I swallow a groan.

"You. Me. You're sure you'll—fit?"

I give a soft laugh and pull her to me. Her arms wrap around me, and her stomach presses against my erection. I push against her.

"We're gonna fit just fine, baby."

Her uncertainty is adorable and a little out of character for her. She can usually hold her own with any of us, but this…it's got her totally out of her comfort zone.

Rye said she was inexperienced, not innocent. I hope the fuck he's right, because after tonight, she's gonna know every fucking thing about what it means to be in my bed.

CHAPTER 17

BREE

I feel like an idiot. A stupid, inexperienced girl who knows nothing about how to attract a man. I'm standing here—*naked!*—with Ajia. He's naked, too, and all I can say is, *You're sure you'll fit?*

Based on what I know about guys, they probably like hearing that they have a big dick. Most of them pretend, even if they don't have it. And it isn't like I didn't have an idea about how big Ajia really is. I saw that chick going down on him. But—*Jesus!*

It looks…different when he's completely naked. When we're alone. When I know I can be the one to touch him, to taste him, and dreams I've had for years are about to become reality.

I feel different. Not myself at all.

Yeah, I wanted—*want*—to make love with him. That's absolutely part of it. But I want so much more. I want everything Ajia has to offer. To be fair, he's given me a little taste of that, too. The man. The friend. The naughty boy. Enough that my thoughts are all over the place.

He backs me up until I tumble down onto the bed. He follows, and then we're spread out over the mattress. I'm on my back, and he's on his side next to me. He's angled up on one elbow, his hair shoved back over his shoulders, and he leans down to kiss me. A serious kiss, long and deep. His tongue plunges as far into my mouth as it can go, and it's still not enough. I want everything there is of Ajia Stone.

"Give me your tongue, baby," he whispers against my mouth, and I don't hesitate. He sucks me deep in his mouth, and I feel it clear through to my nipples, my clit, my core. I press closer.

He drags a light stroke of his thumb over my nipple, and I groan. He does it again, and then his lips and tongue are on my jaw, my neck, my collarbone. Seconds later, he takes me in his mouth and sucks my nipple like it's the sweetest thing he's ever tasted. He swirls his tongue around and around, licks me, then closes his teeth lightly over the crest.

I arch against his mouth without thinking. "Again," I whisper. "Harder." His light touch is suddenly not enough.

He does it again, and this time he bites my nipple with a little pressure. A low sound comes from the back of my throat. *Jesus, that feels good.*

"You like that, baby?" He licks my nipple like he's apologizing.

"Yes." I shove my fingers through the tangle of his hair. "Please."

He does it again, a little harder, and then cares for me with a gentle lick. He shifts, turns his attention to my other breast, and it receives the same treatment. And each time his teeth close over me, an arrow of awareness shoots straight to my pussy.

I'm wet and aching, and only Ajia can take care of it.

He slips down my body, spreading open-mouthed kisses between my breasts, over my abdomen, my belly button, the nicely-waxed mound above my pussy. His fingers stay on my nipples, playing until I think I'm going to come before he ever even touches my clit.

I twist against him. I feel his cock against my leg, still hard, but he seems in no hurry to take his own satisfaction. Instead, he scoots farther down, angles my hips slightly upward, and then he licks my seam from bottom to top. Again. My breath catches, and I arch my hips toward his mouth.

He gives a throaty, thoroughly masculine laugh, and his tongue stabs into my pussy. A tremor shudders through me. It's like he knows my body better than I do.

"You taste like heaven, baby."

His tongue slides up, circles my clit, and I lose all my breath when he pushes one finger in me. He did it before, and that same sensation of fullness returns. It doubles as he keeps the soft pressure against my clit and adds a second finger. The pressure increases, but having seen—and now touched—his cock, I know this is *nothing* in comparison.

He pushes his fingers in and out, again and again. His hand is turned upward, his fingers angled, and he strokes that place of magic within me. I couldn't stop myself if I wanted to, and I move with him. Has anything ever felt so good?

"Ajia."

My fingers flutter over the covers until they reach his shoulders, his head. I don't mean to grip his hair in my hands, but I do. When he scissors his fingers open, my grip tightens and my hips flex. His hand is moving, in and out, and then his fingers open and close. Teasing that special spot against my inner wall. Again.

I'm a writhing mass of sensation.

"You gonna come for me, baby?" he whispers against my pussy, and his tongue gives a quick, hard flick against my clit. He does it again, and I lose my breath—and then his teeth close lightly over the sensitive bud.

Oh, God.

My orgasm follows after no more than a heartbeat, and I come hard, screaming Ajia's name. How is it that he can bring me to the edge so quickly and so completely?

My arms and legs tremble, and he kisses and strokes me through my climax until I find myself somewhat back in my body again. I let out a ragged sigh and urge him upward for a kiss. I need his lips on mine.

I taste myself on him, and excitement shoots through me. It teases me, makes me want to taste him.

My hands slip over his shoulders, down his chest, to his waist and hips, and I stretch to take his cock in my hands. He's as hard as he was earlier, and I stroke unsteady hands up and down his length.

"Can I do that?" I ask as I tighten my fingers around him.

"What, baby?" he asks between kisses.

"Taste you. Do…you know—" I cut the words off. I don't want to say, *do what the girl in the garage was doing.* "Put my mouth on you."

He licks my lips, darts his tongue into my mouth. "Oh, baby." He gives a short, rueful laugh that sounds almost choked. "I want that," he adds as one hand cups my breast and squeezes lightly. "Jesus, do I want that. But not tonight."

"No?" Defeat chokes me.

"You sound disappointed." He kisses me again.

"I…am. I want to make you feel—"

He cuts my words off with a deep kiss. His tongue seeks and destroys any resistance I might have had. "If you make me *feel* anything more, I'll come right here on your hands." His hips flex against my palms. "I'm too close to the edge already. You put your mouth on me, and things'll be over before I've started."

My heart pounds. Can he really want me that much?

"You've got things plenty *started*," I point out breathlessly. "You made me come."

He smiles against my lips. I can feel the movement of his mouth. He pushes up so I can see his expression. Not sure I've ever seen him look so satisfied.

"I did," he agreed with a slight nod. "And I've never seen—heard—anything so beautiful."

I flush with pleasure. "But now I want…"

"What?" His hand sweeps down to rest just above my mound. "Do you want more?"

A new wetness flushes from me, and my hips flex. *"My God, Ajia."* I lift my head to deliver a quick kiss. *"Yes.* I want that more than…anything."

He pulls his cock from my hands, drops another kiss on my mouth, and slips from the bed. After a moment of fumbling in his suitcase, he drops a handful of condoms on the nightstand and then rips one packet open with his teeth. A few seconds later, he's covered and back on the bed with me.

I'm nervous. I can't deny it. But I've never wanted anything more in my life. I've been holding onto my stupid fucking V-card for this man. I'm past wanting to give it to him.

He kisses me again. Licks my lips, bites the bottom one, sucks my tongue into his mouth. His hands caress my breasts, tease my nipples, and then he pinches them lightly. I sigh into his mouth and press against his fingers.

"You like that, baby?" He kisses me again.

"Yes. Oh, God, A." My breath tumbles from my lungs. "I love—want—everything you do to me."

He does it again, pinching a little harder this time. I like it even more. When he does it again, hard enough that it almost hurts, I don't care. It shoots some kind of pure, sharp desire straight to my pussy, and I scissor my legs over the mattress. I'm even wetter than before.

"There you go, baby," he mutters against my mouth, taking a quick kiss while his fingers tighten over my nipples. I squirm against him, my body begging for more as he makes me a creature of pure sensation.

"Please, Ajia!" I run my hands over his head, his hair, his shoulders. I try to reach lower, but he's got me pinned to the bed with his hips.

"What do you want, baby?"

"You. Oh, God, I want you. Inside me." I force my eyes open and to stare into his. *"Please."* The words come on their own. "Please, A. Fuck me."

The words surprise me. I didn't think I'd ever say anything like that—and especially not to Ajia—but he's got me on the sensual edge to nowhere. Everywhere. I can't describe it. I just know the throbbing in my core isn't going anywhere without him deep inside me.

He kisses me long and deep, and then moves between my thighs. I part my legs without thinking, and he rubs one hand up and down the inside of my thigh.

"That's it, baby. Spread your legs for me."

I open them wider, and he pushes me to bend my knees. "There you go, baby. You okay?"

I nod, too caught up in the anticipation to say anything. He keeps calling me baby, and even though it isn't new, there's something deeper, more caring in it tonight.

"I need the words, kitten. You okay?" he asks again.

"No!" It's a sharp denial. "I need you, A! *Please! Inside me.*"

He gives a soft, sensual chuckle, and then I feel his fingers toy with my pussy. He groans deep in his chest and slips one finger inside me. "Oh, baby. You're so wet."

I flex my hips. "For you, baby. You make me that way." I arch against his hand again.

He pulls his finger free, moves onto his knees, and then I feel him *there*. He moves the head of his cock from the bottom of my opening to my clit and back again. He does it again, and then he presses forward just a little. He parts my lips with the head of his dick, pushes in a bit and stops.

"You good, baby?"

I remember before that he wanted the words. *"Yes."* I can barely get that one out. I'm stretched, wider than I thought possible, and I know there's more to come. A lot more.

He pulls out, then presses forward again, going a little deeper. It's pressure—a lot of it—and a feeling of being full that excites me. He does it again, and then he stops.

"Jesus, you're tight." He blows out a breath. "You still okay, baby?"

"Yes." My hips shift. To find a more comfortable position or to get him to move again? Not sure, except I know I want *more.*

He kisses me, another of those deep, sensual kisses where his tongue destroys my ability to think. "It's gonna hurt, baby. I'm sorry."

He surges forward, and then he's all the way in. A sharp stinging tears a soft moan from me, and then an almost overwhelming feeling of fullness follows. It hurts, yeah, but there's something deeply satisfying knowing that Ajia is a part of me now. Fully.

He doesn't move, and my body slowly relaxes to accommodate the sheer size of him. The sting settles to a kind of throbbing tingle, and after a moment, I flex my hips. I want him to move again.

He brushes the hair from my face, trailing the backs of his fingers down over my cheek. He kisses me softly. "You still with me, baby?"

"Yes." I kiss him back.

"I'm gonna move now, yeah?"

"Please." I sigh against his mouth. *"Oh, yes, please."*

I feel his lips smile. He pulls out, pushes forward, does it again. He sets up a slow, steady rhythm that strokes through me and gradually the pain eases. The sting doesn't completely go away, and yet it's combined with something else. Something more.

I shift against him, and then I feel his hands on the curve of my ass. "Up, baby." He adjusts my position. "Good girl. You'll like it better that way."

Better? Holy shit! He's so *deep* within me but still careful with his thrusts. I can feel his control, and yet he fills me in a way I never imagined possible. Along with that comes a slow-building sensation. His sheer girth brushes tight and hard against my inner walls. That special place inside me—my G spot, I guess. My hips flex with his.

"Ajia. Oh, baby. *Please."* I sound like I'm begging, and I guess maybe I am.

"What, baby? What do you need?" I hear a growing breathlessness in his voice.

"More. Faster. Harder." I arch against him again.

He growls a quick approval before giving me a quick, hard kiss. "You're sure? I—goddamn you're so fucking tight, baby."

"God, Ajia." I grip his ass with firm fingers. "I want you to fuck me like—I'm the girl you can't live without." *At least for tonight.* I keep that bit to myself.

He plunges forward, in and out, faster and harder, his hands on my hips like he's holding me in place.

"There you go, sweetheart. Feels good right there, yeah?" His breathing sounds ragged, just like I feel.

"Yes."

He keeps moving, and that delicious pressure starts to build. I try to catch my breath, but a keening moan hisses out.

"You ready, baby? You wanna come?"

"Yes. God, yes." And I realize suddenly that I do. Something is happening in me, different from when Ajia gave me an orgasm with his mouth. This is deeper. It consumes all of me.

He pulls back, supporting himself straight on his knees where he can look at all of me and I can see all of him. His hips keep up that deep and steady pace. I know it, feel it, but I can't look away from his eyes. The whiskey brown color is darker than I've ever seen, and his expression is pure sex.

His fingers are suddenly on me, a new pressure on my clit as he keeps pumping in and out of me. He rubs over me, pressing harder than he's done before, but it's perfect for the heavy sensation running through my body. His other hand is on my breast, plucking at my nipple and sending raw desire clear through to my core.

"You feel so fucking good, baby."

"Ajia."

I can't say anything else, but that's okay as he pounds into me. Harder. Faster. Deeper. His cock and his fingers work their magic, and then an orgasm slams over me like a sledgehammer. His name is a guttural groan that comes from my soul, and I stiffen against Ajia's body as the walls of my pussy pulse tight around him.

"Jesus." He moves harder, faster, if it's possible. "Goddamn, Bree. Baby, I'm gonna come!"

"Yes!" It's a triumphant cry. I made Ajia want me enough to come this way, like his whole life depends on it. I know mine does.

And then he's there with me. He shoves into me, his hips jerking until finally he holds still. I feel that new, different pulsing. The throbbing of his cock as he empties himself into me. A part of me suddenly wishes he wasn't wearing a condom—that I could have him bare and his cum would spill all inside me. That he would mark me that way.

I welcome his weight as he collapses over me. I wrap my arms around him and hold him close. My heart pounds, my breathing is ragged, and it's the same for him. He's still inside me, and it feels *wonderful.*

I don't know how long we lay there, but finally Ajia pushes up on one elbow. He looks at me with a tender expression that surprises me. "How you doing, beautiful?"

I smile. I push his hair back from his face. "Amazing. That was…" I don't have a word, so I lean upward to drop a leisurely kiss on his mouth.

Slowly, he pulls out of me. I wince just a bit. It doesn't hurt, and yet I definitely feel it.

"Stay here, baby. I'll be right back."

He slips away and into the bathroom, and when he comes back, the condom is taken care of and he carries a damp washcloth.

"Here you go, baby. Open up."

"What?"

He sits by my hip and holds up the washcloth. "Spread your legs."

I do, and he wipes me with tender strokes. His touch is light, the cloth warm and damp, and it feels good. Not in a sexual way exactly, but in a way that's very caring. Gentle.

If I wasn't in love with Ajia already, I would be now. Not that I tell him that.

He pulls the cloth away, and I see the reddish-pink stain. Blood. My blood. More evidence, if he'd needed it, just how inexperienced I am. Was.

"Any regrets?"

I feel myself go soft all over, and I reach for his neck. I pull him down until our lips are almost touching. "None. No matter what happens between us, I've always wanted you to be my first. I will *never* regret that."

He gets up long enough to toss the washcloth into the bathroom, then scoots into bed next to me. He pulls the covers over us and cuddles me against him.

"Let me hold you for a bit, baby."

I kiss his chest, right over his Wycked Obsession tattoo. "I'll stay as long as you want me." If only I could convey to him how deeply I mean that.

CHAPTER 18

AJIA

Bree slips from my room a few hours later. It's almost eight in the morning, and we've heard a few sounds from the hall. Little chance it's Knox up so early, but she doesn't want to push our luck.

Me neither. In a way. *Fuck.* I'll be glad when this secret shit is over. Like it or not, Knox doesn't get to control everything. Last thing I want to do is act like he does, and hiding things with Bree gives him more power than he deserves.

He can make your life fucking miserable, a voice of reason reminds me. *It* could *tear the band apart, and you know it.*

I do. We've always known how he feels about Bree. It didn't matter before; she was a friend to us all. She never seemed *quite* like the little sister to me that she did for the others; I knew she had a crush on me, and that always made things a little different for me. And then, somehow, her crush became more, and when shit happened, my feelings started to change, too.

Now I want her as much as she says she wants me.

I didn't fuck her this morning. She wanted to—*Christ, I did, too*—but I'm pretty sure that would be too much for her. Not bragging, but I am bigger than most guys, and her sweet pussy needs a little time to recover. That's about the *only* reason I was able to restrict to kisses and some very fucking erotic touching.

Now I can't stop thinking about it. Her.

Shit. I get up and shower. I head down to the lobby for coffee and find Noah and Rye in the trendy little bistro tucked away in the corner of the entry.

"You're up early," says Noah, and I nod.

164

"Couldn't sleep."

"Thinkin' about Zayne?" Rye looks at me like he doesn't believe that for a second.

"Yeah." Not even close, but I go with it. "He was fucked up last night."

"Ya think?"

The waitress shows up and takes my coffee order before Noah can say anything more. She checks us out with a *fuck-me* smile and gives Noah a wink.

"Don't think it's the first time since we've been on the road," he says when we're alone again.

I shake my head. "Looking back, you're right. What're we gonna do?"

Rye shrugs. "Wait for Knox. We're all gonna have to talk to him."

I nod and sip my coffee. It's hot and strong, better than the average hotel coffee.

"You been online yet?"

I shake my head. "That's Knox's job."

"I check shit out myself." Noah pulls out his phone. "Look."

It surprises me that Noah cares enough about that kind of crap to look on whatever internet gossip sites he checks out. I take his phone and read the headline glaring back at me.

Wycked Obsession and Their Band Wife! Ménage a Cinq?

There's a picture of us, Bree leaned back against Noah's chest, Rye and me on either side of her, and Zayne facing us all, a huge, shit-eating grin on his face.

Last night in the green room. Some fucker took a picture and either uploaded it or sold it to a tabloid. Or both. Clearly, somebody heard Zayne shoot his fucking mouth off about Bree being our *wife*. And the skank he hooked up with has been photo shopped out of the picture.

"Damn." I say it softly.

"Read the first paragraph," says Noah in a tight voice.

I look from him to Rye and see frustration—real anger—in their expressions. I turn back to the phone and scroll down.

"Did Knox Gallagher give the guys in Wycked Obsession a major gift on this tour? Like…*his sister?* Our sources say, *yes.* Reports are that the band is involved in orgies and group sex with

Breeanne Gallagher, Knox's younger sister, who's traveling with them on the summer's Edge of Return tour. The question is...is this simply a case of bandmates sharing the same woman, or are the rumors of *incest* true? Stay tuned!"

I raise my gaze to Noah's, then Rye's. *"Fuck!"*

Noah nods once. "Fucking Zayne."

"You boys ready to order?"

The waitress is back. I've got enough acid eating through my stomach that I order pancakes. I wait impatiently for Rye and Noah to order, and then lean forward when we're alone again. "Knox is going to flip his shit."

Noah smirks. "Takes the pressure off you, dude."

I blink. "What?"

Rye shakes his head. "Fuck, no. It adds to it! Knox is gonna be looking at *everything* now. Even more than usual. Especially where Bree's concerned."

"What are you talking about?" I try to pretend ignorance, but I know. We all know.

"Don't play dumb." Noah frowns. "You fuck her yet?"

"Jesus!" I snap. "Will you fuckers stop asking about my fucking sex life!"

"Saw her come out of your room this morning."

"What?"

Rye shrugs. "Couldn't sleep so I got up early. Went to the gym. I was headed back to my room when I saw her leave your room and go back to her own."

"Fuck." Seems I've been saying that a lot this morning.

"You know we don't give a shit—"

"As long as you don't hurt her." Noah interrupts Rye.

"But this whole thing is now *way* more fucked than if we only had to worry about you sleeping with Bree."

Son of a bitch. I *hate* the secrecy, but no way can we go public with Bree and me being—whatever it is we are. Knox has to know first. And I have to tell her about Lara and Mason and Jill—shit I'd rather *die* than talk about. What I want doesn't matter; Bree deserves to know all my ugly truths before she considers telling the world that she's with me. And now we've got this other shit that needs to be handled.

Band Wife?

Ménage a Cinq? Is that even such a thing?

"Whatever happened between Bree and me stays here." I pin them each with a determined glare. "I'm not talking about her like some slut, and I'm not telling anybody shit." Not yet, anyway. I hope they can read it in my gaze.

They both nod. I swear I read understanding, maybe even pride, in their expressions.

"First we're gonna deal with this shit-storm Zayne unloaded on us. Knox isn't gonna like it. Hell, *Bree* is gonna *hate* it. We'll take care of it and *then* I'll talk to Knox about...whatever."

"Band meeting?" Noah asks as our breakfast arrives.

I nod. "Thirty minutes. Your room." Sure as hell aren't bringing them back to my room. It probably still smells like sex in there.

Noah smirks, like he's reading my mind. "Bree, too?"

"Hell, yes, Bree, too! She's the one who's gonna take the biggest hit here. It makes her sound like—" I cut the words off. I don't want to say it.

"Yeah, okay." Noah doesn't seem to need the words, and Rye nods.

Noah takes a bite of his omelet and grabs his phone. He sends off a quick text, to the others I assume, and I cut into my pancakes. Goddamn, but how did this tour—and my life—just get so fucking complicated?

Thirty minutes later we're all crowded in Noah's room. Zayne looks like death warmed over, and while Knox looks better, he's still not at his best.

Noah's sprawled on one bed, Bree tucked in next to him. It fucking pisses me off to see it, but it's better that way. She knows it, and I know it. I see the way she avoids looking at me, even as I try to look anywhere but at her. I don't like it, but I understand it. Rye and I sit at the table, while Knox sits in the one soft chair and Zayne groans from the other bed.

"Okay, you fuckers, what's this all about?" Knox demands.

Rye hands him Noah's phone. "Read."

It takes like three seconds before Knox explodes. "What. The. Ever. Loving. Fuck!"

I force myself to shrug like it's not a big deal. Anything that might keep Knox from going off like a roman fucking candle. "Somebody took a picture last night."

"Somebody took a picture?" He repeats the words like he can't fucking believe them. "Somebody took a fucking picture—and then made up a bunch of shit to sell to the tabloids?"

Bree looks directly at me for the first time. "Ajia?"

I angle my head toward her. "Give her the phone, Knox."

"Fuck no!" He glares at me. "I don't fucking want—"

"Knox, give me the goddamn phone." She holds out her hand with a scowl.

"It's her life, too, bro," I point out. "You can't keep it from her."

Everything about Knox screams he doesn't want to do it, but finally he hands the phone to Bree. Her eyes grow wide, and then wider as she scrolls through the picture and brief teaser article.

"But..." She looks around the room, dazed. It's the first time *she's* been the subject of tabloid gossip. *"It's not true!* I—the wife thing...it's a *joke!"*

Noah pulls her close against him. "I know, baby girl. We all know."

I wish I could hold her, kiss her, give her something else to think about. My temper sharpens and I take it out on Zayne.

"You listening, asshole?" No response. "Zayne?"

"Wha...?"

"Pay attention!" snaps Knox.

Zayne pushes himself up on one elbow. His eyes are dull and unfocused. "What?"

"You got anything to say?" Knox is relentless when he's in protective mode.

"About what?" Zayne blinks.

"This!" Knox grabs the phone from Bree and reads the headline and article. Then he shoves the phone in Zayne's face. "And there's a picture!"

Zayne squints and looks at the phone for a long time. He glances at Bree, at the rest of us, and says, "When was this?"

"Last night," I snap, "when you were too fucking out of it to know what you were saying."

"What happened?"

"You had some skanky chick with you. You know—the one you fucked and probably woke up with this morning. You were calling Bree our *wife,* the chick started yelling, and the rest of us had to calm shit down. Somebody took a picture."

"Fuck." Zayne stares at the phone some more. "Where is she?"

"Who?" demands Noah.

"Skanky bitch." Zayne holds out the phone. "Why isn't she in the picture?"

"Jesus." Noah grabs the phone from him. "She got photoshopped out. How the fuck do we know? And why the fuck are you worried about that?"

Zayne shrugs. "Just tryin' to figure shit out."

"Nobody gives a shit about her." Rye speaks, finally, and when he says shit, it counts. "What matters is that they're calling Bree a slut—" he jabs a finger through the air, pointing at the phone in Noah's hand "—and sayin' that she's sleepin' with all of us." He pauses. "At the same fucking time!"

Zayne's expression clears, like the truth finally dawns on him. He looks at Bree, stiff and unhappy in Noah's arms. Her hair is pulled back in a nice-looking braid, but it leaves her expression exposed and almost vulnerable.

"Jesus, Bree," he mutters. "I'm sorry. I'm…"

"I know, sweetie." She scoots away from Noah and climbs onto the bed with Zayne, hugs him and gives him a kiss on the top of his head. "You were fucked up. Bad. That worries me more than shit they're saying about me."

"I'm sorry," he says again.

"We'll deal with it," she says and keeps holding him. "But what about you? You were using last night. Weren't you?"

"Bree…" He tries to scramble away, and after a moment she lets him go.

The rest of us look at each other. Bree's like Knox in that she doesn't let shit go. If it's gotta be dealt with, then it's usually done head-on. The only things she's treated differently are the thing with her stepfather and whatever this is between her and me. Doesn't take a genius to figure out why.

"Zayne," she tries again, softly. "We're here for you. We love you. But you got some bad shit going on."

He wants to deny it. I can see it in his eyes. But none of us have ever had a whole lot of luck lying to Bree. She's…special. Our baby girl. The one who loves us, no matter what.

The woman who scares the shit out of me.

The woman I'm falling for.

The sound of Zayne's voice shuts down my racing thoughts. "I…things just got away from me, baby girl. I'll be fine."

She shakes her head. "Not sure I believe you, sweetie. I don't know what you're doing, but—"

"We had a deal," Knox interrupts.

Zayne looks at him with a moment of anger that fades to…I don't know—acceptance maybe? "I'll take care of it."

It's Rye who asks, "You need help?"

"Nah." Zayne shakes his head. "I got it."

Bree reaches for his hand. Zayne doesn't want to take it. It's obvious when he hesitates. But finally he does.

"You call any one of us, day or night, if you can't. Yes?"

He closes his eyes. "Yeah. Okay."

Bree crawls forward for a hug. Maybe she believes him, but I don't. Don't know that I'm ready to call Zayne a junkie, but maybe that's just semantics. Maybe I just don't *want* to call him that. Doesn't matter. I've seen the other side of it, the fake claims and denial, the soul-deep addiction. Last thing I want is for that to be Zayne.

"I'm bringing Baz in on this." Knox pulls out his own phone.

"On what?" Zayne stiffens.

"This fucking tabloid shit!"

"Oh, right."

"Do you have to?" Bree asks softly. "Can't we just ignore it?"

Knox is too pissed off to answer, so I do. "Not this, kitten." It's probably a mistake, but I cross the room to sit next to her and take her hand. "When it comes to sex, the tabloids can be relentless. Even a *rumor* of you sleeping with the band and we're having orgies—" I try to grin, but it doesn't come across very well "—well, that's gonna catch a lot of attention. Add the idea of something between you and Knox—"

"Shut the fuck up."

I glance over at her brother. *"I'm* not saying it. *Jesus,* Knox. But as long as it's out there, we gotta do something."

"What'll we have to do?" I can feel the tension in her. There's plenty to feel tense about, but with the crap she left behind in Austin—her fucking *stepfather*—I know she feels it all more.

I shake my head. "I don't know," I admit.

"That's why I'm getting Baz involved." Knox types something out on his phone. "Maybe the label. We'll see. I'm too fucking pissed to do it myself."

"Maybe we can spin it through our own social media," suggests Rye, always the voice of reason.

"How the fuck do you spin something that *disgusting?"* Knox snaps.

Nobody answers until Noah finally says, "That's why we need a PR person. Like a publicist or something. Somebody to keep up the website, Twitter, all that crap. Somebody who knows how to spin this shit and can do it *right away."*

Knox nods, but he's paying more attention to his phone. "I met with somebody yesterday."

"What the fuck?" We're all surprised, but Noah says it.

Knox shrugs. "After the photo shoot. The label recommended her, and I met her."

"Who is she?" asks Rye.

"Some chick named London. She's supposed to be putting together some information for us or some shit."

"Push it into high gear, bro," says Noah. "We can't afford to leave Bree's ass hanging out there like this for long."

Knox nods and looks like he's sending another text. "I'll see if I can get her an invitation to the party this afternoon."

"What party?" Bree asks.

Knox looks up. "The label party. At four. It's a big fucking deal."

"Oh." She nods while the rest of us mutter a chorus of low *fucks.* "I guess I was thinking I wouldn't go."

Knox scowls. "Goddammit, Bree, you know the rule of the tour! Where the band goes—"

"I go," she finishes for him mildly. "Yeah, Knox, I fucking know."

"You've pretty much gotta go now," Noah points out.

"Why?" She shakes her head.

"You can't fucking hide out after that kind of gossip! You gotta be out there pretending like it doesn't fucking bother you."

She sighs. "I guess."

"And Knox," he adds. "You pretty much gotta stay away from her."

Knox blinks, and I can almost see the wheels turning. "She's my fucking sister," he says finally.

Noah nods. "We all fucking know that. But you're protective as shit about her, and if anything happens—anybody says anything—your temper is gonna fuck it all up."

"So everybody else is gonna look after her?" Knox looks at us all. Even Zayne who's stretched out on the bed again. At least his eyes are open like he's paying attention.

"I can look after myself, Knox."

"No, you can't." It's Rye again. "And if the rest of us pay too much attention, it'll look like the whole *band wife* thing. The orgy bullshit."

Knox nods. "Okay…" He's thinking again.

"She should stick with Ajia," says Rye.

I cough. *What the fuck?*

Bree blinks and looks at me, her sparkling green eyes wide and uncertain.

"Why him?" demands Knox. "He's got a fucking reputation."

His smile in my direction is generally pissed, and I know why. *Ajia Stone, manwhore.* Who'd want their sister around a fucker like me? I don't say a word.

"He's also the face of the band," Rye points out mildly.

"Why not you?" asks Knox. "You're—what do they call it—the tortured one? Troubled bad boy. Whatever. You don't have the same rep."

Rye shakes his head. "I'm too much in the background. You put Bree out there with me, it's gonna look like we're trying to hide something. Put her out there with Ajia, and it'll look like nothing's going on."

Knox nods slowly. "I suppose…"

"It's not like they're gonna be walking around with their hands all over each other, making out in corners," says Noah with an edge to his voice. Knox may not understand the tone—but I do.

And so does Bree. Her hand is still clutching mine, and her grip tightens.

Going to a high-profile party? Together. Pretending like nothing has changed between us?

I close my eyes. I don't think a lot about God on a normal day, but right now I'm convinced He has a lousy sense of humor. He's enjoying fucking with me. Or this is karma, kicking my ass for all the girls I've fucked and forgotten before they're out the door.

Maybe I don't deserve Bree, but she doesn't deserve this bullshit making her out to be some kind of slut, either. I'll do whatever it takes...and try to figure out how the hell I'm going to tell Knox that *I'm* the reason his baby sister isn't a virgin any longer.

CHAPTER 19

BREE

I stare at myself in the closet door mirrors and shake my head. My hair is loose and rustles over my shoulders, catching on the lacey bodice of my little black dress. Crystal-and-pearl earrings flash beneath the length of my hair, and a matching bracelet sparkles on my wrist. My four-inch heels have black satin bows at the ankles, and my makeup is heavier than I normally wear.

All in preparation for the label's Wycked Obsession party.

I head into the bathroom for the last thing—lipstick. It's a berry color that isn't quite red but darker than pink. I can't remember what it's called, and I don't care. *Get Me Out of This Thing!* would be perfect.

I don't have anything appropriate to wear to this kind of party. Or I didn't. I told Knox that, thinking maybe I could beg off that way. Two hours later, Baz sends a few boxes to my room. Two black dresses, two pairs of black heels, jewelry, makeup, and perfume.

Really?

Everything fits perfectly, which is just a little bit creepy. The style suits me perfectly, too. The makeup and perfume are high end stuff. And now I'm dressed up like somebody's idea of a rock 'n' roll Barbie doll to prove to the world that I am *not* sleeping with everybody in the band.

Just fucking the lead singer. But that's private.

I smile a little as awareness races through me. Being with Ajia is something I'm only just *beginning* to be able to accept. I've wanted it for so long—before I really understood what it meant to *be* with him—and now that he's mine, I'm almost afraid to believe it's true.

174

It's a good thing—a *wonderful* thing—that pretty much outweighs all the other stuff that's happened in the last few months. Mom marrying Gabe, Gabe being…disgusting, seeing Ajia with other women, living in close quarters with five rockers who always seem to be on the edge of being out of control, our suspicions of Zayne and drugs…

I could go on, but that's enough. Isn't it? It's a lot for me and—

A knock interrupts my wandering thoughts, and I'm just as glad. Looking through the little peep hole, I spot Knox and open the door.

"You ready?"

I nod and grab the classy little black evening bag. Baz thought of everything, including a way to carry my lipstick, a comb, card key, and phone.

"We're meeting the others in the lobby. Limo's waiting."

I nod again, but my brother doesn't see. He's walking toward the elevator, his back to me.

"Uh, Knox? Could you slow down a little?"

He stops and looks over his shoulder. "What?"

I point to my feet. "Heels. They're like four inches high. I don't wear this kind of shit that often. Give me a break, will you?"

His gaze softens. "Sorry, baby girl." He waits until I'm next to him and then takes my arm.

"You mad at me?" I ask as we approach the elevator.

"No." He shakes his head. "I'm pissed at the situation. That some fucker who doesn't know us would say crap about you like that. That they'd even *joke* about something like you—me…"

He punches the down button like he wants to shove the whole control panel through the wall, and I pull him close for a quick hug while we wait. "Don't let it get to you. You hear me?" I release him and give him the best encouraging look I have. "You're a great brother. That's just somebody's twisted bullshit. It's got nothing to do with us."

"What about Gabe?"

"What about him?"

"Maybe *we're* good, but he—tried shit. I should have fucking killed him. Now there's all this bullshit on top of—"

"Knox…"

My voice trails off as the elevator arrives. We get in—just the two of us—and once the doors close, I start again. "Nothing Gabe tried has anything to do with you. Remember, he didn't succeed. You got me out of there. Just because some anonymous loser out there is saying ridiculous shit about us doesn't mean squat to me. You're my brother, I love you, and that's all there is to it."

"Yeah, well, now we're going to this party, and we have to act like we're not related or some shit."

"We do not. I'm just gonna hang with Ajia so people know we're not hiding anything." I do my best to ignore the rolling excitement in my stomach at the thought of *publicly* spending time with Ajia. "And you—you got that PR lady coming? You said her name is London?"

"Yeah." My brother nods.

"Okay. So you spend the time talking to her, and it'll be like a normal party. If you were busy any other time, I'd be with the guys anyway."

He nods like I'm making sense. And maybe I am. But I'm also wearing these ridiculous heels and a black lacy dress that are nothing like the *real* Bree. This is the rock stars' sister/friend/fake wife on display, and it's the biggest fucking *bullshit* I've seen yet.

How did such a stupid goddamn joke end up being tabloid *gossip?* Except for trying to help make it go away—if that's even possible—I give literally no good fucks about it. The harder thing for me is pretending—for now—like nothing has changed between Ajia and me.

Yes, I've totally complicated things. It's my own damn fault, and I can't pretend that I'm not the one who wanted to steal some time to just *be* with Ajia. To not worry about Knox or Gabe or the rabid fangirls who are gonna hate me when they find out Ajia and I are...well, whatever. We haven't had a chance to give it a name beyond fucking—making love—and *I* was the one who wanted to wait. To pretend we're normal people who don't have all the rock 'n' roll bullshit going on.

Well, I got what I wanted. Nobody's fault but mine if it's turning out to be different than I expected. More difficult. And there's nothing I can do about it now.

I force my thoughts away from Ajia. "You look handsome, you know," I say after a minute. And he does. Knox is dressed all in gray, including shirt and tie. It looks great against his dark hair and I

176

realize in a new way how my once-goofy big brother is a good-looking guy who's become a freaking rock star!

He grins and looks down at himself. "I'm hot, yeah?"

I laugh. "Yeah. You're hot."

The elevator reaches the lobby, and security is there to escort us to the limo. Cameras start to flash the minute we step out through the large glass doors, and I do my best to ignore them and the shouted questions. It's a lesson Baz instructed me about early on in the tour, and one I never thought I'd need.

The rest of the band is already inside the car. I get in first and end up sitting between Ajia and Knox.

"Damn, baby girl, you look hot!" Zayne seems somewhat recovered from last night's party and this morning's hangover. I hope that means things aren't too bad with him, despite his bloodshot eyes.

"Thanks." I smile and look around me. The guys look amazing. Every one of them is dressed in a suit and tie. Almost conservative, even. I'm impressed!

"Where'd you get that fuck-me dress, baby girl?"

I shake my head. "That supposed to be a compliment, Noah?"

He laughs. "Well, I'm probably not supposed to say you look hot as hell—but you do. You haven't worn it before. Didn't know you brought that dressy kind of shit with you."

"I didn't." I shake my head. "Baz got it."

Rye shakes his head with a little grin. "He's like two or three people at once. Wonder how he does it all."

"You look nice, kitten," says Ajia from beside me, and I can't help smiling at him. Talk about fucking hot! I'm surprised he hasn't burst into flames. He's wearing all black—suit, tie, shirt, and shoes—and his dark blond hair is pulled back into a tame-looking ponytail at the nape of his neck. I can't decide if I like that better, or his hair all loose and free and flowing over his shoulders.

The ride to…well, wherever this party is being held—nobody actually told me—is filled with Knox's advice.

"Remember. Talk to the execs. Their wives, kids, whoever they introduce. Baz says there'll be reporters and photographers, but not the paparazzi type. And—"

"What the fuck, dude?" Noah shakes his head. "What kind of loser assholes you think we are?"

"What?" My brother acts like the question has him clueless. And, to be fair, it probably does. His need to control shit goes deep.

"We got this," says Rye calmly. "Maybe this is the first party the label's given *for* us, but we've been to other shit. We know what to do."

"Right." Knox nods. "Right."

"Why're you so nervous, dude?" asks Zayne.

I sigh and say, "Me." Because I know it's true. "The tabloid shit."

"We got that, too." Ajia takes my hand and squeezes. "Nobody fucks with Bree."

They all share a gaze that almost makes me want to laugh. You'd think they were the Sopranos going in on a hit or something. I don't, though, because I don't want them to doubt how serious I take the gossip. Part of me feels kind of removed from it, because it's so far from the truth. The rest of me is just...overwhelmed.

We pull up in front of another hotel, and the limo door opens. Knox is first out, and immediately I hear shouts and people calling his name. So there's a crowd—and that means paparazzi.

"Let me get out ahead of you."

Ajia crawls over me, then turns to help me out. I step from the limo, my hand in his, and the noise almost overwhelms me. The same shouts, people calling Ajia's name, the fast click of camera shutters.

"Ajia, do you have anything to say about group sex with your bandmates?"

"Is that Breeanne Gallagher? Bree, any comment?"

"Wycked Obsession rules!"

"How's the tour with Edge of Return? Any chance you're sharing your girl with them?"

"Get rid of that slut! You want a *real* woman, I'm here for you, Ajia!"

Ajia drops my hand to splay his fingers over the small of my back and guide me forward. *"Ignore it."* His voice commands me like I've never heard him before. "Look straight ahead and smile like you're the happiest fucking woman on this goddamn planet."

I do as he says, but only because it's Ajia next to me. Ajia telling me what to do, reminding me in his own way of every piece of advice that Baz's given me. The weak part of me wants to turn into the man at my side, hide my face against his chest, wrap my arms around him, and steal some of his strength. Bask in the knowledge of what he can do to my body with his touch, his kiss…his cock. But the rest of me—the Bree Gallagher who's put up with the years of longing for him, of being the band mascot, and fighting off my stepfather's advances—wants to make him and the rest of the band proud.

I smile and nod, as though some sort of acknowledgment of those around me. Truthfully, I keep my eyes focused on walking forward with some shred of certainty. When the wide glass doors open and we step inside, I welcome the cool, relative calm of the hotel.

"This way."

Security is there. It's Kel, and he steps up to lead us toward where Knox is waiting. The others trail behind us, and as we wait for the elevator, Ajia drops his head to whisper in my ear.

"You did great, baby."

I look up at him. "Did I?"

He nods and glances at the others. "We got this, right, you fuckers?"

They laugh, Kel smiles, and the elevator finally arrives. It's crowded with all of us but not uncomfortable, and when the doors open, I see a fancy restaurant decorated with a banner announcing *Wicked Is As Wycked Does*.

Kel leads the way. There are other posters inside: album covers; the Wycked Obsession logo; pictures of the band, both posed and live in-concert; and what I can only assume are some of the pictures taken at the most recent photo shoot, if what Ajia told me is true.

There he is, larger than life, reclining shirtless on a bed of white. His leather pants are unbuttoned, his hand tucked into his waistband, and a sultry expression on his face that says, *C'mon, baby. Fuck me now. You know you want to.*

"Holy motherfucking shit," mutters Noah just behind me.

"How did they get those pictures so fast?" asks Rye.

I glance around and see oversized posters of them all. Every one in a seductive pose and looking like they're ready to fuck the next girl to step in front of them.

"Jesus, y'all." It's all I can say.

Zayne laughs in delight, but I forget when I feel a soft breath behind my ear. "I was thinking about you when they took that," Ajia whispers.

My nipples perk up to stand at attention, and my eyes dart from left to right. Nobody seems to notice Ajia and me so close together; they're all staring at the posters like ten-year-old boys hooked on video games.

"There you are! Good to see you!" A middle-aged, somewhat balding man with a round tummy approaches and shakes hands all the way around. He hesitates for just an instant when he gets to me. "And this must be Bree."

I smile and offer my hand. "Yes, sir. I'm pleased to meet you."

"I'm Martin Evans, but call me Marty. These boys are mine."

I recognized the name. "You signed them."

He nods. "That I did." He gestures to the room that's quickly filling with…I don't know, music industry insiders, I guess. "I'm going to steal Knox." Marty smiles at my brother. "Maybe we can get this marketing and PR issue nailed down today."

London. I smile to myself and wave Knox off. I know he'll stay around for me as long as he thinks I need it, but we already agreed to our solution.

"Go." I let the smile spread over my face. "I'll be fine." I slip my arm through Ajia's with a wink. "Ajia said he'd introduce me around."

"Good, good!" Marty seems to like that idea, and then he cocks his head, looking from Ajia to me and back. "You're like a pair, both dressed in black." He turns to wave at somebody—a photographer, apparently, when a guy with a camera approaches. "Get some candid shots of them. They look good together."

Ajia shrugs when I look at him. Far as I know nobody planned for us to both be in black. I didn't have much choice; both dresses Baz sent are black.

Marty leads Knox away as the photographer waves us off. "Mingle. I'll keep an eye out for you."

"Okay," says Noah. "Divide and conquer, bitches." He grins at me. "Baby girl, you're gonna kill 'em dead."

I smile back. "Let's do this," I say with more bravado than I actually feel.

And so it begins. Ajia snags a couple of glasses of champagne for us and leads me around the room. He seems to know a lot of the people from the record label, although it's clear he's meeting some of them face-to-face for the first time. He introduces me easily as Knox's sister—the unrecognized member of Wycked Obsession, he tells them, which I'm not sure is such a good idea. Some of them—the ones who have an idea of the internet gossip—smirk in a real fucking unpleasant way.

I ignore it and remind myself I'm strong all on my own. I don't need to reach for Ajia's hand. I might *want* to, but that can wait until later.

The crowd demands we circle endlessly, or so it seems. After more than an hour and a couple of glasses of champagne, I need a break. Just a few minutes in the Ladies' Room, I promise Ajia, and I'll be fine. I even believe it.

The restroom is empty, but I slip into a stall, anyway. The added privacy beckons, and I sit primly on the commode. Ajia, Knox—all the guys—are made for this kind of thing. They're entertainers, and they thrive in a crowd. Something in them blossoms—they're *on* and playing rock star versions of themselves. Not quite the same people as when it's just us and our fucked up little rock star family, but it doesn't matter. They're good at it. At everything.

Then there's me. I don't have any other version of myself, didn't know I'd need one. I'm just Bree, band mascot, tagalong and, now, Ajia's lover. If I'm going to spend the next couple of months on the road with them—and if I seriously want this relationship with Ajia to have the chance at being something *real*—then I better figure out pretty damn quick just who this *public* Bree is going to be. And, more than that, how to turn her on and off.

The restroom door opens, and I swallow a sigh. Should I flush and exit the stall like I'm done? Or can I get by with hiding out for a few more minutes?

The decision is taken from me when a voice demands, "Did you see her?"

"Who?"

The women sound young, maybe my age, with an easily recognizable entitled boredom in their tone.

"The slut sister. Breeanne."

My breath cuts off and my eyelids snap closed.

181

"She's here?" snorts Girl Number Two.

"The one walking around with Ajia Stone."

"In that awful black fuck-me dress?"

Number One laughs. "The dress isn't so bad. Looks like shit on her, though."

"D'you suppose they're all fucking her?"

"You saw her!" Number One screeches. "What d'you think? Muddy brown hair, little tits, huge thighs. Why the fuck would the Wycked Obsession guys waste their time on *her?*"

Number Two laughs. "Not everybody can afford the boob job you got at sixteen."

"Oh, come on. Her brother is Knox fucking Gallagher. He could buy her twenty boob jobs if he thought it would do any good. It'd be a waste of his money, and he probably knows it. What's that saying? Something about putting lipstick on a pig."

They laugh, take care of Mother Nature, and whatever else they came in for. I hear the water run, the hand dryer roar, and they continue to gossip. How big is Knox's dick? Is fucking Ajia as hot as his voice makes it sound? Can they convince Noah to have a ménage with the two of them?

I hold myself absolutely still. Not sure I even breathe until the door opens again. "Come on," says Girl Number One, her voice fading. "Let's go find Ajia and show him what a couple of *real* women look like."

Number Two laughs, and the door clicks shut behind them.

I realize I've been pressing my hands over my mouth, but the reality of it comes only after the others are gone. The bathroom stall comforts me and yet the metal walls press in on me at the same time. How long have I been in here?

Moving like I'm sick or something, I push myself up and open the stall door. My brain stays checked out until I finally get to the sink to wash my hands. My face—a stranger's and yet oddly familiar —stares back from the mirror, eyes wide and cheeks bright red.

You know how this stuff is supposed to work, I tell myself. I've heard about it, witnessed shit first-hand, even felt the hatred of the groupies when I'm around the band. I've even been preparing myself for it to get worse, once word of Ajia and me gets out.

But this kind of meanness throws what I thought I knew all to shit. It's specific, targeted directly at me, and over nothing but a silly rumor. A joke that somebody took way too fucking far and now has a life of its own. Worse, it shows pure hatred for me and my place in the guys' lives.

Or maybe it's just a combination of everything. Hearing the actual fucking words like I'm such a worthless piece of shit. Wide green eyes stare back at me from the mirror, and I realize that it's true. It has nothing to do with the rumors. It's about me, and it's personal.

Well, personal to me. To them, it's plain old jealousy, and they don't really give a shit about me either way. If I can just remember that, I can make it through the rest of this stupid party, and I won't have to see these people ever again.

What other choice to I have?

"Stop stalling." I say it aloud, snapping at the me in the mirror. "So maybe they hate you. They don't matter. You don't need them. You have Ajia and Knox and the rest of the guys. You don't need anybody else."

You have Ajia and Knox and the rest of the guys. I repeat the words over and over as I freshen my lipstick, fluff my hair to fall over my shoulders, and straighten my dress over my hips.

You have Ajia and Knox and the rest of the guys.

My confidence wavers as I reenter the party. It hits me in an entirely new way just how many beautiful women fill the room. They're all taller than me, with perfect figures, stylish outfits, and they carry themselves with the grace and poise of fashion models. Who am I? A plain, simple girl from Texas who has no business being here with the pretty people.

I suck in a ragged, half-assed breath and that's when I spot Knox. He's talking with a petite woman, about my height but slender. She's wearing a navy blue cocktail dress, conservatively cut, even though it's sleeveless and with an outer layer of lace over the bodice and skirt. Her hair is a beautiful auburn color that falls to her shoulders. I wish she'd turn around so I could see her face. Could it be London, the PR and marketing whiz?

Zayne crosses into my line of sight, distracting me enough so that I follow his progress. None of us quite trusts that he's totally recovered from whatever he had going on last night—or that he isn't possibly doing something more today. I didn't see the guys at their absolute worst, but I saw enough during and after the last tour. Now I know just enough to be suspicious.

Fortunately for us both, he stops to chat with Marty. It's then that I spot Ajia, surrounded by a couple of girls. *Of course.* I wish I could smile about it, but I can't quite manage it at the moment.

I start for him, partly because I'll always be drawn to him, but also because he's my point man in this party charade. I'm *supposed* to stay close. I promised.

"Ajia."

I hear a woman's laugh, and then another joins in. The girl on his right says his name as she reaches for his arm, and I find myself staring at the way her long, red-tipped fingers curl over his forearm. I hear it again. The laughter, the entitlement, the edge beneath the humor…

The girls from the bathroom have cornered Ajia, and I want to puke.

"Bree!"

Turning away, I spin on the ball of my foot. I can hear him calling my name, but I can't stop. Not now. Not after…everything.

You can do it. Face those bitches down! You're better than them. You kick ass!

Something desperate inside me shouts out a hell of a pep talk. A part of me even tries to listen. I *want* to be that strong, resilient woman, but everything I need to be her is just shot right now. Damn if I'm not just a little too exhausted at the moment.

For now, it's just too fucking much, and I'm outta here.

CHAPTER 20

AJIA

"Bree!"

She turns away, and I can't tell if she heard me over the crowd noise. *Fuck.* I look at the vampires around me. Maybe not fair to call them that, but I can feel them sucking the life out of me.

Does Bree think I went back on my word? That these women around me mean something in some fucked up way? She trusts me more than that, doesn't she?

Why the fuck should she? demands my conscience. *What have you ever done to* prove *yourself to her?*

"Sorry, honey." I pull away from the vampire who clutches my arm. "I gotta take care of something."

"Ajia" Her voice is a shrill demand. "You're not going after *her,* are you?"

I turn to look at her full-on. Maybe *vampire* is right. She's pale with long, seriously black hair and goth-looking makeup. Her expression is…well, pretty fucking ugly, if you want to know the truth. Entitled and just plain mean.

"What?" It comes out like I can't fucking believe she questioned me. *"Who* are you talking about?"

"That's the one, right?" The vampire points in the direction of where Bree disappeared, seeming to miss the clues I'm sending out that she's crossed a line. I glance at her friend, who looks like she gets it on some level, at least if her wide eyes are any sign. *She's* smart enough to keep her mouth shut.

"The one what?"

"The slut from the internet. Knox's sister. The one you're all supposed to be hot to fuck."

"The slut..." My voice goes so low it can only fade away.

"C'mon, Ajia." She steps toward me, and I step an equal distance back. I suddenly can't stand the idea of being any closer to her than is absolutely necessary. The distance from L.A. to Austin would be perfect.

She blinks, angles her head, and narrows her heavily made-up eyes. "Don't tell me it's true! You're actually fucking her?" She laughs, but it's an angry, ugly sound. "What the fuck could you guys want with her, when you can have prime pussy like this?" She spreads her arms wide.

The slut from the internet. Knox's sister.

I've never cared what the tabloids say or write about me. It might not be accurate, but there's a pretty good chance there's some underlying truth. I'm a piece-of-shit manwhore who doesn't care about anybody but myself, the band—and now, Bree. Maybe always Bree. Nobody knew much about her before, but now...

A few hours in the spotlight, and she's a slut?

Fuck that.

My temper's on a hair trigger right now, and I don't fucking care. A lot of shit has put me on the edge lately. Traveling, performing, partying. Crap with Bree's stepfather, getting her in bed with me, the secret we're keeping from Knox...and the shit I have to reveal from the past. It's too fucking much, but I can't seem to stop myself from making it even fucking worse.

Disgust narrows my eyes, and I let the expression settle over my face. I shake my head and drag a revolted gaze over the goth vampire chick. "No thanks, honey. Not into sloppy seconds. But you're right about one thing." I lean forward just enough that I can lower my voice. "She's not sleeping with the whole band. I'm keeping her to myself." Spinning on my heel, I stalk off and ignore the shriek behind me.

I should have kept my big mouth shut, and I fucking know it, just like I know this'll come back to bite me in the ass. Honestly? I don't give a fuck right now.

That cunt called my kitten a slut.

Bree left the restaurant, and so I follow in the direction she went. She's not around the elevators, not down the long hall, which leaves me with a shorter hallway that ends with a large, gleaming window. I head that way and find an odd little alcove with a couple of chairs—and Bree.

She's leaning against the wall, her head back and eyes closed. Her arms are loose at her sides, but her fingers are clenched in tight fists.

"Bree?" I say softly. "Baby?"

Her breasts rise and fall as she takes a deep breath, and after a moment, she opens her eyes and settles her gaze on me. It shouldn't surprise me, but the depth of her soft and caring expression does. "Ajia." Her smile is small.

Relief shoves the breath from my lungs. "What's wrong, baby? Why didn't you come back to me?"

She shakes her head, and I step closer. She drops her gaze. "Those *women* were there."

The stress she places on the word sounds like she might as well have said the devil. Demons. *Vampires.*

I pull her into my arms. "They weren't anybody, baby. Less than nothing. They were just talking to me. You know I wouldn't—"

"Oh, Ajia." She strokes my face, her fingers soft. And—are they trembling?

"Bree, baby—"

"I know, A. I know it wasn't anything like that. You promised."

Relief leaves me breathless. "Thank you for that, baby. I…don't deserve it, but it means a lot."

Her palm rests wide over my chest, right at my heart. "It wasn't about you or anything you did. It's them. Who they are and what they represent."

What they represent? "Not sure I understand what that means, kitten."

"I…" She pauses, shakes her head, and I'm caught up for a moment in the way her chocolate-brown hair tumbles around her shoulders.

"They were in the bathroom with me," she finishes after a moment. "I was in one of the stalls, so they didn't see me. They were talking about me. About the rumors, but mostly about me as a person."

"What about you?"

She shakes her head again and gives a sad little laugh. "Well, let's see. I'm wearing a cute dress but it looks like shit on me. My tits are too small, my thighs—maybe my ass?—are too big. There was some other stuff, but they pretty much agreed that trying to fix me up was a waste of time. What did they say? Something about it being like putting *lipstick on a pig.*"

"*What. The. Fuck?*" I smack my hand over hers, where it still rests on my chest, and I press it hard against my pounding heart.

"But the good news is they agreed y'all aren't wasting your time—or maybe your hotness—by fucking me."

"*Holy. Motherfucking. Christ.*"

My voice is deep, growly, and pissed. Exactly how I feel. I can't let myself move or even breathe on the chance that I'm going to do something really fucking bad. Like kill somebody.

I close my eyes, breathe deep into my belly, and try to calm the rage that makes me want to do something really fucking stupid. Somehow, I manage to get my shit together. I think it's my concern for Bree that gives me any kind of self-control.

"Baby." I pull her to me, her tits flat against my chest and one leg tucked between mine. My cock perks up, liking this position a lot, but I ignore that for now and rub my hand tenderly over her back, up and down.

"You know that's all a bunch of shit," I say when I can. "They're just jealous bitches. It's all—"

"Is it?" She pulls back enough to look up at me. "Is it anything but the truth? I'm nobody. I'm Knox Gallagher's sister, plain and simple and very fucking ordinary. I go to college in Austin, Texas, and I have no business being here with the pretty people."

"And I'm a fucking commodity. If you don't belong, I sure as fuck don't. They don't want *me,* they want Ajia Stone, rock star, and he doesn't even fucking exist. He's a figment of those chicks' imagination. You're the only one who wants—who even *knows*—the real me."

And that's a fucking lie. She doesn't know the real me. Nobody does. The fans have one part, the band another, Mason and Jill still another, and Bree has the part that's the me I want to be. But that's still not me, and that makes my whole life a fucking farce.

A farce that I swear to God I'm ending today. Not here, not in public, but when we're alone. No more running and hiding. I'll tell her what I've done, what a sick fuck I am, and then?

Is there any way she'll want to stay with me?

I shift so I can catch her mouth with mine. I have to taste her—now. Our kiss is long and hard, lips and tongues and teeth. My mouth demands her response, and she gives it. Completely and immediately.

"You're my girl," I snarl against her lips. "And those cunts can go fuck themselves."

She pulls back enough that I can see the emotion—hope, desire…pleasure— flicker in her wide green eyes. "I'm your girl?"

"Fuck, yes." My smile is crooked. Will she want to be my girl after she hears everything?

"Since when?"

I give her honesty about this much. "You think I'd have ever slept with you if I wasn't gonna make you my girl?"

She smiles softly. "I guess I never thought that far ahead."

"Well, you don't have to now. You're mine, I'm yours, and we're telling Knox tonight. No more of this sneaking around shit."

Besides, now that I said what I did to the vampire and her minion, the rumors are bound to amp up. Change. I should probably warn Bree, but not here. I can't stand to stay in this fucking hotel, at this party, a second longer.

"C'mon, baby." I loop my arm around her shoulders and lead her back toward the elevators. "We're getting out of here."

"We are?"

"Yep." I pull out my phone with my free hand and text Baz. "The limo can take us to the hotel, then come back for the others."

I glance into the restaurant as we wait for the elevator. The party seems to be going strong, and I thank God I don't see anybody I recognize. Or anybody who's going to try and stop us from leaving. Worse, anybody who'll say something stupid that'll mean I have to punch them. And especially no vampire goth chick or her creepy minion.

Nobody notices us at all.

"I can't wait to get you back to my room." I drop a kiss on top of Bree's head and whisper against her hair. "I'm going to lick you from top to bottom—and then do it again."

She peers up at me, the naughtiness in her expression surprising me. "You aren't going to fuck me?"

I blink. "Do you want me to?"

"Yes."

I shake my head with a little laugh. "Well, no, baby, probably not. It's too soon. You'll be sore."

"I don't care."

"I do." I lean down so we're eye to eye. "I don't want to hurt you." *Any more than I have to,* I remind myself. Any more than I already have. "But I'm still going to make you come."

"Only if I get to—you know."

"What?"

The elevator dings, signaling its arriving. I don't look away from her.

"You know. Put you in my...mouth." She kind of rushes the last.

I can't help it. I drop a quick, fierce kiss on her mouth, and she turns into me. Her arms go around my waist and presses herself against me.

"You wanna suck me off, baby?" I whisper in her ear. "You got it."

We step into the empty elevator, and the instant the doors close, I pull her close for a deeper, more sexual kiss. Maybe I'm not going to fuck her with my cock today—it's my job to fucking take care of my girl—but I'm going to remind her what it's gonna be like the next time we do it.

Her arms are around my back, clutching my suit jacket, and her belly is pressed against my erection. *Fuck.* My mouth waters, pushing me to go down on her right now, at this very fucking second, but I've pushed the boundaries of good luck far enough today.

Nope. Not here in the elevator, but soon, she'll be mine again.

We barely make it through the door to my room before Bree is in my arms and I push her up against the wall. We kiss in that same desperate, open-mouthed way, my tongue searching, seeking, plunging home.

Jesus, I need to be *inside her!* But that's about me, not her, and some sane part of my brain knows she needs a little time to recover. She was a virgin less than twenty-four hours ago, and my cock not only destroyed her hymen, but I stretched her wider than a virgin should probably go. That means, for today, I'll try to restrain myself and show her how much I want her in other ways.

But, first…we should talk. I said we would. I said I'd tell her my truths, and I want to do that before we tell Knox about us. I've been a fucking coward to keep this from her for so long—even the sanitized version. I should have told her that much before she let me fuck her. She deserves that—and more.

It could change everything, and I fucking know it. But she deserved to know everything about the guy she thinks she loves.

"Bree…baby." I step back. "We should talk."

The smile she gives me is wicked, and slowly she shakes her head. "I can think of a *lot* of things I'd rather do than talk."

She reaches up to push my jacket from my shoulders and down my arms, rising up on her tiptoes to drag her tongue along my jaw and up to behind my ear. "Like this," she says, her hands working at the knot of my tie. Shivers race down my spine as her teeth close over my earlobe. Next thing I know, my tie is free, and she slings it across the room. "Or this," she adds as she unbuttons my shirt.

Her head drops back far enough that I can see her eyes, heavy with desire that goes soul-fucking-deep. Can she see the same in me? It feels like it.

Jesus, I need her.

She unfastens my belt, unbuttons and unzips me, and then her hands are on my hips, pushing downward.

"Bree…"

I try again, but my dick is so hard, I don't have any blood flow left for my brain. My voice comes out all hoarse and ragged, and it disappears altogether when she sinks to her knees in front of me. She drags my pants down with her, all the way to my ankles. Lifting one leg and then the other, she gets rid of my shoes, socks, and then tosses my pants aside. She tugs on my boxer briefs, my cock springs free, and then I'm naked.

How the fuck did she do that? And why can't I seem to do anything but stare at the blatant need on her face?

"Oh, baby." She looks up at me so I can see her wide-eyed excitement. "You look different from this position." She leans forward and swirls her tongue around the head of my cock. "Beautiful."

I mean to laugh, but it's a choked-off sound. "Men aren't beautiful."

"You are." She kisses the tip, pulls it just between her lips and sucks gently.

My hips flex forward before I can even think about it. Her soft mouth is like fucking heaven, and I do it again.

Looking down, hair that's come out of my ponytail hangs in my face, but so fucking what? I can only stand there and watch as she strokes her tongue up and down my shaft like it's the best thing she's ever tasted. My cock grows harder, and before I really know what Bree's doing, she sits back on her heels. Angling her head to one side, she licks my balls, sucks them into her mouth. Her tongue circles around them, and she sucks on them with just enough force to drive me wild.

"Jesus, baby!" When the fuck did I shove my hands in her hair? I don't even know if I'm pushing her away or pulling her closer. I groan. "Where the fuck did you learn *that?*"

She releases me with a pop but starts licking up and down my cock again. "The internet."

A laugh chokes out of me as she takes me in her mouth again. "The *internet?* What the fuck did you do, Google blowjobs?"

"Porn."

She takes my dick deep into her mouth, leaning forward and dropping her head down until the tip reaches the back of her throat. She gags a little, but she doesn't let that stop her. She does it again. Again.

"Baby." It's a groan. I force myself to pull out of her mouth and drop to my knees so I can look at her, eye to eye. "Porn, kitten? Why were you watching porn?"

She licks her lips. "So I'd know how to please you." She says it like the answer should have already been obvious.

And maybe it is, but the whole idea kind of fucks with my head.

"You don't have to do shit like that, baby. You know I want you. As…you."

"I know. For now." She drops her gaze. "While we're new and…getting to know each other this way." Her hands rest on my thighs, and she squeezes the muscles there. "But you've been with…a lot of women. Experienced and beautiful women. I'm not like them so—"

"Oh, baby." I lift her chin so she has no choice but to look in my eyes. "Those women don't mean shit. Never did. Don't remember them, couldn't tell you any of their names or what they looked like. Can't even tell you what I did with them."

It makes me sound like a piece of shit dickhead, and I know it, but it's the truth. As fucked up as that is. With all the other shit still unsaid between us, I'm not lying about anything else.

"But you." I lean in so I can catch her lips with mine. "No one is more beautiful than you are, kitten, and I remember every fucking thing we've ever done. I will *always* know, until the day I die."

"But…" She hesitates. "We haven't done *everything.*"

"What do you mean *everything?*"

"You know." She frowns just a little. "Other positions. Other…places. *Everything.*"

"I need better words than that, baby, but it doesn't matter right now. We're *not* doing everything." I cup her pussy through her dress. "Not tonight. You're still sore, and you need some time so I don't hurt you. But you're not even going to know the difference, because I'm going to make you come so many times with my mouth, you'll lose count."

For some reason, it hits me then just how hot it is that I'm naked and she's still fully dressed. I never expected that, don't know why it turns me on so much, and then it doesn't matter. The thought disappears when she flexes her crotch against my hand.

"And you'll let me? Too?"

"Let you what?"

She reaches for my cock. "You'll let me do all of it. And you'll… come in my mouth?"

My dick gets harder. "Is that what you want?"

Her eyes darken to an almost gray-green. *"Yes."*

"All right."

I push to my feet and pull her up with me, dragging her dress up and over her head as we move. She might actually get more credit than me; she wants it off as much as I do and gets the dress over her head in an instant. I bend a little at the knees, just enough to give her foot a resting place when I pull her leg into place.

"Those fucking bows have been driving me insane all night." I unfasten one shoe and toss it aside.

Her smile is as naughty as it is surprised. "They have?"

"Fuck, yeah." I lower one leg, take up the other, and then sling shoe number two across the room.

"I just thought—" her breath comes a little heavier as I curl my palm over her calf and trace a light, teasing line to the back of her knee "—they were…cute."

"Cute, hell." I release her leg and lean in to catch her bottom lip between my teeth. "They're sexy as fuck."

And I'm not wasting any more time uncovering the rest of her body. My mouth is open over hers, my tongue licking and circling, and my fingers imitate the motions as I work my hands over her body. In seconds, her bra and thong are gone, and then she stands before me in nothing but a pair of goddamn thigh-high stockings. Stockings that make my dick like fucking granite, and even that's too much between us.

I drag my mouth down, over her jaw, her throat, her chest, her tits. I lick and stroke my way down until my tongue finds her navel, and she sucks in a sharp breath. I smile against her belly, and then settle back to roll the stockings down her legs and tug them from her feet. I'm rough enough that I probably ruined them, but I don't give a shit.

"C'mon, baby."

I grab her hand and stand, leading her to the bed. It surprises me when her hands come up to my chest and she pushes me back. Next thing I know, she's on her knees before me again.

"You're sure you want to do this?" I force myself to ask the question.

She wraps her fingers around my cock with an oddly secretive smile. "Ajia, baby, I have wanted this for so long, you'd be shocked. You thought little Bree Gallagher didn't think about stuff like this? You were wrong."

"Ye-ah?" The word comes out of my mouth with an odd break in the middle, exactly when she strokes her hand up and down my cock.

"Yeah." The smile is still there as she leans down to kiss the head. "I was still in high school at the time I first fantasized about this."

"Uh…huh?"

It was supposed to be a laugh, but suddenly I can't think. She's licking me again, up and down my shaft, her tongue following a rhythm set by her hand. It was good before, but now, harder and more on the edge, it's fan-fucking-tastic.

"You're too big for me to take all of it in my mouth." Her lips move against the length of my cock. "I'll have to practice that. But, God, baby—"

This time I do laugh, but it's ragged. "I can't think of anything better than your mouth on any part of me. Right now. Just like you're doing."

Her smile is seduction itself, and she leans in to take my cock in her mouth. Her tongue swirls around like she's licking an ice cream cone, and my hips follow her rhythm. Again and again she licks, sucks, bobs her head up and down. Each time she takes me a little deeper, and when the tip reaches the back of her throat again, she doesn't gag this time.

Jesus, no one has ever loved me this way. No mouth—or pussy—has ever felt this good. It feels like I was born to be here in this moment with her, and she must feel the same way. She groans deep in her throat, and the vibration sends me to another level of arousal.

My eyes threaten to drift closed, but I'm driven to watch, to touch her, to be present in every fucking second. I palm her breasts, tightening my fingers around her tits to hold their fullness. Her nipples stiffen, demand more, and I pluck at them eagerly. I close my thumb and forefinger around each one, pulling and pinching. I roll them, palm them, and then do it all again.

I learned early on that Bree's nipples are sensitive, and tonight is no exception. She moans around my cock again, thrusts her tits hard against my hands, and moves her head quicker, harder.

"Oh, baby, yeah. Just like that." My hands are suddenly in her hair, and she groans. "You want me to fuck your mouth, sweetheart?"

She doesn't stop, doesn't pull back, just nods and keeps sucking me with that wonderful, amazing mouth.

I tug on her hair, pull her head back far enough that I can kiss her, and whisper against her mouth. "Hold still, baby, and wrap your hands around my wrists."

She does as I ask, and I kiss her again. "Yes. Just like that. Squeeze my wrists if it's too much, yeah?"

She runs her tongue over her lips and nods again. "Okay."

"The words, baby. I need to hear them, know you understand."

She tightens her grip around my wrists. "I squeeze if it's too much."

"Good girl."

Another kiss, and I stand. She opens her mouth before I can push forward, and I take slow, shallow thrusts. The sensitive front ridge of my cock drags over her tongue, and she groans deep in her throat. Breathing through her nose, I can feel her jaw relax. Her throat follows, and her head moves against my grip as though encouraging me to go deeper.

I do. I can't help it, and I move faster. My breath comes in heavy pants. Jesus, it feels so fucking *good,* her moist heat around me and a twisting, changing desire that softens, then sharpens her expression.

One hand clutches my wrist like I told her, but she drops the other to my balls. She caresses me there, tightens her fingers just enough to urge me closer to coming, and then she releases me with a soft, soothing caress. She does it again and again, and all the while I fuck her mouth with control that's almost gone.

"Baby." I groan, and her answering moan, deep in her chest, spurs me farther. Faster.

I can't hold off much longer. The tingling at the base of my spine and the way my balls tighten warn me I'm about to go off like a rocket.

"You sure you want me to come in your mouth, baby?" I gasp.

She tightens her fingers around my balls, and moves her head in rhythm with my thrusts. *Holy fucking Christ!* Does she really want my cum in her mouth, down her throat?

196

A sharp thrust, this one hard and deep enough to make her gag, and I'm done. My orgasm takes over, and my cum shoots over her tongue and to the back of her throat. She slows her pace, but licks and sucks and carries me through the orgasm like the perfect woman she is.

Gradually, my cock begins to soften, but still she keeps her mouth around me. She suckles easier, lighter, and I know she must have swallowed everything I gave her.

I let her have her way until finally she releases me. She places a soft open-mouthed kiss just above my hipbone and then rests her cheek against my pelvis. She peeks up at me through a veil of lashes and offers a soft smile.

"I love the way you fucking taste," she says with enough satisfaction that I'd have thought she was the one who just came.

I laugh. She hasn't come—yet—but she will. For the rest of the goddamn night.

CHAPTER 21

BREE

Ajia's chest makes a nice pillow. A little hard and muscular, but maybe that's why I love it so much. I never thought I'd get the chance to actually *be* with him like this.

He kisses the top of my head and pulls me closer to his side. "You okay, baby?" he whispers against my hair.

I tilt my head back to look up at him. A floor lamp in the far corner is the only light in the room, but I can see a softness in his gaze that's new. The warmth in his eyes goes clear through me.

"Pretty sure I've never been better." I offer my mouth for his kiss.

He doesn't hesitate, takes my lips with his and sweeps his tongue through my mouth. Again and again. Sending arousal and awareness shooting through me to my very core. I'm so—

"Goddammit, Ajia! Open this fucking door! Right this fucking minute!" It's Knox, and he's pounding on the door like an enraged madman from a straight-to-video movie. My breathing stumbles, and my heart begins to pound.

Ajia's look pierces me until he closes his eyes for a long, slow moment. He lets out a slow, deep breath. "Looks like we waited too long, baby."

"I…you think he knows?"

Gently, he disentangles himself from me and climbs from the bed. "What do you think?" he asks as he pulls on a pair of jeans. Commando. Zipped, maybe, but unbuttoned. He had been getting hard again.

I push myself up as he tosses me one of his T-shirts. A Led Zeppelin classic—one of his favorites. It's a couple of sizes too big for me, but it doesn't matter. I pull it over my head, clueless right now where my dress or underwear might be.

Ajia nods toward the bed. "I don't care if you stay there, but be prepared for it to rile him up."

I look from side to side and then nod and stand. "Right."

The pounding comes again. "Ajia, you fucker! Open the goddamn door!"

"Stay back." It's a command, pure and simple, and I listen—for now.

He walks over to the door, unlocks, and opens it. I can see enough to tell my brother fills the doorway like some avenging angel. It hits me then, in an entirely new way, how equally matched Ajia and Knox are physically. They're virtually the same height and the same build. But Knox is one pissed-off motherfucker, while Ajia is…stoic. Resigned.

What the hell does that reaction mean?

"Where is she?" my brother demands. Ajia's broad, muscular back prevents me from seeing much, but the tension radiating between the men is palpable. I hate it, but I understand it. I've never seen Knox so aggressive!

Nobody moves, and then Ajia slowly steps back. He spreads one arm wide, indicating me, or maybe the room. It doesn't matter, because Knox shoves his way inside. He's still dressed in the gray suit, his hair randomly pulled out of the proper, more formal-looking ponytail all the guys wore tonight. His eyes look bright and wild, darting over me in Ajia's T-shirt, the rumpled bed, and then back to Ajia in his unfastened jeans. I don't have to wonder as recognition settles over him. We all know what it looks like—what Knox expected it to be…what it *is*—and in that second, I curse myself for asking Ajia to keep us a secret. Even for a day.

"You motherfucker!"

Before I see him even move, Knox's fist connects with Ajia's jaw, and Ajia stumbles back against the wall.

"Knox!" I shout my brother's name as I race across the room. "Stop it, right now! Goddammit!"

I shove myself between Ajia and him as Knox pulls back his arm again. His eyes flicker over me, enraged, but I don't think he'll try anything more with me in the middle. And, in some ways, he's almost more controlled than I would have expected. He always punches first and asks questions later—which, I guess, he did.

When—and how—did he figure things out? It could be worse, I remind myself. He must have had a little time to start coming to terms with what's happening.

I don't really trust my brother right now, but from where I'm standing, I know I'm safe to turn my back on him. For a minute.

"Ajia, baby." I reach for his face. "Are you okay?"

He intercepts my hand and lowers it to my side. I swallow back a momentary rejection, but it disappears when he links our fingers together. "That's your free one, bro. Maybe I even deserved it. But any more and I fight back."

"Get the fuck away from him, Bree."

I look at my brother, aiming for a composed expression I don't really feel. "How did you find out?"

"That's your question? You got nothing else to say?"

"Knox—"

"No, A." I cut him off and squeeze my fingers around his. "This is between my brother and me."

"Fuck if it is," snaps Knox. "He's the one—"

"Forget it." I take a step closer to Ajia, not because I need his warmth or his strength—although I'll admit it feels damn good—but I want to make a point. I'm taking a stand, and I want Knox to get it. *No mistake.* "You have *no say* in this."

He moves closer and his lips curl into a sneer. "Oh, baby girl, I have a lot to fucking say about this. And you're going to listen to every fucking word."

Ajia slips his arms around my waist. "Cool the fuck off, man."

"Cool off?" Knox shakes his head, and his laugh is ugly. *"Cool off?* You have no fucking clue what's going on inside of me right now."

"Got a pretty good idea. I get it, man. Let's talk." Ajia lifts a hand to smooth it over my hair. He tilts my head back to look at him. "You okay, baby? Why don't you go on back to your room, and—"

"Good idea," puts in Knox. "You don't need—"

I step away from them both. "Don't fucking tell me what I need to do! Either of you," I snap. "I'm a big girl now. *I* get to decide what I do—and that's *not* leaving the two of you alone to do whatever stupid shit you'd end up doing."

"Bree…c'mon. You—this fucker—"

"What, Knox? What is it you think you have to say? Because I thought I put you on notice in Phoenix. Weren't you listening? My life, my body—*my decision!* You don't get to say one goddamn word about *anything."*

"You weren't talking that way when you wanted help to get away from Gabe."

"Son of a—"

"Knox, you goddamn *asshole!"* I cut off Ajia's curse. "That's not the fucking same thing, and you know it."

I hear the fury vibrating in my voice, but it's suddenly too much to tolerate. All of it. The shit with Gabe. The groupies and the tour. The parties, the rumors, and those bitchy women today. My time with Ajia is private, special…a dream come true. And my brother wants to spoil it?

For once I'm too mad to cry.

I stalk up to Knox until I can't take another step. I stare so furiously, he has no choice but to look at me. I poke his chest with one very stiff finger. "Listen to me, Knox, because this is the *last* time I'm talking to you about any of it.

"That shit with Gabe wasn't about my choices, my life, and you damn well know it. It was about *our mother's husband* trying to force me into something sexual! *Something I didn't—and don't—want.* My relationship with Ajia is completely different."

Knox opens his mouth, seems to hesitate, but then it's like the words force themselves from him. "He's like your fucking brother!"

I can't help it; I laugh. It's a rude, ugly sound and suits me perfectly. "Do you *hear* yourself? I have *never* seen Ajia as my brother, and you damn well know it. Everybody in the fucking band knows it. Hell, probably half of Austin knows it!"

I give my head a sharp shake and force myself to continue. "I thought I was so clever, keeping my little a secret, but y'all knew. Y'all must have thought it was so cute. Silly little Bree with her big crush on a *man* like Ajia Stone.

"Well, the truth is, I've been in love with him since the first day we met. *Love,* Knox, not some stupid teenage crush. It's been five years—*five years*—and my feelings have only gotten stronger."

He doesn't like what I said—I can see it in the way his eyes have gone dark—and that, apparently, puts him on the offensive. "So all that shit you said in Phoenix?" he demands. "It was all fucking lies?"

"No." It's Ajia who answers, and he steps up close behind me again. "It was all true. Every fucking word."

"So you didn't start fucking her until—"

"Knox, I swear to God I'm going to pound the fucking shit out of you!" Ajia's fury burns at my back.

"Get over there, Knox!" I jab my finger toward the table and chairs across the room.

"Fuck you! I'm—"

"Get your ass over there!" I go up on my tiptoes. This is all getting on my last fricking nerve, and though there hasn't been bloodshed yet, there will be if my brother doesn't start cooperating. It'll be *me* who pounds the shit out of him. "You two are *not* fighting over me!"

I glare at my brother until he finally cooperates. Ajia understands me a little differently—as a lover, not a brother—but does he *have* to stroll over to the bed and just sort of sprawl against the headboard? He knows that's going to torque Knox off even more.

I take up a spot perched against the low dresser on the opposite wall. "Okay," I start. "It's time for an actual discussion. An *adult* discussion. You're going to talk—and *listen.*"

His glare is my brother's only response.

"You never answered me. How did you find out?"

Knox opens his mouth like he's going to snap off something nasty, but I'm through with this bullshit. "Answers, Knox. *Adult conversation,*" I remind him.

He shakes his head. "How do you think? The fucking internet."

"Again?" snaps Ajia.

Knox glares at us both. "What the fuck did you expect? You tell some chicks at the party that you're keeping Bree all to yourself, and you think that isn't going to run the room in, like, five seconds? Then the photographer—the legit one—got all kinds of shots of the two of you together."

"It's what Marty wanted," says Ajia stiffly.

"Yeah? Including one of you *kissing* when you got on the elevator together?"

"That doesn't sound so bad," I say carefully, even as I wonder exactly what Ajia said about us and what *chicks* did he say it to? It couldn't have been the ones from the restroom—could it?

"Then maybe it was the video of the two of you making out in the fucking elevator."

"What the fuck?" Ajia straightens on the bed.

I look between the men. "What video?"

"Security footage."

I blink and stare at Ajia. He shrugs, but there's disappointment in his eyes. "Never thought about security cameras in the elevator."

He feels bad. That we made out in public, or that we got caught? I shouldn't be questioning that kind of thing now, but this is all too new to me. *We're* too new. Shit's all over the place, and—

"How'd anybody get that?" I'm as frustrated as I am curious. God, I'm going to have to learn about this stuff if it's going to be part of my life—*our* lives—now.

Knox shrugs. "How do the tabloids get any of that shit? Somebody knows somebody who…fill in the blank. I guess somebody had an in with security at the hotel."

Okay. I nod for myself. Lesson learned, not that it helps right now.

"So. You gonna answer my questions now?"

"As long as they're reasonable." I swallow. "What do you want to know?"

Knox shoots Ajia a murderous look. "How long?"

"Recently." I don't want to say any more than I have to. Not because I'm hiding it—I'm not! It's just none of Knox's business. "A couple of days, actually."

"C'mon, baby." Ajia leans forward and gives me a soft smile. "You know things have been different since we left Austin."

"*Austin!* Jesus, Bree! You saw some chick sucking him off there! He's a goddamn manwhore and you—"

"Who was there to comfort me when I had that nightmare, Knox? It was Ajia, because you were too busy fucking your one-and-done for the night. And last night? *Last night* I came to Ajia's room, because I was sick of listening to you and your fuck of the night. 'Spank my ass, Knox, and make me come on your cock!' Or maybe it was when you said, 'Take my cock down your throat!'"

His eyes get big and even darker, but I don't wait for him to speak. "You're such a goddamn hypocrite, Knox. You're fucking anything with two legs and a pussy. No different from what you say Ajia was doing. Yeah, I get it. But if he and I want to see what we've got between us—you don't get a say!"

"See what you've got?"

I nod. Emphatically. "There are no guarantees, bro. I know that. But we'll never know unless we give it a shot. And we're only a couple of days into *that.*"

"Bree…" He says my name softly, slowly. "You're different from most girls. Different from most chicks we see on tours. You—" He shakes his head. "He's no good for you, baby girl."

Ajia speaks before I can. "He's right about that, kitten. We all know damn well that you're too fucking good for me."

"That is such bullshit, and you both know it!" I narrow my eyes to match my expression with my tone. "You two—" I point between them "—wouldn't be such good friends, and Ajia and I wouldn't have this *connection,* if it were. So don't try to pull any of that crap on me."

I'm so out of patience for all this. As much as I *know* this is none of my brother's business, I want it over. Now. Whatever that means.

Maybe a *little* explanation will end it for good.

"Knox, sweetie…" I give him all my attention. "Here's the deal. I'm twenty in a couple of weeks. Not a teenager any longer! Most girls lose their virginity in high school, the back seat of a car or some party or—who the hell knows? They're with a boy who hasn't a clue what he's doing, they're lucky if he has a condom, and the only thing a girl gets out of it is the fact that she isn't a virgin anymore. I—"

"Uh…Bree. Kitten?"

I ignore Aja and keep my eyes on Knox. "I was actually lucky. That wasn't the case for me. I—"

My brother straightens like he's got a goddamn pole suddenly shoved up his ass. "You telling me he busted your cherry?"

"Son of a bitch." I hear Ajia's sigh.

Shit. I realize my mistake then, when it's too late. Well, I'll have to brazen it through.

"That is *not* what I'm trying to tell you—and it's a disgusting way to think of it—but, yes, Ajia was my first. That's because I *wanted* him to be. I…waited. I had other chances, there were other boys. I didn't take them."

"Because of *this motherfucker?*"

"Because I wanted to be with Ajia, yes. And you're just gonna have to get used to it. Accept it. He's your friend, part of the band. Those things aren't going to change simply because I slept with him."

Knox wants to move. He wants to hit something. I see the barely-leashed emotion vibrating through him. I know this is a lot for him to take in, but it shouldn't be. *I told him!* In Austin and Phoenix. He's had time to prepare for this. He should have known it was coming.

"There's shit you don't know, Bree." His voice is low and rough. "He's not the guy you think he is."

"Knox, let me do it."

Ajia's voice sounds oddly ragged, and I look at him. His whiskey-colored eyes are dark with pain.

"Ajia?"

"I'll tell you everything, baby. I was going to tonight, anyway."

Knox snorts, but I ignore him and shake my head. "I know everything I need to." I look back at my brother. "He's not some stranger I just happened to run across, you know."

Knox glares past me, at Ajia, I'm sure. "He's got secrets, baby girl. Shit you don't know. Shit that—"

"Well, fuck me, Knox." I frown. "We've all got shit, and you know that as well as anybody. Ajia's can't be any worse—"

"Don't kid yourself, Bree. If you knew the truth about this fucker, you wouldn't say that."

"Don't start with your drama queen shit, Knox. Now isn't the time."

"You gonna tell her?" he snaps.

Ajia is sitting so straight on the bed, his spine must be screaming. "Yeah," he says without moving. "I said I would."

"What?" I look between the two of them. "What are you two talking about?"

"Your *boyfriend* here." Knox snarls the word.

"Knox…" He's really pissing me off.

"Let me get the conversation started." I've never heard that tone before, both snotty and demanding at the same time.

"About what?"

"The girl."

"What girl?"

"The one he killed."

CHAPTER 22

AJIA

I don't say anything until Knox is gone. Literally, nothing. What's there to say? He's done his damage, and there's no going back.

Bree doesn't say much, either, except to tell him to get out. She ignores him after that, totally focused on me. I know it, feel it, can't really bring myself to look at her. Yet. We need to talk—alone—and we all know it.

Knox doesn't argue much about leaving Bree alone with me. Why should he? He thinks he's getting his way. And maybe he is. He doesn't even try to hide his satisfied smirk as he strolls out. Fucker.

I wait until the door clicks shut behind him, and even after that. "I should have told you," I finally say, soft enough I'm not sure she can hear me.

"Why didn't you?"

She stares at me as I sit on the bed. She's standing maybe halfway between me and the door. My Zeppelin T-shirt looks so fucking good on her. Her legs are gorgeous, surprisingly long for a short girl and sexy as hell.

She takes a step toward me when I don't answer right away. "Ajia?"

I shrug, because it's all I can do. "I wanted to. Meant to. Knew I should. It's why I told you we needed to talk tonight. Then we—" I break off and offer her a sick fucking smile that she doesn't return, so I give her honesty. "The truth is, as much as I wanted to tell you everything, *needed* to tell you, I was more afraid."

Her tongue darts out to wet her lips, and she takes a step closer. "Of what, A? I don't think I've ever seen you scared of anything."

I snort an ugly laugh. "Oh, baby, if you only knew. I'm the weakest fucking person you'll ever meet."

"Ajia…sweetheart—" The look she gives me is so tender, not at all what I deserve.

"You know how you wanted some time—just us—before we told Knox? It's the same for me. I wanted that kind of time before you found out what a piece of shit I really am."

She sighs and gives a little shake to her head. I love the way her hair brushes over her shoulders. Makes me want to sink my fingers deep and pull her against me for a kiss. Will I get to do any of that after I tell her everything?

"Okay," she says. "So we've both been outed. Now what?"

"Now I tell you everything."

I so fucking don't want to do this, even as I know it's the one thing I fucking *have* to do.

I shift around to sit straight on the side of the bed. I know I shouldn't, but I pat the mattress beside me. An invitation I shouldn't make and one she sure as hell shouldn't accept, but it's out there now. She blinks, looks from the spot next to me and back again. I can't tell what she's thinking, but she finally comes closer. She doesn't sit exactly where I wanted, but she does take a place next to me.

"Okay," she says again. "I'll listen to whatever it is you need to say. I want to hear about the things that give you so much pain."

She's looking at me. I know because I feel the pull of her gaze, but I stare straight ahead. Doesn't matter that I knew this was coming. That I don't want to see the look on her face when I tell her what a weak, disgusting son of a bitch I really am.

"If I do this, it's everything. Shit not everybody knows."

I catch the movement as she nods. "Everything. I want everything you are, Ajia Stone."

It takes me a minute. I haven't actually talked about it in a long, long time. It's never far from my head, yeah, but I stopped saying the words years ago.

"Her name was Lara." I blow out a heavy breath. "We got together when we were fifteen. My first real *girlfriend.* She was just a girl I'd known at school—and then she was more."

I think back to the slim, leggy girl I'd known, and even thought I'd loved back then. I didn't, not in a way that would have made it past high school, but in tenth grade, we were totally into each other.

"She was older than me." My lips twist in what's supposed to be a smile, but I know it isn't. "She turned sixteen a few months before I did, and her folks gave her a car. We gave the back seat a hell of a workout. We were each other's firsts."

Somehow, I'm able to give a soft laugh as I remember. "It was over almost before it started. I knew what to do, even had a condom, but being that close to a girl's naked pussy?" I slant a quick glance in Bree's direction. Her small smile is soft, understanding.

"I went off like a firecracker. After a few more times, it got better, and we tried other shit. It was fucking heaven for a fifteen-year-old kid! And we *were* kids. We did the usual other shit. That meant drinking when somebody could score beer. One night, a buddy got hold of some tequila. Shitty stuff, but who cared?"

"Sure it wasn't Knox who bought it?" Bree asks with a trace of amusement in her voice. "The cheaper the better for him."

My lips twitch. Her attempt to lighten the tension warms me. It doesn't work, but it means a hell of a lot that she tried.

"I didn't know him then, but you're right. He has lousy taste in booze."

I sigh, knowing I have to say the rest. "Lara got wasted, and so did my best friend, Mason, and his girlfriend, Jill. I'd pretty much stopped drinking early on. Kept thinking about her new car and how pissed her parents would be if anything happened." I look at Bree for real this time. "It was totally selfish. That car wasn't mine, but I loved it. It was freedom, a place to fuck. No way was I losing that."

She nods, seriously. She gets it. Every teenager is desperate for independence and privacy. Hell, she's still fighting Knox for it!

"Lara and I fought over who should drive home. I wasn't sixteen so still didn't have my license, but—" I shake my head "—she was too fucking drunk to do it. She only had permission for me in the car, but I couldn't leave Mason and Jill on their own. I thought I was Superman or some fucking thing."

The words die out on their own. I remember how everybody piled into the car, laughing and shrieking. Mason got Jill in the back seat, and they started making out. Lara was in the passenger's seat, pouting, and I was kind of pissed. I was trying to do the right thing, and she wanted to fight about it?

The mattress shifts as Bree moves closer. She strokes one hand down my arm, and the heat of her skin against mine shoots through me.

"It was okay for a while. Lara started messing with the radio, and then *Give it to Me* came on. She loved that song, loved anything JT did, but that one always got her all crazy. Next thing I knew, she was trying to give me a blow-job, and I'm still driving."

A breath huffs from Bree's lungs. Not sure what it means, but I know she's never done anything like that. I look at her, at the fear in her dark green eyes, and I nod.

"I can do a lot of shit now. Done a lot of shit. But a horny fifteen-year-old kid without any real experience or stamina? My reactions were off. I couldn't concentrate on my dick *and* the road."

I swallow so I can force out the rest of the words. "I remember looking down. Seeing her head in my lap. Feeling her lips around my cock. Swear to God, I don't know why I didn't blow my load right then."

Bree's rubbing my arm again, but I barely feel it. Can't bring myself to look at her. "When I looked up—" my breath chokes a little "—there was a deer standing in the road. A fucking deer. I might have yelled—don't know for sure—and must have swerved. Lara's head came up, I couldn't see and.... *Fuuuuck.*"

I close my eyes, shudder like a fucking pussy, but the sounds in my head only get louder. The engine squeals, metal scrapes and twists with a horrible deadly groan, the inhuman screaming. And then…nothing.

Bree's next to me suddenly, hip to hip. Don't know when she moved, or maybe it was me. Somehow, she presses against me and wraps her arms around my waist. I want to hold her, sink into her softness, forget in her kisses, but I can't. Not when there's so much more I have to say.

"Next thing I remember, I was all scrunched down in the seat. Lara was between me and the air bag. She didn't move, didn't answer, even when I screamed her name. I could hear Mason and Jill moaning…and that's the last clear memory I have."

"Ajia. Baby—"

"Except for the blood, everything else is fuzzy," I interrupt. I can't let her say anything else. Not yet. "Like a flash of a dream you really can't remember. I got out of the car and called 911, I guess. And—*fuck!*" Jesus, I hate how hard this is. "I wasn't hurt bad. Lara's body took the full impact. She died instantly."

"Oh, no." I hear tears thicken Bree's voice, but I keep going.

"Mason broke his back. Still has problems. Jill…traumatic brain injury. She has the mentality of a seven year old. Didn't think she'd live for a while."

"Baby, I'm so sorry." Bree runs a hand up and down my back, and she kisses a spot on my chest, right above the Wycked Obsession logo tat.

"What the fuck was I *thinking?* Why didn't I *do something?* I've never been able to answer those questions."

"It's bad, A. No doubt about it. And I know it hurts. But it doesn't make you a killer."

"There's more." I slip my fingers under her chin so I can tilt her head back. She needs to look at me while I say the rest. "Never quite knew how it happened, but the cops pieced together a story that had Lara driving and me trying to—fuck, I don't know—save the day or something."

"You were." Her gaze clings to mine, and I can't look away. "Maybe not in the same way they thought, but you were."

"Everybody kept telling me what a great job I'd done. How I'd tried so hard." I shake my head with an ugly laugh. *Fuck me. I* hadn't done a great job. I caused the whole fucking thing!"

"You didn't tell them the truth?"

I blow out a ragged breath and lift one shoulder. "I tried, but people weren't listening. I was out of it for a day or two. Shock, they said. A concussion. They kept me in the hospital, and I finally saw Mason when I got out. He was fucked up, in the hospital, and there I was, trying to piece all that shit together. He was on some good fucking drugs for the pain, in and out of it, and he gave me advice I wish I'd ignored."

"What?"

I close my eyes. "'Let it go, man,' he said. 'Lara's dead and we gotta live with this shit. Let 'em think she was driving. So what? It won't change a damn thing if they know it was you. It woulda been her if she got her way.' And I listened! *Fuck.*" My chest feels all empty and achy. "Fuck me, I *listened.*"

Bree kisses me again, right in the same place. "You were a kid," she whispers. "Fifteen and scared."

"Fifteen and stupid."

"You're allowed to be stupid at fifteen."

I swallow. "I've been so pissed off at Lara for fucking around like that. Then I'd get pissed off at myself for letting her get drunk. For letting her go down on me in the car. So much shit has gone on in my head. Mostly guilt cause I didn't get everybody home. I didn't even get hurt, except for some cuts and bruises and the concussion. And then—what a fucking piece of shit I am for letting *her* take the blame."

"You never told anybody?"

"I tried, off and on, for a couple of years. First I tried to hide in music, the one thing I always loved. I wrote a bunch of shitty songs about it. Haven't touched the subject since. I was depressed as fuck, and the best I could do was just fucking *survive.*"

I take a deep breath. "I finally got the balls to tell my dad the truth around the second anniversary of the accident, but Mason denied it. Everybody thought it was some sort of survivor's guilt or something. I tried to talk to Lara's parents, but they said the same thing. Nobody would listen."

Bree's arms tighten. "And so, here you are, stuck with the guilt and the pain and all the shit that only makes you feel bad about yourself."

I shake my head. "Here I am, the same piece of shit I was ten years ago. Lara's still dead. Mason's hooked on painkillers and prescription meds, still refusing treatment that might give him a chance at a *real life.* And Jill still lives at home, happy as any first grader would be. And me? Hell, I'm Ajia fucking Stone! A fucking rock star with money and women and a career I don't fucking deserve."

Bree climbs over me then, straddles me and looks at me straight on. Sorrow darkens her gaze, and her lips turn down with pain. "Ajia. Oh, baby. You didn't *kill* anybody."

I stiffen, and she clutches my biceps to stay steady. "Weren't you *listening?*" It's a harsher demand than I meant, but I don't apologize. *"I did!* I killed and hurt people beyond their ability to recover. I destroyed families and lives and—"

"It was an *accident."* She takes my face between her small, gentle hands. "You were young and not prepared when life got out of control. You didn't *try* to make any of that happen. It was a terrible, terrible accident, and you did the best you could."

I shake my head. "My best. What a fucking joke."

She leans in, presses a soft, quick kiss against my mouth. "Don't take this the wrong way. Please don't. But maybe it's about more than just you."

"What?" I blink a couple of times. "What does that mean?"

"Well..." She glances away for a heartbeat. "I'm not sure I know how to explain, but...I had some pretty heavy questions when my dad left. Mom was upset, Knox was pissed, and I only had my grandparents to talk to. Mom's parents. It took years, yeah, but I finally got it that Dad leaving pretty much had nothing to do with me. Sure, I was one of the people left paying the consequences, but he didn't think squat about me when he made any of his crappy decisions. It was all about him, and I was just collateral damage."

I don't know how to respond, and then she continues before I figure it out.

"It was Gram who helped me see that I *could* live with the fallout of what he'd done, because he'd never know or care either way. What he did to me wasn't anywhere on his radar. It just didn't matter, and *I* needed to take responsibility for my life and my choices from there on out. You can do the same."

"Yeah?" I close my eyes and think of all the fucked-up choices I've made and how they've affected other people. Even her! That girl at the party in Phoenix is a perfect example!

"I've done such a fucking outstanding job of it so far," I snort. "Look at all the great fucking decisions I've made and how much they helped people." I swallow and force myself to meet her gaze. "Look how much I've hurt you."

She shakes her head and gives me another sweet kiss. "That wasn't about me. I understand that now. It was about you making *you* feel as bad as you possibly could." She smiles sadly. "And it's proof that this shit isn't easy. I mean, look at how I've fucked up!"

"You?" I've tried not to touch her, but I can't help it anymore. I push her hair back from her face, slide the backs of my fingers down her cheek and rest my palm over her shoulder. "You've done everything *right.*"

She reaches across her chest to lay her hand over mine. "Oh, A, you know that isn't true. I lost myself in the demands of school and didn't really live my life while I—I don't know—*pined* for you. I was afraid to take a chance. And I haven't taken control of anything where Gabe's concerned. I just ran away. Going on tour with you and the guys reminded me it was time to step up and do the right thing for *me.*"

"And what was that?"

"First, to see if my feelings for you were real. And find out if you could feel the same way about me."

I close my eyes and tighten my fingers over her shoulder. Goddamn. I *so* should have left this girl alone.

"And you know what I found out?"

"What?" My voice is hoarse.

"Happy endings *are* possible. I really *do* love you. Not as a friend. Not as my brother's friend. Not even as a rock star. I love Ajia Stone, the man who makes me feel wonderful and amazing things. The man who does wicked things to my body. The man who takes care of me, even when I think I don't need it. The man who makes every day better by just being here with me."

"Baby." I wrap my arms around her and fold her against my chest. "I'm not that man. I'm not that good. I'm a selfish bastard. Can't you see that?"

"I see that *you* want to believe it. That you've tried hard to convince yourself and everybody else. But you're *wrong.*"

"An innocent girl *died.* I let her take the blame for my mistakes!"

Bree snuggles against my chest, kisses me there. "She wasn't innocent, A. That's what I'm trying to tell you. She got drunk, even knowing she was supposed to be driving. She messed around and distracted you when you were trying to get her and your friends home safe. And you *did* try to set it right. Nobody wanted to hear it—for whatever reason. You're all collateral damage of each other's decisions, so let it go. There's a reason for it. We might never understand what that is. All you can be sure of is that you're here doing what you're supposed to."

"So you're saying that God wrecked some lives so I could have this one?"

"No. I'm saying that maybe you couldn't save those lives in the way you thought you should, but maybe you're touching other lives. Helping others get through a hard time. People listen to your songs, and it gives them a reason to go on. A reason to hope."

"I'm not that guy," I insist. "I still drink. A lot sometimes. And until you, I fucked random girls who meant nothing to me. Girls whose name I never even wanted to know. A *good guy* doesn't do shit like that."

"No? Well, maybe a good guy who's trying to prove to the world that he *isn't* so good does. A guy who thinks he's a piece of shit and wants to prove it to anybody who looks his way. A guy who's torn between being self-destructive and wanting to succeed for the benefit of others."

I'm all breathless again. *"Jesus, Bree.* How can you see that shit in me? You make me sound so much better than I really am."

"And you make yourself sound so much worse. What would change if everybody blamed you instead of Lara?"

"What do you mean?"

"If they believed you. You already said it. Lara'd still be dead, Mason'd be in pain and hooked on pills, and Jill would still have a traumatic brain injury. No different, except that everybody would know you were driving and trying to get the others home safe. You would have *still* tried to do the right thing, and it would *still be an accident."*

My heart beats fast and irregular. Bree's saying shit I want to hear. Things I want to believe. But it's just not possible—is it?

No. I didn't want any of that stuff to happen to people I cared about. *Jesus, no!* I want to change it, fix it, take the pain myself so the others don't have to feel it. Except…no matter what I do, all of our realities remain the same.

And that's supposed to be okay?

I close my eyes and let my head fall forward until my forehead meets Bree's. She settles her hands at my waist and sits unmoving. Somehow, in that moment, I know we're connected, and she's letting me try to make sense of everything she said. Of all the hopes and fears that have haunted me for so long.

I don't know how long we stay that way. Long enough that my thoughts settle into something like a ragged prayer set on repeat.

What if she's right? Could she be right? What if she's right?

Finally, Bree moves. She leans into me, and then her lips find mine. Her kiss is gentle and caring. It's like she feels the same about me, no matter what I said, what I've done.

"Ajia. Baby. Listen to me." She kisses me again. "I love you, and you know that. This isn't the first time I've said it. But I mean it more now than I ever have."

"Oh, sweetheart." I reach for the back of her neck, to pull her closer, but she shakes her head and slides off my lap.

"You don't know how bad I want to stay here. Hold you, make love with you, take your mind off everything except *us*. But as much as I want that, you need time alone."

"Time?" I blink and look at her, wearing my T-shirt and her hair falling all around her shoulders. "You sure *you* don't need some time? Away from me."

"For what?" She smiles softly. "To think about how much I love you? No, baby." She shakes her head. "This was...hard. Knox was an ass, and what you told me wasn't easy. I know that. So maybe you need to, you know, work it all out in your head."

She's probably right. Hell, a part of me knows just how fucking right she is. But I don't like it, one damn bit.

"What if you wake up in the morning and change your mind?" I fucking hate the question.

"About what?"

"Me."

Her laugh is easy and pure. "Oh, A. I haven't changed my mind in five fucking years, even when I knew you were with other girls. When I *saw* you with other girls. Haven't you figured out yet that, as long as you want me, you're *stuck* with me?"

I don't know how to answer that. How can she—*my Bree*—make me feel all healed and put together when I've just told her all the worst of my fucked-up sins?

She kisses me, quick and hard. "Sleep, baby. Think. Do whatever you need to put this in the past where it belongs. I'll be here for you when you're ready."

And in an instant, she's gone.

CHAPTER 23

BREE

I don't sleep very well after I get back to my room. It's not just because I'm alone, or because I miss Ajia's hard, warm body next to me. That's true, even after only a couple of days. More than that, I keep thinking about everything Ajia told me about himself and his past.

What happened to him breaks my heart. Worse, it hurts that he sees himself in such a fucked-up way. I can't defend it—at all; he made mistakes. So did Lara, Mason, and Jill. But Ajia isn't the only bad guy in this. He's let his guilt and grief twist the way he sees himself, but how do I get him to see that?

He's been fighting to be heard for a long time, and nobody's listening.

The sun's bright in the room when I finally wake up. I lie in bed, thinking about Ajia, all the things he said and what else I know about his past. He grew up in a small town in the Texas Hill Country, moved to Austin after high school, and met Knox at a concert a couple of months later. They hit it off, and Wycked Obsession was born a few months later.

As far as I've always known, Ajia had just turned nineteen and never looked back.

Now I know that isn't true. I don't know how often he lets himself remember the shit that happened, but he's lived with it in his head all the same. He's been running from it with every decision he'd made.

Just like me.

The thought sneaks into my brain like a drifting fog. It swirls around me, and then it deepens, sharpens, and it's there.

I've run from what Gabe tried to do, hidden it from my mom, and tried to pretend it wasn't important. It didn't matter enough—*I* didn't matter enough—to open up and tell the truth.

I can't hide anymore from what I've been doing. I can't keep this secret and let it do to me the kinds of things that Ajia's secrets did to him. He carried that pain for a long time, did hurtful, self-destructive things to punish himself. I don't want to ruin what we might have by doing the same thing.

I have to tell my mom the truth about Gabe.

I hate knowing that. Hate that I have to be the one. Hate it worse than anything I've ever done in my life. And yet, how can I let my mom stay in a marriage without at least *trying* to be honest about what happened?

I remember what I told Ajia that night in Austin.

There are two outcomes if I say anything. One is that she doesn't believe me and it ruins our relationship. Two is that she believes me and it ruins her marriage. Either way, she loses, and I won't be a part of it.

That wasn't the only time I said something like that—and I believed it then, with all my heart. A part of me still believes it. But the rest of me understands the cost. I'm letting Mom live a lie that can come back and tear her life apart at any fucking moment. Who knows what—or who—Gabe is doing?

Clearer than anything else, Ajia's truth shows me the reality of what my silence could produce. Keeping secrets has torn him to shreds, taunted him into promiscuous and self-destructive behavior, and ruined his self-image. I can't give Gabe Richmond the power to do that to me—or be the trigger waiting to explode his marriage to my mom and devastate her again.

I squirm under the light bedcovers. This new awareness makes me a little excited and a *lot* anxious. I want to run down to Ajia's room and talk it over with him, explain my new understanding, thank him for his part in it.

But—no. He has enough to deal with right now. I'm the one who told him to work it out on his own. Figure out how to put the past behind him. I need to do the same for myself.

If I'm the adult I claim to be, then I have to do this all on my own.

Before I lose my nerve.

I glance at the bedside clock. Eight a.m. That makes it ten in Austin. It's been easy to text Mom whenever the mood strikes, but we video chat only when she's on her lunch hour. I *never* call when she's home with Gabe.

But—telling her this kind of thing when she's at work? My stomach revolts. It seems selfish. Even cruel. But isn't it worse to let her go on living and believing a lie?

Maybe I should talk to Knox. He—

I cut off the thought and shoot straight up in bed. *No.* "Fuck, no." I say it aloud, just to hear the words.

I am not talking to my brother. Not about Mom, about Ajia— nothing. He was a rude, egotistical asshole to do what he did. Ajia is supposed to be his best friend, and Knox threw him under the bus for the sake of being a jerk. To get his own way. To prove some fucking point that doesn't exist.

Nope. Knox gets nothing from me. Not until he apologizes and makes things right with Ajia.

So…I'm on my own.

I crawl out of bed and head to the shower. Seems like the safest way to start the day—until I'm naked under the steamy hot water. Soaping my body reminds me of Ajia's hands and mouth as he learned and relearned every inch of me last night. He stuck to his word and wouldn't give me what I really wanted—him inside of me—but his magical hands and mouth gave me orgasms that defy description.

My core tightens just thinking about it.

God, I want him again. All of him. I want to hold him, prove that his old ideas are screwed up, and that he's the best thing in my life.

But first, I have to clean up my own mess.

I wrap up my hair, towel dry, and head straight for my phone. No more hesitating.

Me: Free on UR lunch hour?
Mom: Sure, sweetie. You want to talk?
Me: Yeah. Important.
Mom: Private?

Me: Definitely!
Mom: OK! Call me at 12:10 my time.

I send her a thumbs up emoji and throw my phone on the bed like it's a snake or something. And maybe it is. *God.* I *have* to do this. For Mom, for me, for everything. If I want Ajia to get over his past, then I have to show him that I can do the same.

Now all I have to do is wait. Two hours, give or take—and then?

It all changes.

♫

"Hi, sweetie!"

My mom's face pops up on my phone. Calling—or video chatting—is a really shitty way to do what I have to do, and I know it. I should have handled things so differently, but I didn't, and now waiting is even worse. I have to step up and own it all.

"Hey, Mom."

"You look good, sweetie! Things going okay?"

I nod and try to smile. "The label had a big party for the band yesterday. It was really fancy. We all went."

Mom smiles. It's like looking at myself in twenty-five years. Well, fifteen, maybe, because she looks at least ten years younger than she actually is. I hope I inherit that part of her genes, as well.

"You brother told me," she's saying.

"You talked to Knox?"

"He called. He said there's been some gossip—tabloid stuff—and since it's all lies, I should just ignore it."

"That's...good."

She shakes her head and wrinkles her nose like something smells bad. "I never expected that when my son got famous, people would makeup stories about him and his friends. What's *wrong* with them? I've learned to completely avoid those gossip sites and stuff on TV. Knox says it's part of the price of fame, but I think those awful people should be sued!"

I can't help smiling. She's been saying that since the first time Wycked Obsession made the tabloid news. I can't remember what the story was; probably drinking or partying or girls. Knox got Baz to try and explain to her that most of the time it wasn't worth following up, especially if there was any grain of truth to it, but she hated that answer.

"I think they're getting a new PR person," I say to make her happy. "That might help. They might not be any more into suing, but they know how to turn the rumors around and put other stuff out. Positive stuff."

I have no idea if that's true. For all I know, they'll just replace the gossip with other information, direct attention wherever they want it, like those sexy pictures from the photo shoot. But I don't want to say anything like that. Not now.

Mom's too smart for me. She gives me a half-smile. "That sounds good, but I know better. Knox already warned me that there are some risqué shots of the boys coming."

I try to laugh it off. *The boys.* She always calls the members of Wycked Obsession *boys.* Does she have any idea of how wrong she is?

"Yeah, I saw a few," I admit. "They're pretty sexy. It's kinda…weird."

"So, sweetie, what did you want to talk about? You said it was important."

My heart pounds suddenly, and the air races out of my lungs. Mom doesn't usually put off the big stuff. I thought I had psyched myself up for this, but now I'm not so sure. Can I do this? Say the things I need to say? I swallow and close my eyes, trying to ignore the tears that prickle behind my eyelids.

"Bree? Honey, what is it?" The concern in Mom's voice pulls my eyes open. "You can tell me anything. You know that."

Yeah, I suppose I do. Knox, Mom, and I became a pretty tight team after Dad left, but then life kind of weakened the bond a little bit. Stuff like Wycked Obsession's success, the demands of my college education, and Mom's new relationship with Gabe. We all let outside concerns occupy our attention.

Now, though, I'm forcing things to change again. We should have never let go of the closeness. And this is too important to let anything get in the way. Not embarrassment, uncertainty, or even fear. This will make or break us as a family.

I swallow it all back. I've been running from the truth about my stepfather for too long. Hiding behind the rigors of life on the road.

Behind testing my feelings for Ajia. Behind *anything* that will keep me from thinking about Gabe.

And then Ajia's truths last night reminded me again why running is never the answer.

"Uh…well, you know I had my reasons for going on tour with Knox." I only say my brother's name. He's the only one Mom is really interested in.

"Yes." She looks confused, but her nod is encouraging enough. "Knox said it would be good for your degree. First-hand experience with a rock band on tour."

I let out a ragged breath. That had been the excuse he'd used when he first told Mom I was going along, and we've stuck to it since then.

"Yeah. That's part of it. But there's another reason."

"What?" She sounds so *normal.* So trusting.

Oh, fuck. My shoulders tingle, sensation races over my nerve endings, and my stomach feels wide and empty. It's like I'm going to get sick—and maybe I am.

"Mom…I left because…I was having trouble with Gabe."

She blinks. Frowns. "What kind of trouble?"

"He…" I take another breath, this one ragged and thin. "He was—touching me."

The line goes silent, and I can't bring myself to do anything except stare at my mom. Her face is blank. Eerily so.

She's quiet for probably ten seconds, but it seems like an hour. Finally, I see her swallow and she says, "What do you mean?" Her voice is hoarse.

"He would try to touch me when we were alone." It's only slightly easier to say the second time. "My back, my waist, my butt. He'd put his arms around me and tried to kiss me a couple of times. Knox caught him once and wanted to do something, but I talked him out of it. I thought it would stop."

"But it didn't." Her voice is stronger than I would have expected. Her tone doesn't sound like she's asking.

"No. That day you came home and he was in my bedroom, I *had* fallen asleep listening to the new album. When I woke up, Gabe was in the room. He…had his hands under my shirt and was touching my breasts." I close my eyes but then force myself to look at her again.

"I got away from him, but I was *so glad* when you came home right after that."

Her expression remains blank and awful. "You went to Knox that night."

I nod. "I told him what happened." I decide against sharing the fact that the whole freaking band knows about it. "We decided I'd go on tour with him. It would be…easier. Safer."

It takes a few seconds, and then Mom asks, "Why didn't you tell me then?"

Real tears form in my eyes, and I struggle to blink them away. "Oh, Mom, I was mad and scared and all kinds of stuff! I didn't want to ruin *our* relationship, and I didn't want to ruin *your* marriage. You seemed so happy with Gabe, and I didn't want to spoil it for you."

"Oh, baby." The sorrow in Mom's voice cuts me deep. I can't keep the tears back now. "You should not have carried this alone, Breeanne. It should never have been your burden. *Never.*" She says the last word with an emphasis that surprises me.

I try to speak around the tears. "I had Knox, Mom. And Ajia." I don't know why I add his name.

"Ajia." She picks up on it right away. She doesn't smile, but the corner of her mouth quirks. "So he finally noticed you?"

"Yeah." But that's all I can say about it. I'm crying for real now and trying to talk at the same time. "Mom, I'm so sorry. I…should have handled things…differently. Better."

She shakes her head slowly. "Don't beat yourself up, sweetie. Of course, I wish you had said something before, but you did your best. I know that."

"How can you say that?" It comes out more like a sob. "I just told you something really bad. About your husband! And I—"

"Bree!" Her voice is sharp, and I try to sniff my tears back. "One thing your father's leaving us taught me was that we're all responsible for our own choices. You, me, Knox—and Gabe."

I nod, remembering my conversation with Ajia. "Yes. I believe that."

"Sometimes we make great ones, sometimes not so great. And sometimes—" her gaze goes unbelievably hard "—they're worse than bad. Now *I* have a choice to make, and it's going to be the best one for my family. You can believe that."

I do. She's always done that. "What're you gonna do?"

"Don't you worry about that." Mom's gaze softens. "The rest of this is on me."

"Mom—"

"Bree." She cuts me off. "Let's not say anymore now, honey. Just believe that I'm going to take care of this—and you. No one will hurt you that way again, if I have anything to say about it."

"It never went far enough that he physically *hurt* me or anything." The frantic explanation pushes itself from me.

"It isn't about that, sweetie, and you know it. He hurt you emotionally, and he damaged our family. I can't forgive that."

"Oh, Mom." I try to swallow the fresh tears. *"I'm so sorry!"*

"It's not your fault, sweetie." Her smile is tender enough, but the steely resolve in her eyes doesn't match it. "You let me go now, and I'll call you tonight. Okay, sweetie?"

"You're sure?"

"I'm sure." She nods decisively. "Go spend some time with the boys and Ajia. Forget all this. I'll take care of things and talk to you later."

"Okay, Mom." I sound five again, but it's the best I can do. "I love you so much."

"I love you, too, baby."

She's gone then, and I do the only thing I can. I throw myself face down on the bed and cry all the ugly tears I haven't shed in longer than I can remember.

I give myself ten, maybe fifteen, minutes to cry. No longer, or I'll be a wreck all day. It feels kind of good to get the emotion out, but I don't want the whole red eyes, stuffy nose, and hung over feeling that follows a long, ugly cry.

With a deep breath, I force myself to my feet and into the bathroom. I wash my face, apply cold compresses to my eyes, and redo the small amount of makeup I wear. I drink a glass of water—I feel so damned dehydrated—and finally work up the stamina to call Ajia. I need to share my—what? Can I actually call it an accomplishment? I feel more like a failure.

I broke my mother's heart and probably ruined her marriage.

Ajia's phone goes straight to voicemail, so I try his room. He doesn't answer there, either.

I look at my phone like some explanation should show up on the screen. Should I be worried? Possibilities nag at me.

He could be sleeping, in the shower, at the hotel gym, meeting with the band. Explanations pour over me. He wouldn't do anything crazy. Not after everything he's been through. What *we've* been through.

He'll surface in a bit. The record label has a Edge of Return party scheduled for tonight, and we're all expected to attend. It's supposed to be a lot like the Wycked Obsession party last night, except bigger and more impressive, according to Baz. Tomorrow and Saturday are two more shows, they have more meetings, and eventually we head north to the Bay area and Sacramento.

A part of me wants to get back on the road and recapture the close camaraderie of the six of us crowded into the tour bus. Except for Knox. That fucker has some apologizing to do, and I'm not giving him a free pass this time.

I grab my key card and stuff it in my back pocket. I'm back to wearing jeans, a Wycked Obsession T-shirt, and flip-flops. I'll slip down the hall to Ajia's room and see if I can catch him there.

I don't even make it to the door when a familiar pounding starts on the other side. Knox. I'd know that maniac's knock anywhere.

"What?" I throw the door open with a scowl.

Knox and Noah stand impatiently in the hall. My brother doesn't wait to be invited but shoves past me. Noah gives me a quick, apologetic hug and follows.

"Come in." I allow the sarcasm to sharpen my voice.

Knox spins to face me. "You called Mom."

"She called you?"

"What the fuck, Bree? Why didn't you tell me?"

"Why should I tell you anything? You can't be trusted."

"What?" He frowns like he doesn't understand what I'm saying. Asshole.

"What do you have to say about it, anyway? You wanted me to tell her from the very first. Oh—wait! You didn't want *me* to tell her. You wanted to beat the shit out of Gabe and be the big, bad I'll-save-the-fucking-day Knox Gallagher."

Noah gives me a small but very distinct shit-eating grin.

"What are you talking about?" Knox demands.

"Jesus, Knox, who the fuck do you think you're fooling? You don't care that Mom knows what her piece-of-shit husband was doing—or trying to do—to me. You just want to be the one to *handle it*. Well, fuck you, Knox. I told her myself, and it's over. I did my part, and now it's up to her."

"Why are you so pissed off? And—have you been crying?"

"Crying?" I make my eyes go wide. "Why the hell would I be *crying?* Just because I had to tell my mother that her new husband is a pervert? That he hit on me and I ran away like a scared kid? Oh, hell, no, that's nothing to upset me."

"Here, baby girl." Noah comes over with a hug and pulls me down onto the bed. The maid hasn't been in yet, so the covers are all over the place, but it doesn't really matter to either of us.

"You wanna tell me why you got Knox on the shit seat right now?"

Knox sputters from the other side of the room, but Noah slashes his hand through the air for quiet. For some reason, my brother complies.

I look at Noah. "Besides the fact that he's an asshole?"

"We all knew that already."

"And besides the fact that he's being a jerk about this thing with Mom?"

"Yeah."

"Because he did something lousy to Ajia, and he didn't apologize. He didn't even feel bad. He just left acting like the smug asshole that he is!"

Noah swings his head around to pierce Knox with a glare I don't often see from him. "What did you do?"

Knox shrugs with that same cocky attitude. "What had to be done."

"What's that?"

Knox just shakes his head, like he's too good to answer. That just pisses me off more. "He told me about the accident."

Noah stiffens. "He. What?"

"Well, let me be fair." I nod toward Knox. "He didn't actually tell me about the *accident.* Ajia did that."

"What did he tell you, then?" Noah keeps staring at Knox.

"That Ajia killed a girl."

Two seconds of silence deafen the room before Noah blows. *"You selfish motherfucker!"*

"Hey, it's true." Knox tries to defend himself, but he won't make eye contact with either Noah or me.

"It's not true, and you know it, *Knox*. It's far from the fucking truth. There's so much more that happened, and it wrecks Ajia to know he was a part of it. He's fought it longer than any of us have known him, and you did *that* to him?"

"It had to be done," Knox repeats, sounding less defiant and more defensive.

"That's such fucking shit." Noah's having none of it.

"It doesn't matter," I say quietly. "I know it all now."

Noah looks at me. "So he told you."

"Everything. Stuff he says nobody else knows."

"Well, that explains it."

"Explains what?"

"Why he left."

CHAPTER 24

AJIA

Baz has a Town Car waiting at LAX for me. I wanted to take a cab, but security won't allow it. Far as I know, nothing new is happening with Edge of Return's stalker shit, but the label isn't taking any chances. I'm just glad it isn't a limo. I don't want to attract any attention. I only want to get back to my life—to Bree—and now I find out I fucked up. Again.

Noah texted me yesterday, and my gut's been in a knot ever since.

I texted Bree as soon as I realized what a douche I must look like to her. What the fuck was I thinking to leave without telling her? She only answered once. *We'll talk when you get back.* Since then, it's been twenty-four hours of phone fucking silence.

Shit.

I knew I'd have to explain when I got back. I'd planned to. I *want* to explain. Especially to Bree. She's the reason I left. To do what I knew I had to.

Put an end to it all. At least in my head and my heart. Exactly as Bree knew I should.

But now I'm nervous as fucking hell. I was so focused on what I had to do, I handled it all wrong. I hurt Bree. Again.

Fuck.

Traffic is typically L.A.-terrible, and I'm missing sound check. I text Noah, cause I'm not saying a fucking word to Knox. It's not so much *what* he did, but the *way* he did it. Smug prick.

Me: On my way. Traffic's fucked.
Noah: Good fucking thing.

Me: Everything OK?
Noah: UR in deep shit.
I don't even try to pretend I don't know what he means.
Me: I know.
Noah: U ready to fix it?
Me: Yes.
A few seconds pass before I see the tiny bubbles that show Noah is replying.
Noah: Good fucking thing.
That must be his go-to response today, and I don't have an answer that fits. I know I have my work cut out for me—and I know I'll do whatever it takes. Bree's worth it, and more.
Noah: Bet U ain't getting any tonight.
I lose a soft laugh, even though I figure he's right. All I really want to do is lose myself in the soft beauty of Bree's body, but I'll do whatever it takes to make this up to her.

So why does my cock keep reminding me that I can't wait to hold her, kiss her, touch her until she comes all over my fingers, my mouth, and then push deep inside her?
Me: U fuckers are still way too interested in my sex life.
Noah sends back an emoji of a bug-eyed grin, and I let it go. Gotta get my head in the right place. The last two days I've been thinking only about me. Letting go of the past so I can make a future with Bree. I'd probably still keep thinking about that shit right now if I could, but I have to get ready for the concert.

We're in L.A. for at least a week yet, and then we get a day on the bus as we head north. A day when I can focus totally on Bree. I don't know whose turn it is in the fucking bedroom, but I'm taking it. Bree and me, and Knox—and whoever's turn it is—can get fucked.

Now, though, I've gotta take care of fucking business.

It takes another thirty minutes before I'm at the venue. Straight there, no stopping at the hotel. The guys are ready when I blast into the dressing room, but there's no sign of Bree.

"'Bout time, fucker," says Noah in greeting. I grin at him.

"All good?" asks Rye from his place on the couch next to Noah.

"Yeah." I nod. "We'll talk after the show."

Rye nods but doesn't say anything else. Knox is on the other side of the room, but I ignore him completely. Zayne's stretched out on the other couch, eyes closed like he's asleep or in a coma. It's typical for before we go on stage, so I ignore him, too.

"I'll shower and then I'm ready."

"Makeup's waiting for you," says Knox, but I don't respond.

I'm in and out of the shower in record time, and then dress in black leather pants, black muscle shirt, and black motorcycle boots. Between things with Bree and that ridiculous fucking photo shoot, I'm done with that open white shirt for a while.

I rush through makeup, toss back a bottle of water for hydration, and I'm ready to go on. I still don't see Bree anywhere, but, fuck me, I'm not going to ask anybody where she is. Not now, when I'm supposed to be concentrating on giving L.A. a kick-ass show. Marty's got a bunch of label people out there for the next two shows. If we want a successful tour and a decent budget for the third album, we gotta impress them.

I stand at the far side of the darkened stage. I always enter from there to avoid Knox's spotlight. The crowd is restless as it waits for the show to begin. I'm surprised to hear the crowd yelling for *us*. Usually they're shouting for Edge of Return, especially Mad, their lead singer, who the chicks think is sex on a stick. *Their* description, not mine.

Tonight, though, I hear chants for Wycked Obsession, *our* names, the occasional, "I love you, Ajia!" It used to give me a feeling of power whenever I heard it. Acceptance. Now it barely makes me smile, because it isn't Bree saying it. Are we growing our fan base because *Tonight* is still hanging strong in the top five on the charts? Or is it because of the fucking tabloid gossip?

Zayne's bass throbs, Noah adds his heavy bass drum beat, Rye runs the scales, and Knox impresses with the guitar intro. Spotlights shine on them all, leaving the rest of the stage dark, and I take my place at the mic. My head drops forward, and I wait for the exact right moment to start.

Run, baby, run.
You cannot hide from me.
Are you really sure you want to go?
You know I can set you free.

We always start with *Run,* and tonight's no exception. It goes off flawlessly, mostly because, in my heart, I'm singing to Bree. I haven't found her yet, don't really think she's running, and yet…my gut twists in a hard knot.

I need to see her, touch her, hold her close. Make love to her.

I drop my head forward as *Run* ends and the lights go off. The crowd is in a frenzy, screaming and clapping and pushing forward toward the stage. I'm aware of it, and yet I'm totally preoccupied with one thought.

I want to make love to Bree.

Not fuck her. *Make love to her.* In the real sense of the words. It will be the first time in my life.

The stage lights come up and I stare out into a crowd of faces. Can't see most of them, but the frenzied screaming and applause tell me they're there. My thoughts energize me, and I smile.

"Hello, L.A.!"

The audience shouts back, and I wave my arm in a wide sweep that includes the rest of the band. "We're Wycked Obsession, and we're here to show you a good fucking time!"

They erupt again, and I decide to egg it on. "You ready to party?" I pause as the noise grows and then demand again, "I said, are you ready to *fucking party?*"

I let it all roll around us for a few seconds before I raise my arm. Noah strikes off the beat, and we launch into *No Doubt*. It doesn't have quite the same meaning as it did before, not when I wrote it and not when I sang it earlier in the tour. That doesn't stop me from strutting the stage so I can search for Bree.

Then, finally, I find her perched on a high stool in her usual spot. The stupid question flashes through my mind—*did that fucker Steve put it there for her?*—but I let it go when I notice another woman, slim and pretty, seated next to her. Who the fuck is *that?* I don't have time for more.

No doubt that I want you.
No doubt that I need you.
No doubt that we'd be good.
But I can't have you.
Shouldn't take you.
Should have left you alone
Right where you stood.

The rest of the show passes so goddamn slow, it's like I feel fucking frozen in place. I want to just walk off. I don't. I force myself to play to the crowd, flirt and laugh and tease, but I steal looks in Bree's direction the whole time. I can feel her gaze on me, but she doesn't smile or move with the music like she usually does. She just *watches*.

I make it through somehow, and we end with *Tonight*. I can't wait to get to her, but she gone from her perch just off stage left. That's not unusual for her, I remind myself. I usually find her in the green room after a show, and I head straight there.

"Ajia! Oh, my God!"

"Ajia, you're here!"

"I love you!"

"Great show!"

"I'm your biggest fan!"

Groupies squeal and hands grab, but I don't stop. Not even for a quick, "Hi, honey," or "Thanks." Not tonight. Noah comes up behind me, almost like he's running interference, while Zayne and Rye hang back to deal with the fans. I don't know where the fuck Knox is, and I don't fucking care.

We reach the green room easily enough, but there are too many fucking people there for me. Still, I find her fast enough. I'll *always* fucking find her.

She's at the beverage table, pouring something into a red Solo cup. Vodka and Sprite, I bet. She's dressed in a long skirt I don't remember seeing before. It's light brown decorated with colorful flowers...and a slit up one side that goes so high, I swear I see a flash of panties. Her top is white with thin little straps and tight enough to leave no doubt about the shape of her beautiful tits.

Son of a bitch!

I slip behind her and wrap my arms around her waist. "Baby. I missed you." I lean down to kiss her just behind her ear.

She stiffens. I don't know if it's because she's pissed at me or because it's the first time I've touched her this way in public. Knox knows about us, so there's no reason not to now.

She drops her head back and turns enough to look up at me. "Ajia."

I take advantage of the moment to drop a quick, hard kiss on her mouth. "Did you miss me, baby?"

She blinks and frowns. "Don't waste your charm on me right now, A. I'm pissed at you."

"I know, baby." I kiss her again. "I'm sorry."

She steps away. I don't want to let her go, but I do. I have to handle this the right way, whatever that is. Got no clue at the moment. I admit I know a hell of a lot about fucking women, but I don't know shit about loving them.

"You should meet London." Bree points to the woman I saw sitting next to her earlier. She's maybe an inch taller than Bree, with long, reddish hair and dressed in black and white. "Marketing and PR," Bree prompts when I just stare.

"Oh! Right." I hold out a hand. "Ajia Stone."

"Ajia." She shakes my hand with a professional-looking smile. "Nice to meet you. I'm London Kennedy."

"So you're taking us on?" I ask as I grab a bottle of water. I'm always so goddamn dehydrated after performing.

"Looks like." Her voice has an interesting sound to it, not quite an accent and yet not like anything I've heard before. "*You* being my current project."

"Me?" I glance at Bree. She shrugs.

"You haven't been online lately?" asks London.

I shake my head. "Not in a day or two. Decided to give it up. That shit gets me in trouble."

Bree laughs, but she sounds more pissed than anything.

"What?" I look between her and London.

A shout distracts me, and I glance over my shoulder to see Zayne, Rye, and Knox wander in, surrounded by chicks. The room's filling up with the usual mix of groupies and fans, and I suddenly want out of there. Bad.

I look back at Bree. London's glaring at the other guys like she could cut off every one of their dicks. Or maybe it's Knox she's pissed at. I'm sure he's her point man.

"Over here," she says before I can process that. I follow her to probably the only halfway quiet corner of the room and grab Bree's hand as I go.

"What?" I say again.

Bree nods toward London, who catches my eye with a very direct gaze. "You don't need to *avoid* going online to get in trouble. You need to pay attention to it."

Fuck. "What happened?"

"Well, let's see. First you pretty much tell a couple of very pissed-off—"

"And vindictive," puts in Bree.

"Female fans that you're sleeping with Bree," finishes London.

"What do you mean 'vindictive'?" I ask, but London waves me off.

"Then there's video of you two making out in the elevator."

"Yeah. I knew about that."

"Great!" London nods with a smile that doesn't go any farther than her lips. "Which totally explains why you then drop out of sight for two bloody days, only to resurface at the airport in Austin."

I look from London to Bree and back again.

"And, of course, *nobody* wondered what was going on when the rest of the band was at the Edge of Return label party last night *without you*. And *none* of your fans had anything nasty to say about Bree when she attended with Rye."

I close my eyes and drop my head forward. *"Fuck."* I take a breath and force myself to look at Bree. She stares at me with those wide, beautiful green eyes that tell me absolutely nothing, and it hits me again, how much I love this girl.

And how much I've done to hurt her.

"I'm sorry, baby." I pull her against me and wrap my arms around her. I don't give a shit that I'm sweaty from the stage or that the room is full of strangers. All that matters is that Bree has to know how sorry I am.

She's stiff against me, but at least she doesn't pull away. I adjust my hold until she has to soften her posture and then, slowly, her arms come around me.

"What do I do now?" I ask London, looking over top of Bree's head. "How do I fix it?"

"We'll talk about that. But not here."

I nod. "Can you get everybody back to the hotel?"

London smiles. "If I can't, Baz will. Or Knox." She frowns and glances across the room.

I don't waste my time following her gaze. It doesn't matter. "Great." I let Bree go long enough to shake London's hand again. "Bree and I'll go on ahead. We'll meet in my room."

"Got it." London turns away, all businesslike.

"And tell those fuckers *no girls!"* I call after her.

235

She waves a hand but doesn't turn around. I swear I hear her mutter the word, "Wanker," under her breath.

Does she mean me or Knox?

I look down at Bree. She's watching London cross the room to where Knox stands, a circle of chicks surrounding him.

"Kitten?"

She blinks and then raises her head to look at me. It takes forever for her eyes to meet mine.

"I'm sorry I hurt you, baby. I didn't mean to. I—let's get the fuck out of here. I'll tell you everything, but not here."

The seconds drag out. I hate that she hesitates, but then finally she nods. "Okay."

Goddamn. I must have scared her off but good with my disappearing act. Fuck, fuck, *fuck*. That's the last thing I meant to do, and I only know one way to fix it.

I wrap my arms around her and jerk her up tight against me. I shove my leg between hers, palm her ass, and then drop my head to catch her mouth with mine. I part her lips and stroke my tongue over hers before she can figure out what the fuck hit her. I give myself only a few seconds to enjoy my success, and then I kiss her like I don't give a fuck who's watching.

Truth is, I don't.

CHAPTER 25

BREE

Somehow, Ajia has a Town Car waiting for us at the back of the venue. A limo is parked behind it—for the rest of the band, I suppose.

A crowd of mostly female fans is being held back by security and a metal barricade. They shout and wave when they see us. Ajia's so easily recognized with his long blond hair and still wearing his stage clothes, all in black.

"Ajia!"

"I love you!"

"Forget that slut! I won't break your heart!"

Pretty much the same shit they've been saying online.

I ignore it as best I can. The gossip is probably gonna get worse after that kiss in the green room. I can only imagine what it looked like, because it went straight through me. To my core, my heart, maybe even my soul. I can *guarantee* that pictures of it are gonna show up on the internet.

Hell, they're probably there already.

Ajia helps me into the car, and I slide all the way across the seat. That amazing kiss aside, I need some distance between us. He gets in next to me but stays quiet until we're on the way.

"Bree—"

"Why'd you do it, A?" I don't mean to interrupt, but the words erupt from me.

"Which part?"

I can't decide if I want to smile because he sees the possibilities that he fucked up in more ways than one, or if I want to be pissed because he isn't sure what he did to hurt me. I stare at him with a death-ray glare that I want him to think should level him.

"The part where you disappeared for two days without telling me where you were going—or why! *That part.*"

He watches me. I can tell he's looking, but the flickering shadows caused by streetlamps we pass don't provide enough light for me to read his expression. Finally, he sighs.

"Technically, I didn't disappear for two days. I texted you yesterday."

I narrow my eyes. Asshole. "You *know* what I fucking mean. You didn't tell me you were leaving *before you left.* And, for the record, you didn't text me until *after* Noah texted you."

He blows out a harsh sigh, rubs a hand over his face, and shoves his hair back. Finally, he nods. "You're right, kitten. I fucked up. And I'm sorry."

"I know you fucked up. That's not the issue, and it doesn't answer my question. *Why?*"

He reaches for my hand, but I don't offer it. He has to take it from my lap, and then he links our fingers. "Baby, I'm so sorry. I wasn't thinking."

I let the words echo between us for a second. "You weren't thinking," I repeat, like I can't believe he said them. In a way, I can't.

That's it? *He wasn't thinking?*

He tugs on my hand, pulling me closer until I either move with some kind of dignity or fall all over him. I don't want that. Not right now. Especially when my long skirt has a side slit that shows off a lot of leg. Scooting around on the back seat is difficult enough without making the thing twist up around my hips.

"That fucking skirt is driving me crazy," he says suddenly and then reaches across me with his free hand. He strokes his palm up my thigh until his fingers slip under the cloth and are practically at my hip.

"Stop it." I shove his hand away. "Don't try to distract me. You were explaining how you *weren't thinking.*"

He sighs and pinches the bridge of his nose. "Yeah, okay. You're right."

He's silent for a couple of minutes, and then his fingers tighten briefly around mine. "I *was* thinking, actually," he says carefully. "I was thinking about everything we said to each other. About the things I'd told you—the fucking secrets I'd held for *so long*—and the amazing way you reacted. I didn't expect that."

"Expect what?"

"You didn't judge me or remind me what a piece of shit I am. You said the opposite. You said things that made sense. You gave me...hope."

It hurts to think that Ajia would automatically expect the worst. Not of me but of anyone. And that, still, he can only see the worst in himself.

That *doesn't* mean I'm letting him off the hook.

"Oh, well, that makes perfect sense," I snap. *"Of course!* I gave you hope, so you ran off without telling me."

"Shit." He shakes his head. "You really *are* pissed, aren't you?"

"What was your first clue?"

"Look, it was stupid, okay?" Ajia shakes his head. *"I* was stupid. I was just so caught up in the whole idea that maybe, finally, I could put all that shit behind me. Or at least not let it drive me to do such stupid shit anymore. I knew I had to do something—and so I did. I raced off to fix it. I didn't think a lot about what I was doing or how I did it. I just wanted to get it over with and come back to you...better. Cleaner, maybe."

He sighs and drops his head forward enough that his hair slides over his shoulders and tumbles down his chest. "I didn't want to drag you through any more of it. I wanted to surprise you with something *good.* I never fucking thought about how it would look to you."

I don't want to be charmed by his explanation, especially by the emotion behind his actions, but I am. Damn, but this man always does this to me! Grabs some special place inside me, a secret piece of me where only he has access. He is the best part of my life—and my greatest weakness.

"And did you do it?" I ask softly.

"Do what?"

"Fix it. Come back...cleaner?"

"Yeah." He sounds thoughtful. "I think I did. And I have you to thank for that."

He pulls me closer before I realize what he's up to, and his mouth captures mine. His kiss holds me uncertain, confused and hopeful at the same time, because it's way different from anything we've shared before. Not the statement he was making in the dressing room—whatever the hell that was—and not a hot kiss of passion. This is seeking and giving and sharing all at the same time.

It almost feels like...love.

Don't get ahead of yourself! My common sense jumps to my defense, even as my body awakens to Ajia's touch. *He knows how you feel—you've told him—and you know he cares for you. But he's never said the words—and don't go expecting them. This is new, and a lot of shit has happened.* Love *is a big step for a guy like Ajia Stone.*

I pant a little breathlessly when he releases my mouth. "Do...you want to tell me about it?" I ask.

"I do, baby. I will. I want to tell you. Everything. But not here. When we get to the room, okay?"

A small slice of disappointment flares through me. He wants to wait. It's silly to be so sensitive. I understand why; we're almost back at our hotel. But I guess a childish part of me wants Ajia to be so anxious to share everything with me, that he really *can't* wait.

We pull up at the hotel a few minutes later. Honestly, it's a relief. As much as I love being in such close quarters with Ajia, I need to keep putting a little space between us. This whole thing with him—becoming lovers, the tabloid gossip, his disappearance—has me off-center enough that I need a minute now and then to ground myself again.

A crowd of—I don't know—fans and paparazzi hover outside the big glass doors of the hotel, and I sigh. They're suddenly everywhere we go these days. It doesn't matter if they're here to catch sight of Wycked Obsession or Edge of Return or any other celebrity who might be staying here. The result will be the same when they catch sight of Ajia. Especially with me.

The doorman opens the car door, and I take a deep breath. Hotel security is there to shield Ajia as he climbs from the car. I follow, grateful for Ajia's hand as he helps me out, and then he pulls me tight against him, his arm firmly around my shoulder.

"Ajia!" Multiple voices shout his name.

"Where did you go, Ajia?" That must be a reporter or a photographer.

"What's in Texas, Ajia?"

"Are you and Bree Gallagher together?"

Feminine squeals followed by, "Oh, my God! I love you, Ajia!"

There are other cries. Threats and slurs and demands that Ajia dump a slut like me, and though I hear them, they don't really penetrate. I've seen enough of it online, and I get the sentiment. Then we're through the automatic doors, blessedly inside, and the noise dies away.

We've all learned not to say anything much in public, and I'm sure as hell not taking the chance of getting close to Ajia in the elevator again. That one bit us on the ass already. We're out of the elevator and in his room before I can really think of what to do or say next.

Wish I'd been able to come up with something, because the first thing I see is the bed. *That bed.* The bed where I gave up my V-card, where Ajia did amazing things to my body, where I learned what he liked and how to do it. And, holy hell, how it all made me *feel.*

My skin heats to roughly the temperature of the sun, my nipples tighten to almost painful stiffness, and tension in my lower body produces a familiar wet heat between my thighs.

Jesus, Bree, not now!

There aren't enough places to sit, especially when I know the rest of the band will show up eventually, so I pick the bed. It might piss Knox off, but I really don't give a shit at the moment.

"Are you gonna forgive me?"

I blink and look at Ajia. He's across the room, by the closet. His eyes are dark, but I'm not really sure why. I mean, he knows I'm gonna get over what he did eventually—doesn't he? We've never had a fight that lasted more than a day or two.

"I probably started to forgive you the second you texted me, A." I give him a half-assed smile. "This isn't about that. It's about the fact that I didn't matter enough for you to tell me you were leaving. It really—"

"Whoa, there, baby!" He stalks across the room like some goddamn predator, but the closer he comes, the less fierce he seems. He sinks to his knees in front of me and lays a palm on each of my thighs. "Who the fuck said you didn't matter?"

I lift a shoulder. "Well…it seems kind of obvious. You didn't text me until you heard from Noah—"

"I didn't tell anybody!" His eyes are narrow. "Hell, I didn't even text Baz until I was on the plane waiting to taxi out."

"But you *did* tell him. Your manager." I don't mean to be a pain in the ass, but I have a point Ajia doesn't seem to be getting. "It just wasn't me you talked to."

His face settles into a full-fledged frown. "I guess I'm not used to answering to anybody for what I do. I don't—"

"That's bullshit, A, and you know it. You've been accountable to the band for five years, and you've never let them down. You remembered to tell Baz what you were doing. You're not an irresponsible jerk. You just didn't tell *me.*"

He sits back on his heels, but he doesn't take his hands from my legs. His expression evens out to one I don't recognize. Understanding and regretful at the same time.

"You're right." He blinks and gives me a single nod. "You're absolutely fucking right. The truth is, I think I was afraid to tell you."

"Afraid?" I stiffen but allow one hand to drop over his. "That makes no fucking sense, A."

He shrugs. "I didn't know if I could do what I wanted to. If I could let go of all that crap I've been carrying around and—I don't know—start fresh, I guess. I wanted to do it—*fuck, did I*—but could I really accept something so different from what I've believed all this time? I was taking a hell of a chance, and I knew it. Maybe I thought…it'd be better if you were pissed at me because of the way I took off, not because I failed."

"Oh, baby." I lean forward and take his face in my hands. "That's never going to happen. The fact that you even tried is amazing."

He turns his face so his lips can brush my palm. "Only you would say something like that."

"Now, tell me." I scoot around on the bed until I'm cross-legged, and Ajia's sitting across from me, his feet flat on the floor. "I know you went to Austin, but I don't know the rest."

He drops his head forward, a habit I've noticed only when he talks about this. I reach for his jaw and turn his face until he looks at me.

"I had to see if I could make any kind of peace with it. I went to see…everybody."

"Everybody?"

"My folks, Lara's family, Mason, and Jill." He wants to look away—his eyes dart from side to side—but he doesn't.

"And how did it go?"

I ask the question as carefully as I can. Instinct tells me it went okay, because of the mostly-calm way Ajia is acting. I also know that he's spent a long time hiding his feelings, which means it's possible I have no clue what might be going on inside his head.

"It went...well. I told Mom and Dad and Lara's family that I'd been carrying a lot of guilt over what happened, and I wanted to apologize for my part in everything."

"You didn't try to tell them the truth again?"

He shakes his head. "I was prepared to, but nobody seemed to want to hear it. My mom cried, and Lara's dad told me that they'd been worried about her getting *wild* back then. Their word, not mine. They'd been afraid she was going to get into trouble with the car, and her blood alcohol level after the accident confirmed their worst fears."

He lets out a deep sigh and his whiskey-colored eyes draw my gaze with their sad acceptance. "I was all ready to say something. To tell them the absolute truth, and then Lara's mom told me that, while they'd always love her and never forget, it had been long enough that they'd reached a peace and acceptance of it. They wanted that for me, and they wanted me to let it go forever."

"And so you did as they asked."

One of his eyebrows shot up. "What was I going to say? Oh, and by the way, your daughter was wilder than you thought. She was trying to give me a blow-job when we crashed?"

He gives a hollow laugh. "It's not fair, and it's still fucking wrong of me to let a dead girl take the blame, but I finally got the idea that they don't *want* to understand anything except exactly what they already know. They have an explanation that they've accepted, and that's enough for them. Can I—*should I*—fuck with that for my own selfish reasons?"

"I told you." I take Ajia's hands between mine. "No matter who knows what, the facts are the same."

"That doesn't make it right."

"So what are you going to do?"

Ajia turns his hands over so his fingers twine with mine. "I *should* talk to our lawyer. Tell him everything and ask him to look into it. But I seem to be the only one who wants that."

"It could mean trouble."

He shrugs. "It *should* mean trouble. I deserve it. But..."

"But, what?"

"I'm the only one who wants it. I can't keep dragging these people through shit that they want to be done with."

I can't just let it go. "And...you're okay with that?"

His gaze slid away and turned inward. I could see him thinking about the question. "Yeah. Or I will be. I made my apologies and asked for forgiveness. The rest will have to come when and how it needs to."

"And what about Mason and Jill?"

Ajia smiles for real this time, and his fingers tighten around mine. "Jill was great. She'd just had a birthday, so we ate leftover cake. I talked with her parents about the accident, made the same apologies, but not to her. It upsets her."

"And Mason?"

"I didn't get to see him. He's in rehab!"

"Oh, A, that's great!" I can smile, too. "I'm so glad to hear it! I—"

Pounding on the door drowns out the rest of my words, and I swallow a curse. "Open up!" It's Knox—and the others, I suppose.

Ajia pushes to his feet and lets them in. London enters first— because they're Texas men, after all—and my brother follows right on her heels.

"You doing okay, baby girl?" Noah asks as he approaches the bed.

"Of course." I nod and smile. "I didn't get to tell y'all at the venue. It was a great show!"

He grins, grabs my hand, and pulls me around to sprawl next to him, leaning against the headboard. He's got his arm around my shoulders, and he smirks at Ajia as though daring him to say anything. For a second, I almost expect A to take him up on it, but then he shrugs and circles the foot of the bed. Next thing I know, Ajia's crawled up on the other side of me, and I'm crushed between the two of them.

"Well, look at this," Noah laughs. "We got ourselves a Bree sandwich."

"Different for you, huh?" I share his laugh.

"What do you mean?"

"You're usually with two girls. I guess that makes you the meat in *that* sandwich."

The instant it's too late, I hear the suggestiveness in my words. *Oh, Jesus!*

I shoot a panicked gaze in Ajia's direction, but he's no help. He's trying to keep a straight face—and failing miserably. I peek around the room. London's sitting at the desk, Knox is perched on top of it, Rye's settled into the room's one comfy chair, and Zayne's stretched out on the floor. Every one of them is trying not to laugh—except Knox, of course. He always looks vaguely pissed.

"Shut up, you fuckers," I giggle and finally give in. They laugh with me, even London.

Knox's expression doesn't change, except to spread a dark, irritated gaze around the room. He finally drops it on Ajia. "Okay, Pipes," he says. "You wanted a fucking band meeting. We're here."

I let out a soft sigh. It's going to be such a fun meeting with Knox acting like an asshole, holding Ajia and me responsible for—whatever. No question that my brother's been irritable as fuck since he found us together.

"*I* called the meeting," says London smoothly without looking at Knox. "This kind of thing is *my* responsibility, and we need to talk about what's going on and plan some strategies."

Knox's mouth tightens, but it's Rye who asks, "Strategies about what?"

"Well, we have a couple of things to explain." London touches the screen on her tablet. "First, we need to talk about Ajia's unexpected trip to Austin."

"It was personal," I say, but he leans over and drops a quick kiss on my head.

"No, it's not a secret. Not anymore."

He gives an abbreviated explanation of his trip, including very minor details of the decade-old accident. London nods. "Any reason you had to go *now,* mid-tour?"

Ajia sits forward, grabbing my hand as he moves. I look down at where our fingers are entwined. I've never held hands so much in my life.

"Bree and I are together. It's not a one-night stand, and we're not fucking around." He looks directly at Knox. "Our relationship isn't open for discussion."

I try to swallow around a pounding heart. What's with Ajia tonight? He's being so—direct about us. It's like he really means to try with me. To make it...*real.*

"About fucking time," says Noah from next to me. I glance at him with a crooked grin.

"What?" Zayne pops up from the floor and looks around like he just joined the human race. "You two are fucking?" He points at Ajia and me.

Knox's jaw clenches, but it's Ajia who answers. "Among other things."

"Huh." He shakes his head. "So she's your...girlfriend?"

"Fuck," says Rye. "You killed too many brain cells, Zayne. Ajia said they're *together.*"

"Right." Zayne nods. "Together—as in girlfriend."

"Right," agrees Ajia. I don't miss the look the others exchange, and it's got nothing to do with Ajia and me. It's about Zayne. He's still...off. Whatever's going on, it's not getting better. Something passes between London and Knox, a look that seems to say, *we're talking about this,* but then it's gone when Ajia continues.

"The truth is half-assed out there. At least the questions are. We haven't confirmed or denied. Correct?" He looks at London.

"Correct. Although you gave a pretty good indication of how things are in the green room tonight."

"What happened?" Knox demands.

"Fuck, Knox, you were there," I snap. "Too interested in your groupies to notice anything else?" I scowl at him. "Ajia kissed me."

"Is that all?" He frowns back.

"You should have been paying attention," London says calmly. "In this case, it's enough."

"I was there," snaps my brother.

London shakes her head. "Maybe physically. But your bloody attention wasn't. A few too many groupies for you to concentrate?"

246

I blink and look between the two of them. Interesting shit, this. I'm the only one who pushes Knox about his shit. Other girls just want to suck his dick or... I shudder when I remember the fangirl who wanted him to spank her.

"Whatever," says Ajia, and I let out a breath of relief. He relaxes back against the headboard and pulls me with him. "I missed my girl, and I wanted to say *hi.*"

London sighs with a nod. "And being a typical Texas man, you couldn't wait. For anything. You had to go to Austin *immediately,* come back just in time for the concert, and then make out with Bree like you hadn't seen her in a damn year."

"Well, yeah." He pretends he doesn't get her sarcasm, but I know better. "Bree helped me see it's time for me to find a way to put the accident shit behind me, so I took the first step."

"All right." London is so *calm* about everything. "Anything else I need to know?"

"Besides the fact that Knox is pissed Ajia and I are together?" I can't help poking at my brother. He deserves it.

"Is that true?" She looks at Knox, but I answer.

"You tell me. He told me things about Ajia—about the accident—in the worst possible way, hoping it would end things. It didn't, and he's been pouting ever since."

"I'm not pouting." Knox's look would incinerate a normal person, but I've seen it too many times.

"Oh, you're pouting, man," laughs Noah, but his hard expression surprises me. "It was a dick fucking move to say that shit to Bree, and now you're twice as pissed. One cause they're together at all—" he points to Ajia and me "—and two because you couldn't break 'em up."

"Well, we aren't going to share any of that," says London quickly, giving Knox a serious frown that has to mean, *shut up!* "And in public, you're going to act like it's the best thing that's happened all tour."

"Fuck me." My brother's voice is cold enough to freeze the room. "Bree is *my* sister, and—"

"And she's an adult," London interrupts smoothly. "Unless you want fans to be worried about problems within the band, you're going to act happy as fuck that your sister and your best friend are a couple. Got it?"

The room falls silent as she stares at Knox. Tension crackles between them, and I can't help watching the interaction with surprised fascination, until finally Knox nods.

"Understood."

"Good." London lets the room go quiet for another moment and then asks again, "Anything else?"

I shake my head, and the guys do, too, while Knox pushes off the desk. "Mom's divorcing Gabe."

It's like all the air is suddenly sucked out of the room. My heart pounds so hard I can't breathe, and tears collect behind my eyelids. I try to swallow it all back, but it doesn't seem to work all that well.

Ajia pulls me into his arms and against his chest, and I realize I'm shaking. *Oh, God.* I've been so torn, wanting Mom to be happy and yet wanting Gabe out of our lives. Now...I don't know how to feel.

"When did she tell you that?" I can barely get the words out.

"This morning." Knox stares at me as he answers, his expression unreadable.

"And you didn't tell me until now?"

"You knew it was coming." I can't tell anything from his tone. "You had to expect it, after you fucking told her about him."

Ajia's stroking a gentle hand over my hair, and he whispers against my forehead. "You told your mom?"

I drop my head back to look at him, but I have to close my eyes for a bit of control. "I had to. After everything you told me, well...I just knew. I had to," I say again.

"Details, please." London's voice is careful, but she's glaring at Knox.

"Bree's stepdad was hitting on her," says Rye, finally, when nobody else answers.

"Okay." She nods briskly. "More personal stuff. Not going there, either."

London stands suddenly. "Let me do a little work. I'll see what I can do to finalize our strategies, and let's meet again in the morning. We'll start our own campaign and direct attention to where *we* want it."

"Thanks, London." I smile from the safety of Ajia's arms.

She smiles back. "Hey, you're stuck with me now. I'll do whatever I can for you."

"Great!" crows Noah as he climbs to his feet. "Welcome to the family! Looks like you got yourself a sister in crime, baby girl."

"It's about time," I laugh.

"And it's about time for the rest of you fuckers to get out of here. I wanna be alone with my girl."

Everybody laughs except, predictably, Knox. Rye shoves him out the door, and the rest of the band follows. Noah's the last to go.

"Night, kiddies. Sleep tight." And then he laughs like a freaking maniac.

CHAPTER 26

AJIA

I turn every fucking lock once we're alone. Maybe it's only been two days and one night since I touched Bree, but I want her. Now. No more waiting.

I reach back behind my neck, pull my shirt over my head, and toss it to the floor as I walk toward the bed. Next are these fucking leather pants that are *way* too constricting.

"You got some plans there, A?"

She's stretched out on the bed with her back against the headboard and looks so goddamn fuckable. Her hair's all loose around her shoulders and most of one leg shows because of that fucking slit in her skirt. She's smiling, but somehow I manage to catch a flash of sadness that darts through her expression.

"What's wrong, baby?" I forget about my pants and sink down next to her.

"Nothing." She shakes her head.

"Kitten..." I drag it out so she knows I'm serious.

"I just...can't really forget. I wish Knox had told me about Mom and Gabe earlier. I would have had time to—I don't know—process it."

Selfish asshole! Not sure if I mean Bree's stepfather, her brother...or me. We've all done shit to hurt her, and then I got so focused on my cock, I didn't even *think* about how she must feel about Knox's fucking last-minute announcement.

"So you told your mom," I say as I slip into place next to her. "How'd that go?"

"Pretty good, actually." She leans against me, and I pull her close enough to cradle her in my arms. "As good as something like that can go. Better than I expected."

"But she didn't tell you what she was going to do?"

When Bree shakes her head, her hair rubs against my bare chest. I don't want to notice how fucking good it feels, but my prick sure does.

"She just said she'd *take care of things* and wouldn't tell me what that meant. Not even when we talked again last night." Bree's sigh sounds a little heavy. "Sounds like she decided on divorce."

"That upsets you?"

She tilts her head back far enough that I can see the uncertainty in her expression. "It's like I said when I first told you about Gabe. She had to make a choice, and neither one was going to make her happy. I just wish I didn't have to own any part in that."

"You don't. It's not your fault, baby." I drop a quick kiss on her lips. "Gabe owns the whole fucking shit storm. You know that, right?"

"Yeah. Most of the time." She presses her lips against my chest. "It's all just so...fucked up!"

"Well, yeah, I guess it is." I give her a crooked smile. "Welcome to my life."

Bree reaches up, curls one hand around my neck and pulls me down for a kiss. I open my mouth to turn it into something more, but she pulls back before I can.

"Sweetheart, I'm sorry." Her fingers brush over my neck. "That was shitty of me."

"What do you mean?" I can taste her on my lips, and I want more.

"I shouldn't be feeling sorry for myself. You've been through so much, and this thing with Gabe is just...stupid."

"No, baby." I steal that second kiss and then twist until I can pin her beneath me. "It's not stupid, and that's not what I meant."

"No?" She brushes my hair back from my face and then rests her hand on my shoulder. "Well, maybe not, but—"

I'm not letting her take the blame for anything else. "We've all got shit in our lives that we gotta deal with, and we do our best."

"We try," she agrees. "But it worries me, you know."

"What does?"

251

Her fingers press hard against my skin. "All this crap. The fame, the groupies, the gossip, and that doesn't even touch anything about my mom, Gabe, Knox. *That s*hit. I don't know—"

"Forget about all that. It doesn't matter. I love you and you love me, and that's what counts."

Her eyes widen, a beautiful green that draws me and holds me still at the same time. "You love me?"

"Well, yeah. Fuck, yeah. I told you. You're my girl."

"That doesn't mean you...love me."

"It does to me." I take a soft bite of her bottom lip. "Never called anybody my girl before. Except maybe Lara, and that was so long ago, I don't even fucking remember." A soft, amazed laugh escapes me. "And that was so goddamn different from what I feel for you."

"But, Ajia—"

"You need the words, baby?"

She gives me a serious look. "I don't know. I guess—yeah, maybe I do. I...wasn't prepared. I didn't expect it."

"Why not?"

She swallows, like she doesn't want to say it. "You've been with so many girls. Women. Love is a big step after that."

"Not with you."

She brushes the side of my face, and I lean into her touch. "I love you. You know I do. But...are you sure?"

I try to smile, but it fucking kills me that I've made this beautiful girl doubt herself—and me. I've gotta keep my shit together here.

"Give me a chance, baby." I turn my head to kiss her palm. "I'll give you the words and the actions to back 'em up. All you need to think about is how good we are together."

"Yeah?"

"Yeah." I grin, mostly because I want her to know how happy being with her makes me. "And I'm gonna prove it to you."

She smiles back for real. "And how are you going to do that?"

I don't waste my time answering with words. Not this time. I kiss her instead. Mouth open, lips seeking, tongue sweeping in to find hers. It's not a long kiss, but I keep going back for more, and she keeps encouraging me. Again and again.

"You taste so fucking sweet, baby."

I feel her smile against my mouth. "I wanna taste you, too. You know…"

I pull back. Her expression is wicked and tempting, but I shake my head. "No way, sweet thing. Maybe later, but not now. I want you too much." I grab her hand and pull it against my crotch to prove my point.

"You *are* glad to see me." Her fingers curl around the bulge of my hard cock.

"Fucking leather pants," I mutter as I surge up off the bed. I unzip and shove them down my legs.

"Commando, A?" Bree grins as she watches.

"Too fucking tight for anything else." I kick them off and turn back to her. "And now it's your turn. That fucking skirt has got to go."

She laughs and reaches around to the side. A couple of buttons, and the damn thing unwraps from around her.

I stare at her pussy, covered by only a tiny pair of white panties, and the skirt spread out under her. I swallow like I haven't had a drink of water in *years.* "Is that all that held that fucking thing in place?"

Bree laughs again and pushes up far enough that she can pull her top over her head. Her tits are barely covered by a thin white bra that matches her panties.

"Jesus, woman." I grab the top, tug the skirt out from under her, and throw them both across the room. I thought my dick was hard when I finally got out of my pants. Now it's like fucking granite.

"Come here, baby." Bree opens her arms and dares me through half-open eyes. "I need you."

I kneel on the bed next to her, demand her lips in a kiss that feels as satisfying as it does punishing. She holds nothing back, not even a soft moan that sounds like nothing less than total approval. I drag my mouth over her jaw, down her throat, and across her chest. Her tits tease me from behind the flimsy cover of her bra, her nipples tight and begging for my mouth.

I can't wait another second. I cover her with my mouth, fabric and all, sucking hard. I run my tongue in a lazy circle around her peak, and then I close my teeth over her nipple in a soft bite. She arches against me.

I laugh but don't release her. Can't release her. I do it again and again, loving that I know what pleases her. She wants more; I can tell by the way she moves for me. I do, too, but first things first. I have to get rid of that ridiculous fucking bra and those cock-tease panties.

The bra's easy enough. Her panties are a little different. "You're wet for me, baby," I say when I touch her there.

"God, yes. I want you, A. Inside me." She arches against my hand where it rests above her mound. "You haven't *really* fucked me since—"

"The first time." I take her naked breast in my mouth, teasing her nipple with my tongue and then bite with enough pressure to earn a hiss of approval.

"Don't make me wait, baby. I was a good girl when you wanted to wait, but now…"

She lets the words trail off, surprising me when her hand palms my dick and her fingers close around my shaft. She strokes me up and down, and I can't stop my hips from thrusting into her grip. "See?" She purrs with satisfaction. "You don't want to wait, either."

"No, baby, I don't."

I fumble in the drawer next to the bed and grab a condom. I rip the package open, but Bree stops me. "Let me do it?"

"Do what?"

"Put it on you."

My laugh is a hoarse chuckle of desire. "No way, baby." I kiss her quick and hard. "Not this time. You put your hands on me again, and I'll come before you even get the fucking thing on me."

She pretends to pout, but then she bites my bottom lip and I forget everything except us. Together.

I get myself sheathed and then slip away, dropping open-mouthed kisses between her breasts, over her stomach, against her hips, and at her mound. "Open for me, baby," I mutter as I kneel between her thighs. She parts her legs as I slip my hands under her ass, and I bring her up to my mouth.

"*Ajia.*" She groans my name.

I swipe my tongue over her slit, bottom to top and back again. She tastes so fucking good, like life and love and everything I need to survive for even one more second. I lick her again and then dip my tongue deep in between her lips.

"Oh, God." Her hips flex, pushing her pussy against my mouth. I stab my tongue in her again, then stroke it up to circle her clit. She can't stay still and squirms against me again.

"I love the way you taste." I scrape my teeth over the bud of her clit and slip a finger into her. I push in and out, add another finger, and then fuck her again and again with my fingers as I suck on her clit.

"God, baby." She groans as much as she whispers. It's like she has trouble talking. "You're gonna...make me come. Your mouth..." Her hands shove into my hair and she holds me close.

"Yeah? You like it, don't you, kitten?" I lick her clit, close my teeth in a sharp bite, and then lick it again.

"Oh, yes, baby. *Please.*"

Satisfaction roars through me, and I pump my fingers harder, deeper. Her breathing is coming labored, faster, and when I sink my teeth into her clit this time, I do it harder. Instead of licking, I pull her into my mouth and suck while my tongue dances and swirls.

"Oh, Jesus! Ajia!" She screams my name and her fingers tighten in my hair. Her pussy tightens around my fingers, and her climax rolls over us both.

I slow my hand but let my fingers fuck her through her orgasm. I keep my mouth soft and coaxing on her pussy, and slowly, adorably, she comes back to herself.

She lets out a long breath. "I don't think it's supposed to be like that."

"Like what?" I kiss the inside of her thigh.

"I don't think I'm supposed to come so fast. What do you *do* to me?"

I kiss her other leg, from thigh to knee and back up again. "Just love you, baby. That's it."

She sighs again, and there's no mistaking her satisfaction. "You weren't supposed to do that, you know. I want you *inside me.*"

"I know. I will be."

"When?" She's so fucking cute when she's demanding.

I push up onto my knees and lean down to kiss her, my mouth hot against hers. I fist my cock, holding it to run the tip up and down over the natural lube of her pussy. She groans against my mouth and arches against me. Holy shit, I *have* to take that invitation.

I move forward, pressing just the tip into her. "Yes, baby," she whispers hoarsely, her lips moving against mine. "I need to feel *all* of you."

I go slow, at least as slow as she'll let me, until I'm seated deep inside her. She's taken every bit of me, even as goddamn tight as she is. Maybe she's not a virgin anymore, but she isn't far from it. I hold still for her to adjust to my size.

"Fuck, Ajia." She licks my lips and then sucks my bottom lip into her mouth. "You're so big," she says after a minute. "You fill...all of me."

"Too much, baby?" My arms start to shake with the effort it takes to hold back.

"No!" Her muscles clench to tighten around me. *Fuuuuck!*

I lose a sharp breath. "I'm gonna move now, yeah?"

"Oh, yes. *Please.*"

I sink my tongue into her mouth as I start a slow, careful rhythm. My tongue imitates my cock, and her legs come up around my waist. Invitation or not, I thrust a little harder, faster.

"God, yes, baby." She moans against my lips. "Please, fuck me. Like you want to do it, not like I'm—" Her voice hisses off to nothing.

"Like what, baby?" I'm moving but keeping it as controlled as I can.

"Like I'm...new. Not good at it." She drags her hands up my back, her nails scoring their way. "I want to be your woman."

"You are, baby" I groan and slam into her hard as if to prove it. "You're my woman, and I'm having a fuck of a time not coming. *That's* how good you are."

"No," she breathes. "That's how good *you* are."

"You want more?"

"Yes!" She arches up, shifts her legs, and then somehow I have them tangled around my arms, her knees pushed up to her shoulders. *"Oh, Jesus, yes.* Like that!"

"You sure, baby?" I stroke deep in her again.

"Yes! *God, yes."* She raises her hips to meet mine. "Hard and deep. Just like that."

I give her what she wants, what *I* want, and step up my rhythm. Her body welcomes me, her pussy tight and wet for my aching cock, and I can't drag my mouth from hers as we fuck.

Fucking. It's what we're doing, and yet it's so much more than that. I think I understand it, but more than that, my soul *knows it.* It's an exchange of pleasure between two lovers, yeah, but that's too easy. Too simple. This is me wanting—*needing*—her satisfaction way more than my own. It's me roaring like a beast inside because I know I'm the only man who's ever been with her like this. The only man who will *ever* be with her like this.

She's *mine.*

And more than that, knowing—and loving—that *I'm hers.*

"Ajia. *Jesus, baby."* Her voice fractures. "You're gonna make me come again."

"Yeah?" I increase our rhythm. "You ready for it?"

"Uh, yeah. But with you. *With you."*

I give a low, hoarse chuckle. "Good thing, cause I'm almost there, baby." I try to breathe, but I can't. *"Fuck, I'm almost there."*

My lower back tingles in that familiar way, my balls draw up tight, and I know I can't last long. My breath is almost gone, sweat covers my chest and back, but I can't stop. *Jesus, not now!*

The muscles of Bree's pussy tighten around my cock, and she cries out. "I'm gonna come, baby. I'm—"

Her orgasm takes over, drives us both, and then I'm there in two more strokes. I come with a roar, as hard as I ever have, and I slam into her until I can't move.

When I find consciousness again, I discover I'm collapsed on her. Her legs are somehow wrapped around my waist again. Our breath wheezes in and out, and I feel my lungs labor for air. My heart pounds with a heavy beat, and I wonder if it's from the best fucking orgasm I've ever had.

More than that, it could be because of the love I feel for this woman.

"Ajia." She smooths one hand against my forehead, brushing damp hair back from my temples and face. Her fingers are trembling, hinting that maybe she's feeling the same things I am.

"I love you, kitten." I have to say it.

"And I love you, A. I always have."

"How did this happen?"

"What?" She gives me a quick, smiling kiss. "This? Don't tell me I need to explain the birds and the bees to you."

I laugh. "Nope. Not *this* this. I mean us. How could you ever have fallen in love with me? Put up with my shit and actually *waited* for me to grow a pair of balls and get smart?"

"Oh, *that* this." She kisses me again. "Well, I'm not sure I can explain it, but I think it had something to do with you being a part of this *wicked* rock band. I mean, who can resist a hot lead singer? There I was, a silly little girl who didn't know any better except to develop this wicked crush, you see—"

"Say no more." I stop her with my mouth, my tongue. "You were a smart fucking girl who knew better than everybody around you."

"Well, maybe." She smiles. "I know one thing for sure."

"What's that?"

"I love you." She kisses me again. "I always have, and I always will."

"And I love you."

And somehow, no matter what lousy shit I've done or how bad I've fucked up, Bree saved me. I'm not a fucking loser anymore. Not the asshole who doesn't deserve a goddamn thing.

I'm Ajia Stone, the guy Bree Gallagher loves, and I'm the luckiest son of a bitch on the planet.

Epilogue

Ajia

The venue is packed. We've been playing to sold-out shows ever since L.A., all through California, Oregon, and now into Washington. We're in Seattle tonight, and it's a special show.

It's Bree's birthday.

My kitten is twenty today, and I'm going to make sure she remembers this birthday above all others.

We just finished with *No Doubt,* always a crowd pleaser. It's my moment, one the band and I planned. Everybody's excited, except maybe Knox, but he isn't saying much these days. He kind of fucked himself with the way he was acting, and nobody's feeling all friendly toward him right now. He's a stubborn fuck and might go through the rest of the tour being an ass.

He ought to know better. The rest of us can wait him out.

Just like we're waiting on Zayne. It's up and down with him. Some days he's there with us; others, he's walking a thin fucking line that's going to bite him in the ass if he isn't careful. Noah and Rye are doing what they can to be there for him, but he's fighting us all every step of the way.

Tonight's a good night. Zayne's sharp, Noah's excited like a little kid, and Rye's quietly satisfied. We'll see how well Knox pulls through for me.

The lights come up on stage, brighter than they normally are when we go to the next song, and I glance over at Bree. She's perched on her stool just off stage, London seated next to her. My beautiful girl questions me with a look, glances around the stage and then out toward the audience. She's seen our show every goddamn night, and I know she's wondering what the hell is going on.

"Before we start to the next song, I want to do something a little different. You fucking with me, Seattle?"

The crowd screams their approval and I grin. I look at Bree and I crook my finger for her to come out on stage. She stares back, her eyes grown so wide they overshadow her face, and then she turns to look behind her. Nothing there, just a wall, and I have to laugh.

I don't give her any more time before I stride across the stage and grab her hand. "Ajia!" She tries to pull back, but I'm not having any of that. I tug her with me, onto the stage.

The crowd erupts, although I'm not sure if they know who she is. Maybe it's because she looks fucking hot—and she does. She's wearing a new white dress I bought for her. I told her it was a birthday present, but it was really because I had this planned all along. It's tight around her waist and hips, and low cut enough to show off her boobs to perfection. It makes me want to stare and then cover her to keep any other guy from looking. Her hair falls loose around her shoulders, just like I love it, and her cheeks are an adorable pink.

I slide my arm around her waist and pull her against my hip. We stop at the mic. Most of the noise dies off.

"In case you don't recognize her, this is Bree Gallagher. She's Knox's baby sister." I wave at him behind us, and he makes a fuss, grinning and waving and faking it for the audience. As long as he steps up and continues to play his part, I don't give a fuck.

"You've been hearing a lot of rumors about all of us." I jerk my head backward, indicating the band. Noah waves from his drumkit. "Well, there's one I want to confirm. It's true. Bree's my girlfriend, and we're *very* happy together."

A few groans and cries of "No!" mingle with a lot of cheers and sharp whistles. I look at her with a smile, and her eyes are still big enough to take over her whole face.

"What are you doing?" she whispers fiercely. She looks at the audience anxiously.

I put my hand over the mic. "Claiming you."

Her eyes soften despite her nerves. "A, baby, you don't—"

I lean down for a kiss, cutting off anything else she was going to say. The crowd goes wild.

I grin at the audience. "And not only is she my girl, today is her birthday!"

More whistles and cheers and shouts fill the auditorium until I raise my arm. "How about it? Y'all want to help us celebrate?"

The noise erupts again, and then I drop my arm. The band launches into *Birthday,* because if Bree's twentieth isn't a good time to cover The Beatles, when is? We all sing, even Noah, and I whirl Bree around in a swing dance routine that she doesn't really know but picks up quick enough. She's laughing, blushing, and looks so goddamn fuckable, I want to drag her out of there right fucking now.

That's not going to happen, and I know it. We've got a fucking show to finish, and I'll do my part. Still, as the song winds down, I do the only thing I can. I give her one big whirl so she spins into my arms and jerk her close. It's not tender, it's not careful, it's not cute. It's kind of a dick move, a stamp of possession, and I do it real fucking deliberately.

I want the whole world to know that Bree Gallagher belongs to me, and I belong to her. Knox hates the idea, but London's in charge of video and pictures, and I want them plastered on the internet like wallpaper on every fucking page. Everywhere.

"You're mine, kitten," I shout over the applause of the crowd. "Now everybody knows it."

Her smile is radiant. "And you're mine. Everybody knows that, too."

"Good."

"So that's it? You're giving up Garage Girl and Tits for good?"

I give her a wicked grin. "Never really wanted 'em in the first place, and I gave 'em up the first time I went down on you."

"Ajia!" She tries to look shocked, but I can see the satisfaction settle over her.

"You're mine, kitten," I say again, just to be sure. Then I do the only thing I can.

I kiss her like it's the end of the fucking world.

THE END

PLAYLIST

These aren't necessarily the songs that I listened to while writing
Wycked Crush, although some of them are. Mostly, my writing
playlist is far too eclectic to make sense to anyone but me. These are
the songs that Ajia, Bree, and the rest of the band listened to during
the course of the book.

Highway to Hell – AC/DC
Welcome to the Jungle – Guns n' Roses
Kickstart My Heart – Mötley Crüe
Every Rose Has Its Thorn – Poison
Here I Go Again – Whitesnake
Heaven – Warrant
Something from Nothing – Foo Fighters
Adventure of a Lifetime – Coldplay
Don't Wanna Know – Maroon 5
Confident – Demi Lovato
Rockstar – Nickelback
SexyBack – Justin Timberlake
Crazy – Gnarles Barkley
Give it to Me – Timbaland ft. Nelly Furtato, Justin Timberlake
Birthday – The Beatles

ACKNOWLEDGEMENTS

Sometimes life throws us a curveball, and that can change your whole direction. It's happened to me more than once in my lifetime, and it isn't always easy to recover. The last time it happened to me, I felt lost, adrift, confused, and alone. I saw no way to go forward, and the things that had always brought me comfort—reading and writing—seemed to have abandoned me, as well. There were times when I wasn't sure I wanted to go on.

Life got better. I got better. It took time, hard work, the love of friends and family, but finally I found my way again. I even found my way back to reading, and then writing. So much had changed! Amazon and the freedom of independent publishing opened avenues that had been missing from traditional publishing, and I found a whole new world.

It wasn't always an easy transition. I was familiar with traditional publishing, thought I should give it another try, but I didn't fit. I'm not sure I ever did. And so, in a fit of temper, I decided to write something that was a total fantasy, something I wrote just for me. It was supposed to open my mind and heart to the freedom of indie publishing, and I never expected to finish it. It was practice.

You now hold that fantasy practice book in your hands. I had such fun writing the first 20,000 words, I kept going. I made a very basic plan: write a 50,000-word book and see what I could do with it. About the time I hit 35,000 words, I knew 50,000 words was a joke, but I also thought I had something. So I kept going, all the way to 89,000 words, and by then I was totally in love with the men of Wycked Obsession.

I didn't do any of this alone. I've had some very wonderful, supportive women in my life who have seen me through everything. Enormous, heartfelt thanks go to my sisters Karen Henderson and JoAnne Mandel, my sister-in-law Kathy Ferguson, and my friends-to-the-end Shannon Canody-Fink, Kathy Hafer, Jenny Hunter,

Mindy Meinking, Kelly Scardino Meller, and Stacy Young. You ladies enrich my life!

I'd like to thank my "team," my beta and ARC readers, brainstormers, and cohorts in crime on Wynne's Way. Here's to you, Kathy Hafer, Nickie Harman, Sherry Goodman Hughes, David Hunt, Rachael Siegel, Karen Wilson, and Stacy Young. Wycked Crush would definitely not be the same book without every one of you!

I would also like to thank Crystal Kaswell, who inspired me to tackle the rock star world in the first place. The men of Sinful Serenade and Dangerous Noise changed my reading and writing life. Tom, Pete, Kit, or Mal? I couldn't decide, so I had to write my own heroes!

Finally, I want to thank you, the reader, for choosing this book from among the many others available to you. I hope you enjoyed your time with Bree and Ajia. Please watch for *Wycked Rumors,* Knox and London's story, coming in the winter of 2017.

ABOUT THE AUTHOR

Reading and writing have been a part of my life forever. I was that odd child who went to the library during summer vacation, and I was reading romances before I quite realized that's what they were. Years later, my habits are still the same.

As Wendy Douglas, I published two historical romance novels, *Shades of Gray* and *The Unlikely Groom,* with Harlequin Historicals. After a long hiatus from publishing, I have returned with new enthusiasm and a different focus. *Wycked Crush,* the first book in the Wycked Obsession series, is the result.

I was born and raised in northwest Iowa and spent most of my adult life in Anchorage, Alaska. When it came time to thaw out my bones, I moved south to the Texas Gulf Coast, where I live with my two very spoiled dachshunds and an assortment of fictional characters who all jockey for position in my head. Sometimes I win, sometimes they do, but it's never dull!

Wycked Rumors

Wycked Obsession Series – Book 2

(Knox's Story)

Coming Winter 2017

[Note: Unedited and subject to change.]

PROLOGUE

LONDON

The restaurant is quiet and dignified, everything I would expect from the finest French establishment in my namesake city. The table is covered with sparkling white linen and set with fine china, silver, and crystal. An elegant silver candlestick holds a flickering white taper, and the mood is perfect.

Colin has already ordered his choice of wine, it's poured and waiting, and so I take a sip. Anything to calm my nerves. They've put me on edge since he picked me up. Something in his voice, his demeanor, his choice of restaurant—everything—tells me he's up to something.

It must be something special, I think to myself. Colin Gilbert is somewhat stoic and unemotional—typically British, he always says—and romantic gestures aren't his style. Could tonight be the night he pops the question?

Do I even want him to? And if he does, how will I answer?

"Have you decided?"

I blink. I haven't looked at the menu.

"No." I shake my head as the waiter approaches. "You order for me. You know what I like."

Colin nods smoothly. He likes it when I defer to him, and in this case, I don't mind. I've been back in England for three days, and this is the first time we've seen each other. I'm hoping our latest separation might drag out of him whatever trace of romance he might have buried deep in his soul.

I can't help watching as he orders. He's slender, not soft but definitely not muscular. The perfect body for an English gentleman, he claims. I don't know if that's true, but I accept it if he's happy with himself. His hair is dark brown, curly on top and short on the sides, and his eyes are a shade lighter than his hair. He's maybe five inches taller than my 5'5", which seems comfortable enough, and dressed in a navy-blue-almost-black suit and coordinating tie.

We're a nice match, he says, although he does complain about my hair being too red. I laughed the first time he said it. Maybe I *do* have auburn highlights in my hair—they're natural—but it's just as much brown as it is red. My eyes are brown, too—hazel, they're probably called—but Colin says they're too gold. They make me stand out, and he'd rather I not draw too much attention.

He isn't the first one to wish that.

For myself, I'm through with that kind of thinking. I've lived most of my life under that pressure, and I'm done with it. Forever. I made myself a promise the day I turned eighteen. By the time I graduated from college, I'd no longer be the shy, innocent girl who faded into the background. I'd be strong and independent, a woman defined by nothing and no one except being my absolute and authentic self.

The time has come. I graduated with my degree in Communications a week ago.

Colin sends the waiter off and looks at me with a distant smile. Is it my imagination, or has he been preoccupied since he picked me up?

"Is everything all right?" I try to smile in an easy, understanding way.

"Yes. Why do you ask?"

"You seem…distracted." He's an attorney—a *solicitor,* I remind myself—and work frequently concerns him.

"No. Although I do want to have a word."

"All right." It's the British way of saying, *we need to talk.* Uneasiness snakes through me. That's not usually a sign of anything good, is it? On the other hand, maybe non-romantic Colin doesn't understand the usual clues. I learned long ago that he sees things much differently than I do.

"What is it?" I ask when he doesn't continue.

He shakes his head. "We'll save that for later. How was your trip?"

"Fine."

"Did you travel with your parents?"

"My mother. Dad...went ahead without us." I don't explain—again—that my father never goes out in public with us. Colin knows the situation. We've talked about the realities of my family dynamic more than once.

"Yes, of course. And your graduation?"

"Uneventful." I swallow the words that I really want to say, mostly because I've already said them—and it was a waste of breath. I asked Colin to attend the ceremony, and he begged off. Too busy. Too far. Too expensive.

It's always too much *something*.

"And your plans now?"

I delay my answer while our waiter places an artfully-arranged vinaigrette salad before each of us. Colin begins eating immediately, while I wait.

"I've submitted a number of resumes, both here and in the States."

"The States?" He looks up. "Southern California?" He says it like he means the very pit of hell. The garbage dump of all humanity. I suppose, to Colin, that's the case.

"It's home," I remind him mildly. "Where I grew up."

"Yes, well..." His nose wrinkles up like he's just noticed a bad smell. It makes me want to push him a little.

"I've had some very promising interest from a record company in L.A. I interned there last summer."

"I thought you were staying in England permanently now."

"That depends."

"On what?"

I rest a flat gaze on his face. He ought to know; we've been seeing each other for months now. But I also recognize his unemotional reserve. Colin Gilbert never assumes *anything*.

"It depends on the job offers." I try to keep my tone patient. How difficult can it be to understand? "And how—fulfilling my life here can be. You know, because of *my father.*"

"Right." He nods and returns his attention to his salad. "Have you thought about *not* working?"

"Not working?" I pick up my salad fork but then drop it back to the tabletop before I take a bite. "Why wouldn't I work? I worked hard for my degree! What would I do instead?"

He finishes his salad calmly and sits back in his chair. He looks at me after a moment, tilting his head as though he wants to see me from a different angle. "I'd like to set you up in a flat. Keep your time available for *me.*"

"I…" The words fall away. "Keep my time available for you?" I blink and pull my head back. "What the bloody hell does that mean?"

His expression tightens, and I know it's my language. Colin doesn't like ladies to curse. Right now, I really don't give a good goddamn.

"Exactly what it sounds like. I want to be your priority."

"My *priority?*" I have to repeat it, hear it again, to believe it. "My priority?" I say once more. "Do you mean *my priority,* or *my only concern?*"

He narrows his eyes. "London…"

Why doesn't he finish?

"What about me, Colin?" I ask stiffly. "Am I *your* priority?"

"London," he says again, and this time he shakes his head.

"What? We aren't engaged. Why should—"

"Engaged?" He frowns. "What do you mean?"

I blink and imitate his expression. "Engaged. As in we've made a commitment to each other. That we will have a future together. Why would I make you *the* priority in my life if I'm not one in yours?"

He stares at me long enough to make me uncomfortable, and then finally he sighs. "London, you must realize the impossibility of what you're suggesting."

"The impossibility of what? My being a priority in your life?"

"Of our becoming engaged."

An odd feeling races through me, like an electric shock sent straight through to my nervous system. I'm hot, then cold, then hot again. "What do you mean, Colin?"

He scowls and shakes his head. "Do I really have to say it?"

"Yes." I nod emphatically. "You do. Absolutely."

"It can't come as a surprise to you that a man in my position can't consider *marriage* to…Hugh Kennedy's illegitimate daughter."

"Hugh Kennedy's illegitimate daughter?" I repeat carefully, my throat suddenly dry. *"And a man in your position?"*

He tries to hold my gaze, but he can't do it. Brown eyes that suddenly appear weak and untrustworthy slide away.

"You know my goals," he finally says. "I have grander plans than to remain a simple solicitor for the rest of my life. With the right connections, the right wife, I can—"

"The right wife," I repeat. I don't give a fuck if I interrupt him. "And that couldn't possibly be *Hugh Kennedy's illegitimate daughter.* So that must mean you're asking me to become—what? Your *mistress?"*

"London…"

I nod as though things suddenly make sense. And they do. They fucking do. "Your mistress," I say again. "You want to set me up in a flat where I can wait for you to have time to come round for a quick fuck."

He flinches but says nothing. I press on.

"This might come as something of a shock to you, Colin, but you overestimate the attraction of your cock, you asshole."

"London!"

His voice is strangled, his voice horrified, and I really don't give a damn. I rise from my chair with every bit of elegance my mother instilled in me, reach for my purse, and drop my napkin on top of my untouched salad. "I'll find my own way home, you wanker."

I don't turn back. Why would I? I may not have an undying love for this man, but my emotions *are* involved. I trusted him to believe that he at least cared enough to treat me *decently.* Hugh Kennedy's illegitimate daughter deserves *some* reasonable consideration. Some respect. Doesn't she?

Don't I?

It doesn't matter. I step out onto the street and look for a taxi. Quickly and oh-so-efficiently, Colin has destroyed whatever there might once have been between us. Shattered any hope that this time—this man—would be different.

I should have known better by now. Men want one thing, and women want another. Sex for security and commitment. Isn't that the exchange?

Maybe for others. Not for Hugh Kennedy's illegitimate daughter. Born on the wrong side of the sheets, as I've heard it whispered, means never aspiring to a *real* relationship apparently.

A man to love me for who I am, and no other reason.

Tears shock me when they begin to prickle behind my eyelids. I haven't cried in years, and I know instantly I'm not emotional over Colin fucking Gilbert. It's the reminder that the accident of my birth makes me…dirty. Not good enough. Someone to be hidden away or embarrassed over.

So maybe London Kennedy, embarrassment to her family and friends, ought to start thinking about herself, suggests a fierce voice from deep inside me.

I choke back a laugh, or is it more tears? Yeah, maybe I should. Instead of looking for trust, romance or even respect, why not accept the obvious that life has laid out for me?

Work hard. Earn respect. Protect yourself, and forget about relationships. For that kind of thing, sex is the answer. Sex doesn't waste its time with love and happily ever after. Sex doesn't take your feelings and smash them into smithereens. Sex fills a physical need. The big O is the reward.

Isn't that how guys look at it? I know it is, so why waste my time expecting anything else? I ought to be *thanking* Colin! He did me a big fucking favor. Reordered my *priorities.*

Relationships? They aren't bloody worth it. I've seen what a mess they cause.

"Fuck love," I mutter as a cab pulls up to the curb. "Who needs it?"

Who, indeed? That's going to be my new motto, and if I do it right, it'll see me through anything.

CHAPTER 1

LONDON

The photographer's studio buzzes with activity. I stop just inside the entrance, keeping well out of the way, and look for a familiar face. I recognize the guys from Wycked Obsession, of course; anybody in the music industry, or who hasn't been living under a rock for the last six months, would know them. They came out of nowhere, a sudden phenom from Austin, and now they're on tour with Edge of Return, the biggest band since Coldplay.

Not bad for a band with only two albums out.

I straighten my spine and resist the urge to adjust my hemline or tug at the fit of my shirt. I'll admit it: I dressed to impress. I'm wearing a white pencil skirt and a teal blue sleeveless blouse, with coordinating jewelry and three-inch blue heels. I don't expect Knox Gallagher, Wycked Obsession's lead guitarist and my contact within the band, to give a damn what I look like...or even notice anything about me. But Baz Calhoun, the band's manager, might, and I'm not taking any chances.

I want this job.

The photo shoot seems to be breaking up. I recognize every one of the band members: Ajia Stone, lead singer; Noah Dexter, drummer; Zayne Prescott, bassist; Rylan Myles, keyboardist...and Knox. I'd recognize him anywhere. He's one of the best guitarists playing right now, and, with Ajia, co-writer of Wycked Obsession's biggest hits. He's also the best-looking guy in a band made up of some of the hottest men on the freaking planet.

The other band members disappear, while Knox continues to talk to the photographer. Baz explained that Knox acts as the band's unofficial leader, and I can see that must be true. From photo shoots to meeting with me about the band's marketing and PR needs, Knox exudes an element of *control.*

So, where's Baz?

I look around but don't see anyone who has that harried, I'm-so-busy-I'm-going-to-tear-my-hair-out look I've seen on other band managers. That leaves me to stare at Knox some more.

He's tall, maybe 6'2", and muscular. His arms and chest are tattooed, revealed because he's not wearing a shirt. The meaning and placement of his tattoos are of great interest to his female fans. I did a little on-line research before our meeting, and it left me both amused and alarmed at the information and speculation out there.

None of what I read about Knox seems to have done him justice. His hair is long, to his shoulders, and a deep sable color that looks so much richer in person. It's like strands of brown, black and ginger all tangled together, and some perfectly decadent part of me wants to discover for myself how soft it is. His lower face is covered with the scruff of a few days worth of whiskers, darker than his hair, and I have to admit it looks totally freaking *hot.*

His facial features are nicely proportioned. His nose is maybe a little wide, but his bottom lip is perfectly *bitable,* according to one on-line fan site. His eyes are lighter colored than I would have expected, sometimes gray and sometimes green, according to his fans. I can't tell the shade today, not from where I stand, and a part of me wants to move forward to see for myself. I almost take a step forward—and then I realize that he's staring back at me.

I can feel my reaction: my eyes widen and my cheeks flush. Damn. I've changed in so many ways from the shy, embarrassed girl I used to be, but I've never quite learned how to control that damned blush.

Knox grins, but it's more of an I-know-you-want-me smile than a friendly expression. Asshole. So he's like all rock stars. Sure of himself and his appeal, and not afraid to take advantage of it.

And why not? an impatient voice snaps inside of me. *He can get by with it. Every girl in America wants him—and if you had the chance, you wouldn't turn him down, either.*

Bloody hell.

I don't have time for this. More than that, I don't *want* to notice him as a man. That wanker, Colin, cured me of that kind of rubbish, and I'm *not* looking at Knox Gallagher any longer.

I pull my phone from my purse and glance at the time. I check emails and text messages. Nothing new. *Now, pay attention,* I tell myself. *You're here to meet with Knox and Baz as a* professional. *Not some daft cow looking for a quick dance in the sheets.*

Properly chastised, I look back only to discover Knox is gone. The photographer is bent over, messing with a camera case at her feet, and so I approach.

"Pardon me. Can you tell me where Knox Gallagher went?"

The photographer looks up at me through a tangle of long graying hair. "You supposed to be here?"

"I have a meeting with him. I'm from the label."

It's only partly true. Wycked Obsession's record label *was* interested in me for an in-house position, but they ended up hiring someone else. They think I'll be a better fit after some on-the-road experience, and so I'm here at their recommendation, hoping that Knox and Baz agree.

She nods her head toward the far corner of the room. "He's in the dressing room."

I turn. *Dressing room* is a generous term. The studio is one big loft, and there's an area partitioned off with a big screen that is, apparently, the dressing room. With Baz nowhere in sight, I head in that direction.

"Hello?" I step around the partition to find some odd pieces of furniture and a couple of rows of rectangular metal racks filled with men's clothes draped on hangers. "Pardon me?"

Clothing rustles, but I hear nothing else, so I try again. Politely. "Knox? Uh, Mr. Gallagher?"

My nerves ratchet up as I wait. I've met my share of famous people over the years, but this is different. Knox has the final say about whether I get this job—and the more arduous this whole process has become, the more I want it.

"Well, hell, honey. If you wanted to see my cock, all you had to do was ask."

He steps out from between two racks of clothes, stark fucking naked.

I try—bloody hell, do I try—to keep my gaze on his face. I fail. Dramatically. His chest is broad, tattooed with a Wycked Obsession logo over one pec, a colorful chest piece over the other—a dragon draped around a Celtic cross—and the words Wicked Is As Wycked Does angled over one hip.

That, of course, leads me lower. To his cock that—*oh, my God*—even in its only semi-hard state, is twice the size of Colin's in full erection.

What must it be like to ride him to orgasm? My panties become drenched and my nipples tighten at just the thought.

Jesus, luv, no more men! Remember?

I force my gaze back to his face and stiffen when I see his smirk. Fucking rock stars.

I swallow. A prissy part of me recognizes how completely unacceptable this is, but most of me knows I have to handle it just right. Rock stars—celebrities of any kind—live by their own rules. They pretty much get by with whatever strikes their fancy. If I want to play the game, I have to learn the system. After all, Baz made it clear that taking this job means working closely with Knox—and I can't do that if he's laughing behind my back at some prudish reaction on my part to a little nakedness.

"Well, hell, baby." I saunter close with an appreciative smile. "I didn't know you were offering such…personal service as part of the interview." I recognize a flicker of awareness in his almost-gray eyes, but that doesn't stop me. My research told me everything I need to know about the Wycked Obsession guys and their manwhore reputations.

I wrap my fingers around his shaft and stroke it up and down, just a couple of times. "I would have brought my camera if I'd known, and we could have posted a few pictures on Tumblr."

His gaze darkens to one of absolute awareness, like the two of us are suddenly and unquestioningly the only two beings on the planet. He closes his hand over mine and drags my palm up and down over his cock a few more times. His grin is a naughty smile that says, *What the hell do we have here?*

"Interview, huh? You must be…Kennedy?"

"London," I correct. "London Kennedy."

I pull my hand from his—and his cock. "I'd shake your hand," I say as casually as I can, "but I think we've already moved past that point."

His eyebrows rise. "Does that mean I get to grab your pussy?"

I can't help it. I laugh. "You taking advice from a certain businessman turned politician?"

He frowns, but then he laughs, too. "No. God, no. Not looking for any controversy here. Forget I said that."

"Good." I nod emphatically. "Now, if you want to put on some clothes, we can talk about this PR and marketing position you have available."

"What if I want to do it naked?"

I shrug. A very surprising—and mischievous—part of me wishes he would. "Your choice. You're the boss."

"And you?"

"Me?"

"Will you be naked, too?"

"Ah, no." I shake my head with as much emphasis as my earlier nod. "My girly bits aren't quite—agreeable to being naked for a first interview."

"Girly bits." He laughs and shakes his head. "Too bad. It might have been fun."

"I'm not sure your manager would agree."

Knox turns and disappears between the rows of clothing racks. "About that," he calls, and I hear sounds that might indicate he's getting dressed. "Baz texted. He got held up at the label. It's just us."

"Oh." I swallow my disappointment, ninety percent sure it means I won't have an answer about the job today. "Are you all right with that?"

"Sure."

He walks back out, fastening a pair of skinny jeans over his remarkable hips. I got so caught up in the sight of his cock, I forgot about the rest of him. The man-scaping, the delicious V that starts above his hips and ends at his pelvis, the elaborate guitar tattooed on his thigh. I remember it all now, as clearly as if he hadn't covered it up at all.

I swallow. Part of me wishes I'd just said, *screw it, let's do this thing naked.* The rest of me fully appreciates the sight of Knox in those dark skinny jeans and vintage Jim Morrison T-shirt.

Hold on there, luv! I drag my thoughts to a halt. Or maybe it's my libido. Whatever, he's *dangerous.*

Knox Gallagher might be the hottest thing this side of the sun, but keep your mind on business!

"There's a Starbucks not too far from here." Thank God, he started to speak. "We can go there and talk."

"Out in public?"

"Why not?"

"Uh…" How exactly do I say it? "Fans? Interruptions?"

He shrugs. "It's Southern California. C-list celebrities are a dime a dozen here."

I smirk. "Not sure I'd classify you as 'C-list,' but you're right about it being common to see celebrities here." I take a breath. "Okay, let's go."

"You got wheels?"

"Yeah." I send him a look. "You don't?"

"I got a tour bus." He waggles his eyebrows. "Otherwise, I hire a car."

"You trust my driving?"

He grins, and my heart stumbles. *Bollocks!* What is it about rock stars, and this one in particular, that makes me all hot and anxious…and *wet?*

And goddamn Colin for being such a douche as to drop the mistress bomb on me before we'd had sex in—what? Three months? Maybe if we *had,* I wouldn't be so…edgy.

"It's only a couple of blocks," Knox says easily. "If the label sent you, you must be safe to go at least *that far.*"

I nod, wrestling my physical awareness of him to the back of my mind. I lead the way from the studio to my coppery-colored Audi R8 Spyder, parked just down the street.

He whistles. "Nice ride."

"A graduation present from my father."

"College?"

"High school."

He gives me a look I've seen before. It means anything from *you must be rich* to *who's your father?* I'm not about to explain anything about Hugh Kennedy and my cocked-up family life until I have to, so I just gesture toward the car as if to say, *get in.*

We do, and we're pulling into the Starbucks parking lot before I can think of anything else to say. Knox hasn't made any effort to speak, either, and I'm glad. It's hard to concentrate with the heat of his big, hard body so close to mine.

I order iced tea, Knox gets iced coffee, and we find a seat at a relatively private table. Well, private for Starbucks. He sits back in his seat and stares at me.

"Tell me about yourself."

I take a deep breath. *This is it.*

"I graduated from UCLA this spring. Communications. I interned with your label last summer. I know this isn't exactly a *publicist* position, that I'll be doing the actual marketing and PR." I pause long enough to organize my thoughts. "Heavy on computer work, which is fine. I'm well-versed with both Mac and PCs. I have experience in most software, and I'm familiar with all the social media sites online. I—"

"Baz can get all that shit from your resume. I want to know about *you.*"

"Me?" Why the hell does my voice squeak like Minnie Mouse? "What do you want to know about *me?*"

"We're on tour for a couple of months yet. You ready to live with the band twenty-four seven?"

"Yes. Of course."

"You ever been on the road living in a tour bus? It isn't easy."

"No." I shake my head slowly. "But I understand the celebrity lifestyle."

"The celebrity lifestyle?" He snorts. "What the fuck does that mean?"

Why does he have to sound so goddamn *appealing,* even in his snark? I am *so* not noticing guys right now! And how many fucking times do I have to remind myself of it?

"Traveling a lot," I say quickly, talking fast so I can pretend that he doesn't make me nervous as hell. "Public exposure. Paparazzi. Fans. Fucking your way through—"

Oh, shit! Heat floods my face as the words die a sudden, humiliating death. *Jesus.* Was I really going to say *fucking your way through your fan base?*

"Fucking my way through...?" he repeats with a smirk. *Bloody hell.*

I fight the urge to close my eyes or hide behind my hands. They're shaking, anyway, and I don't want Knox to see it. *"Oh, my God! I am so sorry!* I didn't mean *you,* specifically, but that was completely uncalled for. I—*Jesus!* I don't know what I was thinking!"

He lifts one shoulder, along with one eyebrow. "Been known to happen."

If only I could smile, make light of it, but I know better. I fucked this up, and I have to own it. "I read some things on the Internet," I admit meekly, "but that doesn't excuse what I said. I'm terribly sorry."

He perks up. "Anything good?"

"What?"

"On the Internet. What'd you read? Anything good about us?"

Part of me wants to laugh. He's like a kid. The rest of me is busy fighting to keep a calm expression.

Don't blush. For God's sake, do not *blush!*

I take a breath. "About you? Just...you know. The tattoos and piercings."

"Which ones?" He flicks his earlobe, and for the first time, I notice he wears a diamond stud and a gold ring behind it.

"Not...there."

"Where, then?"

"Are you enjoying this?"

He shakes his head, his amazing sable-colored hair shifting to cover his earlobe, but I see the devil in his mostly gray eyes. "Nope. Just trying to find out what they're saying about me on the internet."

I settle back in my chair and cross my arms over my chest. *"You know what they're saying.* That your cock is tattooed. Or pierced. Or both."

He gives me a wicked smile that gives away just how much he *is* enjoying this. "Then you already know for yourself that it isn't either."

"That's true." I try to sound matter of fact, but my gaze drops like I'm looking past the solid wooden table and through thick fabric of his jeans. Picturing him naked again. And maybe I am—but he doesn't need to know that. I drag my eyes back upward.

"We don't need to confirm or deny those rumors on the internet," I add desperately.

Knox takes a drink of his iced coffee and considers me with a look. "You say you know something about the *celebrity lifestyle?*" He uses my words again, sounding amused—or maybe irritated. I can't tell which. "Why?"

Here you go, luv. This is it.

I've known it was coming. I don't want to admit much about my past and my family; never have. Still, I thought I'd accepted that I'd have to do this. Faced with it, I'm not so sure.

Normal people with normal families don't run up against this kind of thing. I've whined about it most of my entire life. When your father is famous—*infamous*—it's a whole different ballgame. Full disclosure. In the long run, it's the right thing to do. The easiest.

And the hardest.

"My father is Hugh Kennedy. The movie—"

"Producer."

"Yes. You've heard of him."

"Everybody who's seen a fucking movie in the last twenty years knows who Hugh Kennedy is. His string of hits is unprecedented."

I nod. "Twenty-two years."

Knox blinks. "That's a pretty specific number."

I shrug. "I'm twenty-two."

"Ahh…" He drags the word out. "You're his muse. His lucky charm."

"No." My laugh sounds more bitter than I mean it to. "My mother is."

He watches me for a heartbeat, and I see the instant he puts it all together. The stories and the gossip. Everything that's been said about my family—and me. True or not.

"London Kennedy." He says my name softly.

"That's right." I take a quick sip of my tea, mostly just to steal a few seconds to think. To breathe. "Illegitimate daughter of Hugh Kennedy." I say it like I'm reading a bullet-list of facts from *USA Today*. "The result of his affair with actress Marisol Malone. The relationship that has remained unacknowledged for twenty-two years. The mistress and daughter he only pretends to hide, while he remains married to Adele Southworth Kennedy, his beloved wife, and father to their three legitimate children."

I pause for a breath that takes too long and comes too ragged. *"That* London Kennedy."

Chapter 2

Knox

Fuck me. This girl is trouble…and, deep down, I know I'm going to hire her.

If she wants the job, it's hers.

Not because I want to fuck her—and that much is *so* fucking true. I do. Not gonna waste my time pretending she doesn't make my cock hard as fucking granite. Wanted her from the second I caught her staring at me from the other side of the photographer's studio. Fuck. I showed her my cock, just to see how far I could push her, and she stroked the fucker like a goddamn pro.

Jesus, it makes me even harder just thinking about it, but I can't go there right now. Not sitting in Starbucks in the middle of the day.

Besides, I can already tell this woman is brave, willing to take risks and no bullshit, and she deserves some respect for that.

Exactly the kind of publicist we need.

It isn't a true publicist's job. We're calling it that, but it's marketing and PR and publicity, all crammed together into a pile of shit and done from a seat on a tour bus. It's close, personal, and looking out for the band's interests instead of the label's. Somebody who, when they speak for us, says what *we* want to say and shows what we want to show.

Whatever the hell that means. Still figuring it all out. I'm shit at doing it. I like the control, but don't have the patience or finesse to say, "Fuck you," in a way that they won't figure out is an insult until it's too late.

I get the feeling that London Kennedy can manage that just fine.

She's been through some shit in her life. In some ways, maybe even uglier shit than we have, and for fucking longer. She knows how to keep a low profile. I know fuck all more about what her parents did than anything about London herself. She looks like any man's version of a wet dream, and I can't help running a slow gaze from her head to as far down as I can see.

She's got reddish-brown hair and oddly-colored golden-brown eyes. They see a lot, those eyes, and I want to know what that means. How does the world look to her? A lot of deep shit is going on in there.

A few freckles spread out over her nose and across her cheeks. Can't say I remember hooking up with a girl who had freckles, but on her, they're fucking hot. Her teeth are white and straight, like her old man paid for the best dentist in L.A., and her lips are full. Kissable.

Fuckable.

She blinks those strange golden eyes suddenly. "Is it too much?"

Looking at her without fucking her? Yeah, it's way too goddamn much.

"What?"

"My background. My—father." Her gaze slides away. "More than you want to take on?"

"No. Fuck no. Why would you think that?"

She lifts one shoulder. "Not everybody feels that way."

"Fuck them."

She looks back at me. "You can afford to feel like that." She points in my direction. "You can get pretty much anything you want. Me? Not so much."

I sit back and look at her like I've been wanting to. Deep and hard and seeing every part of her body. A fine fucking body it is, too. Full tits, tiny waist, hips and an ass that a man can really grab hold of when he fucks her, and legs that'd wrap around me real fucking perfectly.

But she's not a groupie, a one and done I'll forget as soon as I come. Or a fangirl who's heard I like things a little rough and wants to find out what that means. If she takes the job, she'll be around all of us *all the fucking time*—and that means a little discretion.

My cock hates the restraint.

"What about your old man? He can't get you what you want?"

She pulls back like I slapped her. I get it. I hate that I understand, but I've got a fucking sperm donor who taught me everything I need to know about *fatherhood.*

"If I asked him, my father would give me whatever I want. It's easy to give...things. I've never asked him and never will, so if you're expecting some kind of special...favors from him—"

"Fuck no!" It's a harsh snap that suits my opinion of fathers just fine. "I don't take help from anybody. Not that kind."

She nods sharply, like we're in agreement, and I let it go. Don't want to fucking talk about *fatherhood,* anyway. Just the idea ruins my fucking mood.

"Moving on," I mutter after a quick drink of my iced coffee. "Tell me what you know about Wycked Obsession."

"What?"

"You said you looked us up on the internet. What'd you find? And not the tattoos and piercing stuff."

She gives me a little smile. "Okay. Well, you're out of Austin, Texas, formed about five years ago. You and Ajia Stone were the founding members. You played the local circuit for a few years, put together an EP that went viral pretty quickly, and got yourself signed by a label. You went on tour after your first album, self-titled *Wycked Obsession.* You were on the road for a long time, almost six months, opening for anybody they paired you with."

I nod, and she keeps going.

"You took six months away from touring, except for local gigs and the occasional national appearance, and released *Wicked Is As Wycked Does* about a month ago. The first single is *Tonight,* hanging solidly in the top five on the charts. The video is concert and tour footage, but rumor has it that your next video will be a bigger production."

She pauses for a sip of iced tea, takes a breath, and then continues when I don't say anything. "You're on tour with Edge of Return, pretty damned impressive for a band less than two years out of Austin." She angles her head toward me like it's some sort of salute or something. "Your sister Bree is touring with you this summer, and your female fans are...not happy."

"What?" That part comes as a surprise. "Why the fuck do they care if Bree's with us?"

"You don't seem to be as…" She pauses as though searching for the right word. "Promiscuous with her around."

I laugh. I can't help it. *"Promiscuous?"* I shake my head. "Fuck me, English. They think we're not fucking enough cause my sister's along?"

"Apparently."

"Then they better be prepared to be disappointed for a while yet." My expression settles into something more serious. I never joke about what Bree means to me. "She's with us all summer, and my sister's a fuck of a lot more important to me than some random fan's opinion."

"The two of you are close."

It's not a question, and I give a sharp nod. "Been there for each other through a lot."

"You could use that to…I don't know. Appeal to a different part of your audience." Her gaze slides away as she pauses. "Connect with the less horny ones?"

I give her a wicked smile that usually gets me my way. "Aren't many of those in our fan base, English. They're all hot for one of us."

"Lucky you."

"Jealous?"

"No." Her snort is fucking cute, but I feel myself tighten up. That's a description I usually reserve for my sister. "Just wondering how we can…upgrade that. Your sister—"

"Is off limits. Not using her for some media attention."

London angles her head, like she's seeing something new. Different. "All right."

I let it go. I'm a little touchy about Bree. She was just a kid when our sperm donor took off. Eight and I was 12. Old enough to take up the slack, and I wanted her to stay a kid, fun loving and free of what the world is really like, for as long as possible. It worked for a while, but now she's complaining how she's grown up, and I'm too protective.

Bree might be almost 20, but…no. Fuck that. Everything in me stiffens. I'm not ready for her to grow up. She pushed back against my *protective bullshit,* as she calls it, and I'm trying. Keeping my mouth shut as much as I can. It's easier when the other guys are there; we all keep an eye out for her and always have. I'm doing the best I can, but shit still gets out of hand.

Jesus! Our asshole stepfather, Gabe, is a prime fucking example. He's been hitting on her for months now, for Christ's sake! Newly married to our mom, he thinks Bree ought to be some kind of sex toy for him.

Fuck, no. Fuck that—and him. He's the reason she's on tour with us, and I'm not letting anybody take advantage of his sick shit for some goddamn publicity!

"So what else do you have in mind for us?" It comes out as a snarky demand, but I don't care. This shit with Bree makes me crazy.

"What do you mean?"

"If you get the job." Deliberately, I make it sound less certain than it is in my mind. "What're your plans to get us…out there?"

"Well…" She blinks, sips from her iced tea, and then relaxes against her seat to look at me. So, her ideas for publicity don't make her tense up. It says *confidence,* and I like that.

"I'd upgrade your website," she says finally. Slow and careful, like she's giving it serious thought before she speaks. "It needs a total redesign. Show off the album covers and your logo. I'd give you each a page, connect directly to merch sales and link to a YouTube channel for some video blogging. You've all got Facebook and Twitter accounts, but none of you use them effectively, so we'd change that. Post new content every day. Interact with some of your fan sites, maybe get the more serious ones to act like old-fashioned fan clubs used to. Start posting to Instagram, maybe some live feed, and—"

"Enough." I blow out a breath. "Jesus, I get it. Plaster us all over the internet."

"Pretty much."

"And where's this *content* coming from?"

She smiles. It's part daring and part naughty, and hardens my dick again, just when it was starting to soften. *Jesus.* I want to know what the naughty part of her is thinking.

"Some from me. Some from you blokes. We'd set up a calendar—a system—and everybody participates. I'd organize and manage it, of course, and take up the slack on the days you don't post."

"Good luck getting those other fuckers to do anything. They don't listen to me."

She smirks. "They'll do it."

"You sound pretty sure of yourself."

"I'll...convince them."

What the fuck does that mean? "Don't know how, but you're welcome to try."

Her smile widens. "Never dare a woman. Don't you know that?"

I drag a lazy, almost insolent gaze from her head as far down as I can see. She notices...and responds. I hear the sharp breath, cut off abruptly, and her nipples tighten beneath her bright blue top. Her smile fades.

"What else, honey?"

She swallows. "What?" Her voice is soft, ragged-sounding.

"What other dares you willing to take?"

Her eyes grow darker as she stares, narrow, and then her eyelids drift shut. Satisfaction mingles with an odd disappointment. I've seen women react that way a million times.

"Oh, you're good." Her eyes pop open, settling back to that unusual golden color, and she levels me with a harsh, serious gaze. "Bloody brilliant, actually. I don't know how you do it, exactly, but I see how you get your way."

"My way?"

She nods, sharply, and a strand of reddish hair falls forward over her shoulder. "You give a girl *the look,* call her *honey,* and she falls in line with whatever you want. Clever wanker, aren't you?"

"Wanker?"

"Fucker. Asshole." She lifts one shoulder in a casual shrug. "I've spent enough time in England to pick up some of their...idioms."

"You think that's what this is about? Some fucking flirting so I can get in your pants?"

"Is it?"

"I don't fuck employees."

"I'm not your employee."

"You might be."

"And is this part of the interview? Deciding if you want to fuck me?"

Don't have to decide that. I wanted her from the second I saw her, and that hasn't changed. I *do* have something called self-control, however.

Why the hell don't people ever see beneath the manwhore reputation?

"Irrelevant," I snap in a cold voice, refusing to confirm or deny. I don't lie, but I don't give anybody any ammunition to use against me. "Who I fuck's my own goddamn business."

Uncertainty flickers in her eyes before she drops her lids to conceal it. I'm faster than that, smarter than that. Had to be, the way I grew up. Satisfaction that she got the message doesn't ease my irritation.

I'm a grown man, I haven't answered to anybody else since the sperm donor took off, and I don't have to tell her a motherfucking thing about who I want to fuck.

Even if it's her?

"Anything else?" I demand.

"Pardon?" She pretends to look at me, but she doesn't really. Her voice is stiffly polite.

"Anything else you'd do?"

She swallows and takes a minute to answer. "Do you have a photographer touring with you?"

"No." I give my head a sharp shake. "Too intrusive."

She nods carefully, like she understands. "I'm not an expert, but I've taken some photography classes. I can manage internet-quality pictures and video. The label would hire a professional like today's photo shoot for the important things, anyway."

I stare at her like I'm expecting something more. And maybe I am. But I don't know what it is, unless it's for her to drop to her knees and tell me she wants to suck my cock—and that just pisses me off more.

"If we take you on," I snap, hearing the double entendre and glad it's only in my own fucking mind, "how soon can you be ready to start?"

"Immediately."

She does her best to hold my gaze but can't really do it. I know why. Been told often enough that my expressions intimidate the fuck out of people who don't know me well. I like it that way, have no interest in being subtle. What you see is what you get with me. I don't spill my guts of everything I know, but I don't pretend to be anything except exactly who I am.

Fuck. I need to get out of here. I shouldn't be pissed off at her. None of this is her fault. She doesn't know I'm pushing her because of how bad I want to see her naked and spread wide open for me, her arms bound above her head while I eat her to more orgasms than she can count.

No, she's thinking any girl will do. And that's usually true. Something is seriously fucked up if I'm thinking I want *her,* specifically, over some random pussy.

My insides tighten, and I want to hit something. Kick it. Knock the ever-living fuck out of it.

Forget all this ridiculous fucking shit, I tell myself. *You played the relationship game once, and it was a goddamn disaster.*

Relationship? What the fuck? Just the thought pisses me off even more.

I learned my lesson, and I have never, ever forgotten. I'm the kind of guy women want to fuck. To tell their friends they fucked a rock star with a big dick and a taste for rough, dirty sex. They don't want anything permanent—and neither do I.

The sperm donor taught Mom, Bree, and me all we need to know about that happily-ever-after crap. After that, Farren took care of any unanswered questions, and now I know for sure.

Romantic love doesn't exist. Pleasure—sex—makes a pretty good substitute, so I might as well get it wherever and however I can get it. That means no emotions except knowing how fucking good it feels to come. No need to explain shit. No reality except exactly the one I want.

Hey, all you motherfuckers. I'm Knox Gallagher. Songwriter, lead guitarist of Wycked Obsession...and manwhore.

Made in the USA
Middletown, DE
31 October 2021